ALSO BY JEFFREY S. STEPHENS

ENEMIES
AMONG US

A NICK REAGAN THRILLER

JEFFREY S. STEPHENS

Post Hill
PRESS

A POST HILL PRESS BOOK

Enemies Among Us:
A Nick Reagan Thriller
© 2023 by Jeffrey S. Stephens
All Rights Reserved

ISBN: 979-8-88845-299-8
ISBN (eBook): 979-8-88845-300-1

Cover design by Cody Corcoran
Interior design and composition by Greg Johnson, Textbook Perfect

Author photo by Chuan Ding

Post Hill Press
New York • Nashville
posthillpress.com

Published in the United States of America

To Dr. Eric Kaplan, his wife Bonnie,
and their sons Jason and Michael…
wonderful people, extraordinary friends,
and a remarkable family,
with thanks for providing guidance, input,
and support on this novel

PROLOGUE

It was a balmy spring afternoon in Paris, the sun bright, the sky cloudless. Two restaurants that face each other, on opposite sides of the intersection between Rue Marbeuf and Rue Clément Marot, were bustling with the usual assortment of patrons seated both indoors and out. When a sleek black motor scooter approached the corner and slowed to a halt, no one seemed to take notice of another young man and woman looking for a place to eat and drink.

Then everything changed.

Neither the driver nor the woman holding onto him from behind removed their helmets as he pulled a butane lighter from the pocket of his leather jacket. He ignited the flame and held it up, as if inviting her to light a cigarette. Instead, the young woman reached inside her oversized sweatshirt and pulled out two large cylinders, each with a string attached to its end. He calmly lit both fuses, then took one of the metal pipe bombs and flipped it underhand across the street, into the midst of outdoor tables that were crowded with diners. She tossed the second off to her right, a shorter throw, aimed at the unsuspecting people enjoying their *al fresco* meals at the other bistro.

Before anyone at those tables had time to react, the driver shifted the cycle into gear. As he sped away, the roar of his engine was almost immediately eclipsed by the sound of two loud explosions, followed by screams of pain and anguish. Innocent people were being torn to shreds by the ball bearings packed inside the two explosive devices and the secondary damage inflicted by flying shards of broken glass from the shattered windows.

1

Leaving the carnage behind, the couple on the scooter raced along a predetermined route, avoiding the usual congestion on the Avenue George V, making a sharp turn onto Rue Z. The driver expected to see a truck waiting for them, with a wooden ramp leading into the rear cargo area, another part of the plan. They were to drive the bike up and into the back of a van that would whisk them out of Paris to the safety of the French countryside.

But there was no truck waiting.

The driver slowed halfway down the street, eventually coming to a stop. He was confused, worried that his timing was off, concerned that he had arrived ahead of the escape vehicle.

But his timing had been impeccable. He was merely unaware that the arrangements had changed.

There were two men on the scene who knew exactly what the young couple expected to find when they arrived but, unlike the young couple, they *had* been informed of the revisions made to those preparations. Watching from a second-floor hotel window just down the street, the first man witnessed the scooter come to a stop, then immediately hit a button on his cell phone to text a single letter: R.

The second man, perched on the rooftop of that same hotel, received the signal. He had already positioned the muzzle of his silenced sniper rifle atop a short stone balustrade. When the text came through he did not hesitate. He fired six shots in rapid succession, one shot each to their heads, two each to their chests, leaving both the young man and woman dead in the gutter.

* * *

AT THAT MOMENT it was still early morning in New York, but the hospital complex on the Upper East Side of Manhattan was busy. Doctors, nurses, and technicians were either arriving for work or leaving at the end of their shifts. Patients were making their way toward the various offices for appointments. Others were coming by to comfort friends or family.

A woman entered the spacious lobby of one of those tall buildings, just off York Avenue but, rather than approaching the desk that assisted visitors and cleared them for entry to one of the many medical departments, she stood off to the left, looking around.

It appeared she was lost or searching for someone, but she did not ask for help. Instead she began walking toward the bank of elevators at the rear of the large entrance hall.

"May I help you?" a uniformed guard asked when she approached.

The woman did not reply. She stopped moving, as if suddenly realizing she did not have one of the paper forms with a printed barcode that were issued by the receptionist—the authorization necessary to pass though the electronic gates to the elevators. She stood still, staring at the guard.

"Ma'am, you need to check in, up front there," he said as he pointed to the main desk.

She offered no response, but did not move.

Among the other people who were beginning to notice this silent woman was a senior officer, who had been witnessing the scene from his station near the front desk. He now came over and asked, "May I help you?"

Again, there was no reply.

"You really need to step aside," he said as politely as he could. "As you can see, this area is getting crowded."

Neither of the guards was alarmed by the woman's odd behavior; it was not the first time a visitor was confused by the security procedures in place. They viewed it more as an annoyance than a real problem as she continued to linger there without moving or speaking.

Just then, a group of physicians and nurses came up behind her, oblivious to any sort of issue as they engaged in early morning chatter while heading for their respective departments.

"Please step aside," the office repeated, but now the woman turned to face the oncoming group.

As they drew nearer, she shrieked, as if gripped in the throes of a sudden frenzy. Then she lifted her right hand, which she had been concealing in the pocket of her jacket, exposing a small detonator. Before anyone had time to react, she squeezed the button on the device, igniting the thirty pounds of explosives she had strapped to her torso, killing herself, the senior officer, the two doctors and the nurse closest to her, and injuring more than a dozen other innocent souls.

* * *

THE STRUCTURES STANDING amidst the concentric circles that form the center of Moscow are at the heart of the city's history and culture. One of the most famous of those buildings is the Bolshoi Theatre, located on Teatralnaya Square.

This evening, at the same time the attacks were being carried out in Paris and New York, a performance of the ballet was scheduled to begin. Well-dressed patrons, arriving in private cars and cabs, headed for the short set of stairs that led to the theatre entrance. As they moved forward, they encountered the inevitable crush of people one experiences when entering or leaving any theater or stadium in any large city anywhere in the world. And, as with any of those situations, there is little attention being paid to others in the middle of such a throng. Even if one had been aware of those surroundings, what would they have done about the odd-looking man in their midst? A man not quite as elegantly attired as those around him, whose gait was not quite as confident.

Nevertheless, he was proceeding in rhythm with everyone else, timing his steps perfectly, like one of the dancers about to perform for this elegant audience that was pushing its way toward the majestic lobby ahead. When he reached the densest part of the crowd, he threw open his coat and gripped the muzzle and handle of the AK-47 that was slung across his chest. Without a word of warning, he opened fire, spraying those nearest him with the searing pain of death.

Terrified people scrambled to get away, causing the circle around him to widen as he turned this way and that, bursts of gunfire tearing into chests and heads and arms and legs, blood everywhere. When the wounded fell to the ground, it only cleared a line of vision for him to fire at the next group of innocent victims.

His first oversized magazine spent, he expertly replaced it with a second, intending to resume the assault. But a Moscow police officer, himself armed with an automatic weapon, managed to break through at that moment, emptying a dozen shots into the man's head and chest, the murderer's lifeless form collapsing to the ground in the center of the horrific massacre that would be his legacy.

* * *

ONLY MOMENTS LATER, word of these coordinated attacks circled the globe, but surprisingly no terrorist organization was taking credit.

PART ONE

CHAPTER ONE

CIA Headquarters, Langley, Virginia
Ten days earlier...

Nick Reagan was seated in the office of his boss, Deputy Director Brian Kenny, inside CIA headquarters at Langley. Kenny regarded Reagan as his most effective field operative and Reagan trusted Kenny with his life. At the moment, however, neither could hide his astonishment at the news Kenny had to share.

"You must be kidding," Reagan said.

Kenny, as buttoned down as they come, was not known for his sense of humor. "I am not kidding, and I'm telling you Nick, this comes from the top."

Reagan was Kenny's polar opposite when it came to things like following the rules and respecting bureaucracy, and absolutely despised expressions like "it came from the top." But he had just been informed that someone from the office of the CIA Director had ordered him to cease his pursuit of Walid Khoury—known to some in the Company as the Handler for his work in recruiting and dispatching young extremists to carry out his vicious *jihad*.

Khoury had been the mastermind behind the recent series of vicious attacks in New York, Las Vegas, and Minnesota. Reagan and his colleagues had some success in doing what they could to prevent the intended genocide, particularly the last of those three, but Khoury had escaped capture. Since then, Reagan had spent the past two months tracking him with no success. Ironically, since most of Khoury's murderous plans had been thwarted by Reagan and his team, the Handler's own brethren in al Qaeda were also searching for him, all the more reason Reagan wanted to find him sooner rather than later.

In response to this news from Kenny—that he had been directed to end his efforts to locate Khoury—Reagan was unable to just sit there, so he got to his feet and began pacing back and forth.

Reagan was thirty-eight years old and stood just over six feet, which made him five inches or so taller than his boss. His complexion was perpetually tan from all the time he spent in the field, his features even, his dark brown hair cut short, and his dark blue eyes capable of conveying warmth or ice-cold ruthlessness, as the situation dictated. He had a trim, muscular build, owing to the strict physical regimen he maintained that dated back to his days in the military.

When he was done walking around the confines of Kenny's office, he sat again, staring across the desk at the deputy director. "You're telling me they really don't want to find Khoury."

Kenny shook his head. "No, what I'm telling you is they want *you* to stop looking and allow them to handle the matter."

"Who the hell is *them*?" Reagan asked. "There's no one in the Company as qualified as Gellos and I to conduct this search."

Kenny sighed. "You know I don't disagree, but this is not my decision."

"Isn't there someone upstairs we can talk to?"

"Believe me, I tried. I asked for a meeting, to give you an opportunity to present your views, but they turned me down. They said they want you to take some time off, that you're too close to the situation."

"Too close?" Reagan asked.

"Let's face it, Nick, you were there trying to stop those attacks. You witnessed what occurred, you saw what happened to the people you couldn't save. They think capturing Khoury is more than personal for you at this point, that you need a cooling off period."

Reagan uttered a short laugh. "That's what they said? They want me to cool off?"

"That's what they said," Kenny replied, his frown making it clear he was as unhappy with the decision as his top agent.

"And how long am I supposed to be on ice?"

"They weren't specific. They suggested you take at least a couple of weeks."

"You want to tell me who exactly gave you this message?"

"I cannot."

Reagan nodded. "All right, I'll take a couple of weeks off if that's what they want. But they have no right to tell me what to do while I'm cooling off, correct?"

Kenny paused a moment before responding. "I know what you're likely to do, just be careful. As I already told you, this comes from the director's office. You get caught coloring outside the lines and we're going to have a problem. A major problem."

"Sir, are you suggesting I might not follow orders?"

Kenny treated him to another of his patented frowns. "I don't want to know what you're doing, I don't want to hear from you, and I also don't want to hear from anyone else that you're creating a problem." Then he repeated, in a softer voice, "Just be careful."

* * *

REAGAN STOPPED AT THE JEFFERSON HOTEL where he had been staying the past couple of days in D.C., pulled together his gear, and grabbed the next Acela Express to New York. During the ride north, he made several phone calls, including one to his partner, Carol Gellos, and one to his long-time companion, Erin David, who was an analyst for the CIA in Manhattan.

In his typically oblique fashion, without providing much detail, he let each of them know what happened and made it clear he had no intention of ending his search for Khoury. He also let them know he expected help from each of them, hoping to build on some leads he had already developed.

Both of them said they would.

Arriving back in his apartment on East 55th Street that evening, he poured himself a bourbon in a crystal tumbler with one large cube, sat on the black leather sectional sofa in his living room, turned on the television to catch the news, and opened his laptop.

Walid Khoury had disappeared in France just before the last of his planned attacks was being carried out. Reagan and Gellos had also been in Paris, close to finding him, but immediately departed when they concluded that the third target was in Minnesota—Khoury's pattern seemed to favor three-part offensives. They reached Bloomington in time and were instrumental in preventing that final assault, saving countless lives in the process. Since then, Reagan had been piecing together any clue he could to determine the Handler's whereabouts.

They had already learned that Khoury had been living a double life—posing as an international banker, he was married to a woman who worked in the State Department, Cyla Khoury, who also happened to be a friend of Erin David. After several interrogations of her by various United States agencies, including the FBI, CIA, and State Department, it was apparent Cyla had no idea that her husband was an al Qaeda operative. They had only been married a little more than a year after a brief but intense courtship, and she had believed he was both a brilliant and well-connected businessman, as had everyone else in their world. She was unaware of his true background as a *jihadist*, or the fact that he previously had a wife and child who were killed in an attack in Aleppo years before. She was now left to contend with the painful realization that their marriage had actually been part of Khoury's master plan to infiltrate her world while organizing his violent strikes on American soil.

Given the personal relationships among Erin David, Reagan, and Cyla, Reagan was only allowed to question Khoury's wife after her innocence had been established. Several days ago, Reagan and Cyla met, and he told her he wanted to discuss what little she knew about her husband that might be authentic, such as his personal habits, people he mentioned that she had not met, and places he said he had been in the past. Unfortunately, Reagan realized that much of what Khoury might have told her was likely disinformation and would have little value. At one point, Reagan bluntly asked why she had married him.

"With everything that's happened," she admitted, "I'm not sure anymore. He is handsome, and worldly, and we shared the same religion and ethnic background. It's not much," she added with a sad smile. "I thought I was in love."

"Love can be strange," Reagan admitted, "but you're obviously a very intelligent woman. Were there no warning signs, nothing that suggested things were not all what they seemed?"

Cyla thought it over. "He never talked much about his business," she finally conceded. "After a while, it almost felt he was purposely avoiding that subject. And yes, I thought that was kind of odd, but he was more than a decade my senior. I just figured he was old school when it came to things like that."

"When you say 'old school,' I take it you mean traditional Muslim."

Cyla winced slightly. "I suppose so, yes."

"This is difficult for me to ask, but do you think he courted you because of the position you held?"

Her eyes moistened, but Cyla did not succumb to tears. "I've thought about little else since that day you and Ms. Gellos came to see me at my office in Paris and told me what was going on." She took a moment to compose herself. "I look back on the dinners we had, the time we spent together, the trips we took before he asked me to marry him. It's hard for me to believe it was all about my working for the State Department. I honestly never gave him any classified information or anything like that, and he never asked. Still," she continued, but then stopped. "I was obviously a fool on so many levels, I don't want to go on deluding myself."

Reagan nodded, realizing that in addition to his murderous assaults, Khoury had also inflicted serious emotional harm on this young woman, injuries from which she might never recover. He returned the discussion to matters such as the trips Khoury took without her after they were married, any people she may have met through him, and so forth.

"No detail is meaningless," he told Cyla, but ultimately the interview came to end. When she apologized for not being more helpful, he disagreed.

"There's value in what you've told me," he assured her. "I'm just sorry you have to go through all this." Then he said, "You can't blame yourself. Evil comes in many forms."

As he sat in his living room this evening, Reagan thought about the few clues Cyla had provided that might be helpful in his search. Whatever lies Khoury told his young wife, Reagan believed there were some things that had to be true.

There were also facts he and his partner, Carol Gellos, had uncovered.

Gellos was tall and trim with short sandy-colored hair, dark brown eyes, and a no-nonsense attitude. Kenny's top female operative, she had taken an unusual route to get there. After a troubled high school experience, she dropped out of college in the middle of her second year and joined the Army. It soon became evident that her difficult childhood had masked a keen intellect and the willpower to succeed. She completed her education and rose through the ranks of the Intelligence Division, until several years ago when she was recruited by the Agency. Gellos quickly advanced to her current status as a clandestine field agent, having worked on numerous missions with Reagan. At thirty-five and single, she kept her private life private, while proving herself a fearless and trustworthy partner.

And she was all business.

Reagan and Gellos discovered that Khoury kept an office in Paris, but there was absolutely no chance the man would ever return there after they raided the place and took custody of his assistant. Cyla said that Khoury had mentioned more than once that he had banking contacts in London, but she had no details. That could have been part of a cover he arranged for himself in order to take trips back to the Middle East, without disclosing that to his wife or anyone else—but now that al Qaeda was tracking him, there was little chance he would risk a visit to that part of the world.

All the other factors analyzed by Erin and Gellos left Reagan with at least one logical possibility—the Handler might be in London—and, order or no order, Reagan was not going to stop looking for him.

CHAPTER TWO

New York City

As Reagan sat on the black leather sofa in the living room of his apartment, going through his computer to review the information he had compiled on the possible location of Walid Khoury, he began thinking about Derek Malone. Now that he was ordered to stop tracking Khoury, Reagan knew he would have to work outside his normal channels. He also realized that, of all the people he knew outside the government he could safely go to, Derek Malone had the sort of contacts that might aid in connecting the dots they had collected so far. He was a man with innumerable friends in a variety of enterprises—including some with connections in the Arab world.

In the unique orbit of Nick Reagan's universe, Dr. Derek Malone was not a likely friend. To begin with, he was twenty-five years older than Reagan. He was also outside the world of intelligence agencies in which Reagan spent almost all of his time. And, as a neurologist who paired his medical background with an entrepreneurial spirit, he had accumulated great wealth and influence. Malone developed powerful contacts who introduced him to opportunities in Big Pharma and led him through various tech investments, all of which ultimately had him mingling with many of the so-called captains of industry who control the American economy. Malone was a classic self-made success story who came from nothing, built a fortune, but never forgot his roots.

That alone was enough to earn Reagan's respect.

But Malone was also a patriot, and several years ago he had provided Reagan invaluable assistance during an investigation into a data breach initiated by the Chinese. Through his far-reaching network, Malone was helpful not only in locating the source of the problem but also in identifying the people capable of shutting down technological invasion.

Unlike so many people Reagan was obliged to deal with in the business world, Malone did not seek any sort of *quid pro quo* for his support. To the contrary, he was pleased to serve his country and enjoyed teaming with Reagan in the process—someone, Reagan realized early on, who shared his values if not his career goals. Malone was fascinated that a young man as bright and capable as Reagan would risk his life working for what he called "coolie wages," rather than parlaying those talents into a lucrative position in the private sector. In his typical fashion, Malone was not shy about voicing that opinion.

Reagan had laughed in response. "If you're worried about my current finances, you better not ask me how much I earned while I was in the military." In *his* typical fashion, Reagan did not disclose which branch of the armed forces he served in, nor did he ever admit to Derek that he was now with the CIA.

"I'm serious, you could make a fortune in the business world," Derek said.

Reagan's smile faded as he said, "Someone has to do what I do. I believe we both prefer that it's someone who has the skills and experience to get it done."

Now Malone also turned serious. "And the focus. Too bad more people in the political arena don't feel that way."

Reagan nodded.

"The way our Founding Fathers set things up, politics was not supposed to be a friggin career," Malone said. "You were supposed to spend some time serving the country, then return to your farm or business or whatever."

"You don't have to convince me."

Malone nodded, as if confirming a thought. "Ever wonder how some of these senators and congressmen get so rich while they're still in office? How they come to own those big houses with security gates, vacation homes, you know what I'm talking about."

"I do," Reagan said, since they had discussed all of this more than once, their shared views contributing to the growth of the friendship. "I wish I had a good answer for you."

"I have answers, my friend," Malone told him, "but you don't want to hear them."

Another positive in their relationship was Malone's wife, Connie. She was intelligent, educated, and as sophisticated as her husband was dynamic, but her road had been even rockier than Derek's. She was an orphan who was raised in foster homes until she was old enough to go off on her own, working her way through college, completing graduate school on scholarships that enabled her to earn a Masters and a Doctorate in psychology. By the time Reagan met her, Connie had given up her private practice but not her penchant for examining everything through the prism of her education and personal experiences. Like her husband, she did not permit their extravagant lifestyle to diminish their kindness or their insistence on treating everyone the same regardless of who they were; she would never forget where they came from.

Reagan decided it was worth a call to see if Malone could provide some help, so he picked up his cell phone, hit the speed dial for Malone's private number, and waited. He heard the familiar voice after the second ring.

"Where the hell have you been? I thought you dumped us for a younger crowd," Malone said.

"An older crowd, actually," Reagan said. "You and Connie move too fast for me."

Malone responded with the raspy chuckle Reagan had heard many times. "All right, we'll try and slow things down next time we see you. Now, what do you need?"

"Is that the way to begin a conversation with a good friend? No clever patter? No questions about how I'm doing?"

"Don't bullshit a bullshitter," Malone told him. "I haven't heard from you in months, and now you're calling me after ten at night. Tell me I'm crazy, but I'm guessing this is not a social call."

"It's always social with you, Derek, that's how you roll. But you're correct, I need to ask you some questions." Reagan paused before adding, "In person would be best."

"Uh huh. Can I ask you where you've been all this time?"

"We can also talk about that in person as well."

Reagan's tone made it clear Malone should resist the temptation to ask anything else, at least for now. "I see," was all he said.

"I'm in New York. Where are you and Connie these days?"

"We're at our place in Florida, but I'm coming up for a couple of meetings in Manhattan tomorrow afternoon."

"Any chance you can take an early flight and meet me in the morning?"

"How about a drink somewhere at noon?"

"Can't I buy you lunch?" Reagan offered.

"First, you can never buy me anything, because you're a pauper and I'm a rich guy. Second, my early meeting is for a lunch in midtown, I'll have to see you before that."

"All right, a drink at noon then."

"Agreed," Malone said, "provided you give me at least one clue as to what we'll be talking about."

Reagan paused for a moment, then said, "A change in the weather pattern."

"A weather pattern?"

"Acid rain in Las Vegas," answered Reagan.

"Understood," Malone said. "Just tell me where and I'll be there."

* * *

THE NEXT DAY, REAGAN AND MALONE met at Il Mulino on 60th Street, just off Madison Avenue. Reagan knew the manager; he told him that he needed a table in the back, but that he and his friend would not be eating. All they needed were drinks and to be left to themselves.

When the maître d' responded with a curious look, Reagan said with a smile, "Don't worry; my friend is a huge tipper, and I have someone else joining me for lunch in an hour."

When Malone arrived, Reagan was already seated in the rear of the modern dining room, which was decorated in cool colors, the pale beige walls adorned with framed black-and-white photographs of celebrities, past and present. He had chosen the last table in the corner off to the left, facing the front of the restaurant with his back to the wall.

Reagan was wearing gray slacks, a black V-neck sweater over a white T-shirt, and black suede rubber-soled loafers. His face was closely shaved and, other than the fact he was handsome with intense, dark blue eyes, his appearance was generally forgettable, which was just as he intended.

Malone, on the other hand, was wearing a custom-tailored suit, dove gray with thin blue windowpane lines. His white shirt was crisply pressed, the collar slightly oversized to accommodate the generous knot of a bright blue Hermès tie. A colorful pocket square was spilling out from the breast pocket of his suit jacket, and his Gucci loafers well shined. He was very tan—living most of the time in Florida, Malone was always tan—his auburn hair cut fashionably long, and his luminous smile revealing snowy white teeth that seemed to glow from across the room.

Reagan stood as Malone approached and the two men embraced.

Taking a step back, Reagan said, "You always look like you just stepped out of a GQ fashion shoot."

Malone responded with an appreciative chuckle. "And you always dress like you're hiding from someone."

Reagan ignored the remark. "I mean it, how the hell can you be so put together if you just got off a flight?"

Malone gave a theatrical look around, as if to ensure that no one would hear what he said next. "Sorry to sound so pretentious, but I flew on a private jet in my favorite college sweatsuit, didn't change until we landed."

"My hero," Reagan said as the two men sat down.

A waiter came by, Malone ordered a Bloody Mary, light on the vodka, and Reagan asked for a Blanton's bourbon with a big cube.

"Little early for something that heavy, no?"

"These are heavy times," Reagan replied with a slight smile.

"Getting right down to it then?"

"I know you've got a schedule to keep."

"Don't worry about me, first things first. When you mentioned Las Vegas, I knew you were referring to that attack at the fountain outside the hotel several weeks ago. Were you there?"

Reagan shared very little about what he did, even with the best of friends, but Malone deserved an answer—especially since it related to the information Reagan wanted from him. After a slight pause, he said, "Yes, I was there. I was also on the Highline in Manhattan when those suicide bombers tried to take out all those people at the outdoor fashion show. And I was in Minnesota, where they attempted to plant an enormous package of explosives in the largest shopping mall in America."

Malone responded with a solemn nod. "You've been a busy young man."

"It's what we do."

"I read enough about those incidents to know things might have been a lot worse if people in our government hadn't reacted in time."

"It was a coordinated effort for sure."

Malone eyed his friend for a moment. "And you were in the middle of that?"

The waiter returned with their drinks, which relieved Reagan of the obligation to respond. The two men fell into silence until they were served and left to themselves again.

"Let me give you a headline or two," Reagan said, "just to get this started."

Malone lifted his glass, said, "First, we're toasting to health and heroism," then took a sip of his cocktail. He waited for Reagan to do the same. "Now, my friend, I'm all ears."

"It appears there was one person behind the planning of those attacks. We did what we could to mitigate the damage, as you say, but we still have unanswered questions." Reagan then added, "The worst part is, he's still out there."

Malone studied his friend for a moment. "And you're looking for him."

Reagan nodded slowly.

"I'm going to guess that you know *who* he is, just not *where* he is."

"You must be head of the class."

Malone showed him one of his toothy smiles. "I didn't get where I am by being slow on the uptake. For instance, you've never admitted exactly who it is you work for, but we both know that I know."

"Fair enough."

"And, just to keep this flow going, the reason I'm here is because you think I can provide some sort of information that will help you find this gentleman," he said, pronouncing the last word with clear sarcasm.

"I do."

"Well then, if those are the headlines, let's not bury the lead. What can I do for you?"

"The man in question is Lebanese with some nasty contacts throughout the Middle East. Together they meant to do some serious harm, as we've seen."

"But his plans didn't work out as intended."

"Correct. And in his world, while success leads to glory, failure is not tolerated. They're not only ruthless murderers of their enemies, but al Qaeda and their ilk are incredibly unforgiving of their own." Reagan drank some bourbon. "His schemes did not go off as planned, as you said, and they don't care why or allow for excuses. That means he's not only being hunted by us, he's also in danger from his own."

"But you have those questions you need answered, so you want to get to him first."

"Right."

"And we're here because you think I can do something to help you find him."

"Precisely. You work with people in high places engaged in international oil deals with the Saudis and others."

"I do," Malone said.

"Those businessmen in the Middle East can be ruthless, but they're not terrorists."

"Most Arabs are not terrorists," Malone reminded him.

"Totally agree, I don't dispute that at all. I just want to know if there's any chance you have contacts that might find a sympathetic ear over there, someone who might help us gather some intelligence on where our friend might be?"

Malone thought it over. "That's a big ask, as you know. The Arabs may not like what this guy has done, but he's one of their own. They might prefer to clean their own house, am I right? Why would they help us find him? From a business point of view, what's in it for them?"

"Depends on who's being asked. Terrorism is bad for business as well as governments. The attacks were an international story, and we're not asking help from people with ties to al Qaeda or ISIS, we're looking for an assist from legitimate sources." He paused before adding, "I'm going to add something that is absolutely classified, that you must not share."

"Got it," Malone said, reaching up with his thumb and forefinger and squeezing his lips shut.

"After all this went down, his own people tried to kill him, but he got away."

"He really *is* in deep shit."

"All the more reason I need to move fast."

"You know me, you don't have to ask twice. I'll do whatever I can."

"Much appreciated," Reagan said, "but you need to be careful. Dangerous people are coming at this from every angle. And all of this has to be completely off the record."

"Understood."

"I also want to be clear you should not say or do anything that puts you in a dangerous or even uncomfortable position."

"Clear as crystal." They were quiet for a few moments, then Malone said, "I have a question that may or may not be related. These people I would go to are involved in a lot more than oil. For instance, they're talking to that Russian guy Mindlovitch, trying to buy an interest in those so-called Ghost Chips he's developing. Rumor has it that some of his prototypes were stolen, but I never heard anything more."

Reagan was impressed. "You really are plugged in."

Malone held up his glass with a smile and had another taste of his cocktail.

"Again, this is confidential," Reagan said, careful not to divulge too much regardless of his trust in Malone. "You're right about that rumor. They say someone took samples from the facility in China, but if it's true there's no word on who was behind it. You're also right about the possibility these actions are linked. Some of us have a concern this technology may be one of the reasons I'm having such a hard time tracking this man. If he's using cell phones without any chance of being traced, that just adds to the degree of difficulty."

"Not to mention the other things they claim these Ghost Chips are capable of doing remotely."

"You're entitled to another gold star, Derek."

Malone paused for a moment, then asked, "When are you going to tell me the name of this man you're hunting? I need that, don't I?"

Reagan nodded. "His name is Walid Khoury. Known as the Handler, for the work he does recruiting and manipulating young jihadists."

Malone sat back. "Khoury? I know that name. Thought he was some sort of banker, married to that young woman in the State Department. I met him a couple of times at affairs in D.C."

Reagan did nothing to hide his surprise. "You really are something, you know that?"

Malone smiled. "You can't buy the kind of contacts I have, young man, they have to be developed over a lifetime."

"Contacts are also the lifeblood of my business. Maybe my boss should consider recruiting you."

"You mean make me a CIA agent?" Before Reagan could utter a demurral, Malone uttered one of his throaty laughs. "My young friend, I thought I already was one," he said.

CHAPTER THREE

New York City

As the lunch crowd arrived, Reagan and Malone remained at their table in the rear of Il Mulino's dining room, identifying the specific sort of intel Reagan was seeking and the people Malone knew from whom it might come.

While Malone had a wide array of investments and relationships, both in and out of the United States, Reagan understood that his principal business activities revolved around medical research and innovations, including a seat on the board of directors at Novak Pharma. His association with the brothers who were the majority owners of that company was by far the most intriguing to Reagan at the moment. To begin with, the Novaks' oil empire was even larger than their pharmaceutical company, which meant they had serious links to OPEC and major players throughout the Middle East. They also engaged in politics spanning a curious mélange of different ideologies, while Malone was strictly a flag-waving nationalist. Their personal styles also differed. Malone was all about people, his loyalty and kindness legendary. The Novaks were famously secretive and aloof, making their friendship with Malone a source of wonder.

"Among these people you're going to reach out to, I assume that will include John and Andrew Novak," Reagan said.

Malone smiled. "That's who you've been hinting at since I got here. Am I right or am I right?"

"You're positively psychic," Reagan said. "Can you speak with them soon?"

"Consider it done."

Reagan nodded. "Just to limit your exposure here, don't even bother to contact me if you come up empty, all right?"

"Got it."

"But if you do find something, just text me a message that you want to talk. Nothing else."

"Done," Malone said.

The commitment made, they spent some time catching up on the social front until Malone realized he was late for his lunch meeting across town, at the restaurant Marea on Central Park South. He and Reagan stood and shook hands, just as Erin David arrived.

Erin was one of the Agency's top analysts and the only woman Reagan had ever loved. Given his profession, he found a permanent relationship challenging, not least because of the potential danger to her. Still, despite the risks, their chemistry was undeniable. She was intelligent, loyal, and beautiful, and had repeatedly made it clear she was willing to face whatever might come as long as they could be together. And that she wanted more.

It was an ongoing debate Reagan secretly hoped he would eventually lose.

Tall and slender, Erin was a devotee of yoga, jogging, and regular workouts that kept her firm and fit. She was sexy in an understated way, exuding a quiet confidence with no need to flaunt her obvious good looks. Her makeup was minimal but effective, highlighting her soft hazel eyes and full lips. She kept her light brown hair cut fashionably short.

This afternoon she was dressed in cream-colored gabardine slacks that were tight in the right places, then flowed down to her high-heeled shoes. Her navy-blue satin blouse was open at the neck, just a button short of too revealing.

As soon as Malone spotted her coming towards them, he broke into another broad smile, reaching out as she approached and enfolding her in an affectionate embrace.

"Damn," he said, as he took half a step back and held her by the shoulders. "If I knew you were coming, I would've canceled my meeting and stayed for lunch."

"And if I knew you were going to be here," Erin replied, "I would have asked Connie to join us."

"We'll all get together soon," Malone assured her. "I'm up here on my own for some meetings, then heading back to the Sunshine State. Sorry that I've got to boogie, but I'm happy I got to see you."

Erin smiled. Malone was probably the only man his age who could get away with an expression like "boogie." "Please give Connie my love. And I'm glad I got to see you too."

Malone insisted on paying for the drinks, left a large tip, and made his exit, as Erin and Reagan sat. She immediately asked, "What was that about?"

"Two friends can't get together for a drink?"

She gave him the look that assured him he would never fool her, not about anything. "Want to try again?"

Reagan looked down at his empty glass. "What would you like?"

"A really good Chardonnay and an answer. I obviously know what you're up to at the moment, which means social drinks are not on your calendar. You're enlisting Derek's help to find the Handler."

"In a third party sort of way." He shrugged. "Malone has contacts that might be able to help."

When the waiter came by, Reagan asked for another bourbon, Erin's glass of wine, and a couple of menus.

After the man walked away, Erin said, "Derek would do anything to help you with anything at any time, you know that. But Khoury is dangerous, and Derek needs to be more than careful if he's going to start poking around."

"I know that, but Malone is as street smart as they come. And I told him to tread lightly."

"Treading lightly is not in his repertoire."

Reagan could not disagree. "I'm only asking for information, and anyone he knows who has an ounce of decency would want to help find this sonuvabitch."

"Unless they have another agenda."

"Meaning what?"

"Not sure. I guess hanging out with you makes me suspicious of everything and everyone. We just don't want Derek getting hurt."

"I'll keep an eye on him," Reagan promised her. "Don't worry."

"Good. And now I suppose you want to know what I have for you."

"Not sure how you mean that."

"Spare me," Erin said, then leaned forward slightly. "As you know, we've been going through various records that Cyla gave us, and I found something interesting in her bank records."

"Interesting how?"

"Cyla says Khoury handled all their finances, even her checking account. According to what she tells me, he was a major control freak, which is not surprising since he was leading a double life he wanted to keep from her. Anyway, there were a number of large transfers she swears she knows nothing about. Hundreds of thousands of dollars being moved around, most of that money ending up in a branch of Coutts bank in London."

"That *is* interesting. She mentioned London to me when we spoke. Carol and I think it's our best lead."

"It may be. Please forgive the ethnic observation, but London has a large Arab population, which also means…"

"If an Arab wanted someplace in the West where he could get lost in the crowd…"

"London would be a good choice."

"Please tell me some of those funds are still there."

Erin nodded. "Loads. In more than one account."

Reagan sat back. "Any interest in dinner at Wilton's?"

"You mean Wilton's as in London? Thank you, my darling, but no thanks."

"Great seafood."

"Undeniably, but you're missing the point. Intentionally, I would guess."

"Enlighten me."

Erin opted for a smile in lieu of voicing something like, "You must be joking." Then she said, "For starters, you're supposed to be on ice. I have no idea how the DD or the brass upstairs might react if they discover you're using this time off to track Khoury in the UK, but I'm sure they will be less than pleased to discover I accompanied you on the trip."

"Is that all that's bothering you?"

"Then there are the people in the chain of command between me and Langley who might be surprised to find that I'm not at my desk for however long this junket would take."

"I see."

"I know you do. Add to the scenario, if you will, that this is a long-shot. The fact that Khoury has significant bank accounts in England is not proof he's there. He could use electronic transfers to move his money anywhere in the world at any time."

"True, but he has to live somewhere. And you know that the more he moves around, the greater the chance he'll be spotted."

Erin took a moment to consider that argument as the head waiter they knew came by for their order. The three of them exchanged greetings before the man said to Reagan, "I know what you want to start."

"Of course. A half order of the porcini ravioli with Champagne truffle cream sauce."

"Excellent."

Erin looked up from her menu. "Not counting calories today, I see."

"Not today. Care to join me?"

Turning to the waiter, she said, "Caesar salad and the veal marsala, please."

"Veal marsala sounds good for my main course," Reagan said, "and two glasses of the Amarone."

After they were alone again, Erin said, "There's something to what you say. I cannot imagine Khoury risking a trip home, and the US would not make sense. What does Carol think?"

Carol Gellos was not only Reagan's partner in the field, she was also trained in criminal psychology and profiling behavioral tendencies. "She tends to agree with me, since we already had certain links between Khoury and the UK. The fact that these bank accounts are still there could be the tipping point."

"Maybe," Erin said, "but we could use more intel on recent withdrawals, transfers, and so forth."

"Then please do what you can to get those details from the bank. Time is not on my side," Reagan reminded her. If he was going to find Khoury, he needed to do it quickly, and under the radar.

CHAPTER FOUR

Washington, D.C.

Andrew and John Novak were born into wealth, but unlike many who celebrate that privilege by draining the coffers for a life of indulgence, they took a reasonably successful family business and grew it into an international behemoth.

Their grandfather, Janusz Nowakowski, had come to America from Poland with his wife and infant son, Pawel, just before the dawn of the twentieth century. Many other immigrants arriving from Eastern Europe settled in the crowded neighborhoods of large cities, but Janusz and his family traveled to Texas. He had spent several years in the oil business back home and believed his best prospects could be found there.

Once they arrived, he Americanized their names, rented a small cabin with the little money he had brought with him, found employment as a laborer on an oil rig, and went to work. Although the pumps, drilling equipment, and derricks he found in Texas were more sophisticated than any he had ever seen, he proved himself a quick learner with an Old World work ethic. Now known now as Jan Novak, he advanced over the years until he became foreman of a group in which he would have once been the lowest ranking member.

But that was not enough for his son Pawel, who had been known as Paul since he arrived in the United States.

As Paul grew, his father taught him all he knew about the petroleum business, but the most important lesson was the one Paul discovered for himself. He understood that a man could make a decent living as an employee of a reputable company, but the real money was never going to flow to the men who faced danger every day as they guided liquid gold from the ground into huge holding tanks. The real money was earned by those who owned those oil rigs and managed the industry from afar.

Large national companies already dominated the industry, but Paul realized there were still opportunities for those who knew the business, understood the technology, and were prepared to set off on their own—and that is exactly what he did. As one of the so-called wildcatters, he was fortunate enough to merge good luck with backbreaking effort. Having saved and borrowed enough money to lease a field in northwest Texas, he struck oil on only his third attempt. Using that early momentum to grow his business, he began to purchase other properties as the years went on—rather than relying on leases—combining a knack for drilling in fertile fields with canny real estate investments.

His strategy proved prescient when the Great Depression descended on the world. His acquisitions were largely debt-free, unlike others who had leveraged their properties too highly and had to forfeit them during the Crash. He even managed to hold onto the few parcels he owned that still had mortgages on them. Banks were in such desperate straits, he was able to negotiate discounts so he could pay them off with "cheap money."

Paul was all about business for many years, marrying late, not becoming a father until he was in his forties. He had two sons, each of whom shared his enthusiasm for the oil industry and, just as he had seen a path beyond what his father accomplished, both of whom saw even greater opportunities ahead. Paul was opposed to diversifying, believing that as long as the world needed petroleum, his company would continue to increase the family prosperity.

His sons, Andrew and John, respected their father, saw his point of view, but thought he was shortsighted. Their company also had those large real estate holdings as well as huge amounts of cash, assets Paul had no interest risking in a stock market he never trusted or fully understood. His sons argued for another approach, pushing him to invest in other industries. Petroleum was not only used to run cars, fly planes, and heat homes, but was necessary in almost every industry in the world, such as plastics and pharmaceuticals. Why not establish positions in those companies, rather than being just a supplier?

The debate continued until Paul's death at which point his sons took control of the business and began to fulfill their vision. Subscribing to their father's suspicions about the stock market, they made direct investments in successful companies and created others, focusing on technology, transportation, and medicine. In just two decades, the breadth and depth of their company's wealth and influence was unrecognizable. Novak Industries had become a conglomerate, its two owners among the most powerful leaders in the United States, as well as the world.

* * *

THE DAY AFTER MALONE MET WITH REAGAN, Andrew Novak's secretary gave him a message that Derek was in Washington and wanted to stop by that afternoon for a brief discussion. There was nothing unusual about the request, since Malone was on the board of their subsidiary, Novak Pharma. They had long regarded Malone as someone as close to them as they allowed any business associate to become. Neither Andrew nor John was much on social interaction, opting for insular lives devoted to their families and their businesses. It was hard, however, not to engage in a relationship with Malone, who supplied most of the energy and all of the entertainment.

They also respected Malone's business acumen. While they had grown their company through cold-blooded tactics and endless hard work, they recognized the head start their father had provided. Malone had no such advantage, building his fortune through intelligence, creativity, and diligence. He was one of the rare people the Novaks listened to, even as they maintained their steadfast adherence to their own principles.

Unfortunately, things had lately taken a bad turn. Malone had aggressively questioned two major projects the Novaks were working on and—regardless of their positive feelings about Malone—they did not abide dissension in their ranks. How that would play out remained to be seen.

Andrew was slightly more than a year older than his brother. He was heavyset, bald, with thick features much like their father, and piercing green eyes. John was taller, not as hefty, with gray hair neatly combed, fine features that were more like their mother's, and dark eyes that were as intense as Andrew's.

As they waited for Malone, they had no way of knowing that he had been in New York yesterday, was on his way back to Florida, and had arranged for a stop in D.C. specifically to see them.

The brothers were in the conference room which, like their executive office suites, was on the top floor of the Janus Building they had named after their grandfather. The room was decorated in a modern, elegant style that managed to be both minimalist and comfortable.

Malone arrived at the agreed time, was shown in by Andrew's secretary, and greeted them with his usual enthusiasm, hugging each of the brothers in turn as if oblivious to how uncomfortable physical contact made them feel.

Taking a stroll around the large mahogany table, Malone stepped to the window that provided a panorama of Washington, and said, "Love this view. Never gets old for me." Giving them no time to respond, Malone added, "And your taste is amazing. This room is fantastic."

"It's good to see you, too," John Novak told them.

Taking a seat opposite them, Malone said, "One of these days you have to give me a complete tour of this place. I want to see the room where you're printing the money." He followed that with a hearty laugh which evoked reluctant smiles.

"What brings you to town?" Andrew asked.

Malone knew his hosts disdained empty banter and was not about to waste their time. "I have a friend who asked me for a favor. It has to do with those recent terrorist attacks in New York and Vegas and Bloomington." The serious looks with which they reacted told Malone no further details about those assaults were required. "My friend is trying to find the individual who was behind the planning and execution of those murders."

John nodded slowly. "I see. May we assume this friend of yours is with the government?" Then he added, "I mean our government, of course."

"He is."

"Since you have not provided a name or affiliation, I'm guessing you are not at liberty to say."

Malone had also become serious. Despite his gregarious nature, he knew when it was time to get down to business. "You are correct," he said. "That's the basis on which I was asked to speak with you."

John nodded again but said nothing.

"Those incidents were horrific," Andrew said. "Anything we might contribute to finding the perpetrator we will certainly do, but what could we possibly know that would be helpful?"

"Here it is," Malone began, using one of his favorite introductory expressions. "The man being sought is Walid Khoury. He is Lebanese by birth and apparently has a long-time association with al Qaeda. He was living in Paris and here in D.C., posing as some sort of international banker."

Neither brother admitted to recognizing the name.

"He disappeared before the third attack in Minnesota," Malone went on. "There's reason to believe his terrorist friends are not pleased with his failure to carry out their plans, but it is possible he still has allies in the Middle East."

"I see," Andrew said, not clear about where this was going.

"With your access to the upper echelons of so many regimes over there, the hope is that you might be able to make a discreet inquiry as to whether this man has surfaced. Anywhere. Anytime recently. That's the bottom line."

"Understood."

Malone quickly added, "Not that I'm asking anything that would cause you embarrassment, or that you feel would be inappropriate."

"Of course not," Andrew agreed. "You're suggesting this is as an act of patriotism on our part."

"Well said."

"Then we will certainly do everything we can to help you," Andrew told him, then added, "And our government, of course."

The three men were quiet for a moment, until John asked, "I take it that this friend of yours specifically asked you to speak with us."

The way the statement was made left Malone feeling a bit uncomfortable. "He knew of our relationship and suggested you might be in a position to help."

"Your friend is well-informed," John said.

"And insightful," Andrew added.

Malone forced a smile. "Information is their business, as I am sure you realize."

The brothers exchanged a brief glance, after which Andrew said, "Let us see what we can do. As you've already noted, this is a delicate matter that must be handled with discretion."

"Naturally, naturally."

"Are you going to be in Washington for a while?"

"No, I'm leaving for home later today."

"We'll be in touch, then," Andrew said.

Malone knew them well enough to realize this conversation was at an end but was not comfortable simply getting up to leave. He spent some time discussing family and Novak Pharma, steering clear of their recent confrontations over the new drug being developed there. The brothers reciprocated with their own pleasantries and asked how Malone's wife, Connie, was doing.

"Connie is great. We're heading to Paris for a few days," he told them. "We're going to have lunch with Benji Solares and his wife."

"That's nice," Andrew said. "Please give them our best."

After a few more personal exchanges, Malone knew it was time for him to go.

"Whatever you can do on this matter," Malone said, "really will be appreciated."

When he was gone, the brothers remained alone in the conference room.

"How are we going to handle this?" John asked.

"First we need to gather information of our own," Andrew told him.

"Such as confirming the identity of Malone's friend?"

"I think we can guess."

"He was involved in that government investigation several years ago. We should have Paszek confirm who he's dealing with," John said.

"We can also guess at Derek's motivation here."

John nodded. "Sometimes Malone is too friendly for his own good."

"Which leaves the matter of Walid Khoury."

"Yes," Andrew said. "Let's also arrange for Paszek's men to keep an eye on Malone while we check on all of this."

"Agreed," John said.

"And let's get in touch with Mindlovitch," Andrew said.

"About the Ghost Chip?"

"That, and our plans about lithium. With all the opposition we'll face, we can use a powerful partner to make it happen."

CHAPTER FIVE

New York City

That afternoon, back in his apartment, Reagan took some time to imagine what a man like Walid Khoury would do once he was on the run.

The Handler's last confirmed sighting was *en route* to Marseilles, during which he deftly avoided the fate intended for him by his cohorts in al Qaeda. After taking out the two men who had been dispatched to murder him, Khoury left their bodies in his train compartment and ran through the Lyon station, where his image was captured on CCTV.

After that, it was unlikely Khoury would have remained in France. Knowing both the French counter-terrorism agency, GIGN, as well as the CIA were after him, he had to assume they saw that video as he left the terminal in Lyon, which would lead to the discovery that he departed Paris by train in a private cabin destined for Marseilles.

All of which was true, as Reagan knew.

Consequently, leaving the country from that port city was no longer a safe option. Even if Khoury found a way to continue south and board a freighter or other commercial ship where cash would buy him passage without questions being asked, where would he go? There was little possibility, as Reagan had discussed with Erin, that he would risk a journey home to the Middle East, at least not yet. The attempt on his life in Lyon made it clear he had some things to square away with his superiors in al Qaeda before hazarding that move.

Reagan figured Khoury would not risk booking a flight, even with a false passport, as Interpol was already circulating his photo.

There were other possible destinations, such as North Africa, but the safer route would clearly have been across the channel to the UK. He would not have to rely on anyone else to take a ferry or rent a car, circle back to Paris, and proceed through the tunnel.

After running through the possibilities again, Reagan sat back on his black leather sofa and drew a deep breath. He was not going to wait for leads that might never materialize since experience had taught him a critical lesson—whether tracking a terrorist, solving a crime, or trying to prevent one, time is almost always of the essence. For now, he was left with same conclusion he had suggested to Erin—it was possible Walid Khoury had chosen London as a place to hide. The bank accounts Erin managed to uncover. Trips Khoury had taken there in the past two years, which Cyla told them about. The ease with which someone of his ethnicity could blend into the metropolitan flow. And, in the end, the difficulty of choosing almost any place but London.

If they were wrong, if Khoury had found a safe harbor in the Middle East, he was already beyond Reagan's reach.

Reagan picked up his cell and called his partner Carol Gellos on a secure line, provided his analysis, and shared the few concrete facts he had that supported his deductions. Then he waited.

Gellos thought it over. As a highly trained criminologist and profiler, she relied less on instinct, as Reagan did, basing her opinions on parameters that combined available facts with past conduct.

"From what we know, he has never done his own dirty work, unless cornered," she finally said.

"Such as taking out those two men on the train."

"Right. But there's more to his methods than simply delegating violent activities. He has proven himself someone who enjoys creature comforts. For instance, he has no history of living in caves with his brethren in Syria or Iran. As he was hatching his plot against the United States, he was ensconced in that comfortable Parisian apartment we visited, living out his cover as an international banker, traveling back and forth to D.C. with his wife."

"Which means he's not likely to go to ground wearing a *thobe*, sporting a long beard and carrying a Kalashnikov."

"That's my point, especially since those would-be assassins on the train make it clear he is no longer a welcome part of al Qaeda."

"That's my thinking," Reagan said.

"The largest factor that has now come to light is the current existence of these bank accounts in the UK, the balances of which are fairly substantial."

"Erin filled me in," Reagan said. "It feels like the last part of the puzzle."

Gellos did not disagree. "Khoury is no one's fool, and it's evident he created an exit strategy for himself some time ago. Whether he had a falling out some day with his friends in the Middle East, or simply tired of their *jihad*, he wanted a means of disappearing, and he was going to do it in style."

"Which leaves us with London as the most logical place for him to be hiding."

"Occam's Razor," Gellos replied.

Reagan smiled. "One of your favorite principles."

"It is indeed. Particularly since there are so many residents In London who are Arab or of Arab descent. Much easier to blend in than other locales."

"Such as a gated community in Boca Raton."

Gellos laughed. "Yes. Then, however, we must still face the small matter of London having a population of over eight million people."

"There is that."

"I've been thinking about what he might have done to alter his appearance by now," Gellos told him. "Cutting his hair shorter, darkening the gray, wearing glasses with clear lenses, the usual."

"I doubt he's gone for plastic surgery. Too chancy."

"And not enough time yet," she agreed.

"Time," Reagan repeated, returning to his basic theme. "It's running out, and I feel I need to do something."

"Despite the fact that you've been ordered to do nothing."

"I'm not sure I heard you," Nick laughed and then said, "Despite that, yes."

"All right, how can I help, other than theorizing about where he might be and what he might look like."

"When you and I searched his apartment in Paris, we found nothing to suggest he had another residence."

"That's correct," Gellos said.

"There wasn't even a hint of the apartment he and Cyla have in D.C."

Once again, Gellos took a moment before responding. "That's true."

"Which means, since he has two sizeable accounts at Coutt's Bank in London, it is not impossible he's already arranged a *pied-a-terre* for himself there."

"Not impossible," Gellos said.

"How about you work with Erin, see what you might else get from the bank. We have to presume he receives his statements online, which is consistent with Erin's investigation to date. Maybe we can hack into his email. And there has to be an address somewhere in his files, no bank opens an account nowadays without one. If it turns out to be the place in Paris, so be it, but it's worth a look."

"Makes sense," Gellos agreed. "What's your next move?"

"Unless you have a better idea, I'm going to London."

Gellos knew her partner as well as anyone, and knew arguing with him would be useless. After another pause, she said, "Have a nice flight."

* * *

CAROL GELLOS' ASSESSMENT of the changes the Handler would make to his appearance was not far off. In addition to shorter, darker hair, and the wire-rimmed glasses she predicted, he had grown a beard.

With access to the funds Erin had discovered, Reagan and Gellos were also right in their assumption that Khoury was enjoying a more than comfortable existence, except for having to live in the shadows. He almost never went out during the day, his nights limited to dinners in small taverns or out-of-the-way restaurants. He was not in touch with anyone, not even those he still believed he could trust.

Because, for now, he could trust no one.

Being hunted by international intelligence agencies was bad enough, with the prospect of arrest and confinement lurking around every corner. But if he were to be located by al Qaeda, the consequences would be far more brutal.

He felt himself growing tired, both physically and mentally, as he constantly grappled with the effects of making even a single mistake, knowing there would be no second chance.

This evening he was seated in the rear of a dark pub, with walls lined in ancient wood, that was only a fifteen-minute walk from his apartment. Even so, just stepping out onto the street involved risk.

He did not mind the loneliness of his current existence, at least not yet. He had long been a solitary soul. It was the ever-present sense of danger that troubled him, something he had never experienced with such immediacy. Even while leading a double life, engineering murderous plots while attending business dinners and social banquets, he always felt certain he would find his way to safety.

This was different. There was no place where he could feel safe.

His escape from France had been dangerous, but he had evaded capture. His real identity had only recently been discovered by the authorities, and even after the confrontation on the train he still had time to organize a route out of the country. He rented a car in Lyon with false papers, took a circuitous route back to Paris, drove through the tunnel beneath the Channel, and made his journey to safety without incident.

Now, as he sat in the rear of this small pub, having a dinner alone, he once again considered his options, which was how he was spending all of his days and nights.

Perhaps there was someone he would have to trust, he knew he could not go on like this forever. Eventually he would be discovered or recognized, and intercepted on a crowded street when he least expected. He knew the odds and so, not for the first time tonight, he even thought about surrendering to the Americans.

He put down his fork and stared out the restaurant window, worrying yet again how it would all end, not knowing that his question would soon be answered.

CHAPTER SIX

London

Reagan landed at Heathrow Airport the next morning, collected his carry-on bag from the overhead bin, passed through customs and immigration, and headed outside to the cab stand. He had booked a room at the Mayfair Hotel, but it was too early to check in and he had other plans. After being assigned a taxi, he gave the driver the address of a five-story apartment building just around the corner from Montague Square and settled back for the ride.

Arriving at his destination, after suffering the usual delays in and out of the London traffic, he made his way inside the building's small vestibule, hit the buzzer, gave his name, and listened as the front door lock released. Taking the stairs two at a time, he climbed up to the third floor. Waiting there, at an open door leading to one of the three flats on the landing, was a tall, burly man just a few years older than Reagan. He had broad features, a thick head of dark hair, and an easy smile. It was Reagan's old friend and fellow agent, Stan Pearson.

"Good to see you, Nick."

"Don't be so sure," Reagan said as Pearson led him inside.

The apartment consisted of two bedrooms, two full baths, an eat-in kitchen, and a comfortable sitting room. Reagan had a quick look around at the nondescript décor, typical of safe houses the Company maintained all over the world.

As he settled into a red brocade armchair in the main parlor, Reagan said, "One of these days I'd like to have a look at Uncle Sam's international rent bills. One year's worth is probably enough money to end hunger in America."

Pearson smiled. "Can I get you something?"

"Coffee, if you have it."

"Sure do," he said. Heading to the kitchen, he asked over his shoulder, "You have a good flight?"

"Slept from the time we took off until we hit the ground."

"Ambien?"

"Bourbon in the first-class lounge." Reagan heard his friend insert a pod into the machine. "Black is fine," he called out.

Pearson soon returned, handed over the mug of steaming coffee, then took a seat on the dark green sofa opposite Reagan. "Your text didn't tell me much. What have you got so far?"

"Not a lot, so there wasn't much to say. Except that I'm here on my own dime."

"You made that clear enough, but you've got to have something solid if you came all the way to merry old England."

"Not sure," Reagan said. He tried the coffee, nodded his approval, then took some time telling Pearson what he knew about Khoury's bank accounts and how that led to the suspicion he might be hiding somewhere in London. When Reagan was done, and about to remind his friend yet again that his mission was unauthorized, his cell phone buzzed with a message. It was from Erin, asking him to call on her a private line.

He punched in the numbers—Reagan made it a habit to never keep his most important contacts on speed dial—and waited. Erin picked up on the second ring.

"You're up early," he said.

"I wanted to make sure we connected."

"Always," he said. "What have you got?"

"Your hunch was correct. We dug deep enough to find an address. No way to know if it's current, but it's a starting place. Bramley Crescent in Knightsbridge. Number fifteen."

"That's great work."

"You be careful," she said. Then, before he managed a sarcastic response, she hung up.

"Something useful?" Pearson asked.

"We have the address he gave the bank when he opened his first account here. Even if it's not current, it could lead to somewhere else."

"Want me to come with you?"

"I do, but only as backup. If this goes sideways, I don't want your ass in a sling with the boys at Langley."

"Understood, but you know that if things *do* go bad, I'm stepping up to the plate."

Reagan smiled. "Then let's get us a couple of baseball bats and head out."

Pearson stood and led him into the master bedroom closet where a large safe contained various weapons and small ordnance. Reagan chose a Glock 10, checked it out, then pocketed an extra magazine, a suppressor, and some other paraphernalia that might become useful. Pearson was already armed, so they each took earpieces with built-in mics for easy communication, locked the safe, and left the apartment.

The address Erin had given was not far from the safe house off Montague Square. They agreed that Pearson should hail a taxi to arrive first and find a suitable position for surveillance. Reagan was going on foot, to give his partner some lead time and to take the opportunity to canvass the surrounding area.

Knightsbridge is the poshest neighborhood in London. As Reagan strolled its tree lined streets, he figured if Khoury really was hiding here he was not suffering. Stopping a block short of the address Erin had provided, he circled behind a row of stately townhouses until he turned left and reached the far corner of Bramley Crescent.

Given Khoury's circumstances, it was unlikely he had any sort of armed protection. He would want to keep a low profile, not parade around with bodyguards, although Reagan assumed any place he was staying would have an alarm system in place and some sort of closed-circuit system to monitor the areas outside his building.

Reagan spoke quietly into the mic as he asked, "You there?"

"In the park directly across the way from Bramley Crescent. I've got eyes on you and the entrance," Pearson replied.

"Any movement?"

"None. Not at the front door or the windows, nothing so far."

"As I mentioned, we have reason to believe he's seen me before, maybe more than once. But he's never seen you."

"What do you want me to do?"

"Walk up to the front door," Reagan said, "hit the buzzer and see if you get any response. Either way, just walk on when you're done."

"Got it."

"I know I don't have to say this, but we're dealing with a dangerous sonuvabitch. Not just the fact he planned those attacks, but the methods he used to murder and maim the innocent people he targeted. Including children. He is utterly amoral, but very damned smart."

"Roger that."

Reagan leaned against a tall light pole, pretending to make a call on his cell. He watched Pearson emerge from the small park across the street and walk toward the entrance of 15 Bramley Crescent. He saw Pearson climb the half dozen stone steps leading to the front door, hit the button, wait for a few moments, then come back down to street level and begin walking in the opposite direction from where Reagan was standing.

Waiting until he turned the far corner before speaking, Pearson finally said, "Nothing."

"Then it's time for me to make a move."

"How do you plan to get in?"

"All of these townhouses are attached, as you've seen. No way to get in from the side. I checked the back from the street behind, and I just don't see a way without going through one of the homes there. Their backyards are fully enclosed."

"Which means the front."

"It's all I've got, unless we want to stake out the place until he makes a move."

"Which could be a long time, and not your style."

"No, it's not," Reagan agreed. "What did the lock look like?"

"Single, fairly standard, but I'm more concerned about an alarm."

"Understood, but it's doubtful he would have a system linked to the local police."

"True."

"I'm guessing it would be an internal signal, together with CCTV."

"What about a remote feed?" Pearson asked. "Let's say he's out but gets a signal on his cell that someone has entered the place."

"Then he doesn't come back," Reagan agreed.

"That's my point."

"Damn," Reagan said, "I hate when you make sense." He paused for a moment. "Tell me about the park. I never saw you until you came out to cross the street. The cover must be good."

"Excellent."

"And if we spot him coming, I can get out and across the street…."

"Before he unlocks the door," Pearson finished the thought.

"I hate to say it, but I guess we're waiting. You ready for this?"

"Unless you have a better plan," Pearson said.

CHAPTER SEVEN

London

Earlier that day, Khoury left his home to stroll through Cadogan Place Park. It provided as much anonymity as he could hope for, the few people there on a weekday morning paying little attention to the solitary figure ambling along the pathways, enjoying the lovely spring weather. In addition to his altered facial appearance, he assumed a posture of an older man, his shoulders slightly rounded, his pace deliberate, just another invisible senior citizen.

He did his best to appreciate the fresh air and exercise but, as usual, his thoughts turned to his predicament and another evaluation of his available options.

He could remain where he was. His townhouse was comfortable enough and, were it not for the specter of being discovered at any moment, life in London was not all bad.

He might move around a bit, but that entailed risk. Leaving the country was possible, but returning across the channel would be another matter. He had succeeded in coming here through the tunnel in a rented car, but the search for him had inevitably intensified. There would be security checkpoints where he might be intercepted by immigration authorities, or he could be recognized by someone who had seen the photographs being circulated to various law enforcement agencies.

If he were to relocate someplace on the European continent, traveling across borders to different countries was relatively easy, but the risk of being recognized was ever present. And where would he go that would be any safer than his current home?

48

He weighed the pros and cons of surrendering to the Americans, which was only a consideration because their legal system was so broken. His case would likely go on for years, with enough of their country opposed to the death penalty that he might even survive in the end, albeit in Guantanamo or some other federal prison. At least he would not face the wrath of his own people, where his "disappearance" would be arranged in a matter of days.

There was the possibility of contacting one of his former allies in the Middle East to see if there was a deal to be made. He could lay the blame for the failed attacks on those who did not follow the instructions he had carefully laid out. He could offer ideas for new assaults and reaffirm his allegiance to the cause. Yet even as he imagined those negotiations, he found himself shaking his head. No matter what agreement was reached, he knew those people could never be trusted. They had already sent two men to murder him, and now there was no going back.

Another route existed—trying to make a deal with an enemy of the United States, such as China. Or Russia. Or even North Korea. The information he had accumulated was valuable, if he could find a way to make contact without revealing himself to the wrong intermediaries.

Khoury exhaled a long sigh, looked at his wristwatch, and decided it was time to go home.

* * *

As anyone in the business of espionage knows, the ability to wait patiently and effectively is an acquired skill. First there is the need to remain undetectable as you bide your time. For instance, Reagan and Pearson were now seated on separate benches in the small public park across from Khoury's townhouse. They were positioned so that the dense bushes and tall trees made it difficult to spot them from across the street, while providing each a good view of the front door of number 15.

Second is the matter of vigilance. You cannot simply wait, you must wait without being distracted. Neither Reagan nor Pearson could afford to lose their focus. They had to remain ready for the moment when

Khoury might arrive so he had no chance to slip inside his townhouse, or even reach his front door before they had time to intercept him.

Finally, there is the need to remain calm and not allow the ticking of the clock to rattle you. They were not sure this was still Khoury's home, but they needed to find out. Then, if the time came to act, they had to be ready to move with speed and efficiency.

Reagan and Pearson had agreed Reagan would be the one to go after Khoury if he should appear. Pearson was already at risk by agreeing to support Reagan in this unauthorized operation. If things went bad, Reagan was the one who should be out front. That left Pearson to stay back and handle any unexpected support Khoury might have.

It was more than an hour after they had established their vantage points when Reagan noticed a bearded man walking slowly along the side of the street opposite them. There were any number of homes he might be entering, or he might just be passing by, but there was something about him that drew Reagan's attention. Perhaps it was his gait, or the fact that he appeared almost too ordinary. Then the man took a look behind him, doing his best to make it seem a casual glance, but Reagan's instincts told him it was Khoury.

And Reagan trusted his instincts in all matters of life and death.

"That's him," he said into the tiny mic, alerting Pearson. Then Reagan got to his feet and moved quickly to his right, circling around a large oak. By the time he emerged from the park and began to cross the street, Reagan was advancing at an oblique angle off to the man's left.

That's when Reagan broke into a trot.

Khoury had his own instincts—one does not survive long in the world of terrorism without having a unique sort of intuition—and he felt Reagan coming even before he heard him. When he turned, he immediately recognized Reagan from the afternoon he had watched him outside the Hotel Bristol in Paris several months earlier. Reagan was moving fast, and Khoury instantly calculated the distance to his front door, the time it would take him to get there, and the closing speed at which Reagan approached. Realizing he would never get there in time, he did not even bother to run.

Instead, Khoury came to a stop.

Reagan kept moving forward, now displaying enough of the automatic he was holding inside his jacket to make his intentions clear. If Khoury made a wrong move, he was prepared to shoot him right there, on the street.

Khoury made a show of holding his hands at his side.

He said, "Mr. Reagan, I believe."

"Lousy haircut, Walid," Reagan replied.

"We do what we can."

They were standing face to face now, and Reagan performed a quick frisk, surprised to find Khoury unarmed.

"You expected me to be carrying a weapon?"

"I knew you weren't going to be wearing a suicide vest. You leave that to the martyrs you recruit."

"Indeed," Khoury said. "Leaders and pawns. The way of the world, is it not?"

Reagan ignored the question, instead having a look behind him, then nodding to Pearson across the street. Turning back to Khoury, he said, "Let's go into your townhouse."

"Excellent idea."

"And believe me when I tell you, if you do a single thing I haven't approved in advance, I'll use this gun and be glad to do it."

"Understood," Khoury said calmly. "Shall we proceed?"

They walked, with Khoury ahead, and proceeded up the stairs to the front door.

"All right if I take out my key?"

"Slowly," Reagan said, "then let me see it."

Khoury reached into his pocket, and Reagan was mildly surprised to see it really was just a key. There was no fob or other electronic attachment that might be used to ignite an explosive device or trigger an alarm.

"Your place wired?"

"Yes, a security system including video cameras. There's a touchpad inside, to the right."

"Anyone else home?"

Khoury's expression made it obvious how absurd he found the question. "At the moment, Mr. Reagan, necessity dictates that I live alone."

"We'll see. Open the door and turn off the alarm."

They entered the foyer, the system began beeping, and Khoury did as instructed. When the noise stopped, Reagan shut the door behind them and removed the Glock so it was in full view. Then he made a show of attaching the silencer.

Khoury eyed the weapon as if it were the source of some mild curiosity. "If you intend to use that, you will be wasting a wonderful opportunity."

"Is that right?"

"For the past several weeks I have considered how I might approach your country and offer a trade, but could not decide how and to whom my proposition should be submitted. It appears your arrival has resolved that issue for me."

"You have something you want to exchange for your life? Keeping in mind," Reagan added, "that you're responsible for the deaths of any number of innocent people, not to mention the serious injuries you inflicted on many more."

"I am well aware of my responsibilities, but when countries are at war..."

"Don't start that war bullshit, or I'll end this discussion right now. Wars are fought by armies, with soldiers who have volunteered or been drafted into service. You and your friends are mass murderers who slaughter innocent civilians, using deranged young people to carry out your plans, never coming near the line of fire yourselves."

"Except at this moment," Khoury corrected him.

"Your misfortune, not your choice."

"What about your generals and admirals? Do they not send young men and women to die?"

"If you want to debate the morality of war versus terrorism, let's start with how these conflicts begin."

"If you propose a review of history, Mr. Reagan, let's remember that man's history is all about war."

"Some justified, most not."

Khoury nodded. "Suppose we continue this discussion in my living room? We'll be far more comfortable than standing here."

Reagan had a quick look around. "Why would I want to do that?"

Khoury smiled his thin, mirthless smile. "Are you afraid I've placed explosives under the cushions of my sofa. Come, Mr. Reagan, I am well aware you can fire your gun at me any time you choose. Before you do, however, I believe you are going to want to hear what I have to say."

Pearson, who had been doing his best to pick up both sides of this exchange on his earpiece from across the street, interrupted for the first time, "You okay, Nick?"

"Fine. Seems the target wants to sell me a subscription to Wikipedia."

"Last time I looked, Wikipedia was free. Need me to come over there and provide additional security?"

Khoury interrupted. "You have backup, I see."

Reagan looked at Khoury, measuring the man from head to toe, before ignoring his question. Speaking to Pearson, he said, "Thanks, but for now I think you're more useful keeping watch outside. Stay in contact."

"Roger that," Pearson said.

Reagan motioned with the automatic. "Hands behind your back," he told Khoury as he pulled out the plastic restraints he had taken from the safe house, using them to bind Khoury's wrists.

"Is this really necessary?"

"Absolutely," Reagan said. "Now lead the way. You have five minutes to convince me you have something to offer that's worth your life."

CHAPTER EIGHT

Palm Beach

Dr. Derek Malone was at home in Palm Beach, sitting in his private office, staring out the large picture window that provided a view of several large palm trees and the intracoastal waterway. He had not heard back from the Novak brothers since his meeting with them two days before. He had placed a follow-up call to Andrew yesterday, but his secretary said that Mr. Novak was out, but that he would get back to him when he returned to the office.

Malone was still waiting.

He was feeling both disappointed and frustrated—he never liked to let a friend down, especially something as important as this. When he and Reagan parted the other day in New York, Nick told him not to make contact unless he had information, so Malone had not left any messages.

He had no way of knowing that Reagan had already found Khoury in London, and was therefore still expecting the help he had requested from the Novaks. Whatever their present business disagreements, Malone felt that finding this man Khoury was important enough for Andrew and John to put that aside and reach out to their contacts.

He wondered if was misjudging the depth of their recent conflict.

Malone had been introduced to the Novaks two decades ago through a mutual friend, Dr. Phillip Roberts, and Malone had since served almost ten years on the board of Novak Pharma. He had been instrumental in the dramatic growth of their business, which resulted in part from his association with Roberts.

Malone and Roberts had interned together in New York City years back, and had been close ever since, at least professionally. While Malone had a solid marriage and two sons whom he and his wife adored, Roberts had no children and was twice divorced for all the usual reasons. Now in his late sixties he was—as Connie Malone described him—an old man chasing young skirts.

His personal life aside, Roberts was a talented physician who took his profession far more seriously than his dalliances.

As neurologists, Malone and Roberts had long ago identified one of the future profit centers for Big Pharma—antiaging medications. They recognized, back then, the correlation between the nervous system and immune system. Malone and Roberts advanced the hypothesis that if you could slow down the nervous system, you can also slow down the aging process.

That was a game changer, especially after they began working with neurotoxins.

A neurotoxin is a substance that can alter the structure or function of the nervous system. There are numerous natural and human-made chemical compounds containing neurotoxins, from snake venom and pesticides to ethyl alcohol and cocaine. The extent to which they affect nerve function depends on the type and toxicity level of the substance, as well as the recipient's age and health. The inhalation of less than one microgram of botulinum toxin is lethal to humans, yet when modified it can be valuable for therapeutic uses.

When those applications were expanded to cosmetics, the new compound became the mother lode.

Malone and Roberts quickly realized the aesthetic potential of a scaled-back form of neurotoxins. If a patient was not successful in slowing the aging process, at least they could look younger without surgery. Simple injections made wrinkles disappear and years melt away.

When the two doctors brought their findings to the Novaks, a lucrative branch of their pharmaceutical company was created.

Beyond cosmetics, Malone and Roberts believed they could develop other compounds that would slow the human biological clock. They conducted studies involving telomeres and the connections between the brain, body, and nervous system. Working with doctors from other disciplines, they experimented with a combination of snake venom, the excretions of the puffer fish, an assortment of B vitamins, and antioxidants, ultimately developing a drug they called *Neulife*. They found evidence it might not only retard the aging process, but could also play a role in treating physical and mental health disorders such as ADHD, Alzheimer's disease, and schizophrenia.

The Novaks were fascinated. Roberts was a cheerleader for the project. Malone, however, who was initially cautious, became increasingly skeptical. He believed the downside risks were far more severe than Roberts was willing to admit, but his warnings were ignored. The Novaks had already commissioned an advertising campaign to be launched for when the drug was ready for FDA approval and global marketing. The slogan, Andrew Novak announced to his medical team, was irresistible:

"NEULIFE will add years to your life and life to your years!"

Meanwhile, Malone continued to ask for a long-term study to gauge the side effects of the drug as well as the consequences of coming off the prescription. While Roberts hailed *Neulife* as a panacea, Malone pointed to data suggesting that patients who began taking the medication and then ended the treatments could suffer permanent damage to their body's cellular structure. In addition to other possible contra-indications, which varied in accordance with an individual's genetic makeup, there was evidence that stopping the dosage might actually accelerate the aging process.

To Malone's amazement, Roberts saw this as a positive.

"Think about it Derek," Roberts said one evening over a dinner at the Capital Grille in D.C., "this is like anti-heroin. Equally addictive, but beneficial so long as the patient signs on for a lifetime of use. We would literally control the population through the promise of antiaging. Just consider the implications. For the future of health care. Slowing disease and reducing hospital costs."

"What about the other hazards we've been studying?" Malone asked.

"Such as?"

Malone reeled off a number of risks. "Even if you put those aside, what about the harm to people coming off the drug because they can no longer afford it, or for any number of other reasons?"

Roberts waved off his questions, then raised his martini as if to make a toast. "We'll address all of that in time, but for now we have to look to a bright future."

"What about our ability to maintain a steady supply?"

"Scarcity is a key source of wealth, is it not? You're telling me that our dosages might only become more expensive for the consumer. Pray tell, how is that a negative?"

Malone's dubious expression made it clear he was more than a bit concerned. "There are years of research needed on this."

Once again, Roberts was not dissuaded. "We'll reach every American, every person worldwide, letting them know that *Neulife* will nourish your cells and maintain a healthy life. The body is an incredible self-healing organism if given the right empirical formula. Now we have that formula. Neulife provides an enhanced process for cell regeneration and protection. Do you doubt the results we've already seen?"

"No, I don't," Malone conceded, "but I'm worried about the things we *haven't* seen."

Over the past twenty years, Novak Pharma had generated enormous profits from the work done by Malone and Roberts on botulism-based compounds, and Malone enjoyed a large increase in his wealth as a result. *Neulife* was another story. It was not about giving people options for cosmetic procedures, it was an unspoken endorsement of a process that would make people drug dependent.

The misgivings shared by Malone and a small group of his colleagues only grew. He monitored the research and trials being conducted, by now convinced that Roberts and his acolytes were willing to ignore the dangers posed by *Neulife*, tailoring their results to fit the narrative they would ultimately sell to the FDA and the public. As a last resort, and unknown to anyone, Malone was retaining copies of the raw data, preparing for the day when he might have to stand up to Roberts, the Novaks, and others in the company.

Yet, despite the issues all this was creating in his dealings with the Novaks, as he stared out his window at the beautiful Florida scenery, he worried about why they were not responding to the request for help he had made on behalf of Nick Reagan. Why would they not provide any assistance they could to bring a ruthless terrorist to justice?

CHAPTER NINE

London

Reagan was seated on a dark brown velvet sofa in Khoury's richly furnished living room, the Glock in his right hand resting on his lap. He was facing his prisoner, who was shifting uneasily in a Queen Anne armchair upholstered in a deep maroon paisley pattern, the restraints binding his hands behind his back making it difficult for him to find a comfortable position.

"Are these really necessary? Do you think I'm going to lunge across the table to take your gun?"

Reagan stared at him for a moment, then said, "From what I've seen, I have no idea what you're capable of. I've given you five minutes, don't waste it complaining about plastic handcuffs."

Khoury moved forward, perched on the edge of the seat. Meeting Reagan's cold gaze, he said, "You were ordered to stop looking for me."

Reagan did not reply.

"I see you must be a reasonably good card player, Mr. Reagan, but your eyes are the tell. You and I know it's the truth and, logically, you're wondering how *I* know."

"Playing games, Khoury? Do you have something serious you want to say, or are you just buying time?"

"You work for a man named Kenny. He passed the order to you, but it did not come from him."

Reagan stared at him without speaking.

"You decided to continue this search on your own, am I right?" When Reagan did not reply, Khoury went on. "You sought the help of

59

a friend," Khoury said, "to see if he might obtain information regarding my whereabouts."

Reagan frowned. "I have a lot of friends who helped me track you here."

"But this individual, he did not."

"Did not what?"

"He provided you nothing that would lead you to me here, in London."

"Your time is running out and that's the best you can do? Pretending you know of a friend I asked about you, who then gave me no help?"

Khoury offered him another unpleasant smile in response. "Dr. Derek Malone," he said.

Reagan worked hard not to betray the wave of surprise that washed over him. First, Khoury claimed to know that Reagan had been ordered to stop tracking him, which was obviously true. Now he had Malone's name. How? He felt the urge to stand up, walk toward Khoury, and crack him across the head with the butt of his Glock, but he resisted the impulse. "Is there something you want to tell me about Derek Malone?"

"I should not need to say anything more," Khoury said. "I've already told you that I know you are not here officially on behalf of your beloved CIA. And I know you went to Malone to see if he could find anything about my returning to my homeland. Come now, Mr. Reagan, is that not enough to pique your interest, at least a bit?"

"My interest in what, exactly?"

"In the wealth of knowledge I have concerning corruption in your government."

Reagan was shaking his head before Khoury finished the statement. "You don't know whether I'm here in an official capacity or not, and Malone has absolutely nothing to do with my government."

Khoury showed him that annoying smirk again. "Your superiors directed you to abandon your search, we both know that to be a fact. And Dr. Malone has been instrumental in assisting you before, in another matter, which means he has everything to do with your government, at least indirectly. But let's move on. To Paris, for instance. When you and I were both there recently, you forced my wife to arrange a lunch meeting with me. It was to be, what you Americans like to call, an ambush. Did you ever wonder why I did not attend your little party?"

Reagan remained silent.

"I was warned by one of your own people, which is why I immediately left the city."

"Only to be met by a couple of your pals from al Qaeda."

"Yes, an unfortunate occurrence, but not a complete surprise. My former associates are an unforgiving group."

"Your reward for not having murdered enough innocent people?"

"Oh my, am I about to get another lecture from a hired assassin about the horrors of killing people? If so, let us resume our historical debate, which should include the highlights of your career, as well as more than two hundred years of slavery, the plight of native Americans, United States imperialism, and so on?"

This time Reagan did get up, taking two strides forward and placing the end of the Glock's suppressor hard against Khoury's right temple. "You're down to sixty seconds. You have something you want to say?"

Without flinching at the gun barrel pressed against his head, Khoury said, "We both know you're not going to kill me, at least not yet. You want to know how I know you were told to stop tracking me, and how I know you went to Dr. Malone for assistance."

Reagan noted that his prisoner was doing a reasonable job of not looking scared. "I don't want anything from you. If you don't force me to kill you along the way, my job is to bring you in for interrogation and to make you pay for the atrocities you committed."

"Then you have no use for the name I was going to give you."

"What name?"

"Ross Lawler," Khoury said.

Reagan backed away half a step. "What about him?"

Khoury looked up at him. "You are obviously aware that the media has recently exposed several incidents of corruption in your government. Little will come of it, of course, which is typically the American way. But these stories are merely the beginning of what I know. Believe me, your CIA's second in command, Mr. Lawler, is at the center of a far-reaching drama that is about to unfold, one that will affect you personally."

CHAPTER TEN

London

After making his vague accusation about Ross Lawler, Khoury advised Reagan he had said all he would until he had a credible guaranty of asylum from someone with the authority to give that assurance.

"I have neither that authority nor that inclination," Reagan told him. "Which is why we're done, at least for now."

Reagan spoke to Pearson. "Everything still all clear out there?"

"As a bell."

"Things got a bit more complicated than I expected."

"I'm catching part of it, what do you need?"

"A flight home for me and a guest."

"Is he going to be upright or horizontal?"

Reagan had a look at Khoury. "Can't trust him to cooperate."

"Roger that. You have the stuff?"

"I do. Let's get a vehicle out front. I can get him to the door, then you can come up here."

"I'll make the call," Pearson said.

"I'll call the DD."

After hearing only Reagan's half of the conversation, Khoury asked, "Are we leaving?"

"We are. Get up."

Khoury managed to stand, his hands still bound behind him. Reagan stood and pushed him forward as he reached into his pocket with his left hand and removed a syringe he had taken from the safe house, keeping it from Khoury's view. The two men made their way toward the front door, Reagan keeping the barrel of his Glock jammed into the small of Khoury's back.

When they reached the foyer, Reagan reached up, roughly stuck the needle into Khoury's neck, and depressed the plunger. "Sweet dreams," he said.

Reagan eased him to the floor as Khoury lost consciousness, then he phoned Kenny.

As careful as Reagan and Pearson had been to stay alert to their surroundings while surveilling the townhouse, they did not see a young man by the name of Odai entering the far end of the park where they had waited. He was dressed in khakis and a blue oxford shirt and carried a satchel, the sum of his appearance being that of a graduate student from some local university. He was far enough behind them, shielded by a stand of trees, to keep himself out of view.

But he was there for the same reason Reagan and Pearson had come.

A week ago, Odai's superior numbers in al Qaeda had received a tip that Khoury might be living somewhere in Knightsbridge. They dispatched the young man to spend time walking around the neighborhood and, after several days moving about the area, this morning he thought he spotted Khoury. Despite changes to the man's hair and the growth of dark beard, he looked enough like the photos Odai had been given for him to take notice when the man entered Cadogan Place Park.

Odai waited patiently from across Cadogan Place until he could get another look at the man. He did not want to follow him too closely. He also did not want to call for help from anyone else until he could confirm it was Khoury and, hopefully, locate where he was living. That would certainly be a reason for *fakhar*.

When the man finally exited the park, Odai trailed at a distance down the long street. He had just entered the small commons across from Bramley Crescent, using the trees for cover, when he saw another man, up ahead, begin running across the street. Odai hesitated as he saw the man accost his target, leaving the young man no choice but to remain out of sight. He waited as the two men spoke, then watched as they headed upstairs together to one of the town-houses, number 15.

Odai pulled out his cell phone and called for instructions.

By now, Pearson had joined Reagan in the foyer of Khoury's townhouse, where they waited for their ride. Discussing their options, Reagan reflected on the truism, that when actions in his profession seemed the simplest and safest, they can be the most difficult.

In this case, they had to get Khoury's inert body down the stairs and into a car without interference from any locals or worse, being seen by hostiles who might be watching this location. Assuming they could get Khoury in the vehicle without incident, they would have to make the drive to Farnborough Airport to board a private jet home. Although Kenny had authorized the flight—after a number of questions and a clear expression of his disapproval—the DD had no control over the British bureaucracy or what issues might arise when Reagan had to deal with customs and immigration officials, some of whom might be a bit testy about bringing a comatose man on board the plane.

All of that was going to be difficult enough without the fact, still unknown to Reagan and Pearson, that his visit with Khoury had not gone unnoticed.

After enumerating the various alternatives, Pearson said, "We need to decide how to handle this now. Our ride is on the way."

"I don't suppose you have access to an ambulance? Take him out on a stretcher?"

"Negative," Pearson replied. "Would take way too long for me to line that up, and there would be too many questions."

"Understood," Reagan said with a nod.

"Too late to buy a coffin and claim you're bringing him home to be buried," Pearson offered with a smile.

Reagan held up a hand. "Maybe not."

"You're not serious."

"No, I'm not." He paused. "I think we have to do the obvious—each grab him under an arm, take him down the stairs like he's drunk."

"A little early for that, isn't it?"

Reagan shrugged. "If you've got a better idea..."

"I don't," Pearson admitted.

"All right, let's just hope he doesn't have a lot of nosy neighbors wondering how he got soused at this hour of the morning."

"What about when we get to the airport?"

"Still trying to figure that out. I've got my diplomatic passport, didn't use it when I arrived, but that could work."

Pearson looked at his phone. "The car is pulling up right now. Let's go."

The sedative Reagan had injected was powerful enough to keep Khoury out for the next couple of hours, which was all they needed. He and Pearson were tall and strong enough to pull Khoury up to his feet and so, with each man on either side, they began the descent down the stairs toward the street below.

Odai had moved toward the front of the commons, an interested observer of these proceedings as he awaited his own ride. He watched as two men dragged Khoury down the steps, loaded him into the rear of the Range Rover, and were swiftly whisked away with their cargo.

Just a minute or so later, a Ford sedan pulled up on Bramley Crescent and Odai jumped in the rear.

"Which way?" the driver asked.

"Straight ahead," the young man told him, and they set off in pursuit.

"Car?"

"Black Range Rover," Odai told him, then recited the license plate number.

"Good work," the driver said.

The man in the front passenger seat turned to face Odai. "Why didn't you call us sooner?" he demanded.

"I was not sure it was Khoury," the young man replied.

"But you're sure now?"

"Very sure. He entered his building with one of the men. Then the second went up there and they brought him down to the street."

"What do you mean, brought him?"

"They had him under his arms, as if he was unconscious. Then they put him into the back of their SUV."

"Is it possible he was dead?"

"Don't be stupid," the driver interrupted. "If they killed him, they would have left him there. Listen to what Odai is telling you. They're taking him somewhere, for interrogation no doubt."

"An airport?" Odai suggested.

"The only thing that makes sense," the driver in the front agreed.

"I saw his condition," Odai told them. "There is no way they are getting him on a commercial flight."

"Good point," the driver said.

Odai was feeling pleased with himself. He said, "It would have to be some smaller airport. Southampton? Farnborough? Some other private airfield?"

Stepping on the accelerator, the driver said, "We're going to find out."

Pearson's fellow agent, Gary Haller, was behind the wheel of the Range Rover, maintaining a legal rate of speed. He figured there was no sense being stopped with an unconscious body that had been bound and stowed in the rear of the SUV.

CHAPTER ELEVEN

London

As Haller maneuvered through the inevitable tangle of London traffic, turning onto Brompton Road and heading for the M4, he said, "I don't mean to sound paranoid." Then he had a third glance at the rearview mirror during the past few seconds. "I think we may have company."

Reagan was in the back seat with Khoury and turned to have a look behind them.

"That dark blue sedan has been weaving in and out," Haller told him. "Seems to be in a real hurry."

Reagan saw the Ford. It was definitely coming on fast, now just a few car lengths behind them. "Just in case, you know any great shortcuts?"

"These London streets are like a jigsaw puzzle, so it may not be a shortcut, but we can try and lose them."

Haller yanked the steering wheel hard to the left, cutting off the car beside him, the driver slamming on his brakes and leaning on his horn. The sudden move caused the Ford to also veer left, but too late for the driver to follow them down Hans Road. Haller accelerated, racing toward Hans Place and a route leading to Kings Road.

"Not the best way to get to the airport," Haller admitted.

"You were right though," Reagan said. He had watched the Ford's failed attempt to make the sharp turn Haller had negotiated. "They're definitely tailing us."

"Where the hell did they come from?" Pearson asked.

"They must have been doing the same thing we were," Reagan said, "casing the townhouse. We just got to Khoury first."

"But you were in there with him for more than five minutes. They could have made a move then."

Reagan nodded. "Maybe they weren't armed for that, or maybe they just had a scout in place."

"Now what?"

"We stick with our plan. Kenny told me the jet will be ready to go when we get there."

They rode in silence for a while, Haller doing his best to pick up as much time as possible. Then, as he followed the side road that fed onto the M4, he saw the Ford again.

It was parked off to the side of the long entrance ramp, just ahead of them. Having lost the chance to follow them, they had obviously taken the direct route ahead, guessing their likely route and hoping to intercept them.

"Just keep moving," Reagan said as he pulled out the Glock and lowered his window.

Pearson turned around to face him. "What're you going to do, shoot it out in the middle of all this traffic?"

"Not unless they shoot first."

Whoever was in the Ford spotted them as soon as they entered the busy highway and pulled right behind the Range Rover.

"I've got this," Haller said, hitting the gas again, swerving into the far right lane, and racing away from the sedan.

"We can't do this all the way to the airport," Reagan said.

"How about I let them pull alongside, then I can try to run them off the road," Haller suggested.

Reagan shook his head. "I can see you're a good wheel man, but this is not *Fast and Furious Part Sixteen*. I know we have the larger vehicle, but you lock up with them and we're as likely to crash as they are. Not to mention the risk to all these other cars."

"What do you suggest?" Pearson asked.

"Next time you have an opening on your left, jump into the lane and hit the brakes." As he said this, Reagan lowered the window on the right side of the rear passenger seat.

"I thought you said you wouldn't make a move unless they fired first," Pearson said.

"I lied," Reagan said. "Now do it."

Haller waited a beat, then swerved to his left and hit the brakes. As the SUV abruptly slowed, a large white van behind them also had to jam on the brakes, the driver blowing his horn as he narrowly avoided rear-ending the SUV. The Ford, meanwhile, had instantly come alongside them, and Reagan could see the man in the front passenger seat was holding a semiautomatic rifle.

Reagan did not hesitate. He fired three shots through the silenced Glock, two of them hitting his target—the front left tire of the Ford.

The sedan, which had been accelerating in the effort to catch them, now swung out of control.

"Move it," Reagan hollered, and Haller hit the gas pedal again as the Ford crashed into the guard rail on the right, then careened back across the lane, striking the van that had been behind their Range Rover, bringing both of those vehicles to a loud, violent stop.

"Nice work," Haller said.

"You too," Reagan replied as he put up the window. "Let's see what surprises for us at the airport."

CHAPTER TWELVE

Farnborough Airport, Hampshire, UK

Farnborough Airport handles most of the private air travel in and out of London. After Haller connected from the M4 to the M3 and they neared their destination, Reagan told him to exit onto one of the back roads that circled around the back of the airfield. The men they had taken off the road undoubtedly phoned for help and, even though they had no way to be sure of the Range Rover's destination, Reagan was not taking any chances. He certainly did not want to roll through the front door if someone was waiting for them.

Haller did as Reagan suggested, finding his way to Ively Road, then coming around through a side gate, eventually pulling up to the hangar for the private company that would be providing transportation home.

It was not a large building, painted white with minimal windows and two glass entry doors. Reagan was surprised to see a pair of security personnel waiting out front, each of them carrying what appeared to be an H&K submachine gun—clearly not standard operating procedure for a private air carrier. The good news was that they were wearing uniforms of British tan.

As Haller slowed to a stop in the drop off area, Reagan said, "You guys wait here. And be ready in case they make any funny moves."

"Funny how?" Pearson asked.

Reagan let himself out the back door of the Range Rover and walked toward the two men. His first impression was that they were not surprised to see him, which was understandable since arrangements

71

for their ride had been made through a deputy director of the CIA. The second impression was that they did not appear friendly.

"Greetings," Reagan said as he approached. "You guys on high alert or something?"

The stockier of the two men spoke up. "We were told you were coming. Then we got word there was a crash on the M4."

"Nothing unusual about that," Reagan said with a smile. "There's an accident on that road about every four hours, am I right?"

The Brit was not smiling when he said, "This was no accident. Seems one of the vehicles had its tire shot out."

Reagan maintained his friendly demeanor. "That so?"

"Highway videos picked it up. From two different angles," the man added.

Reagan finally allowed his smile to fade. "What has that got to do with us?"

The taller man answered this time. "Your Range Rover there, it was picked up in the footage."

"There are a lot of Range Rovers in London. They're actually made here in England you know."

The taller man shook his head. "Not many people call for a private flight to Washington on an hour's notice. We have a pretty fair idea of who you work for."

"Then I'm going to guess you were sent here by someone in MI5," Reagan said, referring to the British domestic counterintelligence and security agency. "You're either military or guns for hire, is that the play?"

Ignoring the question, the first man told him, "Someone's got to answer for what happened on the highway."

Reagan took a moment, as if thinking it over. "We're still allies, right? The US and the UK, I mean. When a group of Americans is being chased by a car full of Arabs carrying automatic weapons, you guys have to pick a side. I think it should be ours."

"If what you say is true, we'll get it all sorted out."

"We're a bit short on time, so we need to sort it out right here," Reagan told them, his tone remaining even but firm. "We have a flight to catch, and a delay is out of the question."

"Your schedule is not our problem…" the stocky man began, but before he could finish, Reagan made his move.

In one swift motion, he pulled out his Glock, took a step forward, and grabbed the taller man around the neck with the crook of his left arm, sticking the barrel of his weapon in the man's side. "As I said, I believe we're allies, but I also said we have a flight to catch, which means you have some limited choices here. This can get real nasty, or you can take my word for what happened, get the hell out of our way, and let us get on the plane. Your call."

As soon as they saw Reagan remove the Glock from inside his jacket, Pearson and Haller were out of the car, guns drawn and moving forward.

"Goddamned Americans," the stocky man growled, but did not make a move as Pearson approached and took his weapon. Haller disarmed the man Reagan was holding.

"This doesn't involve you guys," Reagan said calmly as he released the taller man and stepped back. "We have some baggage to get home, and we're going to do it now, with or without your cooperation. Understood?"

The two Brits exchanged a glance, then the taller man spoke. "You say they were chasing you and they were armed?"

"That's the fact," Reagan said. "I'm sure if you check your video footage carefully, you'll see that there were weapons in their car."

The Englishman nodded.

"For reasons not worth discussing," Reagan said, "it's possible the hostiles we left on the M4 might've called for help and guessed we were heading here. Which means time really is short. I can ensure that you don't interfere with our departure by taking the two of you with me, but I suppose that would qualify as kidnapping. We could tie you up, gag you, and leave you somewhere until the flight takes off, but that would also create an international incident. Which leaves me to ask a simple question." Staring at them, his deep blue eyes unblinking, he asked, "What can we do to convince you that stepping aside is the way to go here?"

"We were told to stop you and bring you in for questioning," the stocky man said.

"The best laid plans," Reagan said. Then he turned to Pearson. "I wonder where that order came from?"

"Something you're going to have to find out," Pearson told him. "We can handle this on our end."

"Consider it done," Haller agreed. "I'll stay behind and keep them company. You two go."

Reagan shook his head. "You're both going to stay," he said, turning back to Pearson. "You're stationed in London, no sense in complicating matters."

"All right. Once you're in the air, you'll be okay."

The three agents led the two Brits to the Range Rover where they did a quick frisk, removing cell phones and handguns. Then they sat them in the back seat.

"We're not using restraints and we expect no nonsense," Reagan told them. "The four of you will have plenty of time to figure out what to tell the people over at Thames House."

After Haller shut the car door, he said "Let's get you moving."

"Thanks," Reagan said. Reaching into his pocket he pulled out his diplomatic passport and handed it to Haller, who went inside to make the arrangements.

"Whatever you need on the other side," Pearson told Reagan, "I'm there for you."

"My mission, my risk. You guys should try and remain invisible."

"Not likely," Pearson said with a smile, as he nodded at the two officers in the back seat of the SUV.

"We'll see. Take them someplace far away from here once I'm gone. I wasn't bluffing about those shooters calling for backup. Guessing we were coming here would not be a huge stretch, especially since they were waiting for us at the entrance to the M4."

"Understood."

Reagan walked to the rear of the Range Rover and opened the tailgate. Khoury was still out cold. Once Haller was back to keep an eye on the Brits, Reagan and Pearson each grabbed an arm, dragged Khoury to an upright position and carried him onto the Gulfstream. Once aboard, they maneuvered him into something approximating a sitting position and strapped him in.

As Pearson was about to disembark, Reagan said, "Thanks pal. No telling how this is going to play out, but I'll be in touch."

"Watch your six," Pearson told him.

CHAPTER THIRTEEN

Over the Atlantic

Once they were in the air and Reagan settled back for the flight home, the first call he made was to Deputy Director Brian Kenny. After giving a sanitized version of what occurred in London—he figured he would deal with the fallout later—Reagan provided a summary of the key claims made by Khoury.

After hearing him out, the DD admitted it was unsettling that the Handler claimed to know that Reagan had been ordered to cease the search for him, and that Reagan had reached out to Derek Malone for help. The most troubling item, however, was the mention of Ross Lawler, the number two man in the Agency.

"He made no specific accusations, is that correct?" Kenny asked.

"That is correct, sir, but as I say, he did know about the order that I…"

"Nonsense," Kenny interrupted. "This is a classic disinformation ploy. He makes two fairly benign statements, then uses them to convince you that the third, more serious claim is true."

"Benign? How would he know about the order? Or Malone?"

"First, we have no idea who Malone might have spoken with about the conversation you had with him. You asked him to have his contacts reach out to influential people in the Middle East for information. Word of that could have easily circled back to Khoury in any number of ways. We have to assume he still has friends in that part of the world with whom he has contact. Did you consider that?"

Reagan did not respond.

"As for the order that you stand down, who knows? It might have been nothing more than a good guess," Kenny suggested, although without much conviction.

"What about the two Brits at the terminal? You obviously didn't alert anyone about who I am or why I was there. So, who did?"

This time Kenny had no answer at all.

"All right, let's shelve all this for now," Reagan said, seeing no point in debating any of it, at least not now. "Khoury claims to have much more to share but will only deal with someone who has far more authority than a mere field agent. He mentioned your name, incidentally, since he's also aware I report to you. Let's see what you think after you have an opportunity to interrogate him. Fair enough?"

"It is."

"Good. Then what's our plan?"

"Whatever Khoury may or may not know, we need to keep both you and him below the radar for a little while." Kenny thought it over, then said, "I'll have a car waiting for you at the airport. By then I'll decide where we'll meet."

After that call, Reagan took some time analyzing what the DD had said, and to consider his next moves. He treated himself to a premium bourbon from the well-stocked bar, then sat back in his comfortable leather seat and watched Khoury sleep through his drug induced stupor. Reagan was in a forward facing seat, Khoury's unconscious form opposite him.

Reagan wondered how someone becomes a mass murderer of innocent people. What could drive someone to that depth of depravity, taking the lives of men, women, and children he does not know and has no personal grudge against, just to make some deranged political or religious point?

Then he thought about what Erin had told him, after doing a deep dive into Khoury's background. He was Lebanese, raised in Beirut, his real name Ghafran Shaheen. As a young man he was, in fact, a banker. Bright, educated, and a devout Muslim, he was recruited by *jihadists* to assist with their cause—not as a planner of murderous plots, but by utilizing his experience in finance. He married young, had a daughter, and was working from Aleppo when the Syrians launched an attack against the rebels there. He was at his office when the counterinsurgency came, learning later that day that his wife and daughter were two of the civilian casualties in the intense fire-bombing of their neighborhood.

Rather than viewing their deaths as evidence that this entire region needed to find a way to resolve their cultural and religious differences and establish peace, he blamed the West for his personal tragedy, particularly the Americans. He could not see past the rage he felt as a Muslim, intent on eradicating the infidels from the world. He was no longer the banker Shaheen, he had become the terrorist Khoury, known in the West as the Handler.

Reagan had another taste of bourbon as he stared at Khoury. After all he did—regardless of what triggered him—this butcher wanted to trade secrets he claimed to possess, hoping to save his life. And in doing so, he seemed almost preternaturally calm, as if the outcome really did not matter one way or another. What was he really thinking?

Then Reagan questioned how he could even engage in these discussions with the man. Would it not be fair to simply strangle him as he sleeps? Would that not leave the world a better place? In a sense, would that not be a greater justice?

Reagan shook his head, dismissing the notion that he could ever be as cold-blooded as the Handler. He had another pull at his drink, then went on contemplating the situation until deciding it was time to call Erin David.

"You all right?" was her first question.

"Never better. I'm on my way home with a special guest in tow."

"So I've heard."

"Who ruined the surprise?"

"Carol gave me an update."

"How would she know?"

"The DD read her in, gave her the right to include me in the loop."

"That Gellos, what a blabbermouth."

"I'm about to leave for D.C. to meet with her, should be there when you arrive."

"That's the best news I've had all day," Reagan told her, allowing himself a smile for the first time in hours.

"I hear Khoury wants to make some sort of deal."

"Yes indeed. Claims to have all sorts of information we can't live without."

"Any previews?"

"He knew I was ordered to stop tracking him."

"How could he know that? Some sort of wild guess?"

"That's what Kenny suggested, but I don't think so. He was too smug in the way he told me. I believe he was telling the truth. He actually knew."

"What else?"

"He mentioned Derek, that I'd gone to him for help."

"He knew about Malone?"

"Yes, he did." Reagan hesitated. "Your line secure?"

"Is there such a thing anymore?"

Reagan nodded to himself. National security was a growing source of concern at all levels. "Let's just say he mentioned someone else, someone higher up in the company who we know."

"I have the name," she told him.

"Good. I'll share more about that when I see you. For now, though, I need some help."

"Now there's a surprise."

"I have Khoury's cell," he told her, then recited the phone number and model. "I know it will be tough to do this remotely, but I need you to start looking at calls he's had coming and going over the past few weeks."

"You mean, since he went missing."

"That's the idea. Someone is obviously feeding him this information. The sooner we identify the source the better."

"It would be a lot easier if I had the phone."

"You will, in a few hours. Just want to get this started."

"I'll get right on it," she said. "An intriguing puzzle, for sure."

And more than a little dangerous, Reagan well knew.

CHAPTER FOURTEEN

Over the Atlantic

A short time later, Khoury began to come around. He was clearly worse for wear after being drugged and then jostled around in the cargo section of the Range Rover.

Shaking his head in an apparent effort to rid himself of the cobwebs, he asked, "Was all of this really necessary? Sedatives? Handcuffs?"

"I certainly thought so," Reagan replied.

"You would not have brought me on this journey if you were not convinced the information I have has real value."

"Let's just say it's enough for me to resist the urge to push you out the door."

Khoury did not take the bait, nor was he about to admit that making a deal with the Americans might be his best option. At least for now. Instead, he asked, "Can we at least do something about having my hands cuffed behind my back? If you're not going to push me, do you think I'm likely to try and jump out of this plane myself?"

"You need to use the facilities?"

"That would be civilized of you."

Reagan stood, took out a knife, leaned Khoury forward and cut the plastic restraints from his wrists. He immediately followed that action by removing the Glock. "After you use the head, I'll bind your wrists in front of you, as well as your ankles for the remainder of the flight."

"But..."

"This is not a negotiation. Just get up."

When Khoury returned from the washroom he took a long drink from the bottle of water beside his seat, then allowed Reagan to secure him once again, this time both wrists and ankles. At least he could sit back comfortably with his hands in his lap.

"You haven't told me anything about Ross Lawler, except to use his name. We have a few hours to kill, why not fill in some blanks."

Khoury nodded slowly. "Lawler was the one behind the order that you give up your search for me." Before Reagan could respond, he asked, "Have you not wondered why that direction was issued?"

"I'll ask the questions here. For instance, how would you know that?"

Khoury resorted to his thin imitation of a smile. "That would be a major leap forward in our discussion, something I intend to divulge only to your superiors. However, the reason *why* that order was given should be obvious to you by now."

"Someone didn't want me to find you."

"Not just someone. Mr. Lawler."

"Which raises another 'why' question."

"Yes it does," Khoury agreed, "although that answer should be equally clear."

"You have information someone does not want you to share."

"Again, not someone. Ross Lawler."

"You're accusing him of treason?"

"Treason is a judgment based wholly on perspective. Mr. Lawler may have very good and valid reasons for objecting to my having this discussion with you. Or with others. Those motives remain to be seen."

"Why didn't he just have you killed, if you pose such a danger to him?"

Khoury took some time thinking that over. "The first thought that comes to mind is that he was not as clever as you in locating me. But there is more to it than that."

Reagan anticipated the Handler's next claim.

"I have made arrangements for what I know to survive my death," Khoury said. "I assume you understand what that means."

"You've left your story with someone or at some place that will become available in the event of your demise."

"Despite my unfortunate circumstances, I am not without resources. As I have demonstrated, I know about you having been directed not to continue your search for me, as well as the involvement of Dr. Malone. A man in my position develops various channels of communication in the course of a career."

"Career?" Reagan replied in disbelief. Leaning forward in his seat, he said, "You kill innocent people, what kind of career do you call that?"

"Please, Mr. Reagan, let's not go through all of that again."

Reagan sat back. "Go on."

"Many of my connections are highly placed, in government, industry, and so forth. Only a few knew of my role with al Qaeda, most did not. Since you have met my wife, you realize that I move in rarefied circles, internationally as well as within your country. I realize you will find this hard to believe, but I am trusted by many of those with whom I have had dealings."

"Which really is incredible," Reagan said. "I hate to admit it, but you must be good."

"I believe it is your American writer Mark Twain who said, 'It is easier to fool someone than to convince him he has been fooled.' How else can you explain the huge deceptions perpetrated by people such as Bernard Madoff, who swindled billions from people who believed him to be their friend? Or that young fraud who engaged in similar activities involving cryptocurrencies? Even while in hiding I have been interacting with people, albeit remotely, enriching the extent of my knowledge as well as my influence."

Reagan responded with a look of disbelief.

"I see that you think I'm posturing, but I assure you all that I am saying is true. Your government chose not to publish reports of who I am, to whom I am married or to provide photographs of me to the media. That decision should have you asking the same question."

"The question, why?"

"Exactly."

Reagan was not buying it. "As I'm sure you understand, our motive was to find you before your former colleagues got their hands on you. Turning you into a celebrity would not serve our purposes."

"Apparently not, and congratulations to you since you succeeded in locating me and taking me into custody. But publicizing my face and background would certainly have made me easier to find, would it not?"

"Maybe, but that doesn't matter now, does it? Regardless of who or what you know, you were behind three murderous attacks in the United States, and our system requires that justice be done."

Khoury smiled again. "I know much more about you than you could ever guess, and one of the qualities for which you are well-known is an overdeveloped sense of right and wrong. Some have even described you as a Boy Scout, based on your allegiance to the ideals you still see in your country. You refuse to recognize that a new order is coming, and that your morality will soon become outdated."

Reagan did not respond.

"There was a time when the common currency in this world was actually grain. People needed to eat before indulging in any other activity, and so agriculture ruled the land, along with hunting. As populations became more comfortable, food more plentiful and people more sophisticated, they indulged in other occupations. The basis for trade turned to coins of gold and silver, as well as bartering for services or goods. Ultimately, nations agreed on the myth of legal tender, some currencies more valuable than others as we know, and thus the concept of money was born. The accumulation of this fictional wealth allowed those who had the most to run countries, build armies, and control their people, while establishing large homes and making purchases far beyond the reach of ordinary men and women. Now it seems information, and the means by which it is spread, has become the key to power, and I possess significant intelligence that your superiors will find worthy of trade."

"We'll see."

"Yes, we will. How they react will depend entirely on which side of any given debate these individuals stand. Some will want to share the information, some will want to suppress it, and still others will want to use it for their own gain."

"All of which brings us back to the need for you to suffer for what you've done."

Khoury uttered a weary sigh. "The predictable response from someone who sees the world in black and white, right and wrong, without an appreciation for the nuances of what real power is about. You are nothing more than a law enforcement officer who, in your parlance, is bringing me in. I, on the other hand, know how to negotiate for the result I seek."

"Which is?"

"My life, Mr. Reagan. I thought that was clear. And as I've said, you are not the person with whom I should be discussing this any further. You are hell-bent on vengeance rather than understanding what is truly at stake in today's world."

"Maybe so," Reagan said as he got to his feet, "but if we really are done talking, we have a few hours until we land, and I need to get some rest. I'm going to have to put you to sleep again."

"You're not serious."

Now Reagan smiled. "Afraid so. You don't think I'm going to take a nap with you sitting there wide awake, do you?" With that, Reagan reached into a bag on the seat across the narrow aisle and withdrew another syringe. "This will put you out for the next few hours. If I'm asleep, I've instructed the copilot to keep an eye on you, just to make sure you don't give me any nightmares."

"You are a very melodramatic young man."

"Mostly I think of myself as careful. And by the way, as for my desire for vengeance or your interest in trading for your life, you're absolutely right, that's not my call. But you're also correct about my view of the situation. If I were sitting on any sort of tribunal with your life on the line, I wouldn't care if you could tell us where to find the Holy Grail, you know how I'd vote."

CHAPTER FIFTEEN

Washington, D.C.

John Novak was in his brother's office, the door closed, no one else present. It was a large room, furnished in a postmodern style featuring glass and metal tables, a highly polished rosewood desk with a chrome base, and chairs upholstered in black leather. The walls were covered in various examples of abstract art, the overall effect consistent with John's adherence to the Nietzsche maxim, "From chaos, comes order." The quote could be found in the background of one of the paintings John had commissioned, if studied carefully enough.

There was also a framed calligraphic piece bearing the Novak motto, which came from Gandhi:

Be the Change You Wish to See In the World

Andrew and John were seated across from one another in Eames armchairs of chrome and black leather, with an irregularly curved table of smoked glass and stainless steel between them.

"What has Paszek told you?" Andrew asked.

"Malone is still in Florida. He hasn't had any further contact with his friend in the government."

"No texts, phone calls, nothing?"

"None that Paszek has detected," his younger brother confirmed.

"And he's confirmed that..."

"The friend is Nicholas Reagan. CIA. Same agent Malone was involved with during the investigation of that Chinese computer hack a few years ago."

"As we surmised," Andrew said as he leaned back and stared up at the ceiling. "Seems odd, Malone coming to us with that sense of urgency, then dropping the ball this way."

"Not really," John disagreed. "He called the office the other day, but Lisa told him we were out."

Andrew began nodding. "Good, although that does not address the larger problem."

"Why is Malone even having those discussions?"

"Precisely. And how strong is his connection to this fellow Reagan? We need to know if he's going to persist with this little mission of his."

"Paszek says they've remained in touch over the years. Only social, apparently."

"Mr. Sociability," Andrew said.

John could not suppress a smile. "Yes he is."

"Let's return to the matter of Dr. Roberts," Andrew suggested, as he sat up and faced his brother. "He and Malone were thick as thieves when we rolled out our line of cosmetic injections. Lately they've been on separate trajectories."

"Wealth is an interesting thing, on many levels," John observed. "Some can never get enough, while others reach a point where they feel it's their obligation to do some good with all they've acquired."

"And Malone has become one of those do-gooders."

"Which causes him to ask too many questions."

"Such as his performance at the last board meeting," Andrew said.

"I assume you're referring to more than the questions he raised again about *Neulife*."

"Correct," Andrew said. "I mean all those objections he raised when we discussed our efforts to secure sources for lithium. He went on and on about how we would be taking advantage of third world countries, damaging their environment, and victimizing their people. He sounded like a rabid do-gooder."

"He did," John agreed.

Andrew paused before saying, "Contact Paszek. Tell him to tighten his surveillance on our friend, Dr. Malone. We want to know about *anyone* he communicates with."

"Including social interactions?"

"Especially those. As we've already said, Derek tends to be too friendly for his own good."

"Consider it done."

"The mention of the lithium raises another interesting thought."

"Anatole Mindlovitch," John responded, demonstrating how adept the brothers were at finishing the other's thought.

"We've not heard back from him."

"He's playing his cards close to the vest on this Ghost Chip he developed."

"Yes, he is," John agreed.

"Let's set a meeting then, this is better handled face-to-face anyway."

"Here or at his place in California?"

"See what his schedule allows for," Andrew told him. "We can be flexible."

"I'll take care of it."

"And tell Paszek to find out what he can about this Nicholas Reagan character, and how close he is to locating Walid Khoury. I thought he was ordered off that search."

"He was."

"Then Paszek should persuade him to do what he's been told."

"Already in the works," John assured him.

CHAPTER SIXTEEN

Outside Union Station, Washington, D.C.

Erin David took the Acela Express from Penn Station in New York for her meeting with Carol Gellos in D.C. After their telephone conversation, which followed Kenny's discussion with Gellos, they concluded it would be best if they could work together at Langley with the support staff on hand.

Union Station in Washington is a majestic facility with ceilings soaring ninety feet high, the architecture and design from a classic era. Tourists and shoppers frequented the various stores and restaurants that had been installed in recent years, making this a popular destination even for those not traveling. After Erin stepped off the train, she weaved her way through the crowd toward the taxi stand outside.

When she emerged from the building and neared the area where a line of cabs waited, a short, dark-skinned man approached from her right and said, "Taxi lady? No waiting."

Before she could reply, a second man came up from behind her, pressed something hard into the base of her spine, and said, "Let's go, or you'll never see your friend Nick Reagan again."

Erin felt her face flush and her pulse race as her mind shifted into overdrive. There were obviously police all around the station, but none she could see from where she was standing. If she cried out for help or tried to run, she feared they would carry out their threat to kill her, then disappear into the crowd, as the gunfire would create an instant panic. If she went with them, there was no telling what she would face.

The man on her right had taken hold of her arm, his grip firm, as he said, "Move now or die, bitch."

He pointed to a black sedan waiting at the corner, with the rear passenger door open.

"Let's go," the man behind her said.

It was all happening too fast for her to improvise any reasonable means of escape. She remained standing there, managing to ask, "Why?" which was the only thing she could think of to say.

Neither of these men was interested in conversation.

The man behind her said, "Move," then shoved Erin toward the car.

She took a step, feeling herself falling off the edge of the curb when—as if events were happening in slow-motion—everything suddenly changed.

As she began to stumble forward, the pressure at the small of her back, which she assumed to be the barrel of a gun, disappeared. Then the man behind her was also falling, while the man to her right let go of her arm. She reached out to steady herself against the side of one of the waiting taxis as the man who had been behind her toppled into the gutter.

Struggling to regain her balance, she turned to see what was happening as people all around began hollering and screaming.

Leaning against the cab, she recognized Alex Brandt, the young agent who often worked with Reagan and Gellos. He had the man on her right in a choke hold that was so tight his face seemed to be turning blue. Looking to the man in the gutter, she saw he was now face down with Carol Gellos' knee in his back and her gun pointed at the side of his head.

"Federal officers," Gellos called out to the people around them. "Everyone stay back."

A uniformed police officer arrived with his gun drawn, and helped Erin onto the sidewalk. "You all right, ma'am?" he asked as he placed his hand gently on her shoulder.

"I am now," she said with a weak smile.

She heard the sound of screeching tires and looked up, seeing two police cruisers arrive at the corner, preventing the sedan that had been waiting for her from moving. Armed officers jumped out, but found there was no one in that car.

"Oh my God," Erin said.

By the time the two would-be kidnappers were handcuffed and taken into custody, a group of federal agents drove up, announced that the matter was in their jurisdiction, and carted the prisoners off. Gellos and Brandt took Erin to their Chevrolet sedan, which was parked just around the side of the large building, and drove away.

Erin was in the back seat, bent over, working to steady her breathing. She finally asked, "What just happened?"

Gellos, in the front passenger seat, turned to face her. "Nick and I were concerned after you spoke with him. The guys downstairs had intercepted some random chatter, and Sasha thought your call might have been intercepted. That's why Nick asked Alex and me to meet you at the station."

"I'll remember to thank Sasha," Erin said with a wan smile, then drew another deep breath and sat back. "What a world. My boyfriend can't even have a private conversation with me from a private jet."

Gellos also smiled. She wasn't sure she had ever heard anyone refer to her partner as a "boyfriend," not even Erin. "Unfortunately, Nick has concerns that the interception of your conversation may have come from inside the Agency."

"Seriously?"

"Nick told you some of what Khoury had to say."

Erin nodded. "He knew about Nick being ordered to back off his search, and that Nick asked Derek Malone for help."

"He also claims there are people in the Company who are not what they seem to be," Gellos said.

"What a polite way to put it. And yes," Erin said, "he mentioned that, but didn't give me a name over the phone."

Gellos nodded. "We'll see what else Khoury has when he gets here. Our plan was to meet you at the train, but it took us a lot longer to get there than expected."

"Seems you got there just in time."

"True enough," Brandt agreed from the driver's seat.

Erin was still for a moment, then said, "I think that's as close as I've ever been to dying."

Gellos reached out and took her hand. "You don't ever want to get any closer than that."

"No, I don't. Thanks again guys."

"Don't mention it," Gellos said, then turned to face forward again.

"What now?"

"We're not taking you to Langley, not yet. We're going to meet Nick somewhere else."

CHAPTER SEVENTEEN

A safe house outside Langley, Virginia

When the Gulfstream landed at Montgomery County Airpark, Nick Reagan was wide awake following a refreshing sleep, but his fellow passenger was still groggy from the second dose of sedatives he had been given.

Reagan leaned forward and slapped Khoury lightly across the face. When that did not rouse him, Reagan followed with a hard smack. "Time to go," he said, and the Handler nodded his head.

The plane taxied to a stop outside a private hangar. Reagan could see a black Chevrolet Suburban waiting for them, one man standing outside beside an open door, a second inside at the wheel. Reagan undid the restraints on Khoury's ankles, but left his hands bound in front of him.

"Get up," Reagan said as he pulled Khoury to his feet, then moved him toward the hatch that was being opened by the copilot. "Thanks guys," Reagan said as the pilot also came out of the cockpit. "Smooth ride."

"We aim to please," the pilot told him.

Reagan had Khoury walk down the stairs first, holding him from behind by the collar of his jacket so he didn't fall face forward onto the tarmac. They were met by the agent who had been standing across the way, near the Suburban. Reagan recognized him and they exchanged greetings.

"Good to see you, Elliot."

"You too." As he helped Reagan put Khoury in the back of the SUV, he said, "The DD is waiting for us."

"Then let's not keep him waiting," Reagan said.

The Central Intelligence Agency's most elaborate safe house in the United States was an imposing stone structure nestled in the midst of a large tract of land situated some forty miles southwest of Langley in suburban Virginia. Once jokingly referred to by an agent as The House of the Seven Gables, the estate had since become affectionately known to insiders simply as the "Gables," used only for the Company's most important guests.

The property on which it stands extends for more than a hundred acres, the perimeter bordered by a wood fence discreetly fitted with high intensity electrical wiring and surveillance cameras. The fortifications at the gatehouse and outbuildings were also well disguised, leaving the property with the overall appearance of a stately manor, which actually concealed a variety of tracking devices, round the clock surveillance, a full complement of armed guards, and enough weaponry and communications paraphernalia to withstand an assault by a well-equipped battalion.

Reagan thought they would bring Khoury there, but he was informed that Kenny had decided otherwise.

The "Cottage" was another CIA safe house, further west than the Gables, deeper into the rural part of Virginia. Less elaborate with fewer men on site, the DD felt it would be easier to control the flow of information in and out of there while they tried to decide what to do about Khoury and his claims.

Elliot drove through suburban Virginia into an increasingly countrified area, the journey pleasant enough with almost no conversation, just as Reagan wanted it.

He spent time on his phone, confirming by text with Pearson that he and Haller did not encounter any problems after he took off. In their brief exchange, he also told them he had no intention of bringing their names up when reporting to Deputy Director Kenny, realizing it was an assurance he would find hard to keep. Kenny would want details and Reagan would have to give them.

They approached their destination from a small side road that led to the front gate. As was the case with the Gables, the perimeter of the Cottage was fenced in with a variety of electronic devices and high voltage wiring. After being cleared through the checkpoint, they drove along a stretch of curved driveway that led to a large brick colonial where they pulled to a stop.

"Please take our guest inside to a holding cell," Reagan said to Elliot, "I'll meet with the DD."

Elliot did as requested, helping Khoury out of the SUV, then leading him up the few stone steps toward the front door. Reagan remained behind, waiting until they had disappeared down some interior stairs, before he made his way toward the main foyer. Waiting for him at the door was Deputy Director Kenny.

"Nice of you to drop by," Kenny said.

Reagan drew back slightly. "Is that irony, sir?"

"Spare me the sarcasm, Reagan. You had specific orders to cease any operation seeking the whereabouts of this man." Kenny's tone sounded more annoyed than upset. "I suspected you might act on your own and admit that I'm impressed you located him. Perhaps, if you had eliminated him in London, there would be less of an issue. Instead, you involved two other agents who apparently had no idea you were directed to stop your hunt for Khoury. Then you engaged in some sort of Wild West shootout on a London highway, disarmed two British operatives from MI5, and then brought Khoury back here."

Reagan knew Kenny well enough not to make light of anything that had occurred. It was bad enough it was already known Pearson and Haller had participated in the abduction. "I was confronted with certain information that suggested it would be more valuable for us to interrogate Khoury than for me to liquidate him and leave him in his townhouse. I made that clear on our call. Once you speak with him, I believe you will agree, sir." Before Kenny could answer, Reagan added, "And if I may say so, you did authorize our transportation back here."

"As if I had any damned choice," Kenny said, which was about as angry as he ever became.

"If this is going to be a problem up the chain of command, I take full responsibility for my actions."

"A lot of good that will do either of us, Reagan. You disobeyed an order, I am your direct superior, and people are going to demand accountability."

Reagan said nothing.

"There are other events that have taken place," Kenny said in a softer voice. "Come inside."

Kenny opened the door to the left and they entered a large sitting room where Carol Gellos and Alex Brandt were seated in the upholstered armchairs.

Erin, who had been on a large sofa, jumped up, ran to Nick, threw her arms around his neck, and murmured, "Oh Nick."

Before Reagan could ask, Gellos described what had occurred earlier that morning at Union Station.

When she was done, Reagan expressed his gratitude, kissed Erin on the forehead, then took her by the hand and led her back to the plush sofa covered in a forest green fabric.

After they sat down, Reagan said, "Unfortunately, this is consistent with the things Khoury has been telling me." Looking at Kenny, he said, "If I may review a couple of examples for everyone."

"I wait with bated breath," Kenny said.

Reagan then gave a summary of what Khoury had shared with him so far, as well as his interest in trading further information for his life.

When he was done, Kenny said, "Tell us why you involved Dr. Malone."

"He works with the Novak brothers, sits on the board of their pharmaceutical company, participates in their charities, and so on. Maybe I was grasping for straws, but I thought Malone might get me a lead on Khoury through them."

"Did he?"

"I told Derek he should only contact me if he had something to say. I haven't heard back."

"But Khoury claims to know that you spoke to Malone."

"Any chance of a connection between Malone and Khoury?" Gellos asked.

"Zero."

"All right," Kenny said. "How about his accusation against Ross Lawler?"

"As I've said, Khoury never gave any specifics about Lawler, just that he's a traitor and involved in things he is willing to describe if there's a deal to be made." Reagan paused. "He did say that Lawler was involved in the order to take me off the hunt for him."

"Did he actually say that?"

"In so many words. Whether that's true and how he knows is up to you to find out." Reagan paused, looking at the man he trusted above all others within the Agency. "It's true, isn't it? Lawler was the one who issued the order to have me back off the hunt for Khoury."

Kenny met his agent's intense gaze. "I'm not sure, but yes, damn it, it might have been."

CHAPTER EIGHTEEN

Palm Beach

After an early dinner, Derek Malone retired to the office in his waterside home in Palm Beach. A few minutes later his wife Connie walked in. He was seated in the black, ergonomically designed chair behind his desk, so she took a seat in the armchair opposite him.

"What's going on?" she asked.

Malone managed one of his easy smiles. "What do you mean, sweetheart?"

Connie was not smiling. "We've known each other too long for you to brush me off with a wink and a grin, Derek. Something is troubling you, so let's have it."

Malone uttered a long sigh, then stood and began pacing slowly around the generously sized room. It was airy and light, the walls adorned with various awards, citations, and photographs of the Malones with celebrities and politicians. "I'm not sure."

"Well my darling, *I'm* sure it's not like you to sit here by yourself brooding these past couple of days. If there's a problem, let's discuss it. Maybe there is something I can do to help."

Malone stopped moving in front of the large picture window that looked out over the intercoastal waterway. He perched on the sill facing Connie, his hands at his sides bracing him. "The Novaks," he said.

"Is this about your meeting the other day?"

He nodded.

"You never told me what it was about and I haven't asked. But I'm asking now."

After a slight pause, he said, "I saw Nick when I was in New York."
She waited.

"He asked for a favor. He wanted me to speak with John and Andrew about something."

When he hesitated again, she offered up a warm smile. "You're a neurologist and I'm a psychologist. Neither of us is a dentist, so can you please forego the teeth pulling and just tell me what this is about?"

He stood, came around the desk, and sat in the chair beside her. "Nick swore me to secrecy, but I assume that doesn't include my better half, meaning you."

"I hope not, or I'll have to take that up with Nick the next time I see him."

Malone nodded. "That recent series of terrorist attacks, in New York, Las Vegas, and Minnesota. Nick was involved in trying to prevent them. Now he's hunting down the man who planned them."

Connie waited again. As a trained therapist, she was skilled at waiting for people to speak.

"This man, he was born in Lebanon, became part of al Qaeda. Nick thought I might be able to get some information on him through the Novaks. As you know, they obviously have significant connections in the Middle East. He figured they could make some inquiries."

"Makes sense."

"That's why I stopped in D.C. It was not a discussion I was comfortable having on the phone."

"Understandable. Were they helpful?"

"That's what troubles me. They said all the right things, but I've heard nothing back, and that's not like them. Even if they came up empty, they normally would have been in touch. I followed up with a couple of calls, but never got past their assistants."

"Did they understand how serious this is, and who was behind the request?"

"That's two questions," he said with a weak smile. "I told them it was about the monster behind those attacks. I mean, does it get any more serious than that?"

"I suppose not."

"In answer to your second question, I didn't give them Nick's name, or even mention the CIA."

Connie thought it over. "Maybe they came up empty," she said, almost immediately changing her mind. "I don't buy it, Derek. With all of their connections?"

"I agree, sweetheart. They never come up empty when they want something, whether it's information, a business deal, whatever. And, even in the unlikely event they did, why not just call and tell me that?"

"A valid point."

"But it's more than that," Malone told her. "You know that Roberts and I are on different sides of the argument about *Neulife*."

"I do."

"Which is why things have become cold between Phillip and me. I just didn't think that extended to the Novaks. I keep telling them, you can't play fast and loose with pharmaceuticals, and I thought they understood."

Connie had never been a fan of the Novaks, a fact well known to her husband, so she was careful not to advance any criticisms of them now. All she said was, "They should understand."

"Right. But now they want to buy up all those lithium mines in South America, since lithium is a key component of this new drug, as well as several others. At the last board meeting, when they discussed their plans, I raised questions about the environment, the economic impact, what would happen to the locals. They cut off the discussion as if I'd called them a dirty name."

"You told me."

"More and more I feel like an outsider rather than part of their inner circle."

Connie thought it over. "How do you think all of that relates to the assistance you were requesting on behalf of Nick? I mean, we're talking about providing help to find a vicious terrorist who murdered and maimed innocent people in our country. *Their* country."

"I'm not sure, which is a big part of what's bothering me. I know their idea about the lithium market involves medications, but also batteries. In much larger quantities. That brings Anatole Mindlovitch into the picture, which is a whole other level of concern."

"Is all this why you decided to postpone our trip to Paris?"

Derek nodded. "I thought I should be here, in case I could help Nick. Hope you're not upset about that."

"It's fine," she said, "although Benji and Sondra are going to be disappointed."

"I know," he said glumly.

"Let's get back to Nick. Why wouldn't anyone who might give Nick help in capturing this man do everything they could?" The answer was obvious, but she let her husband respond.

"Only if the capture of this man would somehow pose a risk to them or their interests."

"Which raises the next question," she said.

"Yes," Malone agreed. "How is that even possible?"

CHAPTER NINETEEN

A safe house outside Langley, Virginia

When Kenny, Reagan, and Gellos entered the small room in the basement, Khoury got to his feet. The plastic restraints on his wrists had been removed, and he extended his right hand.

"Mr. Kenny, I presume."

Kenny ignored the gesture. "Sit down," he said.

The room was lined in white-washed cinderblock, with no decorations or windows, and recessed fluorescent lighting overhead. There was a rectangular gray metal table in the middle of the room surrounded by several gray metal chairs. As Khoury sat, the three of them took seats across the table from him.

"A lack of civility is unnecessary," Khoury said.

"I understand you want to speak with me, and your time is short," Kenny replied. "I suggest you get to the point."

"May I assume Mr. Reagan has provided you some preliminary information?"

"You may assume nothing," Kenny told him. "You're going to be charged with causing the murder of numerous people in this country, as well as serious injuries to dozens more. It is unlikely you have anything to share that will mitigate your punishment, but if you have something to tell us, now would be the time."

Khoury sat back and studied each of them in turn, ultimately returning his gaze to Kenny. "Is it necessary for all of you to be here?"

"I trust these people with my life," Kenny replied, "and I believe they feel the same. We are all going to hear what you have to say, or this interview is over."

"Very well. You will recall that Mr. Reagan attempted to lure me to a lunch with my wife in Paris in an attempt to capture me there. Have you wondered why I never showed up, about who might have warned me?" Khoury paused but received no reaction. "You have nothing to say about that?"

"Why not dispense with the games and tell us?" Kenny said.

"I will," Khoury said as he showed them his thin smile, "but since the source of that information is part of what I have to trade, until we have reached an arrangement of some sort, I will keep it to myself."

Kenny nodded without speaking.

"I am merely attempting to establish my credibility," Khoury said, then cleared this throat and went on. "In the matter of Mr. Lawler, did any of you question why he ordered Mr. Reagan to cease his search for me? I suspect not, since that is how bureaucracies work. Orders are given and followed, and so we end up with Nazi Germany, communist China, and now, the CIA."

Reagan, who had been silent up to now, other than the sound of gritting his teeth, asked, "Can I just get up and cave his head in now?"

Without taking his eyes off Khoury, Kenny said, "You were the one who brought him all this way for interrogation. We are going to hear him out before we decide what to do with him."

Carol Gellos spoke up for the first time, addressing herself to Khoury. "You appear to see this as some sort of negotiation, but you are mistaken. Regardless of whatever information you have, or claim to have, no one knows you are here. There is no prospect of escape or rescue, and you are not entitled to the constitutional rights afforded the citizens of this country, whom you have chosen to slaughter without cause. Do you understand?"

Unlike the anger he saw in the eyes of both Kenny and Reagan, Khoury noticed that Gellos remained remarkably calm as she stared him down. His smile having faded, he said, "You misunderstand my situation. You are my only viable option for rescue, as you call it. Ross Lawler is part of a large cabal that supports a new world order where individuals have no voice, governments do not matter, and everything will be run by a group of wealthy elitists. All you need to do is review his actions over the past two years and you will see that they are consistent with this vision of the future. Do I have your attention now?"

They waited.

"If I end up in Lawler's hands," Khoury continued, "I will be as dead as if my former associates in al Qaeda had apprehended me."

"You're making a serious accusation against one of the top people in the Agency," Kenny said.

"I don't make any of these statements lightly, or because I think they will save me. The understanding I have of my situation is far more acute than that."

The interrogation room was soundproof, but they all heard someone knocking on the door. Kenny got up and found it was Alex Brandt.

"We have a situation, sir," he told Kenny.

Stepping into the corridor and pulling the door closed behind him, Kenny asked, "What's up?"

"I got word from your assistant. There's been grumbling upstairs at Langley. Someone got word that Nick grabbed Khoury."

"I didn't tell them," Kenny said. "Do they know we have him here?"

"Not sure. They apparently know about the flight from London, so they're likely to make calls to the Gables and then here, among other places."

Kenny nodded. "Go upstairs and see if they've heard anything. I'm going to put an end to this interview for now."

Back inside the room, Kenny sat and stared at Khoury. "I have some bad news for you. There are others who already know Reagan brought you in, and they may be on their way as we speak."

For the first time, Khoury's expression betrayed a measure of concern. "Even if you're telling the truth, we may be at an impasse. Unless you have the authority to trade my information for a promise of clemency, I have no reason to say anything more."

Reagan began laughing. "You're kidding right? You think we give a good goddamn if you've reached an impasse?"

Khoury did his best to ignore Reagan, fixing his attention on Kenny. "You know the name Klaus Schnabel?"

"Of course."

"Do you consider him an enemy of the United States?"

"My views on world…"

"Please, Mr. Kenny," Khoury interrupted. "You say we do not have much time. Will you concede that Schnabel's vision for a new world order is contrary to the ideal and doctrines of your country?"

"If I do?"

"What if I told you that Schnabel and his collaborators have arranged for the placement of men and women in some of the highest positions in your government. Not just elected officials, since they are becoming increasingly irrelevant. I'm talking about the bureaucrats that actually run the United States, along with the wealthy and powerful in the business sector. Together, these people have practical control over what happens in education, medicine, vaccine mandates, finances, all of the day-to-day decisions that affect your people and your economy. Am I getting through to you?"

"What has all of this got to do with you?"

"These people not only fix interest rates, tax rates, energy costs, and manipulate the much-discussed supply chain. They also make life and death decisions and, believe me as someone who knows, they have little regard for the great unwashed. They work with anyone who will create the hierarchy that will serve as a means to their end."

"Which is?"

"Total control, of course."

"And you have access to information that proves the existence of this grand scheme?"

"You don't need me to prove it exists. You don't even need to look past the people funding your elections." Khoury paused, slowly shaking his head. "What if I told you that there are individuals in your own beloved government who actually work with al Qaeda, with ISIS, even with neo-Nazi groups that still wield power all over the world?"

Kenny frowned. "We've been dealing with these conspiracy theories for longer than I can remember."

"I believe one of your statesmen said, 'When something is true it is no longer a conspiracy theory.' I say it is a plot against the welfare of your nation."

"And you have evidence this is all true?" Reagan asked.

Khoury sat back, realizing he finally had their attention. "I've met with your Mr. Lawler, here in Washington, when I was in town with my wife, Cyla."

Kenny nodded. "You had a successful cover as an international banker married to a woman in our diplomatic corps. If you met Lawler, that would not be uncommon."

"It would if he knew I was working with al Qaeda at the time and did not disclose that to anyone in your Agency. And I can prove that he did."

"We're listening," Kenny said.

Khoury described Lawler in detail, as well as the date, time, and place of their most recent meeting in Washington, just a couple of months earlier. It was at a State dinner, and Khoury claimed that Lawler took him aside to have a private discussion.

"Lawler knew exactly who I was but took no action to expose or arrest me. As he put it, he thought I might be useful."

"You're claiming he knew you were planning attacks on our country?" Reagan demanded.

"Of course not," Khoury said. "He was interested in the contacts I had. It was only later that he realized the mistake he had made. That's why he warned me about the lunch meeting Mr. Reagan had arranged in Paris. He did not want me taken into custody and questioned. When I left Paris, I believe it was Lawler who suggested to my own people that I should be removed." Khoury sighed. "That last part is supposition, I admit, but it makes sense."

"This is all rather far-fetched," Kenny said. "Even if I believe you met Lawler at some point which, as I've said, is not surprising since you and your wife moved in those circles, the suggestion that he's in league with Schnabel and al Qaeda is quite a leap."

Khoury hesitated, then gave them a name of an agent with the FBI. "Victor Turnquist was in Paris when I was there, something you can check with the Bureau."

"And he's supposedly another member of this conspiracy," Kenny said in a tone that made his skepticism obvious.

"Very much so. And far more dangerous than you would imagine."

CHAPTER TWENTY

A safe house outside Langley, Virginia

There was another knock at the door, and Kenny went outside to speak with Brandt, leaving Reagan and Gellos with Khoury again.

This time, as soon as the door was shut behind the DD, Reagan leaned forward. "Listen, asshole, my boss may be interested in what you have to sell, but at the moment I only have one question. Who went after Erin David?"

Khoury's look was as blank as a sheet of paper, and Reagan thought if he was acting he was very good. "Who is Erin David?" he asked.

"A close friend of mine, who also happens to be a close friend of your wife, Cyla."

"Ah, yes," Khoury replied, nodding his head as if he had just recalled the name. "I met her in Washington once or twice. Attractive. Intelligent. Likable."

"I'm thrilled that you remember. Now tell me, who tried to have her kidnapped today? Was it something you planned?"

"Don't be ridiculous, Mr. Reagan. I've been in your custody with no access to any sort of outside communication since you found me in London. And what possible motive would I have?"

"Maybe they intended to hold her as a bargaining chip for you."

The Handler responded with a look that suggested the idea was absurd. "Of all the people in the world, why would I have Ms. David kidnapped?"

"Because she's a friend of mine?"

"Come, come, Mr. Reagan, don't exaggerate your importance. As I have repeatedly said, you do not have the authority to make the sort of arrangement I'm seeking. No offense, but if I were inclined to use someone as a bargaining chip, as you put it, I would aim much higher than your lady friend."

Reagan glared at him, resisting the urge to reach across the table, grab him by the collar, and hit him with a series of quick jabs. But he took a deep breath instead and stood up. He knew Khoury's logic was right, so he left him there with Gellos and joined Kenny and Brandt in the hallway.

"Brandt was just filling me in," Kenny said. "Bottom line it for him."

"There's a group on their way here from Langley," Alex said.

Kenny turned to Reagan. "What do you think?"

"I think Khoury's the scum of the earth," Reagan said, "but I believe him. He has too much information he should simply not have. Malone. The fact I was ordered to stand down. Even if his claims against Lawler are bullshit, there are just too many coincidences."

Kenny thought it over. "Perhaps, which creates an obvious dilemma. If Khoury's telling the truth about Lawler and his people take custody of him, we may never get the rest of the information he has. On the other hand, Lawler is our superior and we can't ignore his instructions."

"You can't, but I can," Reagan said. "I already have." Turning to Brandt, he asked, "How much time till they get here?"

"Not certain. Twenty minutes, maybe thirty."

"All right," Reagan said. "Let me bind Khoury's hands, tape his big mouth shut, and take him to my place on the Chesapeake. That'll buy some time for me to get more answers from him."

Kenny gaped at Reagan as if he had just asked him to commit professional suicide. "What am I supposed to say when these agents arrive? There are too many people upstairs and at the security gate who know Khoury is here."

"Tell them I took Khoury to FBI headquarters for questioning. After all, the three attacks he arranged were all on US soil, so the Bureau has a jurisdictional right to interrogate him. You can say my role was only to bring him in."

Kenny considered that for a moment. "It might work."

"At least it'll buy us some time."

"What if this is all some sort of ruse and Khoury's made other plans?"

"For instance?"

"He's no one's fool, and may have some sort of contingency," Kenny said. "For all we know, he may have allies who know you brought him here from London. Leaving you alone with him in your cabin when his friends show up? I don't like the odds."

"It's always nice to know you care, chief, but I've searched him three times. He has nothing on him that could be traced, no cell phone, no microchips, and he wouldn't want that anyway. He has no friends anymore, and he's more afraid of al Qaeda than he is of us."

"Maybe, but there might be others outside al Qaeda still loyal to him."

"Then why was he so isolated in London?"

"Maybe he wasn't, maybe you just caught him at the right moment."

Reagan shook his head. "Not likely, believe me, and we don't have to involve anyone else in what I'm doing. I'll handle this alone."

"We're all involved at this point, Reagan. You can take Khoury, but you're bringing Brandt with you." When Reagan began to voice another protest, Kenny cut him off. "That's an order, and it's an order you're going to follow."

"All right," Reagan said turning to Brandt. "Let's get moving. We'll take one of the rigs out front."

"If you get a call from me," Kenny said, "don't answer unless I text you a hashtag first. Then you'll know I'm in a position to talk."

"Got it," Reagan said. "Except for Gellos, no one else here needs to know what we're doing. Alex and I are just going to walk him out the front door and hit the road."

"All right," Kenny agreed, "get his hands bound good and tight and take a couple of friendly tranquilizers with you, might make your life a bit easier."

"The way I keep jabbing him, he's going to turn into a narcoleptic." Then, far more seriously, Reagan said, "Please take care of Erin. She's still badly shaken."

"Don't worry," Kenny told him, "I will."

* * *

AFTER REAGAN SECURED KHOURY'S WRISTS with another pair of flex cuffs—behind his back, over the man's objections—they did exactly as planned. Gellos handed Brandt a small leather bag containing weapons, additional ammunition, and a couple of syringes. Then the four of them took Khoury upstairs and out the front door, where Brandt buckled him into the front passenger seat of one of the SUVs in the driveway.

Kenny and Gellos had walked behind, watching as Reagan got behind the wheel and drove off.

After exiting through the security checkpoint at the front gate, Reagan turned to their prisoner. "We can do this the easy way or the hard way; that'll be up to you. I've already made it clear I would just as soon be rid of you, and I will not hesitate to do just that if you make even the slightest move we have not approved. Are we clear?"

"Yes," Khoury said. "May I ask where we are going?"

"No, you may not. In fact, I have tape here that I can slap across your mouth, but I decided to give you a break, especially since there may be things you want to tell us along the way. No time like the present to improve your chances of survival."

"Mr. Kenny has yet to give me any assurance of what will become of me once I have divulged more of what I know. There's no reason for me to say anything else at this point."

"Maybe, but we have you in custody and there doesn't seem to be anyone who's going to care if you come to a bad end, especially your friend Lawler, if what you say is true. Which means you may want to be a bit more forthcoming." Reagan shrugged. "Just a thought."

They rode on for a while in silence before Khoury said, "That FBI agent I mentioned."

"Victor Turnquist."

"You know him?" Khoury asked.

"Not yet, but I will."

"He's extremely dangerous."

"I'll be careful."

"I mean dangerous to me, and not in the way you might guess."

Reagan took a quick glance at Khoury but said nothing.

"Also, do you know a man named Bogdan Paszek?"

"Can't say that I do," Reagan replied.

"Turnquist and Paszek are connected."

Reagan glanced in the rearview mirror at Brandt, who was seated behind Khoury, weapon in hand. "How are they connected?"

"You'll find out." Khoury paused before adding, "Paszek is even more dangerous than Turnquist."

"I'll keep that in mind too."

"There's a point to my telling you this."

"Which is?"

"The more you learn about these people," Khoury said, "the deeper you will find this treachery runs." Then he added, "Perhaps you will even come to trust me."

"Trust you," Reagan said. "I doubt that."

Khoury stared at him, but for now it appeared he was done talking.

CHAPTER TWENTY-ONE

A small town in Virginia on the Chesapeake

Reagan owned a small, gray cedar-shingled house in a remote town along the Chesapeake. Several years back, he engaged a broker using an assumed name, purchased the place through a shell company as owner, and had since used it exclusively as his personal retreat. Although Gellos and Kenny knew it existed, neither had asked for the location and he never brought a visitor there other than Erin. There was no name on the door, and the only thing he ever found in the mailbox were throwaway advertisements addressed to "Occupant." It was a completely anonymous sanctuary.

Heading there through the back roads of Virginia, Reagan braked to a halt at a stop sign well before he was near the house and had a quick look around. The large SUV had dark tinted windows, but he made sure there was no one else on the road. Then he turned to Khoury and said, "Hold still for a moment, and close your eyes." Tearing off a large piece of the duct tape he'd brought with him, he reached across with both hands and placed it across his prisoner's eyes.

"What in the name of…" Khoury began to protest, but Reagan stopped him.

"You don't need to know where we're going. You'll be lucky if I take it off when we get there."

Then Reagan drove on.

An hour later, they pulled into the long gravel driveway leading to Reagan's home. There was no one else around, and all seemed quiet. Brandt got out, opened the Suburban's passenger door, and unbuckled

Khoury. Reagan came around the front and they dragged Khoury out. Leading him to the front door, with Brandt behind them, Reagan hit a series of numbers on an electronic touch pad and led them inside.

"Follow me," he told Brandt, taking Khoury down a narrow wooden staircase to a small room he had built just for this contingency. It had no windows and a door he could lock from the outside.

When Reagan tore the tape from Khoury's face, the man uttered a pained shriek, but said nothing. He looked around, seeing a bed, a chair, a small table, a plastic bucket, and nothing else.

"Make yourself comfortable," Reagan said as he freed Khoury's hands.

"Under the circumstances, I can do without the sarcasm," Khoury said, as he rubbed at the raw skin around his eyes.

"Under the circumstances, you should be grateful for not only my hospitality but for the fact that you're alive," Reagan told him. "I'll be back in a while with some food, and I'll let you know our next move."

"Can I at least get a bottle of water?"

Reagan did not bother to reply as he led Brandt out of the room and locked the door behind them.

Upstairs, Reagan went to the kitchen and checked the cabinet where he kept minimal supplies, then had a look in the refrigerator. He had not been here in a while, and, although there was not much on hand, it would have to do for now.

"Not exactly the Ritz," Reagan said to Brandt, "but I love the place."

"Great views," the younger agent said as he looked out the window.

"I never have anyone here, Alex. This is a special circumstance, so…"

"I get it. I've never been here, and I have no idea how to find the place."

"Good. Now make yourself at home," Reagan said, then went out to the back porch overlooking the bay, sat on one of the Adirondack chairs and pulled out his cell.

The first thing he did was text Kenny a single word, SECURE. Then he checked his messages. Nothing had come from Kenny or Gellos, which was fine. Erin had sent a text checking on him, to which he responded with a thumbs up and a heart. Then he made a call to Dick

Bebon, a long-time agent in the FBI with whom he had often worked, and who had risen to the position of deputy director.

"Reagan, long time no see."

"I've been kind of busy, tell you the truth."

"That's what I've heard. To what do I owe the honor?"

"I'm going to give you a name. Say whatever you want or say nothing. All right?"

"I'm listening."

"Victor Turnquist."

The silence on the other end told Reagan what he wanted to know. Then Bebon spoke up. "You in town?"

"I'm in striking distance."

"How about some oysters at the Sequoia? We can sit outside on the patio, get some privacy."

"I can be there around an hour and a half or so?"

"Make it two," Bebon said.

"I'll see you there," Reagan said, then went back inside. "I've got to go see a friend at the Bureau," he told Brandt. "I mentioned the name Khoury gave us, and he suggested we get together. You going to be all right?"

"No worries."

"Come with me," Reagan said, leading him into a small den off the master bedroom. On the desk were three monitors which Reagan switched on. "I have cameras set up along the edges of the property and the entrance to the driveway. They're all fitted with alarms, so we don't have to sit here staring at them, they'll start beeping if there's any activity."

"Got it."

"I don't have anything set up along the water, but that's easy to keep an eye on."

"You're not expecting an amphibious landing?"

Reagan laughed. "Not likely, but these days who knows. I like to think this place is totally secure, but with drones and microchips, you can't be sure." He walked over to what appeared to be a closet, but when he opened the door Brandt saw the tall safe behind it. Reagan entered the combination and pulled on the large steel door, revealing a small arsenal of weapons.

"Secure or not," Brandt said, "you're certainly prepared for unwanted company."

Reagan nodded, then said, "Help yourself."

Brandt was already armed with a Sig Sauer P226 Legion, but removed an M16 assault rifle and an extra magazine. "Just in case."

"I like your thinking," Reagan said as he shut the metal door. "I'm not locking this for now. Also just in case."

Back in the kitchen, they put together some food, grabbed a bottle of water from the refrigerator, and together brought it downstairs to Khoury. Brandt stood back, gun in hand as Reagan unlocked the door. They found their man seated on the bed.

Putting the plate and bottle on the table, Reagan said, "Best I can do for now."

Looking at the serving of sardines, cheese, and crackers, Khoury asked, "You expect me to eat that with my hands?"

"You don't think I'm giving you a fork or knife, do you?"

Khoury frowned. "Am I going to be here long?"

"A lot of that will depend on you. The more information you provide, the better chance I can get you someplace more comfortable."

"I assume you've already begun checking on the names I gave you."

Reagan did not respond.

"The people I've mentioned would like to silence me. And they have accomplices."

"You may be right, which is all the more reason you should be giving me the information you're holding back."

Khoury appeared to be thinking it over. "Come back with whatever you learn about Lawler, Turnquist, and Paszek. Then we can talk further."

"I'm supposed to take instructions from *you*?" Reagan asked.

"No, Mr. Reagan, you're supposed to take the help I give and use it to uncover this conspiracy."

CHAPTER TWENTY-TWO

Georgetown, Washington, D.C.

Reagan reached K Street in Georgetown just before five that afternoon. He parked the Suburban in a lot a few blocks from the restaurant and walked the rest of the way.

Sequoia features a sleek modern bar with gray low-backed seats and an elegant dining room with chairs upholstered in red fabric, tables covered with white tablecloths, and neon and glass vacuum lighting fixtures overhead. Situated along the shore of the Potomac with garden sculptures and a patio, it provides dramatic views of the Kennedy Center, Roosevelt Bridge, and the Virginia skyline across the way.

When Reagan entered, he found Dick Bebon seated at the far end of the bar.

Bebon was tall and trim, with thinning gray hair, a fair complexion, and bright blue eyes. He was more than twenty years Reagan's senior and, as he was fond of saying, he had seen it all.

The two men shook hands, and Bebon told the bartender, "I'm going to take this drink outside. We all square?"

The young man behind the bar nodded, so Bebon picked up his scotch on the rocks and led Reagan down to the patio.

"You still drinking Macallan 12?" Reagan asked.

Bebon smiled. "My father told me that life is too short to drink cheap booze."

The staff knew Bebon and, although the place was already filling up, the waitress managed to seat them at a table on the far end of the terrace, away from other patrons. Nick ordered a Bulleit bourbon with a large cube and watched the young woman walk away.

"I hear you were the one who prevented that attack at the mall in Minnesota," Bebon said. "That was some kind of work."

Reagan smiled. "Right down to it, huh? No, how are you, how's life treating you, none of that opening chit chat?"

Bebon had a taste of his drink. "If you wanted to meet so we could catch up on our social lives, you wouldn't have started that conversation by mentioning Victor Turnquist."

"I see. Struck a nerve, did I?"

Bebon fixed him with a serious look. "Yes, you did Nick. Now you show me your cards and I'll show you mine."

"Fair enough. Let's start with those attacks. New York and Las Vegas as well as the attempt in Bloomington."

"I'm listening."

"There was one al Qaeda operative behind the planning and execution of those assaults. He had a deep cover, including here in D.C."

"That's what I've heard. Name of Walid Khoury, better known as the Handler."

Reagan nodded. "What I assume you have not heard is that I apprehended him yesterday."

Bebon responded with an appreciative smile. "Why am I not surprised you would be the one to grab him. Can I ask where you found him?"

"In a fancy townhouse in London."

"And they say crime doesn't pay. You have him in the States now?"

"We've got him buried someplace not far from here, at least for now. Seems a lot of people would like to bury him permanently."

"What's next for him? Gitmo?"

"Maybe. He claims to have information about corruption in our government, but not the usual accusations about politicians on the take or that sort of thing. He claims there are actions underway that can impact our national security. Treason. Traitors. He wants to make a trade for his life."

"His life, not his freedom?"

"So far."

"After what he's done, he better be holding some large bargaining chips."

"He's already mentioned some names," Reagan told him.

"Including Turnquist."

"Correct."

"Anyone else I should know?"

"We'll get to that," Reagan said.

The waitress came by with Reagan's drink, he waited until she was gone, then lifted his glass and said, "Cheers." They each drank, and Reagan went on.

"It goes without saying I trust you, or I wouldn't be here. So, let's start with Turnquist. It feels like he's part of a puzzle and I'm trying to put the pieces together."

"All right, then let me first say something about today's Bureau." Bebon paused. "The overwhelming majority of agents are hardworking, honest, and patriotic. Unfortunately, every large barrel inevitably has a bad apple or two. Most of the time we can deal with it in-house, but the higher up the chain of command the problem exists, the tougher it is to resolve."

"And Mr. Turnquist is pretty high up. I did a quick search online. Executive assistant director, just three rungs from the top of the FBI ladder."

"You've got it," Bebon said. "You know what's been going on with whistleblowers the past couple of years. There are agents who see our system being polluted by politics, but when they dare to speak up, the entire narrative gets flipped. Rather than getting credit for trying to clean up the mess, they're accused of betraying the Bureau."

"That's an age-old story," Reagan said. "No one likes a rat, even when they're telling the truth."

"Correct."

"But, if what you say is true about most agents being loyal to our country—and I believe it is—why doesn't the rank and file rise up when these bad apples are exposed?"

"Because they don't feel supported by the bureaucrats at the top. The men and women who speak up are reassigned, forced into early retirement, or simply manipulated into clamming up. Working for the government is no longer a safe haven for anyone. We've been infiltrated by people advancing interests that have nothing to do with the work we're supposed to be doing."

"Which brings us back to Mr. Turnquist."

"Yes it does. He's at the top of the list of those stifling dissent.

"What's his agenda?"

The way Bebon hesitated made it clear this discussion was more painful than he wanted to admit. "Turnquist is an appointee from a couple of administrations back, which means I don't need to say anything more about his political affiliations. From what I've seen, and I've seen it close up, he doesn't view himself as part of an organization that was created to investigate criminal activity in an effort to protect our citizens and uphold the law. He sees his position as an opportunity to weaponize the Bureau against his enemies, which is anyone on the right, or even close to the center."

"This may be unfair of me to ask, but how far do you think he's willing to go? I mean, how does a man like Khoury have anything to do with him?"

Bebon had another taste of scotch as he thought it over. "There could be any number of answers," he suggested. "As we've already said, this guy Khoury had an excellent cover here in D.C. They could have met someplace, or he might just have heard his name."

"True," Reagan agreed, "but you say that you already have your own issues with Turnquist. There's not a single thing I like about Khoury, but my read on him is that he didn't just pull the man's name off the internet."

"You're probably right. I'd have to do some careful digging to see if I can unearth a connection."

Reagan looked him straight in the eyes. "You willing to do that?"

Bebon thought it over. "I am. To be honest, I would be happy to find something on him. I just have to be careful, he's a powerful force."

"Understood."

"Which raises another issue that concerns me. I realize this entire conversation is off the record, and as far as anyone else is concerned, I know nothing about you taking and holding Khoury. But those attacks happened on American soil and he should be in our custody for interrogation."

Reagan smiled. "As a strict jurisdictional matter, I cannot disagree. But Khoury has made it clear he's afraid of what someone like Turnquist might do to him. He has the same view of someone highly placed in my agency."

"Are you going to share?"

Now Reagan picked up his glass and drank. Then he said, "Ross Lawler."

Bebon drew back slightly. "You're kidding. Isn't he Director Spinelli's right-hand man?"

"He is, which is part of my problem. It seems Lawler issued an order directing me to stand down in my search for Khoury."

"But you have him."

"I acted on my own, the consequences yet to be determined. The point is, Khoury knew about that order."

"How?"

"I intend to find out. What I do know is that Khoury does not want to be taken into custody by either Turnquist or Lawler. Which raises the next question."

"What the hell could they all have to do with each other?"

"Precisely."

Bebon shook his head.

"Let me throw one more name at you. You ever hear of Bogdan Paszek?"

"Sounds familiar," Bebon said. "How does he fit in?"

"Not sure, but our boy Khoury says he's even more dangerous than Turnquist. Can you run a check on him for me? I already used my laptop to research Turnquist, but I'm not sure who might be watching me, and I need to be careful."

"Consider it done."

"You be careful too," Reagan said. "As you've said, these are power-ful people, and if anything Khoury is telling us turns out to be true, they're also very dangerous."

Bebon picked up his scotch. "Nothing more dangerous than those closest to home.

CHAPTER TWENTY-THREE

CIA Headquarters, Langley, Virginia

As Reagan and Bebon progressed from cocktails to an early dinner, while continuing their discussion, Deputy Director Brian Kenny and Carol Gellos were not far away, seated in the fifth floor conference room at CIA headquarters. Also present were Director Anthony Spinelli and his second in command, Ross Lawler.

Spinelli looked nothing like one might imagine the leader of America's key intelligence network should look. He was short and pudgy with wavy gray hair, a dark complexion, tortoise shell eye glasses, and a perpetual expression of dissatisfaction. Lawler, in stark contrast, was tall, reasonably handsome, trimly built, and looked very much like a successful corporate executive.

The director's assistant came in, spoke quietly in his ear, then took the seat to his left.

"Leonard has just checked again with the FBI," Spinelli reported to the group. "Your men and Walid Khoury have yet to show up. Please tell me, how is that possible Brian?"

"I have no idea, sir," Kenny replied.

"You've called your agents and received no response?"

"Several times. Called and texted."

Spinelli rubbed his chin, one of the mannerisms of which he was so fond. "Let us take a guess, then. To start with, Agent Reagan disobeyed an order issued from this office." He took a moment to glance at Lawler. "Reagan flew to London of his own accord, somehow located Walid

Khoury, apprehended him, and brought him back here—on an agency jet that you approved, I should add. You disagree with any of that?"

"No, sir."

"Then he took Khoury to one of our safe houses but, shortly after he arrived, he apparently concluded that was not the right place for this prisoner to be held. He then announced to one and all that he would turn Khoury over to the FBI." He took a moment to clear his throat, his voice rising as he said, "Now, several hours later, he is nowhere to be found, perhaps having taken an international terrorist to dinner and a movie, is that the story?"

No one in the room spoke, giving Spinelli an opportunity to collect himself.

"Do I have all of this right, Brian?" he demanded.

"Sir, I have no idea where Reagan is. I assume he's on his way to the Hoover Building."

"Really? Is he going by way of Samoa?" Spinelli asked, ending again in a shout. "I can assure you, once all parties have been accounted for, I am going to have your man Reagan on a spit."

Kenny took a moment to sit a bit taller in his chair. "I understand you're upset, sir."

"Do you really?"

"Nick Reagan is my finest agent," Kenny told him. "Regardless of having ignored the order from your office, which I assure you I passed on to him," he added with a quick look at Lawler, "Reagan managed to bring in the world's most wanted terrorist. That, sir, is an indisputable fact."

Spinelli, having calmed himself, said, "Go on."

"Reagan could have eliminated Khoury in London and come home without anyone knowing what he had done. However, Khoury claimed to have valuable information and, based on the little he shared, Reagan believed it to be worth the risk of bringing him here for interrogation."

The director was nodding. "Then why the hell didn't he bring him directly here? Or hold him for questioning at the Cottage?"

Kenny drew a deep breath, then said, "All I can tell you in Reagan's defense is that he has his reasons."

Spinelli slammed the palm of his beefy hand on the walnut conference table, the impact so hard it sounded like a gunshot. "First, he flaunts my order, then he decides what should or should not be done with a man you call the world's most wanted terrorist. Who's running this agency, Agent Reagan or me?" When no one risked a reply, Spinelli said, "I want Reagan and Khoury, and I want them here tonight. As in, right now."

Kenny began to respond but it was Lawler and not Spinelli who interrupted him. "Perhaps we should allow Reagan some leeway," he suggested. "He's come this far, let's give him until the morning to produce Khoury. I'm sure by then he'll be in contact with his deputy director. Wouldn't you think so?" Lawler looked at Kenny for agreement.

Lawler's suggestion was more of a surprise to Kenny than Spinelli, but all Kenny said was, "Yes, I do."

"All right, all right," the director agreed, "wherever they are now, I suppose there's no sense forcing the issue tonight. I wouldn't want to upset Nick Reagan, would I?" Then he leaned forward, staring at Kenny. "But tomorrow morning, his period of grace expires. If he and Khoury have not surfaced by nine o'clock, it's his ass. Am I clear, Brian?"

"Absolutely, sir."

"And you'll have to answer for it as well," the director reminded him. Then he stood, ending the meeting, and the others got to their feet and followed him out of the conference room.

Making their way down the long corridor, Gellos said to Kenny, "I don't get to spend much time with him of course, but I never realized the director was so, uh, passionate."

"That was a tame performance," Kenny replied. "You should see him when the White House gets involved."

A few moments later, when they turned the corner toward the bank of elevators, Kenny asked Gellos, "Were you watching Lawler?"

"The entire time."

"What do you think?"

"I wonder why he was willing to give Nick until the morning to bring Khoury in. Was it his decision alone or was there someone else involved?" Gellos asked.

"My questions exactly," Kenny said. "Send Reagan the signal and then a text in code. I don't want to speak with him for obvious reasons, but tell him what both the director and Lawler said." Then he added, "And remind him to keep his guard up."

CHAPTER TWENTY-FOUR

A small town in Virginia on the Chesapeake

By the time Reagan left Bebon and got on the road, he was feeling a bit guilty about enjoying a delicious meal at the Sequoia after leaving Brandt with a meager selection of canned and frozen items, so he texted a hashtag, then gave him a call.

"How's it going?"

"All quiet here," Brandt said. "Except our guest banged on the door a few times. Wants to use the bathroom, but I wasn't about to let him out on my own. I told him to use the bucket."

"Good man," Reagan said. "I'm on my way back, can I get you something to eat?"

"Are you kidding? With the wonderful culinary choices on hand? I'm still deciding between a can of baked beans with a date that expired a year ago or some ancient looking chicken tenders in your freezer."

"There's a Chick-fil-A not far from my place?"

"Perfect," Brandt said.

It was dark when Reagan pulled into his driveway. He had left the outside floodlights off, and everything seemed quiet. He came to a stop in front of the house and killed the headlights. Grabbing the bag of food, he made his way up the porch stairs and inside.

"How did it go?" Brandt asked as they removed the sodas and placed the chicken sandwiches and French fries on plates.

Reagan frowned. "It seems our friend downstairs knew what he was talking about when he mentioned Victor Turnquist. My contact in the Bureau certainly didn't have anything nice to say about him."

"Did he recognize the other name?"

"Paszek? He said it sounded familiar and he's running it down for me. Let's pay our guest a visit."

They went down and unlocked the door, Brandt once again staying behind Reagan with his gun drawn.

They found Khoury seated on the chair, his legs crossed, staring straight ahead. His face wore a scowl. "Can I go to the bathroom now?"

Reagan stepped inside the room, placed the plate of food and the soda on the small table, and said, "Let's go."

After they had all gone upstairs and given Khoury time in the bathroom, the two agents prepared to escort him back to his room.

At the top of the stairs, Reagan stopped and said, "Before we lock you up for the night, I have a couple questions. To start with, what do you have to do with Victor Turnquist at the FBI?"

"I've already told you, I am done talking for now."

"That's your choice but remember, according to you the two of us are the only thing standing between you and almost certain death."

The three men remained standing there for a few moments before Khoury spoke again. "Turnquist is a traitor to your government. For now, that is all you need to know, the rest is for you to figure out."

"What about the other name?"

"Bogdan Paszek? I would have expected you to identify him by now."

"I've been busy," Reagan told him. "Enlighten us."

"He is former Polish military, their version of special forces, and currently a gun for hire."

"Currently hired by whom?"

"That is one question I cannot answer with certainty, but I can tell you the last I saw him was in the Janus Building in Washington."

After they led Khoury back to his room and locked him in, Reagan kept Brandt company while he had a late dinner and they discussed their next move.

"We've heard nothing from Kenny, correct?" Reagan asked.

"No call preceded by the agreed signal." Brandt said.

"I got a text from Gellos. She and Kenny met with the director and Lawler. Spinelli is not happy. He wants us to bring Khoury in by tomorrow morning at nine."

"Which is not good," Brandt said.

"No, it's not. We need to get Khoury to someone we can all trust. I actually like Spinelli, but he's all about delegating, and he'll pass Khoury to Lawler, which may be game over. We need to get Khoury in front of someone he's willing to reveal whatever he has to sell."

"He was ready to speak with Kenny until we ran out of time."

"True, but only on a limited basis. He knows the DD doesn't have the authority to make the kind of deal he wants. Certainly not without the director's office involved."

"Which brings Lawler back into the conversation."

"Precisely," Reagan said.

"How about your friend in the Bureau. He's in a position of authority, right?"

"He's going to speak with some people there."

"Without allowing this guy Turnquist to get in the way, I assume," Brandt said.

"That's the idea."

"What about Khoury's claim he met this guy Paszek at the Janus Building. Isn't that…"

"The headquarters of Novak Enterprises."

"Is it just me, or is this becoming a bit surreal?" Brandt asked.

"Far as I'm concerned, this entire country has become surreal in the last few years." Reagan shook his head.

"I can't disagree."

"I hate politics. The United States should be about the people, not the people we elect. They're supposed to work for us, not to make things worse while they get rich. I feel like it's getting harder to tell the white hats from the black hats."

"Not to mention some people aren't wearing any hat at all," Brandt said.

"Well, we're not going to solve the world's problems tonight, and we need to get some rest. Tomorrow is going to be a big day, as they say."

Reagan had a look around the room. "As I've explained to you, this place is off the grid, but there's nowhere completely safe anymore. I'll take the first shift, let you get a few hours' sleep."

"All right, but if anything…"

"Don't worry, I won't let you miss anything."

A couple of hours later, Brandt was sleeping, Reagan was sitting in his den working on his laptop with the lights out, and the sounds of crickets were chirping in the distance when the first alarm began to beep.

CHAPTER TWENTY-FIVE

A small town in Virginia on the Chesapeake

Reagan had a quick look around the den, making sure the blackout shades were pulled tight as he switched off the audio on his alarm system. Then he pulled out his Glock and checked the chamber and the magazine. He knew it was loaded, but he never left things to chance.

He stood, picked up the M16 assault rifle that was leaning against the wall, and ran through the same routine with that weapon. Entering the safe, he pulled out two ATN PVS night vision goggles and placed them on the desk, grabbed two earpieces, then stepped noiselessly through the living room to the guest bedroom.

Reagan leaned over and placed his left hand across Alex's mouth. As Brandt awoke with a start, Reagan whispered, "We've got company."

Brandt got up and went through the same security sequence Reagan had, beginning with the Sig Sauer P226 that had been on the night-stand, then the M16 he had placed on the floor beside the bed. Brandt had slept in his clothes, so when he was done checking his weapons he had only to slip on his rubber soled shoes to be ready. Taking the earpiece Reagan handed him, the two men headed for the den.

Standing in front of the monitors, they studied the feeds being provided by the various cameras positioned around the property. Fitted with nighttime capability, the screens were filled with images in black, gray, and green. Everything seemed still.

"Alarms went off," Reagan explained.

"Any chance an animal could have set it off?" Brandt asked in a whisper.

"Possible but not likely. I've adjusted these sensors more than once," Reagan told him. "And there were multiple hits before I shut off the sound. See those red flashes? Those are visual alerts. Looks like they're coming up both sides of the driveway."

They waited in silence, not seeing any more movement until another couple of red flashes went off and some vegetation moved off to the left of the driveway, which was on their right from inside the house.

"They're coming in low and slow," Reagan said.

Brandt nodded. "No sense in rushing towards us if they believe they can take us by surprise."

"Agreed," Reagan said as he pointed to the image on the upper left of the largest monitor. "That's the entrance to the driveway. Nothing there. They must have parked someplace down the road, which means they might have backup. Grab one of those night goggles and come with me," he said as he pointed to the desk. "And stay low."

Reagan's house was a small one-story structure with an attic above. All of the windows on the main level were covered, but the two agents were careful to keep down as they made their way back through the living room to the access door at the top of the stairs leading to the basement. Reagan locked it and, as the two men kneeled beside the door, Reagan pointed to an overhead hatch with a pullcord.

In the darkness, he looked into Brandt's eyes and spoke softly. "Whoever these people are, they're here to take Khoury, and we're in their way. I have no idea how they found us, maybe they followed me, goddamnit, although I was sure I came in clean." He shook off the thought. "But they didn't walk up and knock on the door, so we know they mean us harm. Whatever happens, you don't hesitate, you shoot to kill."

"Got it." Brandt hesitated. "Should we do anything about Khoury?"

"Negative. He's locked in down there, it won't help to have him on the loose."

"Understood."

"There are a couple of small windows and two air vents in the attic. Unless they have explosives or intend to burn us out, you'll be fine."

"That's comforting," Brandt replied with a nervous smile.

"You'll be fine, and I have more defenses here than they imagine. The good news, once you're ups there, is that you'll have an excellent line of sight. You have a suppressor for the Sig?"

"I do," Brandt said, pulling it out and securing it to the barrel of the automatic.

"The targets may be too far out for you to be accurate with that, but you may want to start with it anyway, keep your position hidden as long as you can. They'll expect me to fire from ground level, but I doubt they'll be looking for you up there, which gives you an edge. It's just that once you start firing that M16, the noise…"

"Understood," Brandt told him.

Reagan stood, pressing himself alongside the wall between two windows on that side of the house. Reaching up for the cord, he pulled down the steps that provided access above.

"Go," he told Brandt, then watched as Alex climbed up and pushed the hatch closed behind him.

Hurrying back to the den, Reagan inserted his earpiece and had another look at the monitors. Speaking into the mic, he told Brandt, "I'm seeing movement both left and right now. Maybe twenty yards out. You in position?"

"I'm at the window facing the front of the property."

"Good. We have to assume they also have night vision capability, so stay out of sight best you can."

"Should I have a look at the rear?"

Reagan checked the screens. "I don't see any activity there, but they may circle around. For now, stay focused on the front yard."

"Got it."

"They may not care whether they take Khoury alive or not, so we can't let them get too close, we need to act as soon as we have a shot."

"Understood," Brandt told him.

Reagan had a better chance of spotting the hostiles on the monitors than from any of windows at the front of the house, but he had no way to act from inside the den. He had a final look at the images—

confirming that the house was being approached from both sides—then made his move.

"No time like the present," he said, as much to himself as to Brandt. Crouching down again, he rushed into the living room and knelt beside the window to the right of the entrance door. Adjusting his goggles, he slowly moved a corner of the dark gray drape aside to have a look.

Things appeared still outside, until he saw a slight disturbance of the bushes off to his left. "On the left," he said into the mic, then lifted the assault rifle, knocked out the bottom pane of glass of the sectioned window, and opened fire.

The stillness of the night was instantly shattered with the loud report of the M16, enemy fire being returned almost immediately, which was exactly what Reagan wanted.

The flash of the weapons coming from the front yard gave Brandt a great look at their targets from above. There was no sound coming from the attic yet, which meant Brandt was doing as instructed, firing with the silenced Sig Sauer in the hope their pincer move would find a mark. Reagan continued his fusillade to the left until, just moments later, he heard a man scream in pain as the gunfire from that side of the property stopped. Meanwhile, shots from his right began to strafe the front of the house as shards of shattered glass from the window above rained down on him.

Reagan crawled swiftly toward the window to the left of the door. Positioning himself on his left knee, he knocked out the lower pane of that glass and resumed firing, this time aiming toward the flashes of gunfire on his right. "Hostile on the right," he said into the mic.

In the next instant he heard the sound of Brandt's automatic rifle from above, both of them now firing at whoever was hiding in the hedges off to their right. After their relentless attack, there was no scream, but the return gunfire ceased, and suddenly all was returned to silence.

Still on his hands and knees, Reagan hurried back to the den to check the closed-circuit system. Remaining low, he looked from one image to the next, seeing no movement and no red flashes.

"I'm back in the den," he told Brandt.

"You see anything?"

"The monitors are clear. What about you?"

"Nothing," came the reply.

"Let's wait before we make another move."

Just then, both agents heard a loud crash, the sound of the back door to the house being kicked in.

"Check the rear," Reagan hollered into the mic, racing from the den to a position at the entrance to the master bedroom. There was only one short corridor leading into the house from the rear, and this was the best position to greet unwanted visitors.

Moments later, Reagan saw the barrel of a weapon coming from around the corner of the living room wall. Taking a deep breath to steady himself, he waited until the shooter came into view, then opened fire, tearing the man to shreds with a loud barrage from his assault rifle.

Without hesitating, Reagan returned to the den, checked the monitors again, and then flipped the switch that turned on all of the outside floodlights. The entire area around the house and along the driveway was instantly illuminated.

"What do you see?" he asked Brandt.

"Hold on, I'm pulling off the goggles and checking from the widows up here." After less than a minute—though it felt to Reagan like an hour—Brandt reported back. "Seems to be all clear."

"Don't come down yet. Let's wait and see if they've arranged a second wave."

Reagan remained in front of the screens in the den, but the images all remained still. He could hear Brandt upstairs, shuffling from one window and vent to the next. Otherwise, it was quiet.

They allowed five minutes to pass, then ten. Reagan finally said, "Time to have a look outside. Come on down."

Brandt lowered the attic ladder and returned to the main level inside the house with his weapons and night goggles. He joined Reagan in the den.

"We can't just sit here waiting to see if they have reinforcements," Reagan said, as if responding to a question Brandt hadn't asked. "I'm going to kill the outside lights, then we'll leave by the back door, use our goggles, and sweep wide along both sides of the property, moving forward."

"That was a lot of noise, any chance your neighbors called the police?"

"Not likely. Most of the properties are large parcels, basically vacation houses, all pretty spread out. There's no telling if anyone is even here."

Brandt nodded. "What if someone is waiting for us to leave the house so they can come in and take out Khoury?"

"That's quite a double-think, Alex. You must be hanging around with me too much."

Brandt smiled. "I'll take that as a compliment."

Reagan thought it over. "You may be right, but I don't see either of us going out their alone. If they get to Khoury, then shame on us."

"Fair enough."

"Let's get some ammo and go."

After they loaded their handguns and assault rifles with new magazines from the safe, Reagan hit the master switch for the outdoor floodlights, and darkness once again descended on the property. They raced to the back of the house, took a few moments to check the rear deck and property leading down to the water, then made their way into the warm night.

Other than the long gravel driveway and the closely mown area that surrounded the house—which a local landscaper handled for Reagan without ever having met him—the balance of the property was overgrown with trees, bushes and hedges. Reagan pointed to the left, and whispered, "Stay low, meet you at the entrance." He watched as Brandt moved out, then hurried off to his right.

CHAPTER TWENTY-SIX

A small town in Virginia on the Chesapeake

Reagan was obviously more familiar with the terrain and managed to move swiftly outside the edge of foliage surrounding the side of the house. He remained low, his weapon at the ready, tracking an arc that soon brought him near the shooter who had been firing from that side of the property. The man was about five yards away from where Reagan stopped. He was on his back, having difficulty breathing, but still alive. His automatic rifle lay at his side.

"If you want to have any chance of surviving," Reagan said, his voice piercing the quiet, "you won't make a move." The man did not appear to be in shape to be moving anywhere, but Reagan had no way of knowing if he was fitted with explosives, holding a grenade, or had some other surprise in store.

"Drop dead," came the raspy response.

"I can finish you off right now or I can get you help, it's your call."

The man tried to speak but broke into a chest-rattling cough before he managed to say, "Bleeding out."

Reagan moved closer, confirming the man's arms were at his sides, his hands empty. Reagan had seen enough people die, in military combat and other armed confrontations, and knew this man did not have long. "You want me to have a look or not?"

"Look," the man said.

Reagan came forward, near enough to see the wound on the side of the man's head where he had been grazed. That might have knocked him backward but did not appear to be life-threatening. It was the blood covering his chest that indicated a serious wound. Approaching from the side, Reagan picked up the man's rifle, tossed it a few feet away, then placed his own weapon behind him and took out his Glock. Holding the gun in his right hand, he managed to tear the man's shirt open with his left. There was no explosive device strapped to the man's chest, just a gaping hole on the right side of the man's abdomen.

"Not good," the man said in an accent Reagan could not identify, garbled as it was by his coughing.

"No," Reagan agreed as he took off his goggles. "We need to stop the bleeding."

The man choked out a gruesome laugh, followed by a congestive moan. "How?"

"I'm going to do my best to apply pressure, but it's going to hurt. You ready?"

"Do it."

Reagan pulled off his jacket, balled it up, shoved it on top of the gaping hole and pressed his weight down.

The man groaned but said nothing.

"Who sent you?" Reagan asked.

"No one."

Reagan pushed harder, his jacket immediately soaking up blood. "Who sent you?" he repeated.

"Friends of Walid Khoury," the man told him.

"What friends?"

It seemed the man was about to say something else, but his words were obscured by another choking cough, followed by a violent spasm. Then he was gone.

Reagan felt the man's neck for a pulse, but there was none. "Damn," he said, then pulled his goggles on, lifted his automatic rifle, and continued ahead.

He did not encounter any other hostiles as he neared the front of his property. From there he could see Brandt on the opposite side of the driveway and waved him over.

Brandt dashed across the opening and knelt beside Reagan.

"Anything?" Reagan asked.

"That man on the left was dead when I got there," Brandt reported. "Nothing else."

Reagan told him what he had found, then said, "I don't hear any sirens. If someone called the authorities, they're awfully slow in coming."

Brandt nodded his agreement.

"Let's find their vehicle."

Using the trees at the front of the property for cover, they moved parallel to the road. Just fifty yards down they spotted a car parked in a thicket. Taking their time to approach until they had a clear line of vision, it became evident the vehicle was unoccupied. Inside, they found the ignition key on the floor of the driver's side.

"For whoever made it back," Reagan said as he picked up the key. Then he checked the glove box and found a rental agreement. "No surprise there. Probably used a phony credit card, but we'll check it out. Let's go. You drive."

Brandt got behind the wheel and Reagan took the passenger seat as lookout. They turned onto the driveway, stopping short of the house to get out and retrieve each of the two bodies they had left outside, together with their weapons. After a quick search turned up no identification on either man, they deposited the two bodies in the trunk, then drove around the side of the house.

They went inside, carried the third man out, went through the same fruitless search, then dumped him with friends and slammed the trunk shut.

"Now what?" Brandt asked.

"We'll check on Khoury. Even if none of my neighbors heard anything, he certainly did. Then we have to prepare for a second wave. When this crew doesn't call in, more company may be arriving."

CHAPTER TWENTY-SEVEN

A small town in Virginia on the Chesapeake

Reagan and Brandt once again entered the house the way they left, through the back. Making their way into the living room, the first thing Reagan did was head for the den and restore the audio for the alarms and crank the volume up. Then he came back, unlocked the access door to the basement, and he and Brandt headed downstairs. Opening the door to Khoury's room, they found him standing there, gripping the back of the chair, holding it above his head as the only weapon at his disposal.

"Easy," Reagan said. "It's over, at least for now."

"I don't suppose you're going to tell me what happened."

"Three men stopped by for a visit, but we've taken care of them," Reagan said.

"Who were they?"

"Not sure. One of them lived long enough to say they were friends of yours, but neither appeared to be of Arabic extraction, in case you're wondering if they were from al Qaeda."

Khoury finally placed the chair on the floor. "Don't be racist, Mr. Reagan. Not all al Qaeda sympathizers are from central casting."

"Fair enough," Reagan said. "You figure that's who they were?"

"Actually, I do not," Khoury admitted. Then he said, "Paszek."

"You think one of them was this Bogdan Paszek you mentioned?"

"He would not have come himself, he would have sent some of his people, but I can try to identify them for you."

"Let's wait for morning light. They're not going anywhere, and we don't want to venture outside if others are on their way. You get some rest, we'll be leaving early," Reagan told him.

"To go where, exactly?"

Reagan studied him for a moment, then said, "We'll figure that out in a couple of hours, after I make some calls." Locking him in again, he and Brandt returned to the living room.

Dawn was not far off, and it was obvious neither agent was going to sleep. Reagan made coffee and they took their ceramic mugs to the den, where they sat in front of the monitors.

"I'm going to have to do something to secure that back door they kicked in," Reagan said.

"What about the windows that were shot out?" Brandt asked.

"I don't have any plywood here, going to need to deal with that later."

"You can't just bring anyone in," Brandt said. "There are bullet holes across the entire front of the house. People are going to ask questions."

Reagan grinned. "I have friends."

Brandt had a taste of the hot coffee, then gestured to the video screens. "Looks quiet out there."

"For now," Reagan said.

They waited until just after sunrise when, with weapons drawn, the two agents ventured outside to the car parked alongside the house. Reagan opened the trunk, allowing Brandt to take photographs and fingerprint all three bodies. Then they went downstairs and brought Khoury along to have a look.

After studying the corpses from different angles, Khoury shook his head. "Never saw any of them before."

"You're sure."

Khoury, who was still leaning over the grisly montage of death in the trunk, looked up at Reagan. "Why would I lie? They came here to kill me, isn't that what you said?"

"That seemed to be their plan."

"Then if I knew them, I would say so."

Reagan nodded. "I believe you would." Turning to Brandt, he said, "Let's get the hell out of here before any of their friends show up."

CHAPTER TWENTY-EIGHT

En route to Washington

Reagan took Khoury in the Agency's SUV, bound and blindfolded again to his dismay, while Brandt followed in the sedan with the three bodies in the trunk. It was still early and there was no one else on these back roads. They drove more than ten miles from the house when Reagan stopped alongside a marshy area with no houses in sight. He got out and had Brandt pull the sedan as far as he could into the high reeds, where it could not be seen from the road. Then they locked it up and took the keys.

As Brandt got into the back of the Suburban, Reagan said, "We'll call it in later. I just don't need a bunch of feds rummaging around anywhere close to my house."

"Understood," Brandt said.

They rode in silence until they reached the highway, when Brandt asked, "Where are we going?"

"Not sure yet. I figure someplace near D.C. We certainly can't go back to the Cottage, but I thought we might walk him right into Langley. Not much Lawler can do there with everyone in the building a witness."

"Please do not underestimate Mr. Lawler," Khoury said.

"I won't," Reagan assured him, then had Brandt lean forward and remove the tape from Khoury's eyes—far more gently than Reagan had the night before.

"Thank you," Khoury said.

"You have a better idea about where we should go?" Reagan asked. "Want me to book you a suite at the Hay-Adams?"

Brandt's phone buzzed and he had a look at the screen. "It's the all-clear signal from the DD," he told Reagan.

Moments later the call came through. "Where are you?" Kenny asked.

"In the SUV, on our back way to town," Brandt told him.

"Destination?"

"Negotiable at the moment. We were thinking of bringing him to the office."

Kenny took a moment. "That might make sense. How far out are you?"

"More than an hour."

"Have you seen any television, or listened to the radio?"

"No, we we've been busy. Some unexpected guests showed up for a visit last night." He hit a button and said, "You're on speaker now, sir. Khoury is obviously in the car with us."

"Understood. Everyone all right?" Kenny asked.

"We're good," Reagan told him. "The intruders didn't have such a great time."

"We can talk about that later. First, you better put on the news," Kenny said. "There have been three terrorist attacks this morning. All at approximately the same time."

"What the…" Reagan began, but the DD cut him off.

"As far as we can tell, a suicide bomber hit a hospital in New York City, pipe bombs were detonated at two outdoor cafés in Paris, and a shooter in Moscow took out a number of people in front of the Bolshoi Ballet."

"My God," Reagan said.

"All of the perpetrators are dead. In Paris, someone gunned down the bombers a few blocks from the scene. The early read is that they were likely set up by their own people. A Moscow police officer took out the gunman there, and the suicide bomber, well, you get it."

"Anyone claiming responsibility?" Reagan asked.

"Not yet, it all just happened a short time ago. I was just wondering what Mr. Khoury might know about this. His distinct *modus operandi* is to package hits in threes, which would fit this pattern."

Khoury was shaking his head before Kenny had finished. "I know nothing of these attacks, nothing."

"Why do I find that so hard to believe?" Kenny asked. "Since you were located by Reagan you've been a paradigm of cooperation. Could it be you wanted us to keep our focus on you, rather than your colleagues or any of your plans?"

"I tell you I had nothing to do with this."

"Three perfectly timed terrorist assaults," Kenny said, "where none of the assailants survived so there's no risk any of this can be connected to their handler. Sounds very much like your work."

Khoury began to protest again, but Kenny cut him off. "Reagan, your leave of absence is officially over."

"Yes sir."

"You bring Khoury to Langley right now, that's an order."

"On our way."

"But Lawler…" Khoury began to protest until Kenny interrupted him again.

"We'll sort all of this out, including your accusations, once you get here."

With that, Kenny ended the call and Reagan immediately turned on the radio. The attacks were all over the news, and the three men listened to the gory details in silence.

Reagan began driving a lot faster.

*   *   *

THE MALONES WERE IN THEIR DEN in Palm Beach, watching the news as videos were being played of the carnage that had just occurred around the world. Derek was switching channels, looking for as much coverage as he could find about the pipe bombings at the two Parisian cafés.

Almost every time an image of those street corners appeared on their large screen television, Connie said, "Impossible."

She said it again and again.

Derek agreed. "That was his favorite place in Paris. Everyone knew that."

"We all did," Connie said. "So why aren't they giving the victims' names?"

Derek reached out and took her hand. "They have to notify next of kin, there could be security reasons, we need to be patient."

She turned to her husband. "Patient?"

"You're right. This is awful."

"You called again?"

"I keep getting his voicemail."

"What are we going to do?"

"I need to speak with Nick Reagan."

"What can he do at this point?"

"He can get us answers. But I'll have to see him, face to face. We can't trust any of this on a phone call."

"I'm coming with you," she said.

"All right," Malone said, then began nodding slowly, as if confirming a thought he had been reluctant to face up to now. "We'll go together. This involves both of us."

Connie turned back to the television. "Impossible," she said again.

PART TWO

CHAPTER TWENTY-NINE

CIA Headquarters, Langley, Virginia

Reagan passed through security and proceeded into the well illuminated and tightly controlled underground parking garage at CIA headquarters in Langley. By the time he pulled the Suburban into an authorized spot, three other agents were there to meet him. He only recognized one of them.

"Hey, Sam," he said as he stepped out of the SUV, "why the reception committee?"

"Director Spinelli wants us to escort your guest to one of the rooms downstairs."

"Don't suppose you want us to join you?"

Sam, who was clearly uncomfortable with the situation, said, "We'll take it from here, Nick, they want you upstairs. Things are a bit tense, after the news broke on those three attacks.

You get it."

"I do," Reagan said. He looked at Khoury as if he was about to say something, then turned toward the elevators and walked away with Brandt beside him.

Upstairs, they went directly to Kenny's office where the DD was waiting with Carol Gellos.

Before anyone else spoke, Reagan told them, "The director had three agents meet us to take Khoury downstairs. Why do I have the feeling Lawler had something to do with that?"

"Sit down," Kenny said, and the four of them took seats around the small conference table.

Turning to Gellos, Reagan asked, "Is Erin all right?"

"She's fine, I had her stay at my place last night. She's down the hall now, working with Sasha on these attacks."

Sasha Levchenko was an Agency technology expert Reagan and his team regularly called on.

"Tell me about last night," Kenny said.

Reagan gave a brief description of what happened and told the DD that they had photos of the three men and their fingerprints. "The bodies are in the trunk of their rental, out by a marsh near the Chesapeake. I have coordinates, not sure if you want our people to handle this or if we should bring in the FBI."

"You moved them away from your place?"

"I did. Wish one of them had lived long enough to tell me how they found us."

The DD sat back. "I'd like to know that too."

Reagan saw the look on Kenny's face. "What's up?"

"Gellos and I met with the director and Lawler last night. Spinelli wanted me to call you in, right then and there, but Lawler suggested we wait for you to bring Khoury here this morning. I thought it was a little odd at the time, now it feels even worse."

"Did you tell them where Alex and I were taking him?"

"For god's sake, Reagan, I didn't *know* where you were taking him. You treat your address like it's a state secret."

"But you might have mentioned that I was bringing him to my place, or something like that."

"I did," Kenny admitted, "but he didn't ask where that was. Looking back, I suspect Lawler might have already known."

"How?"

"Come on, Nick," Gellos chimed in. "He's second in command at the CIA. We don't intrude on your privacy because we're your friends, but finding this retreat of yours is…"

"I got it. And now my friends are telling me that the second in command at the CIA not only located my house, but gave the address to three assassins while making sure Alex and I would be there overnight with Khoury, three ducks in a shooting gallery."

Gellos was as tough as Reagan and had no problem looking him in the eyes as she said, "I can't be sure he knows where your place is or that he had anything to do with the shooters, of course, but I was there last evening. I watched him, I clocked the entire discussion. There wasn't enough reason at the time for me to send you any kind of warning, I assumed you would be on high alert. But now that it's played out…"

"It looks like he set us up."

"I can't believe it," Kenny said.

"Only because you're too moral to imagine that sort of betrayal," Reagan told him. "And what about Khoury? If he really has the goods on Lawler, he's already as good as dead."

"Not that he doesn't deserve to die," Gellos said.

"But not at the hands of a traitor intent on silencing him," Reagan said.

"You're right," Gellos admitted.

"And keep in mind, whoever sent those shooters last night wasn't just targeting Khoury. They wanted to take all three of us down, probably guessing Khoury had already been sharing some of his juicy stories with us. Which means Alex and I are also still in danger."

No one at the table disagreed.

"I have some ideas," the DD told them. "But first I want to know if you believe there's any chance Khoury was behind the three attacks this morning."

"Anything is possible," Reagan said, "but he would've had to plan them well in advance. He's been incommunicado since I grabbed him in London."

Brandt spoke up. "The attacks in Paris, Moscow, and New York were well coordinated, which means they had to be orchestrated long before today."

"You're right," Kenny agreed. "There was no need for him to make a call or push a button in the past day or two."

"You're right, of course," Reagan conceded, "but when we heard the news from you this morning, he seemed as surprised as Alex and I were. He might have been faking it, but that's not the sense I got."

"I had the same impression," Brandt said.

They all took a moment to consider their next move.

"Have Erin and Sasha come up with anything?" Reagan asked.

"It's all too new," Gellos told him. "We don't even have the names of casualties in Paris or Moscow."

Reagan's cell buzzed and he had a look. "Malone," he said. "All right if I take it?"

Kenny nodded and Reagan got up and walked to the window. "Hey Derek, this is not a great time."

"I understand, but we need to talk. In person. Where are you?"

"D.C."

"I'm already on my way north, I'll call when we land."

"All right. Want to give me a hint what this is about?"

Malone hesitated. "Connie and I were supposed to be there."

"Supposed to be where?"

"Paris."

CHAPTER THIRTY

Washington, D.C.

Information was pouring into Langley from local experts who were combing the sites of the three terrorist massacres, as well as from the various intelligence agencies of America's allies. Kenny sent Gellos downstairs to get an update on Khoury, figuring it was best to keep Reagan and Brandt away from the situation, at least for now. Reagan headed down the hall to join Erin in the small conference room there—more to see how she was doing than for any of the early intel being gathered. When he walked in, Sasha greeted him, then tactfully left the two of them alone.

"You all right?" Reagan asked.

She stood and he took her in his arms. "I'm still not sure. It certainly was traumatic," she said, "I admit that."

"Of course it was," he said.

"On so many levels, as you would say. For starters, why would anyone want to kidnap *me*? If it's about my relationship with you, how would people like that even know about us? Now I'm worrying, have we been followed? Is my phone bugged?"

His immediate reaction was to think "Lawler," but all he said was, "We're going to find out, Erin. I promise you that. They have both of those creeps in custody, and we're going to get answers."

As they sat down, she asked, "What about you? I didn't get any details, but I heard you had trouble at your place last night."

"Nothing Alex and I couldn't handle," he said with a reassuring smile. "You don't need to worry about me."

"But I do, Nicholas. I do worry. I realize you often face dangerous situations, but this all seems so—it's hard to explain—so different...."

"So personal?"

"Exactly."

"We'll get answers, as I say, and things will be fine in no time."

She managed her first smile of the day. "You may be the love of my life, but you're a terrible liar."

"Am I?"

"Like you always tell me, when someone is a bad liar it's because they don't get much practice." Then she added, "Although that may not be great for someone in the espionage business." Before he could respond, she leaned forward and gave him a tender kiss on the lips. "You need to be especially careful right now."

Reagan nodded, anxious to change the subject for all the obvious reasons. "I got a call from Derek just before I came to see you. He sounded upset, says he needs to speak with me in person. He's on his way to Washington right now."

"That sounds serious. Any idea what he wants?"

He paused, then decided to tell her the truth. "I think he and Connie were supposed to be at one of those cafés that got hit in that terrorist attack with the pipe bombs in Paris."

"What?"

"When we met in New York the other day, when you showed up at Il Mulino, he mentioned that they were taking a trip Paris. I had totally forgotten, with everything else going on. He obviously didn't go, but now I'm wondering who else knew of his plans."

"Are you sure he meant that café, did he actually mention its name?"

"No," Reagan admitted, "he just said Paris. But why else would he be jetting up here to meet me in person?"

"It could be any one of a number of reasons that he didn't want to discuss on the phone. Wait to hear what he has to say."

"Good advice coach." He thought it over. "Connie is coming with him, the four of us should have dinner. But maybe there's a discussion I should first have with Derek on my own."

"Agreed, not to mention I really am up to my neck here."

"Then what do you say we have dinner this evening, with or without the Malones?"

"Sounds great, either way, as long as I'm with you."

Reagan responded by kissing her gently on the lips.

* * *

MALONE AND REAGAN EXCHANGED TEXTS, setting a time and place for them to meet. Rather than naming the restaurant, Derek alluded to a prior dinner at one of his favorite spots, the time based on a calculation using their recent meeting in New York City. Reagan smiled at his friend's attempt at tradecraft, but got it all.

The place was Ocean Prime on G Street. Not only was it an elegant setting with a sumptuous menu, but it featured a selection of private dining rooms, as do many fine restaurants in Washington. When Reagan arrived, the maître d' led him to the smallest of those spaces, where Derek and Connie were already seated at a table for four. Derek liked special treatment at any of the many restaurants he frequented and, as Reagan realized, it was all part of his style. When Reagan entered the room, however, it was immediately clear that Derek was not in his usual jocular mood.

After kissing Connie on the cheek and shaking Malone's hand, Reagan sat and asked his first question. "I take it you have something serious and delicate to discuss. Do you think this is the best venue?"

Speaking just above a whisper, Malone said, "A private room in a noisy restaurant is the best possible cover." Forcing one of his signature smiles, he asked, "What kind of a spy are you, you don't know something like that?"

"All right," Reagan conceded, "we'll assume the room is not bugged." He waited a beat before saying, "I have a serious question before we get started. Whatever answer you give, I know it'll be the truth."

"You can always count on me for that."

Reagan nodded. "Other than the people you were going to ask for help on my behalf, did you tell anyone else about our discussion in New York?"

"Not a soul," Malone replied. "I didn't even tell Connie until last night."

"That's true," Connie said.

"There was no one else in the room when you explained to them what you were after?"

"No one," Malone said.

Reagan decided to file that information away for a discussion on a later date. "Fair enough. Then you already know what my next question is going to be."

"Why are we here?"

"Precisely."

Derek Malone became as serious as Reagan had ever seen him. Leaning forward, he said, "I mentioned Paris when we spoke earlier today, but I was actually referring to one of the two cafés those bastards hit. We had plans to meet our good friends at one of them, Benji Solares and his wife Sondra. Benji works for Novak Pharma at their lab in France, he was a physician who conducted research and experiments on some of their new drugs."

"When you say, '*was*' a physician…"

"We didn't make the trip to Paris, as you can see, but I have reason to believe he kept the reservation."

"You're worried he was one of the casualties?"

"I'm asking you to find out."

"You want to provide some context?"

"First, we decided to cancel our plans on short notice, for reasons I'll explain. When I told Benji, he joked about how they would miss us at lunch, so I'm assuming he kept the reservation. Second, it was his favorite bistro. Third, since I saw the reports on television showing Café Angelique was one of the targets, I've been calling and texting him."

"And getting no response."

"Zero."

Reagan nodded but said nothing.

"There's a lot more to this, Nick, things I have to explain to you about Novak Pharma, the work Benji was doing there, and how it all relates to me."

"You're suggesting that this Dr. Solares was not a random victim of a terrorist attack."

"I don't know that for sure, not yet, but my sense is that this was no accident, that he was a target."

"Which means…"

"Which means I might also have been a target of someone who knew I was going to meet Benji there. Someone who had no idea Connie and I had canceled our plans."

"I take it you have someone in mind."

"More than one someone."

CHAPTER THIRTY-ONE

Washington, D.C.

That evening, John and Andrew Novak were seated at the large, polished mahogany table in their conference room atop the Janus Building. They were hosting a private meeting with a congressman by the name of Freundlich, who had long been a recipient of generous donations from the Novaks. His political positions were well known—he was soft on crime, encouraged an open border to the south, believed entitlement programs could be endlessly funded despite the realities of a government teetering on financial disaster, and was in all other respects a poster child for the far-left progressives within the Democrat Party.

Which did not mean he never cast a vote that contravened those views when it was useful to his benefactors.

Freundlich was a friendly man who had used his easy style and liberal rhetoric to build a career that began with a seat on his town council, advanced to a ten-year stint in the state capitol, and had now led to a fourth term in the nation's House of Representatives.

Unknown to Freundlich, the Novaks thought him weak, less than intelligent, borderline incompetent, and self-deluded. But he served their needs, and as long as he did, they would help pay for his campaigns.

In that way, Freundlich was no different than many of the mayors and prosecutors across the country to whom the Novaks provided funds through political action committees, third parties, and other means of indirect payments. These people all served the same basic purpose—to undermine the fabric of an already damaged society that would ultimately lead to a new order that was already moving ahead. The Novaks were among those who did not trust the constitutional republic on which the United States was founded, working instead to seamlessly and invisibly convert the nation into an oligarchy controlled by the rich and powerful.

Local politicians had begun the process, followed by governors and congressmen, most too dense to see the ultimate result they were facilitating. Felons were being let out of jail without any bail. Repeat offenders had their prior actions ignored and were likewise released. Peaceful protests, once a proud tradition in American politics, had all but disappeared. Now there were endless mob scenes where violence ruled, cars and buildings were burned, and people attacked—including law enforcement officers. And what was the solution offered by the left to this destruction and anarchy—defund the police and leave the streets of major cities to criminals, the mentally ill, and illegal aliens.

In Freundlich's case, the reason for his allegiance to the Novaks transcended their campaign contributions. It seemed they knew of the congressman's affair with a Chinese woman who, he was embarrassed to discover, turned out to be an agent for the CCP. Whether that liaison had been engineered or by whom did not matter. Freundlich's loyalty ensured that his dalliance would remain their little secret.

"It's so good of you to ask me here," Freundlich said. "It's been too long."

"We've been keeping an eye on you," John Novak said. "You've gained some impressive committee assignments. Congratulations."

Freundlich responded with an "aw shucks" shrug, and Andrew feared the man might actually say something like, "Tweren't nothing." Instead, he told them, "I do what I can to help."

"Which is exactly what we wanted to speak with you about," John told him. "You have a seat on the Committee on Natural Resources."

"I do."

"We are in the process of acquiring long-term leases on some lithium mines. As you probably know," he added, suspecting that Freundlich did not know anything about this, "there are not many accessible locations. Lithium is rare and difficult to raise from the ground."

"But a very important component of long-term batteries, as well as pharmaceuticals," Andrew added, something else about which they assumed the man did not have a clue.

"Yes, yes, I've heard something about this."

Both Novak brothers assumed it was a weak bluff, but John said, "Good, because we are going to need your assistance."

"Whatever I can do," Freundlich said. "You know you can count on me."

"Excellent," John said, "because there may be a couple of thorny issues. Andrew, why don't you fill us in."

Andrew Novak reached for the file folder in front of him, opened it, and had a look. The move was more for show than necessity, since he was intimately familiar with the detailed reports he now picked up and briefly scanned. "There are two aspects of this with which we would like you to familiarize yourself. The first would be the leases themselves. Two of the locations are in the United States, which will bring the Department of the Interior and your committee into play. Others are in Canada and South America. That means we are also going to have to deal with the State Department and the Committee on Foreign Affairs. You'll need to touch base with your friends in the Senate that have seats there. I'm going to provide you with a written summary which will bring you fully up to speed."

"Happy to do all of that," Freundlich replied, forcing one of his mannered smiles.

"There will be a number of issues, other than the leases themselves. One of them being Laura Russo. As you know, she is the Secretary of the Interior."

"Of course. She's appeared before our committee more than once. Seems a bright woman." Then, with a sly grin he added, "Quite the looker, too."

"Perhaps, but she is no friend of ours, and we are already getting word she's going to oppose the granting of these leases."

"Apparently," John added, "she has the idea that we are trying to corner the market on lithium." He followed that with a smile that suggested the idea was ridiculous.

Freundlich immediately responded. "Totally, totally outrageous. Not even possible, right?"

The brothers shook their heads at the obvious absurdity of the idea.

"Even so, as we are all aware," Andrew said, "in politics, perception is more important than reality."

"You've got that right," Freundlich eagerly agreed.

"Just want you to be aware up front," Andrew said, "that you're going to have to deal with this."

Before Freundlich could reply, John said, "The president is fond of Secretary Russo. They've been friends since back when, and she has his ear. You have any sort of relationship with her, I mean apart from the committee appearances you mentioned?"

Freundlich thought it over for a moment. Never wanting to disappoint his benefactors, he said, "I've run into her at various functions. The exchanges were always cordial." Then he added with another smile, "You guys know me."

"Yes, we do," John said. "That's why you're here and that's why we're counting on you. If she begins to voice opposition, you've got to get to her before that noise becomes too loud. We want as little attention as possible on this, and we want to get it through as quickly as you reasonably can."

Freundlich nodded his understanding. "I'll get started right away, put out some feelers, see what other members of the committee think."

John leaned forward slightly. It was a large table, so the gesture was again for effect rather than any real attempt to get close to the congressman. "You're going to have to be realistic about how this is likely to play out. People in your own party may have problems with some of our plans. Environmentalists will ask the usual questions. Activists worried about an American company taking advantage of underprivileged people overseas might kick up a fuss. And, of course, our competitors are going to use their lobbyists to line up votes against us."

For the first time, Freundlich's vapid smile had completely disappeared, replaced by a look of concern. "You already have information on who we'll be up against? Other than Laura Russo?"

"Not yet," Andrew lied. "We can make some educated guesses of course, but up to now we have kept this entire plan totally under wraps. You're the first person we're trusting with this data, and we expect you to proceed accordingly." Then he added, "As always, we will support you in every possible way."

Freundlich nodded solemnly, realizing this was not the typical favor he was asked to do for the Novaks on the Hill. This was a major enterprise that would be a stretch for what little influence and currency he held in Congress. "You can count on me," he said again, not knowing whether that was true, and nervous about what might happen if he did not deliver.

CHAPTER THIRTY-TWO

Washington, D.C.

In the small private dining room at Ocean Prime, Reagan and the Malones concluded their discussion about the attack in Paris, at least for now. Reagan suggested that Erin join them for dinner and the Malones agreed it was a wonderful idea.

"You're going to tell her everything anyway," Malone said with a knowing smile, "am I right or am I right? She might as well get it straight from us and let that analytical mind of hers start working."

"Glad you agree, because I have her waiting outside at the bar," Reagan informed them, then left the private dining room and came back with Erin.

The Malones were genuinely glad to see her and, after exchanging hugs and greetings, Malone summoned a waiter and they ordered dinner. When the four of them were alone again, Derek got back to his concerns about Paris.

"What the two of you have to understand is that we're at war. Benji Solares knew that, along with some others I can name for you later."

"At war with whom?" Reagan asked.

"In general, I would say the entire pharmaceutical industry, but for the purpose of this discussion let's use Novak Pharma as an example."

"But you're on their board."

"Guilty as charged. When I began my tenure things were all right. We developed some terrific products and, I admit, we made a lot of money. Now I only stay because I'm better off having access to information than being cut off. Benji felt the same. Big Pharma is creating a world of drug dependence. Whether it's statins, blood pressure medication, or any number of other prescriptions, they're turning us into a world of addicts."

"But those medications are good for people, right?" Erin asked.

"Most of them," Malone conceded, "but you have to look at the entire landscape. Tens of millions of people have taken a vaccine before all of the side effects were identified or studied, and now they want to push regular booster shots. You have any idea how much money these companies are making from those injections?"

"I've seen the reports," Reagan admitted.

"I'm not saying that the most vulnerable were not helped by the vaccines, but there are studies emerging that suggest natural immunity is just as effective as the drug for most people."

"I've been reading about that," Erin said.

"What about supplements that may or may not have any effect?" Malone asked. "They're advertised all over the place. Television, social media."

"Give us an example" Reagan said.

"You ever hear of resveratrol?"

"The healthy ingredient in red wine," Erin said.

"High marks," Malone replied. "But the research on whether they really are beneficial in the ways being promoted are inconclusive. Does it work as an antioxidant? Does it help circulation? No one is sure yet, but here's an interesting factoid for you. Most people take a daily capsule containing two hundred and fifty milligrams, some may even take it twice a day. The experiments being done, however, generally involve no less than two full grams, which means you would have to take eight of these pills every day to reach the level they're studying, and there's still no proof you're deriving value."

"It's not harmful though, is it?" Erin asked.

"No, it's not, but it's expensive and the benefits, as I say, are questionable. And what about the drugs that *do* create problems? Xanax can be addictive. Opioids can be fatal. There are medications intended to combat acid reflux, but they're indicated for only eight weeks of use, yet people take them for years. And what is all this about?"

"Money," Reagan said.

"Bingo," Malone replied. "Health care spending in our country exceeds three trillion dollars, which is greater than the amount spent on national defense and something like fifty times the amount spent on homeland security. That raises a basic question because, as Erin has already pointed out, there are any number of medications which are helpful and even necessary."

Erin nodded. "But you're saying that there are too many medications that are not."

"Correct," Malone said. "As I'm pointing out, some may be useless and others are downright harmful."

Connie spoke up now. "Tell them about *Neulife*. That's the real issue at Novak Pharma right now."

Malone had a taste of his Midleton, one of the Irish whiskies he favored. "Yes, let's talk about *Neulife*."

"You've mentioned it to me before," Reagan said. "It hasn't gone to market yet, has it?"

"Not yet, but the hype is already building. It's supposed to be the Fountain of Youth, an antiaging compound that will change the world. They also claim it might not just retard the aging process, it might also help with physical and mental health disorders such as ADHD, Alzheimer's disease, and schizophrenia."

"I'm guessing you're about to tell us about the downside," Erin said.

"Here it is. Benji Solares and I have been leading a small group of doctors at Novak looking at the potential side effects, but no one else in the company wants to listen. They say we're speculating, that we're getting in the way of a miracle drug." Malone took a moment to look from Erin to Reagan. "Believe me, we're not. We are seriously worried."

"What are the risks?" Erin asked.

"I'll start with the biggest. Once you begin taking the drug," Malone said, "there is no way to get off."

"You mean it's addictive, like heroin?" Erin asked.

"Worse, with heroin you can go through withdrawal or take methadone. With *Neulife*, once you stop taking it, your cells become weakened and your telomeres are drastically compromised."

"Explain it as if you're talking to people who are not doctors," Reagan said.

"You want the bottom line? Once you're on this drug, if you stop using it the aging process actually accelerates."

Erin paused before asking, "How fast?"

"We don't know that yet, that's one of our main concerns. But the data suggests that's what happens."

"What if you continue to take it?" Reagan said. "Does it work?"

"Who knows what the long-term effects will be? That's what Benji and I wanted them to take time to study, but this train is rolling down the tracks toward a multibillion dollar bonanza."

Reagan shook his head.

"Before your eyes glaze over, let me throw just a few more facts at you." After another taste of his whisky, Malone went on. "I mentioned that we have three trillion dollars in annual health care costs in the United States. More than eighty percent of that come from the treatment of chronic diseases. Putting aside accidents and mistakes in medical care, the major causes of death are heart disease, cancer, stroke, and issues caused by diabetes. Novak Pharma claims *Neulife* will provide a ninety-three percent reduction in risks from diabetes, eighty-one percent lower risk of heart attacks, fifty percent reduction in risk of stroke, and a thirty-six percent overall reduction in the risk of cancer."

"That's mind-boggling," Reagan said.

"If it's true. And remember, those claims relate to people not already afflicted by any of those conditions."

"Even so…" Reagan said.

"Even so, those claims will make this drug worth billions."

"Assuming it really works long-term," Erin said.

"Exactly."

"But if you're right about the downside of stopping the treatment, it could control a population."

"That's my point," Malone said. "Given the costs of medication and treatment, if you control the drugs, you control the economy, and if you control the economy…"

"You control the people," Reagan said.

"That's why they want to push this through. When Benji raised issues from the studies being conducted in Paris, they tried to shut him up every way they could. They offered to give him what they called a promotion, to get him away from his research."

"He refused?"

"He did. They couldn't fire him, of course, for fear he'd go public with whatever we've learned to date."

"Which is why you think he was targeted in that bombing of the Parisian café. That's pretty extreme," Reagan told him.

"Let's just say it's what I fear. They couldn't murder him outright, or make him disappear. Too many questions, too many other people knew of his concerns."

Reagan was thinking it over. He hated coincidences. "But now they can mourn him as an unfortunate victim of senseless slaughter."

"You got it," Malone said, glancing at his wife whose tense look needed no explanation. "They'll delete his findings while they're praising his contributions to Novak Pharma."

"But that was only one of three attacks," Erin reminded them.

Reagan nodded. "Which means we need full lists of all the casualties in New York and Moscow, as well as Paris."

"That's how I see it," Malone said. "I have no way of knowing if anyone else was related to Novak Pharma, but we have to get those names." Turning to Connie again, he took her hand as he said, "We're worried, Nick."

"I understand," Reagan told him, as he looked across the table at them. What he did not say was that he shared their concern about who might be targeted next.

CHAPTER THIRTY-THREE

Washington, D.C.

Reagan had booked a room at his favorite hotel in D.C., The Jefferson on 16th Street, not far from the White House. The Malones were staying in a suite at the Ritz Carlton in Georgetown, a short ride away. When they finished their dinner and their discussion, Derek offered a ride in their limo, but Reagan declined. He grabbed a taxi and he and Erin headed downtown.

"Nightcap at the Ebbitt?"

"I'm exhausted," she said. "In case you hadn't noticed, it's been a long couple of days for me."

"Helping me bring in the Handler, working on three terrorist attacks around the world, almost being abducted at gunpoint? Is that what you mean?"

"Sometimes, Nicholas, your sense of humor is, uh…"

"Inappropriate?"

"Just put a sock in it."

He placed his arm around her shoulders and held her close. "This has been rough on everyone."

"And now Derek might be in danger." She pulled back slightly to have a serious look at him. "Do you believe what he's saying is true?"

"Let's say I'm becoming a believer."

"That's awful."

They were a quiet for a few moments. Then Reagan said, "I have an idea. You should stay with me tonight."

"I left my bag at Carol's."

"At least yours is local. I left mine in a safe house in London. I figure the sooner we get out of these clothes and let them air out for tomorrow, the better off we'll be."

"Is that your plan?"

"I think it's excellent. You need a hot bath and a back rub. It'll relax us."

She smiled at him. "Us?"

"Sure. We can pick up your things in the morning."

Reagan knew the manager on duty who arranged a quick check-in, then they rode the elevator upstairs.

The room was not large but it was well appointed. There was a small desk, a dresser, an armchair in the corner, and a king-sized bed. He switched on the indirect lighting, the room suffused in a soft glow as he headed for the bathroom and began to run hot water in the tub.

"You weren't kidding about the bath," Erin said when he came back into the bedroom. She had placed her purse on the dresser and kicked off her heels.

Reagan took her in his arms. "I never kid around about being naked with you."

They kissed, slowly and passionately, and then he stepped back and sat on the bed.

They had been lovers for several years, but Reagan never lost the thrill of seeing Erin undress. She moved slowly but purposefully, an erotic dance whether she meant it or not, and the vision of her when she was done was breathtaking. For Nick Reagan it did not get any better than this. She was slender and firm, with contours that made him want to put his hands all over her. And he loved how comfortable she was with their intimacy.

After she carefully hung her skirt and blouse in the closet, she turned toward him wearing nothing but her bra and panties. "You just going to sit there gawking at me while the bath overflows?"

"It's difficult for me not to just sit here and admire perfection," he told her, then got up and quickly disrobed. After hanging his clothing over the back of the chair, he held her again. "You drive me crazy, you know that?"

She responded with a soft smile. "Don't blame me, you had a head start on crazy."

This time when they kissed it felt as if they might not stop.

Finally parting from him, she slipped out of her undergarments and said, "Come on," then took his hand and led him into the bathroom.

* * *

THE FOLLOWING MORNING BEGAN early for them. They were having coffee in bed when Gellos called.

"I assume Erin is with you," she said.

"Yes, dinner ran late, didn't want to bother you," Reagan said.

"Might have let me know. With everything going on…"

"Sorry," Reagan said. "Our conversation with the Malones was kind of…"

"Whatever, you can tell me about that later. As long as she's all right."

"She's fine. Any news?"

"I think we have a problem with Khoury," Gellos told him.

"Such as?"

"Kenny had me keep an eye on him in the holding room downstairs. There were two other agents outside keeping an eye on him as well."

"You find that unusual?"

"I do. Two agents? All night?"

"I take it you checked more than once."

"I did," Gellos said. "Why would anyone post two agents outside a totally secure cell? Khoury certainly has no way to get out."

Reagan nodded to himself. "Which means they don't want anyone speaking with him."

"That's my read."

"You know the agents?"

"There were a couple of shifts," she said, "but I recognized one of them."

"Let me guess. Lawler's men?"

"They are. He obviously wants him incommunicado."

Reagan sat up against the upholstered headboard. "He's not going to try anything while the Handler is at Langley."

"Agreed, but he may not be there for long. I've already spoken with the DD. They're moving him to the Gables for interrogation."

"When?"

"Not sure, but the real question is, why not just question him where he is?"

"I think we know the answer," Reagan said, then paused. "If he's being moved, we need to figure out a way to be involved. Otherwise…"

"Got it," Gellos said. "I'm calling Kenny again, then I'll circle back to you."

"Good. You back at your place?"

"I am."

"Do you ever sleep?"

"Only when I need to," Gellos said.

"Erin's coming by to get her bag, but I'm heading to Langley. Whatever happens to Khoury, our first priority is to gather all the information he claims to have."

"I got word there's a lot of chatter coming from upstairs at Langley," she warned him.

"Any specifics?"

"Just that they want your scalp," she told him.

CHAPTER THIRTY-FOUR

CIA Headquarters, Langley, Virginia

Kenny arrived at his office early, and was already there when Reagan walked in. "We have a problem," he told his agent.

Reagan sat in the chair across the desk from the DD. "I would say that's an understatement, sir."

"I heard from the director that they're thinking about citing you for insubordination."

"For bringing Khoury in?"

"Spinelli says there are people upstairs wondering if Khoury had something to do with the three attacks yesterday."

Reagan shook his head. "I don't believe he did, but how would my apprehending him play into that scenario?"

"I have no idea," Kenny admitted, "but you've obviously made some powerful enemies."

"For capturing someone who might have intel that's making them uncomfortable?"

"I don't know, Nick," Kenny replied, his frustration evident by the fact that he addressed Reagan by his first name.

"Suppose I had left Khoury in London, and suppose he did have some involvement in those murders. Would we have been better off if I hadn't brought him in? Or if I had taken him out right there? I don't think it would have mattered."

"Neither do I."

"At least we can interrogate him."

Kenny did not disagree.

"What about them moving Khoury to the Gables?"

"I don't understand that either," the DD conceded. "No one has even begun questioning him here, why take him to another location?"

"When they take him from here, I want to be involved."

"Impossible."

"We need to learn whatever Khoury has before Lawler gets to him."

"All right," Kenny agreed, "I'll find out what I can about the transport."

"I'll be discreet," Reagan said.

"That would be an interesting change of pace. Now tell me about Malone. Gellos said you met with him and might have information."

"He was supposed to be in Paris," he said, then began to summarize what Malone had told him.

Gellos arrived, took a seat, and Reagan continued. When he was done, she said, "He's claiming the pipe bombing of those cafés was not random."

"That's his theory."

"Organized by whom?" Kenny asked.

"He never came out and said, but he believes it has something to do with this drug Novak Pharma intends to release."

Kenny stood, as if his day was already getting off to such a bad start he could not take any more of it sitting down. "The Novak brothers? Two of the most respected businessmen and philanthropists in the country? He thinks they're behind a terrorist plot to protect a new medication their company is developing? What's next, a passage from *Alice in Wonderland*?"

Reagan remained calm, looking up at his chief as he said, "I realize how far-fetched it sounds, but what are the odds?"

It was Gellos who replied. "The odds of what? One of the people who died in the explosion was Malone's friend, and Malone says he was supposed to meet him there that day. There are probably hundreds of people with stories like that. Near misses, canceled reservations, people stuck in traffic. Come on, Nick, Malone's a bit out there, don't you think?"

"Meaning what?"

"He gave us some help on that case a few years ago. Since then, you've become friends and he's become a wannabe intelligence agent. I'm not even sure I trust him." She looked to Kenny for support, but the DD said nothing. Turning back to Reagan, she said, "You asked him for help finding Khoury, and who did he go to? His friends the Novaks, right? But he never got back to us. What does that tell you?"

"I'm not sure where you're going with this," Reagan said.

"One minute he's asking them for help to track down the Handler," Gellos replied, "then he accuses them of terrorism. Seriously?"

"At some point the two of you should hear him out, but let's table this for now," Reagan suggested. "At the moment I'm more concerned about who'll be taking Khoury from the building. And why."

* * *

KENNY RECEIVED WORD that Khoury was not being taken to the Gables any time soon, and Reagan felt he had better use for his time than sitting around waiting to be handed a formal reprimand.

Instead, he phoned Yevgeny Durov.

Durov was former KGB. Through political shrewdness, a long list of influential friends, and a talent for self-preservation, he had fashioned a second career for himself as an envoy without portfolio for the new Russia.

Durov and Reagan had met years before at a diplomatic function in Washington, which was an ironic setting for two clandestine operatives to cross paths. Since then, they had sometimes joined forces when their interests aligned, and a friendship was forged as it can only be in the fire of battle. On one occasion, Durov provided assistance when Reagan departed Aleppo, after leaving the bodies of several terrorists in his wake.

The conflict between Russia and Ukraine had put a damper on their relationship and their get-togethers had become infrequent. But whenever they met, Durov never failed to mention "the time I saved your life," often parlaying that into an expensive lunch or dinner for which Reagan always paid.

Today there would be no dinner, no lunch, not even drinks. When Reagan called, he made it clear he only needed a few minutes of the Russian's time but needed it now. Durov knew Reagan well enough to know when he was all business and so he obliged without hesitation, agreeing to meet on the National Mall, outside the Air and Space Museum.

Durov was in his late sixties, tall and burly, his physique living proof of a love for good food and drink, his friendly style designed to conceal the cold-blooded assassin he could be if the need arose. Nevertheless, his eyes rarely relinquished their look of cynical amusement—he was, above all things, a pragmatist with a practical view of realpolitik, and a healthy perspective on how lucky he was to still be alive.

Reagan had arrived early for their meeting and was seated on a bench outside the museum when the Russian climbed out of his taxi and sauntered over. As usual, he was wearing a well-tailored suit, the jacket buttoned to cover what it could of his enormous girth, and a pink dress shirt opened at the neck.

"Nikolai," he exclaimed as he approached, and Reagan stood to accept one of Durov's classic bear hugs. Stepping back, he said, "I am so happy to see you, even if you made it clear this is not a social call."

"I wish it could be, my friend."

Having a good look at Reagan—who was dressed in a black, long-sleeved polo, gray slacks, and black suede rubber-soled shoes—he asked, "Don't you ever wear anything that isn't dark?"

Reagan laughed. "You ask me that every time I see you."

"But on such a sunny spring day?"

"I always wear a white shirt with my tuxedo, does that work for you?"

"I'll just have to live with it."

"Come on," Reagan said, "let's take a walk."

As they strolled slowly, side by side, along the grassy median, Durov said, "I take it you want to get right to business."

"Time may be short."

"Rumor has it that you were in London and that you brought company back with you."

"Walid Khoury. You know him?"

Durov shrugged his broad shoulders. "We've met, here in Washington. I heard rumblings that he was not all he seemed to be. I thought he might be a dishonest banker. No idea he was al Qaeda."

Reagan smiled. "I have a feeling those rumblings went deeper than bad loan practices."

"Does it matter now? You did what you could to stop those attacks, and now he's in your custody."

"Attacks are what I want to discuss," Reagan said.

"Ah yes, these recent tragedies."

"I'm going to be even more direct than usual."

"That's hard to imagine," the Russian replied with a chuckle.

"I assume by now your government has a list of the casualties and injured outside the Bolshoi."

"I am certain we do."

"I want a copy of that list, along with whatever you have on the shooter."

Durov responded with a deliberate nod of his leonine head. "That *is* direct. Am I entitled to know the reason for such interest in those of my countrymen who suffered at the hand of that lunatic?"

"I have reason to suspect that the pipe bombing in Paris was not random, that one of the fatalities may have been an intentional target."

"I assume you are seeking that same information from the French?"

"My next assignment."

"And you will be combing the list from New York."

"I've been busy with Khoury, as you say, but I'll be getting to that."

"Will you be sharing those names with me, as you ask me to share mine?"

"If there is anything to this—anything at all—I will indeed be a good sharer."

"All right, I'll get you the names," Durov said, then stopped walking and turned to Reagan. "Do you mind telling me the identity of this unfortunate individual in Paris?"

"I promise I will, when I have more information. As I say, at present this is only a suspicion, and I don't want to provoke unnecessary action if this lead turns out to be false."

"Or especially if it's *true*," the Russian said with a sly smile, then resumed walking.

CHAPTER THIRTY-FIVE

Virginia

Reagan was driving back to Langley when he received a call from Gellos.

"They're moving Khoury to the Gables."

"When?" he asked.

"It's in process."

"I don't like it."

"Neither do I," she said, "but you've been ordered to stay away."

"This is becoming a habit," Reagan said. "What about you?"

"What about me?"

"You haven't been warned off. What if I swing by and pick you up. No one said I couldn't be your driver."

"What's the point?"

"The point is to keep an eye on what's going down. Don't you think that's a good idea?" Before she could answer, he said, "Bring Brandt and some hardware. I have a bad feeling about this."

"Me too," Gellos said.

"See you in about twenty."

Reagan met Gellos and Brandt in the parking lot across the street from CIA headquarters. They decided to take Brandt's vehicle, a Ford Escape SUV, since he had already placed a number of weapons in the back. Leaving Reagan's car behind, Brandt took the wheel and began the forty-minute drive to the safe house.

"You're certain they left already?" Reagan asked.

"Kenny got word," Brandt told him. "Two agents took him away, they're just a few minutes ahead of us."

"Perfect. What about Lawler?"

"He's scheduled to arrive there later."

Gellos, seated in the back, said, "This entire thing makes me uncomfortable."

"No argument from me," Reagan said.

"We're spying on our own people."

"Don't think of it as spying," Reagan told her. "Think of it as providing them an armed escort they don't know about."

"I'm with Carol on this," Brandt said.

"Look, my analysis is simple. If it's true that Lawler is some sort of collaborator, then moving Khoury from Langley to the Gables is suspicious at best. The agents escorting him there may not have any idea there's an issue, but we do."

"What if it's all bullshit?" Gellos asked.

"Then we haven't lost anything, right? We make sure Khoury gets to the safe house, then do whatever we can to see that the interrogation goes according to Hoyle."

"But you've been told to stay away from this entire operation," she reminded him.

"But the two of you haven't," Reagan countered.

*　*　*

THREE MEN IN A LINCOLN TOWN CAR had arrived in time to position their car amid some trees north of the intersection of Old Dominion Drive and Bellview Road, about four miles from the Gables. A fourth man was behind them in a pickup truck.

The area consisted of huge tracts of land with no homes that could be seen from the road and almost no traffic. They had received a text telling them that they would only have to wait twenty minutes or so.

*　*　*

KHOURY WAS SEATED IN THE BACK of an Agency Suburban being driven by Sam, the agent Reagan knew. Khoury's hands were cuffed behind his back and his ankles chained. As uncomfortable as he was, contemplating what might come next was even more unsettling.

"How long until we arrive?" he asked.

"You were told there would be no conversation," the agent in the front passenger seat told him. "Just sit back and be quiet."

"These handcuffs make it impossible for me to sit back."

Neither agent responded.

* * *

BRANDT HAD BEEN DRIVING for a while, the three of them quiet until he said, "Not long to go, less than ten minutes. My guess is we're less than a minute behind them now."

"How do you figure?" Reagan asked.

Brandt smiled. "I'm driving faster than they would."

"Everything looks clear," Gellos said. "So much for the need to have backup."

Reagan shook his head. "Maybe, but I'm more concerned about what's going to happen when they get him inside the Gables."

CHAPTER THIRTY-SIX

Virginia

The driver of the Lincoln had the best angle to see the road behind them, and he was the first to spot the approaching Suburban. Speaking through the wireless connection he had with the driver of the pickup truck, he said, "They're here, coming up fast."

The driver of the pickup threw his vehicle into drive, spun out into the street, and sped toward the Suburban. Before Sam could swerve out of harm's way, his large SUV had been broadsided, the impact striking the front passenger door and front right panel.

"Damn," Sam hollered, having lost control as they spun violently to the left, angry at himself for not having reacted quickly enough to avoid the collision.

The agent in the passenger seat of the Suburban had been shoved hard to his left, but managed to hit the radio transmitter attached to the dash. "We're under attack," he shouted, then did his best to provide their location.

Khoury had been jostled, first to his left as the vehicle was struck, then to his right as it spun, ultimately falling to the floor between the front and rear seats.

The driver of the pickup truck was stunned by the force of the crash he had caused, but his three accomplices were already exiting the sedan and coming towards the Suburban with automatic weapons drawn. They waited an instant, as the driver of the truck collected himself and managed to back up a few yards to give them a clear sight line at the SUV.

Then they began firing.

The Suburban was one of the few Agency vehicles with bullet-resistant glass, but the two agents inside knew that the protection would not survive the sort of onslaught being unleashed. They were holding their weapons but could not risk opening a window or exiting the vehicle to return fire.

Then they saw one of their attackers pull out a grenade.

"Oh shit," Sam said.

Before the man could pull the pin, everyone turned toward the sound of screeching tires as another vehicle joined the battle.

"What the hell," Brandt shouted as he brought his small SUV to an abrupt stop.

"Weapons," Reagan hollered to Gellos, who was already stretched over the back seat and began passing automatic rifles up to the front.

"We're dead if we stay in here," Reagan told them. He threw his door open, weapon in hand, jumped out, and—using the door for cover—began firing.

The customary quiet of this bucolic country neighborhood was now shattered by the explosive sound of several automatic weapons being discharged at top speed.

Seeing that help had arrived, Sam shoved his door wide, got out, and crouched behind the front of his vehicle as he also opened fire.

One of the men from the sedan, who had been holding the grenade, was Reagan's first target. He scored with several shots to the man's chest and head, leaving him for dead before he hit the ground. The second casualty was the driver of the pickup. He had yet to make it out of his vehicle, and Sam sent a series of shots at him, first shattering his windshield, then hitting him in the face before the man had a chance to raise his gun.

Brandt and Gellos were also outside now, providing their own barrage of shots. Together with Sam, who was far off to the left behind the Suburban, and Reagan to the right behind the door of Brandt's SUV, they were unloading a lethal crossfire at the two remaining assailants. One had already been hit in the leg and was limping toward the rear of the pickup truck. The other was making a move back to the sedan when Reagan called out.

"Stop where you are. Drop your weapons and put your hands on your heads or we'll finish you off, right here, right now."

The man who had been shot in the leg did as he was told, but the other made a dash for his car.

"Aim low," Reagan yelled out as he fired at the man's legs. "We want these bastards alive."

It was all over a few moments later when the man fell under a spray of shots from Gellos and Brandt that hit too much of his upper torso.

Meanwhile, the man who had dropped his rifle now collapsed to the asphalt.

"Damnit," Reagan said, as he and Gellos moved cautiously toward the three bodies on the ground. "We need one of them alive."

Sam had circled around the side of the pickup and cautiously opened the passenger door. "This one is gone," he called out.

"Be careful everyone," Reagan ordered. "If one of them is still breathing, they might have a gun. Or they might be wired."

Moving slowly, Reagan confirmed the first man he took down was dead. He carefully picked up the grenade that was laying in the road beside the body, made sure the pin was secure, then placed it in his pocket.

Gellos was standing over the shooter who had made a run for the car. "Also gone," she told them.

Which left only the attacker who had been shot in the leg.

Reagan and Gellos approached him, staying several yards away, as Reagan said, "Keep your hands where we can see them."

He managed to show his hands were empty.

Gellos asked, "Who are you?"

"Drop dead," the man hissed.

"I assure you, we're your best chance of survival," Reagan told him.

The man turned on his side and stared up. "Survival? In a dirty cell at Gitmo?"

An interesting reaction, Reagan thought. Turning to his partner, he said, "Likely not our friend's first rodeo."

"Go to hell," the man said.

"This can only go one of three ways," Reagan told him. "I can shoot you in the head. I can leave you here to die slowly. Or we can get you some medical attention if you're willing to cooperate. All I want to know right now is who you are and who sent you."

The man was obviously in pain, but managed a grim smile. "You'll never know," he said.

"Why is that?"

"Because I have nothing to tell you."

"You'd rather die than answer my questions?"

"What sort of fool are you?" the man asked. "You think I'm someone who would know such an answer?"

Gellos and Reagan glanced at each other.

"You don't know who sent you?" Reagan asked.

The man shook his head slowly. "What do you think, I get a written invitation?"

"We'll find out who invited you," Gellos told him. "For now, let's try and stop that bleeding." She asked Brandt to get a first aid kit from the Suburban.

Reagan said, "After we call this in, we need photos and prints, and let's collect whatever IDs they have. Forensics can clean up the mess when we're done."

Sam, who was standing behind them, said, "My partner already called it in and, from what I've heard, Nick, you may not want to be here when the cavalry arrives."

Reagan sighed. "Too late for that. I want to be sure this dirtbag is kept alive so we can find out what he knows. And I want to be sure that Khoury remains safe. At least for now."

The second agent had climbed over the console of the SUV and out the driver's door. Now that the shooting had stopped, he brought Khoury out to join them.

The Handler took a moment to survey the carnage, then turned and said, "Nice of you to stop by, Mr. Reagan."

"We just happened to be out for a drive in the country," Reagan told him. "Good timing for you guys, it seems."

"Yes, it was," responded the agent.

Turning to Khoury, Reagan said, "Someone is working very hard to kill you, Walid. Let's have a look around and see if you recognize any of these gentlemen."

After visiting the three bodies and returning to the man on the ground that Brandt was working on, Khoury said he had never seen any of them before.

"That's a shame," Reagan said. "Would be nice to know who's behind this."

Khoury looked him in the eyes as he said, "We both already know, don't we?"

Before Reagan could respond, they all heard the sound of approaching sirens.

CHAPTER THIRTY-SEVEN

Washington, D.C.

Anatole Mindlovitch was born to a wealthy family in what was then the Soviet Union. His family sent him off to be educated in London and the United States and, by the time he returned to his homeland, it had returned to its historical roots as Russia—albeit under the rule of a secular tyrant rather than a tsar.

As he tried to acclimate himself to life in Moscow after so much time in the West, Mindlovitch immediately showed signs of a gifted businessman as well as an innovator. He parlayed his father's wealth from the oil industry into a far-reaching business enterprise that won him both admiration and envy from the most powerful people—a sort of Russian parallel to the Novaks' story.

He even gained access to Vladimir Putin's inner circle, but ultimately his ideas were too modern and his success too great—Putin was not inclined to share the spotlight with anyone—which led to Anatole's decision to relocate somewhere less threatening. He did his best not to have his move viewed as either a rebuke of Putin or a defection from his country, traveling the world for a few years before settling in California, choosing Silicon Valley for his home, not far from where he attended graduate school at Stanford.

All the while, Mindlovitch was expanding the breadth and reach of his business interests. He moved into the communications sector, then into sources of environmentally friendly power, such as solar and wind. He bought up large tracts of real estate in California, invested in apartment buildings in New York City, and owned one of the world's largest microchip factories in Suzhou, China.

That was where his scientists were developing something that came to be known as the Ghost Chip—intended to render a smart phone or computer totally hack-proof and their communications untraceable. It was said these chips could also be programed to emit a signal that would remotely detonate explosives and could even cause the battery in the device of the receiving party to ignite.

Several months ago, Nick Reagan visited the Suzhou lab in the hope of gaining information about these chips. He came away empty, his efforts earning him an arrest and brief detention in the hands of the Chinese secret police. He subsequently learned that some of the microchip's prototypes had been stolen but, when he sought out Mindlovitch in the hope of working together to recover the stolen technology, someone made an attempt on the Russian's life.

Reagan saw to it that he was afforded special protection during his convalescence, but thus far the Ghost Chip remained nothing more than an urban legend. And the prototypes were still missing.

There was a long list of governments, intelligence agencies, and large communications companies interested in the Ghost Chip, none more than the Novak brothers. They had a history of dealing with Mindlovitch, especially given their respective oil interests and other intersecting business ventures. As a proponent of environmentally friendly energy sources, the Russian had made large investments in the future of electronic vehicles while understanding the public's two major concerns—the cost of these cars and the range of use before their batteries ran down. A key component to lightweight batteries was lithium, and that is what brought Mindlovitch and the Novaks together this afternoon.

Mindlovitch was in Washington for meetings with various politicians on an array of topics, and his get together at the Capitol Grille with Andrew and John Novak was part of his schedule.

Mindlovitch was already at the bar when the Novaks arrived. A celebrity among lawmakers and businessmen, he was engaged in discussion with a handful of well-dressed men who were pleased to have a few casual words with him.

He was in his late forties, stood at six foot five and, even after his recent ordeal, his trim long-limbed physique looked to be in top physical shape. He was known to befriend professional athletes, especially American basketball players with whom he regularly worked out, and had two full-time trainers on his payroll.

His features were plain, his complexion clear and remarkably unlined, his thin, sandy colored hair cut short and neatly combed. His look was more pleasant than handsome, but his eyes spoke of both intelligence and ruthlessness.

The Novaks were equally well known among this crowd and joined the conversation after exchanging greetings with Mindlovitch and the others. Ultimately the three men retreated to a table in the rear of the restaurant that furnished a measure of privacy.

"How are you feeling?" John Novak asked. "We haven't seen you since that awful incident."

"I'm doing well, thank you. It was an ordeal, but fortunately the drug administered has had no permanent effect. It was intended to kill me—nothing more or less. I think it is safe to say, they failed."

"Thank God," Andrew said.

"I give my thanks to an extraordinary medical team and their quick response. Whatever role God played remains to be seen."

"Sorry to dwell on this unpleasantness," John said, "but have they captured the people behind it?"

"We believe we know who actually did the deed, as the expression goes, but the individual has yet to surface. Given the people behind him, who either paid for his services or found some other means of compelling his actions, it is unlikely that he survived the event. Ironic, is it not?"

Both brothers nodded, acknowledging that the Russian's tone made it clear the subject was at an end.

"Any progress on the microchip?" Andrew asked. "Any word on the missing prototypes?"

"Nothing to report," Mindlovitch said, hoping to shut down that discussion as well, but the Novaks were not so easily deterred.

"What about our offer to buy into the program?" Andrew asked.

Mindlovitch smiled. "I assure you gentlemen, I have all the capital necessary to continue my work on the Ghost Chip."

"We don't doubt it," John said, "but it would be nice for you to bring some friends along for the ride."

"Perhaps," Mindlovitch said without making any commitment. "We shall see." Then, after a brief pause, he said, "I take it the two of you are doing well."

"We are," John said. "And we have a couple of exciting projects on the boards we want to share with you."

"Let's begin with lithium," Mindlovitch said in a quiet voice. "I believe that's why we're here."

Before they could respond, a waiter came by holding menus. Mindlovitch held up his hand.

"Gentlemen, I am sorry to say that I cannot stay for lunch, my dance card is quite full today." Turning to the waiter he said, "I'd like a sparkling water with a wedge of lime, please."

"We'll have the same," John Novak said. "You can leave the menus, we'll order lunch afterward."

The waiter did as instructed and left them alone again.

"These proposals you're advancing, to mine lithium here and abroad," Mindlovitch said. "You have quite a hill to climb."

"We're hoping for your assistance."

"We shall see."

"Lithium ion are the best batteries for EVs," John said, realizing that fact was well-known. "Not to mention, it's still used in some of our key pharmaceuticals, including a new drug we're quite enthusiastic about."

"Understood. But the environmentalists are going to have a field day talking about how you'll be raping the land, using insane amounts of water, killing local agriculture, and so on. Then there's the economic damage and health risks to the locals."

"People want electric cars that can run over three hundred miles without a charge," John said. "We need the lithium."

Mindlovitch smiled. "You don't have to convince me, I have over a billion dollars invested in EVs. But there's another aspect to your applications—you seem to be interested in controlling the entire lithium market by leasing mines in Australia, South America, and here, in North Carolina."

"We have no real choice, we have to go where we find it," Andrew said.

"Leaving behind pollution, compromised water tables, contaminated water basins, and destroying farms for miles and miles around."

Andrew said, "You sound like one of them, Anatole."

"Not at all, but I *am* a realist. It's one thing for governments to tap into these resources. They can at least claim they're mining responsibly while considering all of these harmful factors. Forgive me for being blunt, but you, on the other hand, are successful capitalists who won't give a damn about the locals, the damage you do, or the devastation you leave behind."

The Novaks were silent for a few moments. Then John said, "Perhaps I was mistaken, but I thought you were interested in joining forces on this."

"I am," he replied, "but I have no interest in setting myself up as a piñata for the woke media and the loony left. They all claim they want electric vehicles but turn a blind eye to what is really involved. They act as if plugging a car into their garage socket comes with no environmental cost, as if the electricity does not have to be produced somehow and somewhere. Then there's the issue of how to recycle these batteries once they become useless, something they never seem to consider. Once you open this conversation and they begin espousing the perils of mining lithium in this country and elsewhere, they will come at us from every angle."

"What hypocrisy," Andrew said.

"I don't disagree," Mindlovitch said. "Remember, these are the same people who want to outlaw plastic straws, which they might use once in a week, while downing a half dozen plastic bottles of water every day. Their stupidity is mind-boggling."

Both brothers nodded in agreement.

"I am not opposed to your intention to increase the acquisition of the lithium we need to sustain the advance of EVs and, as you say, production of related drugs, and other uses. Quite the contrary. However, my political connections will run the other way if we do not have a responsible plan to offer."

"What do you suggest?"

"There's an old saying I think is appropriate here." Mindlovitch paused. "You don't always have to tell the truth, but if you're going to lie, make sure it's a lie you can sell."

CHAPTER THIRTY-EIGHT

Washington, D.C.

Later that afternoon, Kenny and Reagan were seated in one of the booths toward the rear of the dining room at the Old Ebbitt Grill on 15th Street. Opened before the Civil War, the dark, comfortable setting was the oldest saloon in Washington. Only steps from the White House and a watering hole for politicos and bureaucrats, they agreed it was best at the moment for Reagan to meet with the DD in public and avoid Langley.

"Lawler is furious," the DD said after they were served beers and bowls of chili. "You were specifically ordered to stay away from Khoury."

"Again," Reagan said, then had a taste of his draught. "But if Gellos, Brandt, and I had not showed up in time, Lawler would have two dead agents to answer for, and his friend Khoury would also be taking a dirt nap, or in the hands of who even knows?"

"I don't disagree."

"Doesn't Director Spinelli have something to say about this? Is no one upstairs suspicious about the attack? For instance, how many people knew the Handler was being transported to the Gables? How did those shooters just happen to be there, right at the moment Sam reached that intersection? When did everyone in the Agency get so goddamned dumb?"

"Excuse me?"

"I'm sorry, sir, I obviously didn't mean everyone."

"I get it, and I share your frustration, believe me."

"This is a whole lot more than frustration. Three hitters tried to go through Alex and me to get to Khoury the other night. How did they know where we were? Pretty obvious, right? Then Erin was almost abducted at gunpoint when she arrived at Union Station. We get anything from those two yet?"

"Nothing. Same story you got from the survivor of the roadside attack. They claim to be guns for hire, several levels of communication removed from whoever is actually paying and sending them out."

"It's probably true. I think we should call Bebon at the FBI. Get them to do their own background checks of all of these players, dead and alive."

"Good idea, I'll do that."

"But keep it away from Turnquist."

"Who?"

"Victor Turnquist, an executive assistant director at the Bureau."

"I recognize the name. What's your problem with him?"

"Khoury gave me the same warning about Turnquist that he gave me about Lawler," Reagan explained. "I have an off-the-record confirmation that he might be one of the bad guys."

"Obviously from Dick Bebon, right?"

Reagan managed to laugh for the first time in hours. "That's off-the-record for now, okay sir?"

Kenny nodded.

"What about Khoury? Have we verified he's still at the Gables?"

"Gellos has eyes on the situation."

"I want to see him."

"Impossible," the DD said.

Reagan tasted the chili, then added some Tabasco. "Nothing's impossible, sir, you taught me that a long time ago."

"He's going to be interrogated."

"When?"

"Tonight, at seven."

"Who's going to be there for the interview?"

Kenny responded with a look that said he did not want to answer.

"Why am I not surprised? Is Lawler going in there alone? Maybe he'll bring a hypodermic? Or something less subtle, like a hatchet?"

"The entire interview will be on video, you know that. What do you think Lawler's going to get away with?"

"I have no idea, but so far I believe he's gotten away with organizing several attempted murders, and one of these days his friends might just succeed." Reagan's phone buzzed. He pulled it out and looked at the screen. "I should take this. It's Durov."

Kenny nodded.

"Yevgeny," Reagan greeted him. "Should I be glad you're calling so soon?"

"Interested, that would be the better word," the Russian replied. "Where are you?"

Reagan looked across the table at his boss. "Having an early lunch with my superior officer."

"Damn, another lunch you're doing me out of. I was hoping to entice you into a good bottle of red and a large plate of sumptuous pasta."

"Let me guess. L'Ardente?"

"You know me too well."

"Then I promise you lunch or dinner there soon. Right now I'm up against it."

"Understood, my friend. But we need to speak in person. I have the information you requested."

"Where are you? I'm near the White House."

"My turn to guess. Ebbitt?"

"Touché."

"The bar there, twenty minutes, all right?"

"I'll have a booth for us."

CHAPTER THIRTY-NINE

Washington, D.C.

As Kenny finished his lunch, he told Reagan, "Be careful with Durov."

"I always am."

"I'm serious. He was KGB, and you know what they say about a leopard and his spots." Kenny drank the last of his beer. "At the moment, you don't need any additional accusations coming your way. We're not exactly friendly with Russia at the moment."

"I understand the geopolitics, sir."

"I know you do, Reagan, that's not my concern. It's that sometimes I think you rely too much on friendship. For all of your cynicism, you tend to assume people have your sense of integrity." Kenny stared at him. "I'm here to tell you they don't."

"Not even the good guys?" Reagan asked.

"Not even them. You're the outlier when it comes to loyalty."

Reagan sat back and grinned. "Sir, I think you just paid me a compliment."

"Don't be a horse's ass," Kenny said with a frown. "I share the doubts Gellos voiced about Malone yesterday, and I can name other past instances where you've been disappointed in people."

"I get the drift."

"Good," Kenny said as he got to his feet. "Just keep your eyes open."

"Will do. You heading back?"

"In a bit. First I'm going to take your advice and call Dick Bebon. If he's in, I'll stop by and see him."

After Kenny left, Reagan told the waitress clearing the table that he was waiting for another guest for drinks. He described Durov, told her he would be hard to miss, and a few minutes later she brought him to the table.

They exchanged greetings, Durov ordered a martini, and Reagan asked for another beer.

As the young woman walked off, the Russian took a seat. "The booth is a good idea, Nikolai, this is a bit more private."

"In this town, nothing is private," Reagan replied.

"Too true."

"I take it you found something."

"Make that plural," Durov said.

"I'm all ears."

"Let's begin in Paris. My friends in the GIGN provided their list of casualties, injuries, and background summaries."

"I thought you were waiting for my help on that."

Durov smiled. "Let's just say I became impatient. I found several names that might be of interest, but one in particular piqued my curiosity."

"Dr. Benjamin Solares," Reagan said.

"Quite so. I take it that was the name you were going to share with me."

"Correct. A research scientist working for Novak Pharma in their French facility."

"That's what I'm told. What they did not include in their report, of course, was that Dr. Solares was also a close friend and colleague of one Derek Malone."

Reagan nodded.

"As I recall, Dr. Malone assisted you in an assignment involving a breach of American data by the Chinese several years back."

"That's correct. They had plans for a massive cyberattack that we successfully prevented."

"Along the way, I should point out, you also stepped on some Russian toes."

Reagan responded with a puzzled look. "Is that true?"

"Our relationship with the Chinese is complicated, and although we had nothing to do with those plans to hack your systems, there was a belief among some in the CCP that my country had helped in your defense of that attack. Looking back, do you find that odd?"

"I find it very surprising, especially since I knew nothing about that until now." Reagan paused. "You have to admit it is a bit ironic, though. The Chinese were engaging in international cyberterrorism, but were upset Russia might have helped prevent it?"

"I agree, and I also believe you did not know, Nikolai. That is why I felt no need to trouble you about before. Now, however, more questions are likely to be raised since Dr. Malone's name has come up again."

"I admit my confusion. Are you saying the Chinese believe it was Malone who was somehow connected to the Russian government, and that's how he was able to provide the assistance he did?"

"I share your confusion, and we may have to wait to see how things play out with the investigation into these three terrorist attacks until we have answers. For now, let me turn to the tragedy outside the Bolshoi."

The waitress returned with their drinks, giving them a moment before moving to the next subject.

"I have a list of the names, and I will share these with you, as well as those I received from Paris. Once again, there is a single name that stood out to me in the report from Moscow. Grigor Kuznetsov." Durov waited for a reaction but received none. "A wealthy businessman, whom you in the West would call an oligarch."

"Not unusual for a wealthy man to be attending the Bolshoi Ballet. You obviously have something else."

"He was one of the more aggressive rivals of one Anatole Mindlovitch."

"That *is* interesting. Businessmen have rivals, but is there any reason Mindlovitch would want him dead? Did he have other enemies?"

Durov responded with a melancholy smile. "All wealthy people have enemies, whether here, in Russia, or elsewhere. But to engineer such a horrific attack to hide the fact he was the real target seems extraordinary, do you agree?"

"Savage and extraordinary," Reagan said. "Is there any indication Mindlovitch knows he was killed?"

"I can't be sure. There are a few names we have yet to release, and Kuznetsov is one of those."

Taking a moment to think it over, Reagan asked, "Have you found any connection between Kuznetsov and Solares?"

"Not yet, but we are looking."

"My gut is telling me there must be a link."

"Despite the fact that my sad gut is empty of the delicious meal I was looking forward to, I would agree. Time for us to take a look at the list of victims from New York City."

"I already have," Reagan told him.

"Good, what have you found?"

"I'll tell you, but first I want to know what you have on a man name of Bogdan Paszek."

CHAPTER FORTY

Washington, D.C.

Reagan walked from the Old Ebbitt to his hotel. Arriving at his room, he called Gellos on an encrypted line and shared what Durov had told him.

"Did you tell him what we've discovered about New York?"

"Not yet, but I'm going to," Reagan told her. "Right now I have to figure out a way to see Khoury."

"Not likely. The agents there have been told you're not allowed entrance to the Gables, and certainly not allowed to speak with him."

"I assumed that's true about me. But what about you?"

"Me again?" Gellos asked, then took a moment. She had an analytical mind, not given to quick reactions when she had the time to think things through. "It's possible," she finally said.

"Would you say it's worth a try?"

"Yes," she agreed. "Lawler's focus has been on you, and Alex to a more limited extent. He hasn't turned his guns on me yet."

"That's my thinking."

"He might have given orders that *no one* is allowed to see Khoury but him," she suggested.

"Do we know that?"

"Actually, no."

"All right then. What if you bring Kenny with you? There's not going to be anyone at the Gables who can override a deputy director."

"You think he'd do it?"

"I think he's fed up with the interference from the director's office. While I met with Durov, Kenny was going to speak with Bebon at the FBI. He wants an update on the questioning of that shooter we brought in, and the two thugs who tried to take Erin. I just heard from him, and he's even getting body-blocked there. If you agree, I'll call him about the Handler right now."

Gellos took another moment. "Why don't you let me call him?"

Reagan uttered a short laugh. "Because he thinks you're more level-headed than I am?"

"Something like that," she said, but wasn't laughing.

* * *

IT TOOK SOME WORK for Gellos to convince Kenny the idea made sense. Reagan had given her a list of the questions he wanted them to ask Khoury, and when Kenny heard what his agents were after, he agreed. He wrapped up his meeting with Bebon, picked up his car, and set off to pick up Gellos.

During the ride through the Virginia countryside, they reviewed their intended approach. Even assuming they got to the Handler, they figured Lawler would immediately get a call and head to the Gables in force.

Whatever happened, Kenny told her, he would take responsibility for the decision.

On arrival, they had no problem getting through the main security gate, as expected. Inside the large house, things were different.

"I'm sorry, sir," the agent in charge told Kenny. "We've been instructed to keep the prisoner in solitary."

Kenny nodded patiently. There was nothing physically imposing about him, but he was as tough as they come, and his voice was like ice as he said, "I'm a deputy director of the CIA. You have absolutely no authority to interfere with me."

The agent stood there, blinking. "But Assistant Director Lawler ordered us…."

"I don't care what you were told, or by whom. Now take us to Khoury or I'll write you up so your next assignment will be in the cafeteria at Langley."

The agent glanced at one of the other men on duty, an obvious signal that someone had better make that call to Lawler. Then he led Kenny and Gellos downstairs to the cell where Khoury was being held, where the prisoner's look of relief was evident.

"That'll be all for now," Kenny told the agent and waited for the door to be shut behind them. Turning to Khoury, he said, "It appears you were expecting someone else?"

"Very true."

"That meeting is going to occur shortly, I can assure you. Your best chance is to cooperate with me before it does."

Kenny and Gellos took seats across the metal table from the Handler. They saw that his wrists were still cuffed, but his ankles had been freed. Gellos took out a small recorder, placed it on the table and turned it on. She assumed this meeting was being recorded but was not taking any chances the video might disappear.

"Our first questions have to do with Lawler. You told Reagan, in effect, that he's a traitor. Is that correct?"

"A traitor to your government, yes."

"You realize that is an extremely serious allegation. On what do you base that charge?"

"Before I begin, I need guarantees...."

Kenny banged his fist on the table. "You are in no position to negotiate. If what you've been telling Reagan is true, the time has come to provide us proof. Otherwise, we'll get up and leave you to whatever comes next. The decision is yours."

Gellos watched Khoury carefully. Sociopaths and criminal behavior were her specialty, and she was surprised to see that he actually appeared to be weighing his options.

"How can I be sure, once I tell you what I know, you will be able to protect me?"

It was Gellos who responded. "You can't, but if you choose not to talk, do you think your silence will be rewarded by others?"

As Khoury stared at her, Kenny got to his feet.

"We're wasting our time," he said, looking down at Gellos. "Whatever is true or not about Ross Lawler, he is undoubtedly on his way here now." Turning to Khoury he said, "If you want protection, we need cooperation."

"There are people known as globalists," the Handler said. "They are called by other names as well, elitists who believe in a one world solution to national conflicts. They are powerful, well-placed in government and business, and very wealthy. They work from the inside in various countries. In yours, they do all they can to undermine the basic tenets of your constitutional republic. One of those men is Ross Lawler. I came to know that during my time in Washington."

Kenny lowered himself back into his seat. "How did you come to know it?"

"You people talk about my work as an international banker as a cover, as if there was nothing to it but artifice. That is far from the truth. I worked with many of these people and, more significantly, those that fund them. We provided financing for any number of projects that advanced their aims. With highly placed bureaucrats like Ross Lawler of the CIA and Victor Turnquist of the FBI affording us protection, it was almost impossible for our plans to be uncovered or stopped."

"Who do you claim are these people behind them?" Gellos asked.

"In our previous discussion, I mentioned the name Klaus Schnabel to Mr. Kenny. He and his allies fund the campaigns of numerous local politicians. They are already successful in turning your largest cities into lawless wastelands, allowing criminals to run wild through the streets while emasculating their own police. Your southern border no longer exists, as people from any number of countries, many with criminal backgrounds, enter the United States carrying narcotics, engaging in human trafficking, and spreading violence throughout the land. The result, as you've seen, is that your citizens suffer from a growing number of violent crimes, drug overdoses, senseless murders, and suicides, especially among the young."

"An interesting civics lesson," Kenny said, "but you've yet to provide any proof."

"You are from the Central Intelligence Agency. You have colleagues in the FBI whom you trust, I overheard Mr. Reagan discussing that with his fellow agent the other night. Investigate the banking records of both Lawler and Turnquist. Not their local checking accounts, of course, but the far-flung assets they have amassed in the names of shell companies they have created here and abroad. That will provide a wonderful starting point for you to seek further information, which will lead you upstream to the source of money. Then, look through their history of action and inaction. Examine the things they have done and the steps they should have taken but failed and refused to move on, even in the face of your country's enemies."

"You have never denied that you worked with al Qaeda," Gellos reminded him. "Are you saying these people are behind terrorist attacks on their own country?"

"No, I am telling you that their plans are far more damaging and devious than that. They are perverting the principles of your government from within."

No one spoke for a few moments. Then Khoury resumed.

"Your beloved President Ronald Reagan predicted how this would happen. Forgive my paraphrasing, but he said that fascism could only come to the United States of America in the form of progressive liberalism. He said that, just like the Nazis, these so-called liberals want to control everything, from education to energy, from guns to medical care, from the military to the dialogue on race. Once that is accomplished, a privileged elite will ultimately take full power through their treachery. The irony here is that your so-called conservatives are just the opposite. They argue for less government, less interference with their rights, and the right to live their lives and conduct their businesses without the heavy hand of a corrupt government pressing on their shoulders or reaching into their pockets."

"You've mentioned Schnabel," Kenny said. "His view of a new world order is well known, but he is neither American nor a member of our government or intelligence community. If you've had the financial dealings you describe, you must know the identity of others involved."

Khoury nodded. "Of course. If you want to begin at the head of this polluted river, just look at the attendance list for Schnabel's international world forum. Another is coming up very soon, in Aspen." He paused. "I understand your Agency was kind to Anatole Mindlovitch after his recent mishap."

Kenny did his best not to react, despite his surprise that the Handler could possibly know that.

"You might want to have a closer look at the company you keep."

"Are you suggesting that Mindlovitch is involved with Lawler?" Gellos asked.

"They're all of a piece, as the saying goes. In the meantime, how much do you know about John and Andrew Novak?" When Kenny and Gellos exchanged a quick glance, Khoury added, "Perhaps you should speak with Mr. Reagan's friend Dr. Derek Malone. Ask him about them, as well as Mindlovitch and his Ghost Chip."

CHAPTER FORTY-ONE

The Gables, Virginia

Kenny, Gellos, and Khoury heard a commotion outside in the hallway before the door flew open. In burst Ross Lawler, followed by his lead agent.

"What the hell do you think you're doing?" he demanded as he glared down at Kenny.

Both Gellos and Kenny stood.

"Mr. Khoury has some intelligence he wanted to share," Kenny said in his unflappable style. "Why are you interrupting?"

"Interrupting? How dare you? This man is my prisoner."

"*Your* prisoner?" Kenny asked, his eyebrows lifting slightly, which for him was a strong show of emotion when dealing with a superior. "Are you claiming some proprietary right here?"

Lawler was too astonished to reply.

"As you may recall, Mr. Khoury was apprehended in London by Nick Reagan, who undertook that mission at great personal risk."

"And against my orders," Lawler said, his voice almost rising to a shout.

"A directive we will need to examine at some point. For now, Mr. Khoury is being held by the CIA, for whom we all work. Presumably we share the same motive, which is to gather as much intelligence from our prisoner as possible. Do you have an issue with that?"

Lawler hesitated before saying, "Your interview of this man is done."

Kenny looked around, as if noticing the others in the room for the first time. "We have two agents as witnesses, so I suggest you rethink that, unless you are prepared to give a reason. In the absence of that, I am going to call the director."

Lawler also scanned the room now, looking as if he was hoping an appropriate answer might be written on one of the walls. Failing that, he said, "I scheduled an interrogation of this prisoner for seven this evening."

Kenny made a show of studying his watch. "Which gives us more than two hours to complete our work here. Now, if you'll excuse us?"

"You haven't heard the end of this, Kenny."

"I suspect not," he said, then waited until Lawler shot a menacing look at Khoury, after which he and his aide retreated, slamming the door behind them.

Leaning toward Gellos, Kenny whispered in her ear, "Call Reagan, tell him to pick up Brandt, give him a heads up, and tell them to get out here. I'm going to call the director."

Ignoring Khoury, they each went to the far corners of the room which left their backs to the door—as well as to the position of the closed-circuit camera they were both well aware of—and pulled out their cell phones.

* * *

As DIRECTOR OF THE CIA, Anthony Spinelli was by definition a political appointee loyal to the President. Some of the Assistant Directors such as Ross Lawler, positioned just below him in the chain of command, were his personal choices and by definition loyal to him. They were old friends or business associates whom he trusted enough to give these assignments.

On the other hand, Spinelli was no one's fool and had political aspirations of his own. As a leader of the controversial agency, he wanted an efficient and effective operation and—at all costs—to avoid mistakes or even worse, scandal. He knew there were thousands of capable and intelligent executives, agents, and other personnel supporting his efforts. During his tenure, he had come to know many of the people atop that hierarchy, including Brian Kenny.

He knew of Kenny's reputation as hard-nosed, serious, and highly competent. Kenny was not likely to call out one of his superiors unless he had good reason, especially when he knew that individual to be as close to Spinelli as Lawler. When the director received Kenny's urgent phone call, he was therefore more than a little surprised.

Kenny began by apologizing for having to engage in this dialogue, but explained that he had no choice. In his typical style, the deputy director began with a headline and then provided a series of key facts.

Spinelli made it clear that he was astounded by the accusation.

Kenny did not wait for the director to offer defenses for his friend or to ask questions. He went ahead, in a hushed tone, cataloging the events that led him to believe Khoury was telling them the truth. When he was done, he simply waited.

"You're saying that Ross was behind the attack at Reagan's home, the attempt to murder Khoury on the way to the safe house, and that he's interfering with your interrogation as he isolates the prisoner for his own purposes."

"I regret to say that your summary is correct. There were only a handful of people who knew where Reagan and Brandt were taking Khoury the other night. As you will recall, sir, Lawler was the one who disagreed with your suggestion that we call them in immediately, arguing that they should not be called until morning. What possible motive would he have for that position, other than to leave them in place for the attempted assassination? Likewise, how many people in your office knew that Khoury was being transported from headquarters to the safe house?"

"Ross was not the only one who knew that," Spinelli protested, without much vigor.

"Perhaps not, but it might be prudent for a list of those who *did* know to be compiled."

Spinelli paused. "What else has Khoury mentioned?"

"Not what, sir, but who. Victor Turnquist of the FBI, and a man named Paszek, apparently a gun for hire. We are working with the Bureau to track him down."

"I've met this fellow Turnquist. An executive deputy at the Bureau, correct?"

"Yes, he is."

"Let's cut to the chase, Kenny. What do you expect me to do on such flimsy evidence? Arrest a man I've known for more than fifteen years?"

Kenny was not pleased at the pale description of what he believed to be a credible list of questionable actions. "I want to finish my interview with Khoury. I want to ensure that the prisoner remains accessible for further interrogation. And I want permission for agents Reagan and Brandt to join me here."

Spinelli took a moment. "You know I'm going to have to call Lawler and advise him of your accusations."

"I would prefer that you not, sir. Not yet. I'm not asking for a lot of time, but I want to continue questioning Khoury, and I am requesting that you authorize my agents to enter the safe house."

"You're requesting for me to betray my friend."

"Respectfully, sir, this is not about friendship. From what I've heard so far, I believe this is a national security issue."

There was another pause. "I know your boy Reagan is good at what he does, but can tend to be a bit, shall we say, impulsive." He hesitated again. "But I've never heard anything like that about you. Your record is unblemished, and you've always struck me as a serious man." Kenny heard him draw a deep breath. "And it *was* Reagan who brought this man in."

"Yes, sir."

After another hesitation, Spinelli said, "All right, I'll take this situation under advisement, at least for now."

"Thank you, sir."

"Before we hang up Kenny, I have to say that this is a career threatening move on your part. You realize that, do you not?"

"I'm willing to take responsibility for my actions, sir. And for everyone on my team."

"Very well, but believe me, you and your team are on a short leash here."

CHAPTER FORTY-TWO

The Gables, Virginia

When Gellos and Kenny returned to their seats across from Khoury, the DD told his agent, "We're in deep shit."

Gellos realized that without knowing the substance of his call with the director. She nodded and said, "Nick and Alex are on their way."

Then they returned their attention to Khoury.

"You've got to give me more," Kenny told him. "We're out on a limb, and your position is even worse. Whether you're telling the truth or playing us, either way you're in serious danger."

"Bogdan Paszek," Khoury said. "I gave that name to Reagan. Have you identified the men who came for me at the house or on the road?"

Kenny was not there to answer questions. "What about Paszek?"

"Run a check on him. My best guess is that they were sent by him."

"At whose request?" Gellos asked. "You're not suggesting that he was acting on his own."

"No, I'm not."

"Then who do you claim he's working for?" she asked.

"There's no way for me to be sure. When it suits your purpose not to involve your military, your country has used private contractors in the Middle East, Afghanistan, and elsewhere." Then he added, with one of his wicked smiles, "You've actually taught the world how to outsource war, which in turn has created a new breed of fighter. They're usually trained in the armed services, and become highly efficient and highly paid killers. Paszek is an extreme example."

"It's apparent you have some sense of who pays him," Gellos said.

Khoury thought it over. "He was born in Warsaw and served in the Polish army. His talent led him to a few tours in their special forces. Then he came to the United States, which is where I first came to know him."

"Did he know who you really are?"

"I would say he suspected, but he's Catholic and no friend of the Muslim cause."

Gellos was unable to restrain herself. "You claim to be part of a Muslim cause?"

"I certainly do. Not any part of the moderate majority, I admit that, but the *jihad* is a sacred quest."

"Let's forego the ideological debate for now," Kenny suggested. "Otherwise, I'll turn you over to Lawler and walk away."

Khoury stared at him without speaking.

"Who did he work for when you met him?"

"He was in charge of security at the Janus Building in Washington."

"That would seem a rather passive role for someone you accuse of running a team of assassins."

"I assure you, Mr. Kenny, he wasn't assigned to check identification at the front desk."

"What was he doing, then?"

"Keeping an eye on the enemies and competitors of John and Andrew Novak."

"He was running an intelligence operation," Gellos said.

"In a sense."

"That's still not the same as heading a group of guns for hire."

"One role does not make the other impossible. He is skilled at recruiting illegal aliens from the many candidates that have poured across your border. When you identify the men Mr. Reagan took care of the other night, I am certain that is what you will find."

Gellos shook her head. "You're making claims without proof. You've already called the assistant director of the CIA a traitor, as well as an executive director of the FBI. Now you seem to be implicating two of the most successful businessmen in the country. I don't know about you, sir," she said as she turned to Kenny, "but unless he's going to give us some credible evidence, I think this interview really is done."

Khoury sat back and had a long look at Gellos. It was clear he realized they had reached a critical point in their discussion. He was out of time and out of options and, so, after a pause, he said, "Unlike Mr. Reagan, you're asking the wrong questions."

"Please enlighten us," Kenny said.

"You've asked about Paszek, but you have not asked what I was doing in the Janus Building, which I told you was the last time I met him. More important than that, you have not asked how I know John and Andrew Novak."

CHAPTER FORTY-THREE

En route to The Gables, Virginia

As Reagan and Brandt drove back to the Gables, Erin called from her office in Langley.

"You all right?" Reagan asked.

"I'm okay," she said. "Worried about you."

"We're fine."

"Rumor has it they want your head on a platter."

"Not the first time," he told her.

She decided to let it go for now. "The GIGN gave us the full list of victims from the bombing with background info. Malone's friend Dr. Solares and his wife are the only casualties that stand out. The rest were locals or tourists who were unlucky enough to be in the wrong place at the wrong time."

"Sad."

"Yes," she said. "GIGN also identified the man and woman who tossed those pipe bombs."

"Who got rewarded by being mowed down as they came around the corner a few blocks up."

"Right. Well get this. They were members of a neo-Nazi group. Antisemites, anti-Israel, a couple of real beauties."

"How odd. From what I've read about Solares, neither he nor his wife were Jewish."

"Correct. So I cross-checked the list of victims. There were a few Jewish sounding names, but no one connected to government, either in France or Israel, no clergy or anything like that."

"No one from a Zionist group, a leader of a local temple, nothing?"

"Zero. Which makes me guess our two bombers were sold a bill of goods."

"They thought they were going after someone deserving of their hate."

"That's how I read it."

"Which means they were likely recruited by one of their own."

"More likely, someone pretending to be one of them."

"Right," Reagan said. "I think I know where you're going with this."

"Yes," Erin said. "Other than what those two on their motor scooter might have believed, the attack was not really motivated by a political or religious agenda. It's exactly what Malone thought. A targeted murder disguised as a terrorist act."

After Reagan and Brandt passed through the security checkpoint and walked through the main entrance of the Gables, Ross Lawler and his top agent were waiting for them in the large foyer. No greetings were exchanged.

The assistant director walked up to Reagan and said, "I don't know what stories you and Kenny have been feeding the director, but when I get done, the two of you are through." Turning to Brandt, he added, "That includes you."

Reagan smiled. "Someone has tried to have us killed. Not once, but twice, and failed both times. We still can't prove who was behind those attacks, but we can clearly see the pattern, so I assure you we'll find out. In the meantime, you do what you're big enough to do, sir, and I'll continue to do my job until someone can stop me."

Lawler did not answer.

With that, Reagan and Brandt headed downstairs and knocked on the door. Both Gellos and Kenny came out and the four of them huddled together in the white-walled corridor.

Kenny began by saying, "This is not good."

"Alex and I received the same warning upstairs. From the assistant director himself."

Kenny nodded, then provided a synopsis of what Khoury was saying. When he was done, he added, "It's just not enough. He throws out names and tells us to track them down, as if he's leading us on a damned scavenger hunt."

"His portfolio of intel may be wearing thin," Gellos suggested.

"But for now, you're saying it's Paszek and the Novak brothers?" Reagan asked. "They're the headliners?"

"Yes," Gellos told him, "assuming they have some sort of connection to Lawler and that executive assistant director at the FBI."

"Turnquist," Kenny said.

Reagan bit at his lower lip while considering their options. "First thing we have to do is press Khoury for anything else he has. Far as I'm concerned his time is up."

"That's what we've told him," Kenny agreed.

"Then we have to locate Bogdan Paszek, which shouldn't be that tough. Private security, guns for hire, whatever he's up to he must be leaving footprints somewhere." No one disagreed, and Reagan paused. "But getting to the Novaks, that's another story. They're wealthier than wealthy, with all sorts of political contacts."

"Which translates to political protection," Gellos said.

"Precisely. If anyone here thinks accusing Lawler was a big deal, wait till we take on those two." Reagan hesitated, then added, "But I may have an idea."

"Let's have it," Kenny said.

"The Malones are still in D.C. They came up to see me, but also mentioned some big charity event they're supposed to attend tomorrow night. They don't even want to go, after what happened in Paris, but I'll ask them to attend, and to have Erin and me at their table."

"I take it the Novaks will also be there," Gellos said.

"That's the idea."

"You intend to interrogate them during cocktail hour?"

Reagan smiled. "No, Carol, I just want to meet them."

"Oh sure. Well maybe you should take me instead of Erin. She's been through enough this week, and if things get rough…"

"She'll be fine," Reagan said. "And the Malones know her, which should relax the situation. Anyway, it's a charity ball, things aren't going to get out of hand."

Gellos stared at her partner with a frown. "Famous last words."

CHAPTER FORTY-FOUR

The Gables, Virginia

Even if Walid Khoury had already divulged all he was willing to share, Kenny wanted to keep him alive, at least a little while longer. They had not even begun to discuss the attacks Khoury had engineered a few months earlier, his list of contacts in al Qaeda, or any other of the wealth of information he doubtless possessed. These past couple of days, all they had focused on were the Handler's accusations about corruption in the United States government, and for now that was enough to keep them busy.

However, as Director Spinelli warned, Kenny's team was on thin ice. With no idea what Ross Lawler might be planning, the DD had to make a tough decision.

"I don't like leaving any of you to confront a senior executive in the Agency on your own, but someone's got to remain here and keep an eye on things."

"Forgive me, sir," Reagan said, "but what we need to do next will be in the field, not the office. What if you stay here while we check things out? We'll give you regular reports until this gets straightened out."

Kenny began nodding slowly, something he did when forced into an unwanted decision. "It makes sense."

"No matter what Lawler's done, and regardless of how tough his agents want to play it, they're not going through you."

"I should stay, too," Gellos said. "The DD should not be left here on his own."

"That's very good of you..." Kenny began, when Brandt interrupted.

"You and Nick are a team," he said to Gellos. "I'll stay, you two go."

The four of them looked at one another until Kenny said, "Alex and I can spend some more time with our pal Khoury, you hit the road."

Gellos got behind the wheel of the car Brandt had driven out here. Of the three agents, she was by far the best driver, and the fastest. As soon as they passed through security and exited the property of the large estate, she stepped on the gas.

"Should have had you with me in London," Reagan said with a short laugh. "We could've outrun the bad guys on the M4, and I wouldn't have had to shoot out their tire."

"Where to?" Gellos asked, already in her all-business mode.

"We have a couple of phone calls to make, but we might as well go to the source. If Khoury is right about the security gig Bogdan Paszek has…"

"We should start at the Janus Building. He controls the guards there. Let's go meet some of them."

"Bingo," Reagan said, then pulled out his cell and called Erin David.

"How goes it?" she asked.

"I'll provide details later. The Reader's Digest version is that Lawler is at the Gables with one of his agents. Alex and the DD are still questioning Khoury, and making sure our prisoner does not have a fatal accident. The director has given us a short reprieve to see if we can validate any of the accusations the Handler's been making."

"And you're in the car with Carol."

"Yes, the female version of Lewis Hamilton has the wheel and we're heading for the Janus Building."

"To see if you can learn anything about Bogdan Paszek."

"That's the starting point, which is why I'm calling."

"Not to see if I'm all right? Or to tell me how much you care?"

"That too, but for now I need to know what you've found on him."

"I have a few tidbits, some of which are interesting. He was in the Polish special forces, something of a prodigy in spreading mayhem and death."

Reagan put her on speaker so Gellos could hear, then said, "That comports with Khoury's story."

"Since he's been in the States," Erin said, "which is more than twenty years, he's been known as Bogdan Paszek—the name we're working with—but back in Poland he had a different moniker."

"That so?"

Erin recited the full name as Reagan wrote it on a small notepad from the glove compartment.

"Any idea what the alias is about?" he asked. "Did he have a criminal record in Poland, a dishonorable discharge, anything like that?"

"The absolute contrary is true," Erin told him. "All sorts of medals, commendations, no problem with our immigration. One day that name disappeared off the radar and poof, Bogdan Paszek appeared."

"Wife, children?"

"Not here and not back in his homeland, far as Sasha and I can tell. A loner with a heart of stone."

Reagan turned to Gellos as he said, "Carol is going to love this one. Sociopaths are her specialty."

"I know, and she has you for a partner, which speaks volumes," Erin said with a brief laugh. "But seriously, this guy is dangerous."

"You still have our attention."

"He owns a legitimate security firm, or at least it looks legit. Hires nothing but former military, from here and abroad. Prefers men with special ops experience. Women too."

"How egalitarian of him."

"His people have all seen action, whether in Iraq, Afghanistan, Syria, you name it."

"Then we'll be polite when we meet him, I promise."

Erin went on. "He has contracts with a couple of large companies, but there's another layer here, at least according to the rumor mill. The chatter we get from the Dark Web is that he hires illegals for cash. People from all over the world, most of whom have walked across our southern border and disappeared around the country. They have no papers, we have no means of tracking them, and they have no hesitation using the weapons Paszek and his lieutenants supply in exchange for cash. It's as if he controls an underground militia."

"That's exactly what it is."

"The shooters who came for you and Alex the other night, and the ones involved in the roadside attack…"

"Could very well be part of Paszek's brigade."

"Not only that," Erin told them. "Word is that he has layers of protection between him and these henchmen. Even if the shooters are caught, they have no idea who paid them, or from whom their instructions came. It's always the same story, the orders were sent from an anonymous source along with an envelope of desirable cash."

"And since these illegals are arriving in this country on a daily basis…"

"They pick out the criminal types and recruit them," Gellos finally said.

"An endless source of shooters for hire," Reagan said. "How charming."

CHAPTER FORTY-FIVE

The Janus Building, Washington, D.C.

By the time Gellos pulled to a stop in the outdoor parking lot of the Janus Building, it was after seven in the evening, the sun was setting, and things were relatively quiet. Across the way they saw the entrance to indoor parking, with a large moveable barrier and a man still on duty in a small guardhouse. It was evident they were not getting in there, but that was not their interest, at least not tonight. They wanted to make a statement—and get some questions answered if that was possible.

Gellos parked, they checked their weapons, then got out of the car, and made their way to the front of the building.

Reagan had to admit the façade and lobby were nothing short of magnificent. He believed that an effective way to put real money on display is through architecture, and this was a fine example. The structure was modern, but went far behind the plain, geometric designs of the contemporary period. It incorporated some classical touches such as moldings and arches, and impressive murals hung on the interior walls.

Making their way through one of three revolving doors, they strolled across the expanse of granite floor tiling to a massive front desk where two uniformed guards waited for them without greeting.

It was even quieter inside than it was outside.

"Nice place you have here," Reagan said.

Neither man responded.

Based on this inauspicious beginning, it appeared Erin's intel was correct. These were not the typical rent-a-cops one finds in most office buildings, malls, or other public places. When the silence went on for a few more moments, Reagan spoke up again.

"We're looking for Mr. Paszek. Bogdan Paszek."

Neither man blinked, but the reaction in their eyes was clear. The beefy man on their left said, "There's no one here by that name."

Reagan smiled. "Come on fellas, you work for the guy, for god's sake. I'm told he stops by here all the time."

The man to their right must have felt it was his turn to speak. "He already told you, there's no one here by that name."

"But you both *know* the name, that's obvious. If he's not here right now, how about you get him on the phone."

It was time for the guy on their left to speak again, and Reagan was suddenly reminded of an old cartoon series where two blackbirds took turns like this, but couldn't recall the name.

"We clear visitors who want to see people working here," he said, obviously straining to stay calm. "You've asked for someone who does *not* work here, so it's time for you and your lady friend to leave."

"Are you seriously telling me you can't get Paszek on the phone?" Reagan shrugged. "Okay, just give me his phone number then."

Heckle and Jeckle. Reagan suddenly remembered the name of the cartoon, just as Jeckle on the right piped up again.

"As my associate indicated, it's time for the two of you to leave or we will be forced to escort you out."

"That so?" Reagan asked. "Not a very hospitable show you're running here but, just so you know, we're not leaving until we get an answer."

The two men stood in unison and began moving around their respective sides of the curved counter, all very synchronized, as if it was a move they had practiced quite a bit.

"You boys are making a mistake," Reagan said.

Heckle, off to their left, said, "You're the ones who've made the mistake."

As they approached from the left and right, Reagan and Gellos did not hesitate. Although both men were large and muscular, the two CIA agents knew their business. As soon as the guard on the right made a threatening move to grab Gellos, she had probable cause to act, instantly pulling the expanding metal baton she'd been holding under her jacket. In one deft move, she snapped it to its full length, then swung it back in the opposite direction, smashing the man behind his knees and dropping him to the floor. He fell with a short yelp of pain, as she followed up with a quick crack of the weapon across the back of his head.

Meanwhile, Reagan's man rushed forward, trying to grab him by the collar. When he was just close enough, Reagan engaged in a classic maneuver, using his attacker's weight to knock him off balance with a leg sweep. As the man stumbled ahead, Reagan shoved him to the floor, dove on his back, grabbed him by the hair, and smashed his face into the hard stone floor.

It was over before the two guards knew what happened.

"You guys are really good at this," Reagan said as he got to his feet. "You just need some practice." Looking up he pointed to the spots where video cameras were likely concealed. "Hope the guys in the security office got the full picture of you attacking two innocent people." Reaching into his pocket, he added, "Especially since we're federal agents." Then he removed a card with his information on it—excluding any mention of his affiliation with the CIA—and tossed it at the man he had just taken down, who was still writhing in pain. "Have your boss give me a call," he said, "or we'll be back." Then he turned to Gellos. "All good?"

"Ready to go," she told him.

As they walked out, Reagan said, "Our work here is done, unless one of their friends is stupid enough to follow us."

"We can only hope," Gellos said.

CHAPTER FORTY-SIX

The Ritz Carlton, Georgetown, Washington, D.C.

"Nice work, partner."

"You too," Gellos told him.

"Didn't know you had that baton under your jacket."

"I had no idea how things would work out at the Gables. If it came down to it, I preferred knocking a fellow agent on his ass, rather than having to shoot him."

Reagan laughed. "You think those two goons are going to call the police?"

"I wish they would."

"That would certainly work for us. Two federal agents defending themselves, with a video recording to prove it."

"Assuming they don't erase it."

"Not likely," Reagan said. "Whoever sits in front of their security monitors saw the whole thing. Going to be embarrassing for them when their boss finds out."

Gellos agreed. "You think this Paszek character is going to be in touch with us?"

"I don't think he's going to call and ask us to dinner, but we'll be hearing from him, that's for sure. He doesn't want us coming back during work hours." Pulling out his cell, he said, "Let's find Malone, he's our next stop."

After a brief call confirming Derek and Connie were in their suite at the Ritz Carlton in Georgetown, they agreed to meet downstairs in the bar.

The lounge is a large, comfortable room, with brick walls, leather chairs, and velvet sofas. When Reagan and Gellos arrived, the Malones were waiting in a loveseat off in the corner.

"You remember my partner…."

Malone was already up, enfolding her in a warm hug. "Are you kidding, I never forget a good-looking woman." He hesitated. "Especially one who carries a gun."

They greeted Connie, then sat in the two leather chairs facing the Malones.

There was no one else near, but Reagan kept his voice low as he said, "Tell us everything you know about Bogdan Paszek."

Malone stuck out his lower lip and nodded slowly. Then he said, "Let's order some drinks first."

Over cocktails Malone told them what he knew about Paszek, which was not much different than the intel Reagan had already gathered— with one important exception.

"At this point he works exclusively for the Novaks," Malone said. "That's my understanding."

"What about the security company he built?"

"Far as I know, he's still the owner," Malone said. "But I don't think he gets involved in managing anything. Unless it has to do with any of the Novak enterprises."

"You've met him?" Gellos asked.

"Many times." Malone smiled. "Not a huge guy, but scary. The way he walks, the look in his eyes. The military background I've heard about. He just has that kind of appearance."

"What kind?" Gellos asked.

"I don't know, threatening maybe?"

She turned to Connie. "Have you met him?"

"Not formally, but I've seen him. We've been at functions with the Novak brothers and their wives." She glanced at her husband before adding, "I once asked Derek who the scary looking man was in the background."

"Background," Malone repeated. "That's a good description of how Paszek operates. He's not like a bodyguard who stands right next to John or Andrew, he's more like someone surveying the whole situation, know what I mean?"

Both Gellos and Reagan nodded.

"Sometimes he becomes invisible."

Which is when he's most dangerous, Reagan thought.

"What about this charity event tomorrow night?" Malone said, trying to lighten the mood. "You coming with Erin?"

"We'll be there, I just need the details."

Turing to Gellos, Malone was about to apologize for having failed to invite her, but Reagan cut him off.

"Don't worry pal, Carol will be there too," he told him with a smile, "and she's all business all the time."

CHAPTER FORTY-SEVEN

The Gables, Virginia

The tension inside the stately safe house in Virginia was unprecedented. Over the years, the CIA had held innumerable people there, ranging from cooperative witnesses to individuals being protected from outside peril to any number of those accused of the most heinous acts, such as the Handler, whose ultimate fates might range from an indeterminate stay in the prison at Guantanamo Bay to something worse. But Brian Kenny could not recall any time when there was this level of open hostility among the Agency's own personnel.

As a political appointee, Ross Lawler did not command the loyalty and respect so many of the agents felt for Brian Kenny, especially those who had worked with him on missions he oversaw. Nevertheless, Lawler was still the number two man in the hierarchy, and very few of the men and women on hand wanted to risk their own careers without a better understanding of what was in play.

Lawler's senior agent managed to enlist the support of a few agents with whom he had worked over the years, but the others were treading carefully, since no explanation was being provided by either side as to why Lawler and Kenny appeared to have their swords drawn.

After Reagan and Gellos left, Kenny and Brandt spent some more time questioning Khoury, who provided some additional leads on Lawler and Paszek.

"Do you have any proof Lawler has communicated with Paszek?" Kenny asked.

Khoury thought it over before saying, "I wish I did. That's something you'll have to discover for yourselves."

"And if you're lying?" Kenny asked. "Or even if you're not, but no proof can be found?"

"Then I would say we both have a problem."

"You say that you knew Reagan reached out to Dr. Malone for help in finding you," Brandt said, "but you've never told us how you found out."

Kenny agreed. "A good point."

Khoury pressed his lips together and nodded before saying, "I suspect you will not believe this, but it came as an anonymous text."

"You're right," Kenny told him, "I don't believe it. You were in hiding, remaining incommunicado by your own admission. How many people who had your cell phone number could have passed on that warning?"

"I've given it a lot of thought, whether you believe that or not. I simply don't know."

Kenny leaned forward. "Have you ever spoken on your cell or texted with either of the Novak brothers?"

Khoury seemed to be considering that. "They certainly had my number, when I was engaged in banking transactions for them overseas. But that phone was long gone by the time I got to London."

"Then who could have reached out to you?" Brandt pressed him.

"I'm telling the truth, I don't know. I only received that message the morning your Mr. Reagan showed up. In all likelihood, whoever sent it had only just found out."

"And you regarded it as a warning?"

Khoury managed a smile. "Not really. I could not imagine what sort of help the Novaks could provide to Dr. Malone, or by extension to Mr. Reagan. They had no idea where I was."

"Maybe not," Kenny said as he sat back. "But without more, there's nothing I can do to prevent Lawler from interrogating you. The best I can provide at this point is round the clock protection."

"That would consist of agents outside this room, monitoring our discussion?"

"That's correct."

Khoury drew a deep breath and let it out slowly. "You think that will be enough of a deterrent? That it will prevent Lawler or one of his men from attacking me? Perhaps inventing some claim that I moved first, or some such allegation?"

"You'll be watched in real time, and the session will be recorded. It's the best I can do."

Khoury's look of utter defeat was clear. "Please do what you can."

Kenny got to his feet. "We owe you nothing, you understand that? What actions are eventually taken against you for your crimes are not up to me. But I will do my best to protect you while you're here."

Before Khoury could respond, Kenny and Brandt left and headed upstairs.

Choosing two of the agents he knew best, the DD gave them the order he promised Khoury. Round the clock observation, starting with them, to be followed by others, all on four hour shifts outside the cell.

"Brandt will be back and forth and available on his phone to coordinate things," Kenny told them. "And to be apprised of any problems." Then he left Brandt and made his way to the office where he was told Lawler was waiting. He knocked on the door and entered.

Lawler was seated in an armchair, waiting. "Are you done?"

"I'd like to speak with you," Kenny said. "Alone."

Lawler hesitated, then told the two agents in the room to leave them.

After they shut the door behind them, Kenny sat in the chair facing the assistant director. "I am going to be blunt, because I believe the situation requires it."

Lawler, who was dressed in a dark suit and patterned tie, looking very much the corporate executive he was before he took this position, remained silent.

"The prisoner has made a series of accusations, some of which we have already verified as true." Then Kenny added, "Some of which involve you."

Lawler folded his arms across his chest as he gazed at Kenny, doing his best to appear incredulous. "You have allegations concerning me from a genocidal terrorist, is that what you're telling me?"

"I am."

"Do you intend to share whatever fairy tale he's invented in an obvious attempt to save his own skin?"

"Not yet, but I will. We are in the process of gathering our own data."

"Then why are you telling me anything at all?"

"I felt I owed you that. And I believe, if any of what he says is true, you should have the opportunity to come clean."

"Come clean?" Lawler got to his feet and stood over Kenny as he said, "Who do you think you're dealing with here? When I get done with you and your agents…"

"Don't waste your time threatening me," Kenny said as he also got to his feet. "You'd be better off using that energy to prepare the answers you're going to provide when you're the one being interrogated." Then he turned and walked out of the room.

CHAPTER FORTY-EIGHT

Washington, D.C.

The following morning, Gellos joined Erin and Reagan in his hotel room at The Jefferson to review intel coming in from various sources. They were seated around the large bed, the fluffy duvet covered with papers and the two binders Erin had brought with her. As Reagan liked to say, the puzzle was coming together.

The first group of pieces they collected related to the recent attacks in Paris, Moscow, and New York. Dr. Benjamin Solares and his wife Sondra had died in the café bombings, as the Malones feared. Whether Derek and Connie were also intended victims was not certain, but there was no doubt Dr. Solares was employed by Novak Pharma or that he had voiced concerns about the drug being developed, to be known as *Neulife*.

Yevgeny Durov had furnished a list of everyone murdered and injured outside the Bolshoi Ballet. As he indicated at his meeting with Reagan, the name generating the most interest was Mindlovitch's rival, the Russian oligarch Grigor Kuznetsov. It did not take much effort on Erin's part to determine the large investments he had made in various enterprises, but why someone would want him dead—other than one of the enemies rich Russians collect over the years—remained unclear.

The list of those who died or were injured in the suicide bombing in New York yielded various names involved in the medical community. After all, as Gellos pointed out the obvious, it took place in the lobby of a hospital. Erin identified one of the physicians killed as Dr. Emil

Fontaine, a neurologist engaged in research for a company that was a direct competitor of…

"Let me guess," Reagan said.

"Right. Novak Pharma," Erin told him.

"That's a thread that seems to be running through everything," Gellos said.

"Yes, it does," Reagan agreed. "The invisible Bogdan Paszek is head of the Novaks' security. Khoury believes Paszek is behind the two attacks on him, both at my place and on the road to the Gables. Malone went to the Novaks for help in finding Khoury—at my request I admit—but swears he told no one else of our discussion, not even his wife Connie. So how would Khoury know I reached out to Derek?"

"Either the Novaks told him," Gellos said, "which seems unlikely."

"Or the Novaks spoke to someone about it who then contacted Khoury," Brandt finished the thought.

"But who?" Reagan asked. "And why? Was someone warning the Handler that I was coming for him?"

Gellos thought it over. "He told Kenny it was an anonymous text that basically meant nothing to him since neither the Novaks nor Malone had any idea he was in London."

"Can we all agree," Erin said, "that whoever sent it did not want Khoury apprehended? I mean, whatever value he ascribed to that warning, someone sent it for a reason."

Gellos and Reagan agreed.

"Then let's work backwards," Erin suggested. "Khoury has accused Ross Lawler and Victor Turnquist from the FBI of being traitors. He claims Bogdan Paszek attempted to have him killed since he arrived in the States. Those are the only three people he has directly implicated in any way."

"Your theory," Gellos said, "is that one or more of them would prefer that Khoury remained in hiding, and therefore would have tried to warn him Nick was coming for him. Once he was apprehended, killing him was the only remaining option."

"If we believe any of what Khoury says, that's what makes sense to me," Erin told her. "Putting aside Paszek, if Khoury's lying about Lawler and Turnquist then this is all some elaborate scheme with a motive I've yet to see."

"Let's not forget," Reagan reminded them, "Bebon already had his own questions about Turnquist. And our pal Lawler has made some unexplained moves over the past few days."

"Meaning that you believe Khoury," Gellos said.

"Yes, I do. Throw in there that I also believe Malone didn't tell anyone else about my request, which narrows the possible pipeline of information."

"And brings the Novaks into play again," Gellos pointed out.

"As you've already stated, they seem to be the common thread that runs through everything," Reagan agreed.

Erin nodded. "Add to it the fact that they never did get back to Derek, not even to say they weren't able to help."

"Apparently after sharing with someone else what he had asked," Reagan added.

"Now what?" Gellos asked as she stood up to have a quick stretch. "You've captured the Handler and he remains in custody. He is going to be made to answer for what he's done, but meanwhile he's levied these allegations at two highly placed law enforcement directors with nothing more than anecdotal events to support his claims. We have three recent attacks, one in our own country, with all the perpetrators conveniently deceased. Director Spinelli is furious with us and with the DD, and time is short. What's next?"

"Great question," Reagan admitted as he sat back in his armchair. "Alex and some other loyal personnel are keeping an eye on Khoury, so he's alive for now. We've left our calling card, literally and figuratively, at the Novaks' headquarters. Hopefully we'll be hearing from someone there fairly soon." He reached out and picked up the file Erin had brought on Paszek. It contained a full dossier and a couple of photos. "Not a friendly looking bloke, is he?"

"I would say not," Gellos agreed, as he displayed one of the pictures.

"Our next move is to find this guy and see what sort of answers we can get from him."

Gellos laughed. "Given that photo and his career path, sounds like he's not likely to be the talkative type."

"Maybe not, but I'm known to be fairly persuasive."

"Assuming you can get to him before we all get suspended," Gellos said.

"We'll get to him, all right, and soon. I'm going to dust off the tux I have stored back at your apartment," he told Gellos. "You two are going to get a couple of beautiful evening gowns, and tonight we're all going to a ball."

"I already feel like Cinderella," Gellos said.

"Except there won't be any glass slippers," Erin reminded them.

"More important than that," added Reagan, "there won't be any fairy godmother watching over us."

CHAPTER FORTY-NINE

Washington, D.C.

Throughout the rest of the morning, Reagan received updates from Brandt, who for the moment was stationed at the Gables. He reported that things were quiet since Lawler and his assistant had departed the night before, not long after Kenny left. It appeared Lawler was foregoing the opportunity to question Khoury. At least for now.

Reagan phoned Kenny and shared their plan for the evening. The DD responded by stressing the need for the team to come up with something substantive to support Khoury's allegations, and soon. The director had made it clear that their careers were in jeopardy and, if they came up empty, they could be sure Lawler was going to press the issue. Kenny also reminded them to tread lightly at the gala that night, which was going to be attended by an array of Washington luminaries.

Reagan told him not to worry.

Kenny found the advice less than comforting.

Carol brought Erin to her apartment where they spent time going through the closets looking for something that might be appropriate to wear that night. They finally agreed they needed something special and headed off to a shop that rented gowns for the runway. They enjoyed the brief time away from the job, each choosing an outfit and then treating themselves to lunch at The Lafayette in the Hay-Adams Hotel.

Erin texted Reagan from there to tell him her dress was beautiful but expensive, even for the one night rental, but Reagan told her not to worry, this was his idea and he would be happy to cover it.

Malone called Reagan twice. He and Connie were nervous about the upcoming event, since the Novaks were going to be there, as well as Anatole Mindlovitch. Derek had a positive nature and was not comfortable with the prospect of a nasty confrontation. Reagan tried to assure him everything would be fine and not to worry, but first he had to convince himself.

The title of the gala was "A Night in Celebration of Children," which Reagan thought was perfect. Who could possibly argue with that? Millions of dollars would be raised for a variety of charities, as the rich and famous got to feel good about themselves. There should be nothing political about the event—a rarity in Washington—and people from every philosophical persuasion would have an opportunity to mingle together in a spirit of kinship and generosity.

Reagan thought of a quote, something about the rich being different, recalling that it came from Fitzgerald. Although Reagan agreed with the basic premise, in his experience he found there were all sorts of rich. Those born to family fortunes, the hardworking self-made types, the recently mega-rich tech entrepreneurs, and so on. Each of those was so different.

He never cared much about money himself; it did not hold the fascination for him that it did for so many people he had met. He understood there are comforts and extravagances serious wealth can buy, but he never found evidence of any correlation of great materiality with true satisfaction.

I probably got that wrong, he thought with an inner smile.

Still in his hotel room, he made some calls to confirm his final arrangements, then studied the guest list for tonight's gathering. It was a staggering collection of affluence, influence, and fame.

"This is going to be interesting," he told himself.

Done with this last part of his research, Reagan headed downstairs, enjoyed some quiet time with a bourbon for company at the hotel bar, then took a cab to see Erin and Carol and collect his formal wear.

Arriving at Carol's apartment, Reagan gave Erin a hug and kiss, then began removing the plastic covering from the dry cleaning package she left out for him.

"You keep clothing here?" Erin teased. "Should I be jealous?"

He looked up and asked, "Carol, should Erin be jealous?"

Gellos gave the two of them a you-must-be-kidding look, then retired to her bedroom to get dressed. Erin used the guest room but told Nick she wanted privacy. As she explained, she did not want him to see her until she was "all put together."

That left Reagan with the powder room. It was not large, but he managed to change into his pleated shirt, insert the onyx cufflinks he had also stored here, and put on his tuxedo. Then he secured a Walther PPK in a slimline holster at the small of his back and returned to the living room to wait.

When the two women emerged, Reagan stood, placed his hands on his hips, and said, "I'm speechless."

"Well there's a first," Gellos said.

Erin was in a strapless, floor length charmeuse gown, deep blue with a slinky, formfitting cut, and a neckline that would be low enough to distract Reagan for the rest of the evening.

"Gorgeous," he said, and Erin smiled.

The real surprise, however, was Gellos. Reagan was accustomed to working with her in the field, where she favored loose fitting slacks, man-tailored shirts, and thick-soled shoes. Tonight, she was wearing a pale pink chiffon gown with a scoop neck, a suppressed waist, and a flare skirt.

"Gellos," he began, but she promptly cut him off.

"Say the wrong the thing, and you're going to find out I'm hiding my nine-millimeter under all this fabric."

"I just wanted to say that you look beautiful."

"Maybe if you didn't sound so surprised it would be more of a compliment."

"Tough audience," Reagan said, then led the women downstairs to the waiting limousine he had hired.

"Nice touch," Gellos admitted.

"When in Rome," he replied as they got in and heading to the gala.

On the ride over they discussed logistics. They had obtained a layout of the large room, which was arranged with round tables that were each set for ten guests. The Malones had purchased one that was up front on the edge of the parquet dance floor facing the orchestra. Reagan and Erin would be seated there, along with six other guests the Malones had invited. Although Gellos had been assigned a seat at the rear of the ballroom, Kenny had approval for her to be part of the security detail, something Bebon helped set up.

They were unfashionably early when their car pulled up to the front of the hotel, just as Reagan intended. Security was not yet backed up with a line of guests passing through metal detection and undergoing handbag reviews, which gave Reagan and Gellos time to present their credentials and receive approval to enter with their weapons.

There was another checkpoint, where their names and table assignments were verified, then the threesome was permitted to pass through one of the large entry doors into the palatial ballroom.

The ceilings were thirty feet high, the crystal chandeliers hanging from them were enormous. The walls were adorned with a cream-colored fabric that both augmented and softened the illumination from above. The tables were set with dinnerware for several courses and crystal for a variety of drinks, including wine glasses, water glasses, and aperitif stems. There were dozens of flower arrangements, one at the center of each table, all different, a unique collection of vibrant colors and greens.

"Glad I dressed up," Reagan said.

Gellos had taken in the opulent scene and was ready to get down to business. "I've got a seat over there, in the back, to our right," she said without any sort of gesture in that direction, "but I expect to be on my feet most of the evening."

Reagan nodded. "We're up front there," he said, but before he could say any more about his intentions for the night, they heard a familiar voice.

"What a great looking group," Derek Malone exclaimed, as he slapped Reagan on the back.

The three of them turned to greet their host and his wife.

"Carol, you can sit with us, you know," Malone told her. "They'll squeeze another chair in there if I ask."

"Thanks," Gellos said, "but I've got some things to take care of."

Malone responded with a knowing look as he held up his hand. "I don't want to get in the way of whatever you and Nick have planned." Then, because he could not help being Derek Malone, he added, "You'll stop by for a drink though, right?"

Gellos smiled.

"Speaking of a drink," Malone said, "let's get one." Taking Connie by the hand, he pointed off to his right, at one of the four large bars that were set up in the corners of the room.

Reagan nodded. Patrons were beginning to arrive, and he figured that was a perfect spot from which to observe the procession.

CHAPTER FIFTY

Washington, D.C.

The five of them were standing at the bar in the far right corner of the ballroom, where Malone saw to it that they were all promptly served. Moving off to the side, beside one of the windows than ran twenty feet up from the floor, they chatted while watching the growing wave of people make their way inside. Having studied the guest list, Reagan knew there should be no surprise visitors at A Night in Celebration of Children but, if there was one thing Reagan had learned, taking nothing for granted is a valuable policy.

He spotted Director Spinelli and his wife, who were accompanied by Mr. and Mrs. Ross Lawler. What or how much the director had told Lawler by now was anybody's guess, and Reagan knew that Brian Kenny was not going to be here to run interference if that became necessary.

The Novak bothers and their wives entered through another door, instantly surrounded by a large group whom Reagan silently dubbed the Captains of Industry Coalition.

He next saw Anatole Mindlovitch, who was hard to miss at six foot five. The Russian was accompanied by a tall young woman, who looked stunning in a sequin gown that was skin tight from thighs to torso, but hung casually at the revealing low-cut neck. There were a few other people walking beside Mindlovitch and his date, two of them staying close enough to make it evident they were his bodyguards.

Reagan knew the total attendance was to be just under five hundred people, which included scores of politicians, businessmen, philanthropists, and even some Hollywood types. He continued to study the incoming crowd when Malone moved beside him.

"Everything okay?" Malone asked.

"Sure. You just need to relax and have some fun, nothing's happened yet."

"Yet," Malone repeated with one of his patented laughs.

But Reagan did not respond. His focus had zeroed in on a man who had entered behind the Novaks and was hanging back, keeping a polite distance from the Captains of Industry. "I'm not going to point, and I don't want you staring, not even from this distance. But you see where the Novaks are, in the back of the room, off to our right?"

"Of course, I saw them when they came in."

"Ten people or so behind them. There's a man by himself, looks like he's without a date, looking all around the room, like his head's a slow swivel."

It only took Derek a quick glance to confirm his identity. "Bogdan Paszek."

Reagan looked in his direction again, and in that moment he and Paszek locked eyes. Reagan did not blink, staring him down as he said to himself, "Mr. Paszek, we are going to meet at last." Turning back to Malone, he said, "He wasn't on the guest list."

"I suppose he's here as the Novaks' head of security."

"Right," Reagan said.

Gellos had moved toward them, asking, "What's up?"

"Back of the room, off to our right, near your table," Reagan said. "Bogdan Paszek."

Gellos spotted him in an instant. "Should we go have a talk with him?"

"Yes, but not yet. Let everybody get drinks, then settle in for dinner. Before the speeches start we'll have a chat with our friend."

Doing her best to appear as if she was surveying the entire room, she said, "He's looking here, no doubt about it."

"Good. Let's give him some time to worry."

The growing throng continued to filter into the ballroom, crowding the bar areas which soon became ten deep with people in search of Champagne, chardonnay, rosé, martinis, mixed whiskey drinks, and, for the truly chic, exotic cocktails and mocktails.

Malone knew a lot of the patrons in attendance, so he and Connie excused themselves and waded into the sea of people, shaking hands, sharing air kisses, and slapping backs.

"Be a little tough for us to mingle," Reagan told the two women. "Unless you want to stop by and say hello to Lawler."

Gellos frowned. "I think I should take a position toward the rear, near my seat."

"I don't care what sort of security they have here, I don't want you alone near Paszek and his gang."

"Looks like he and the Novaks are moving toward the center of this mob scene. I'll be fine, and it'll be better for us to have two views. You have your earpiece in?"

"All set, coach."

"You just take care of Erin, we'll circle back later." With that, Gellos set off around the perimeter to get a second vantage point.

"What now?" Erin asked. "You really think there's going to be trouble in a place like this?"

"Probably not," he conceded. "Unless we cause it."

She turned to him, concern clouding her lovely hazel eyes. "Nick, it looks like everyone in Washington is here except the President. You've got to be careful. You're in enough trouble already."

Reagan finished his bourbon and placed the empty glass on a nearby tray. "That man tried to kill you and me and Alex and—for that matter—took two runs at Khoury. We don't know who put him up to those attempts, at least not for sure, but he and I are going to have a discussion tonight. What happens after that," he added with a shrug, "is in the hands of God."

The Malones returned following their brief social tour, and Derek told them, "Time to sit down, our other guests are here."

Reagan could see that the patrons were heading for their tables. Having studied the seating chart, he knew the premium tables were at the edge of the dance floor, which included the Malones, as well as the Novaks and Mindlovitch.

"I'm going to wait a minute," he told Malone. "Why don't you take the ladies, I'll be there soon."

"Nick, this is…"

"It'll be fine. Go on."

Reagan waited and watched. When Mindlovitch and his entourage were seated, he strolled across the parquet floor, stopping in front of the tall Russian.

Mindlovitch stood, breaking into a broad smile. "Nicholas Reagan." Holding out his hand, he said, "Federal salaries must have substantially increased for you to buy your way into this bash."

"I won an entry ticket in a lottery they held for the bourgeoisie," Reagan said with a laugh as they shook hands. "Good to see you, Anatole. Last time we met you weren't looking so fit."

Slapping his firm stomach, Mindlovitch said, "Back to fighting shape."

"Glad to hear it," Reagan said.

"Owed in part to you," he added, referring to the special protection detail Reagan and Kenny had arranged after the Russian was betrayed by one of his own people several months before.

Reagan nodded. "You look so good, why you need these two gorillas with you?"

The entire table fell quiet as the two bodyguards, who had been seated on either side of Mindlovitch and his date, made a move to get up, but the Russian held up his hand.

"You must understand," he told his guests. "My friend Mr. Reagan has a quintessentially American sense of humor. Propriety be damned in the name of a good laugh. Am I right?" he asked Reagan, then forced a chuckle.

"Sometimes, Anatole. In this case, I really am wondering why someone like you would need two goons at an event like this." Without awaiting a reply, he added, "Maybe you're seated too close to the Novaks?"

This time, not even Mindlovitch was amused. "This visit is done," the Russian said.

"All right," Reagan replied. "But remember, Anatole, people are judged by the company they keep, so there will be a conversation yet to come." Then he turned and headed back to the Malones.

"What was that about?" Derek asked.

Still standing, Reagan said, "I was reopening diplomatic relations with my friend Mindlovitch. Now how about introducing me to the Novak brothers?"

Malone stared up at him. "You're serious?"

"As a heart attack."

Connie got to her feet. "I'm coming with you."

"But sweetheart—" Derek began, until his wife cut him off.

"If he won't bring you over there, Nick, I will."

Malone stood, turned to the rest of his guests at his table, and excused himself. Then, taking Connie by the hand, he led Reagan back across the dance floor, this time to the table just past Mindlovitch.

Reagan knew it was tough to make Malone nervous, he had come up from the streets and had seen it all, but as they walked side by side, he said to Nick, "I hope you know what you're doing."

Reagan smiled but did not reply.

When they reached the Novaks, they found the group at their table engaged in a friendly discussion. Andrew looked up first.

"Derek, Connie," he said, sounding as friendly as someone running for the local Town Council. "I was looking forward to saying hello this evening."

There followed a series of greetings. Since the Malones knew everyone at the table, Derek made the introductions for Reagan, which included his old colleague, Dr. Phillip Roberts. Malone had reverted to his usual affable style, Connie less so except in her exchanges with the Novaks' wives.

Eventually, Andrew said, "Nick Reagan. We've never met but I know your name."

Before either of the Malones could respond, Nick replied, "I'm the person who asked Derek to see if you could obtain information about an international terrorist who turned out to be hiding in London. By now I'm sure you've heard through the grapevine that we apprehended him." No one answered, so Reagan went on. "I'm also the individual who was attacked by the security guards in the lobby of your office building the other night. But I'm certain you know that too. Didn't work out that well for them." Not waiting for a reaction, he made a show of looking at the others at the table. "I see that Mr. Paszek didn't make your guest list. Wonder where he's gone, just saw him a short while ago."

"Derek," Andrew Novak began, his voice firm, but Reagan went on.

"Don't blame Dr. Malone for my bad manners, Mr. Novak. I've worked hard to hone theses skills over the years."

"It seems you've succeeded, young man," Andrew Novak said.

"Proudly so," Reagan told him. "Hope you all make the best of the evening. The real fun is about to start."

With that, he turned and walked away, happy that the Malones followed without offering any sort of apology on his behalf.

"Was all that really necessary?" Derek asked as they caught up to him.

"It's known as lighting the fuse," Reagan said.

Connie smiled. "Then all I can say is, well done, Nick."

CHAPTER FIFTY-ONE

Washington, D.C.

Back at their table, Derek and Connie took their seats, but Reagan remained standing, looking across the room for Gellos. Not able to see her, he adjusted his earpiece and asked where she was.

"Sitting for a moment."

"You hear all that?"

"Mostly your end," she said. "Right out of the Nick Reagan play-book for making friends and influencing people."

"Something like that. You have eyes on Paszek?"

"I did. He's been moving around the room, out of sight for now."

"Time to pay him a visit."

Reagan saw her stand. "I'll be back," he told the Malones.

Erin looked up at him. "Be careful, Nick."

"As ever," he said with a smile he hoped would relieve some of her anxiety, as well as the Malones', then began walking toward the back of the room.

* * *

WHILE REAGAN HAD AN IDEA of how the evening should go, Bogdan Paszek had plans of his own.

Like Reagan, Paszek also had a seating chart, and knew where the Malones would be seated. He had arranged to have one of his men posing as a server at the bar nearest their table, providing him detailed instructions about what to do when their group took their seats and ordered drinks.

The man had been shown several photographs of Derek Malone. He had also been given a small ampule containing liquid, which he now held in his pocket. When the time came, he was to snap open the tiny container, pour the fluid into whatever beverage Derek Malone had ordered, and be sure it was delivered to his target.

*　*　*

As Reagan approached Gellos, she tilted her head slightly, pointing him off to the far side of the room, near one of the large entry doors.

Paszek was standing there, surveying the room.

"You walk directly towards him," Reagan said. "I'm heading out through the door to my left, I'll come around from behind."

Gellos turned and began walking. By the time she was just a couple of paces from Paszek he saw her coming.

Paszek stood just under six feet tall with broad shoulders and arms that filled the sleeves of his tuxedo jacket. He was bald, with broad features and blue-green eyes that were as cold as death.

She kept moving ahead, stopping right in front of him, but before either of them could speak, Reagan was behind him.

"Good evening, Bogdan," he said as he reached up and yanked the tiny headset from Paszek's ear.

Paszek spun around, his reflexes ready to lash out, but he stopped as Reagan held a hand up in the man's face.

"Not the sort of place for your usual tactics," Reagan said. "You make the wrong move here and there'll be ten agents on you before I get the chance to rip your fucking throat out. Which, incidentally, would be very disappointing for me."

Paszek glared at him without speaking.

"We just want to have a little talk, so what say we move off to the side there?" As he gestured, Gellos came around and stood beside him.

"I don't have to talk and I don't have to move anywhere," he said, the accent clearly Eastern European.

"You afraid of something?"

"Fuck you, tough guy."

"Ah, so we *are* talking. You see, not so hard. Let's pick a topic that's of interest to both us. For instance, who put you up to killing Walid Khoury?"

Paszek did not answer, but he did blink, and Reagan figured that was a start.

"We took care of the three shooters you sent to my house the other night, unfortunately they all breathed their last before they could tell us anything. However, we do have a survivor from the roadside attack, not to mention the two clowns who tried to abduct Erin David. They all say they have no idea where the orders came from above, but they all claim to have been hired by you."

"Bullshit?"

"You think so?"

"I know so," he said with a nasty smile. "I'd be under arrest by now."

Reagan shook his head. "See how wrong you can be? We have you arrested and then what? You lawyer up, deny the charges, we go back and forth, and all that time is wasted. We leave you out here, we're going to learn more than anything you'd be willing to tell us during an interrogation."

To Reagan's surprise, the man seemed to be thinking it over. Finally, he said, "I don't know any Walid Khoury or Erin David. We done here?"

"Not hardly, since you *do* know Andrew and John Novak. Your employers, as we understand it."

"My business is my own. You got questions, ask them."

"You're sure that's what you want me to do?"

"I saw you at their table just now. Looked like you didn't get the answers you wanted?"

"Quite the opposite, and I suggest you listen carefully to this." Reagan took a half step closer, until he was right in Paszek's face. "When the time comes, they'll give you up like a bad habit. Just like your filthy little henchman did. It's the way of the world, Bogdan. The guy in the middle always gets squeezed. A smart guy like you should know that."

Paszek remained silent, the two of them so close that Reagan could smell his lousy breath.

"They're going to say you're nothing more than a security guard, that anything you did outside the law has nothing to do with them. You'll take the hit, and they'll go on eating caviar and drinking Champagne. The bigshots always walk away."

"What do you want from me?"

Reagan smiled. It was the question that every interrogator hopes for, in one form or another. He did not expect Paszek to talk, not here, not tonight. But it was a beginning. "All we want is the truth," he said. "About the Novaks, Lawler, Turnquist. There's a deal to be made."

But Paszek was shaking his head and Reagan knew that, for now, the moment had passed.

"You have nothing on me. Nothing. And I don't know anything; I just run security. Now get out of my way before I break your nose and leave you here to bleed all over your fancy shirt."

Reagan took a step back. "I thought you'd be smarter than this, but you're just another stupid thug. An empty-headed puppet who thinks the people pulling the strings are going to protect you when things go south. Wrong, Bogdan."

Paszek turned to walk away, but Reagan grabbed his arm. "And remember this, we're watching every move you make now. Every move. And for me it's personal, which is going to make it worse for you when the time comes."

Paszek pulled his arm free and headed off.

Gellos, who had been quiet, said, "That went well, to use one of your expressions. You think you scared him?"

Reagan shook his head. "He doesn't scare that easy. But we got him thinking, which is all we need for now."

* * *

BACK AT THE TABLE, Malone had given up trying to see what was happening across the room and was doing his best to be a gracious host to Erin and the other guests. They had ordered a fresh round of drinks and when they arrived the server was careful to place each glass in front of the proper patron. Especially Malone.

Reagan had yet to return, so after the waiter walked away, Derek got up and moved to the seat beside Erin. She did not know any of the other people, and he thought it would be helpful for him to include her in the discussion going around the table. Connie moved to his empty chair to assist in the effort and, in doing so, picked up the drink intended for Derek.

CHAPTER FIFTY-TWO

Washington, D.C.

The next day, Reagan, Gellos, and Brandt were in Brian Kenny's office. Word had already come from upstairs that Reagan was continuing his inappropriate actions.

"The director claims you harassed Mindlovitch and the Novaks last night," the DD reported.

"I would be interested to know who made that claim," Reagan replied. "For instance, did the Novaks pass that through their toady Ross Lawler?"

"The source was not shared."

"Of course not. How about some specifics about how they were harassed?"

Kenny waved away the question. "Are you going to deny that you and Gellos assaulted two of their security guards the night before last?"

Reagan looked to his partner, then said, "I'm sure you mean defended ourselves, right? Ask for the video of the little tango we did and share that with Spinelli."

"Director Spinelli to you."

"The Malones introduced me to the Novaks and I told them I was the person who asked Derek to enlist their help in finding Khoury. That was the substance of the exchange. As for Anatole Mindlovitch, ask him yourself if he was put off by what I said. This is all nonsense, stemming from the fact that I rousted their man Bogdan Paszek."

Kenny had clearly not heard about that encounter and asked for details. It was Gellos who obliged, after which the DD asked, "Your thesis, if I have this right, is that you're getting too close for their comfort, is that the idea?"

"Precisely," Reagan said. "If we can get Paszek to cooperate, there's no telling what secrets he can spill."

"What are your thoughts on this?" Kenny asked Gellos.

"In principle, Nick is right, but my read of Paszek is that he'd be a tough nut to crack. He's got sociopath written all over him, not to mention the possible level of involvement he may have in any number of criminal acts. He's not likely to believe there's any deal we can offer that he can live with. But Nick's act last night might get him thinking."

"Sounds like our situation with Khoury," the DD said.

"And what about him?" Reagan asked. "I assume we still have someone keeping an eye on things at the Gables."

"I'm thinking about turning him over to the FBI," Kenny said. "Bebon and I spoke, and at my request he's making the appropriate noises about jurisdiction, which is a valid issue. The Bureau should be interrogating Khoury for crimes against this country."

"Which will move him away from Lawler but closer to this Victor Turnquist," Gellos said.

"They'll have to deal with that, I can't go on arguing with the director about someone he trusts."

Reagan sat back and took a moment to review the options. "We need to set Lawler up."

"Excuse me?"

"I don't mean frame him, sir—I mean put him in a position where it's clear to everyone that he's a traitor."

"You keep throwing that word around, Reagan. It's a very serious allegation."

"It is, sir, but you haven't been shot at twice by people he put into play through his friend Paszek. Not to mention Erin's experience."

"All right, just on a theoretical basis, what did you have in mind?"

* * *

Although botulism is one of the most toxic substances known to man, it does not work immediately on its victim. It attacks the nervous system, which takes some time.

Malone had done extensive work on the subject, having worked with these poisons, and if he had been infected it might be considered an accident of some sort. Although he had not been in the lab for some time, it still seemed a clever way to get rid of him, since foul play would be difficult to prove.

Poisoning Connie Malone was another matter.

The afternoon following the gala, she was still in bed, fearing she had caught that flu. Later that night, despite some over-the-counter medication Derek suggested, she was worse. The next morning, when she awoke, she could barely move or speak or even swallow.

Seeing her condition deteriorate so quickly, Derek called an ambulance. He thought it might be a stroke, or some cardiological event and, as he rode with her to the MedStar Hospital on Irving Street NW, he held her hand, trying to encourage her.

But her symptoms were becoming too familiar.

As they sped through the streets of Washington, Malone made two calls. The first was to the Center for Disease Control in Atlanta, connecting with Dr. Alan Cooper, a specialist he had worked with and who shared his negative view of the recent work being done at Novak Pharma.

Malone provided all of the pertinent information about Connie's condition, to which Dr. Cooper said, "I know you understand it's impossible for me to be sure without proper tests and bloodwork, but it sounds like your diagnosis is correct. I'm so sorry, Derek."

Malone was not interested in sympathy. "What are our options?" he asked.

"I'll assemble my team immediately and take our plane up to you this morning."

"Thank you, Alan."

"And Derek, I know I don't have to tell you this, but keep her quarantined. From this moment forward."

As soon as Malone signed off, he followed Dr. Cooper's direction by ordering the two attendants in the back of the ambulance to mask up. Then he made a second call, to Nick Reagan.

CHAPTER FIFTY-THREE

Washington, D.C.

Reagan was still at The Jefferson Hotel in Washington when Malone reached him. He could hear Malone was doing his best to remain calm as he reported the situation in a concise, scientific manner. Reagan could also tell that his friend was devastated.

"You're certain this was a toxic poisoning?" Reagan asked.

"There's no doubt in my mind."

"I know these things tend to progress slowly, but how bad is she at this point?"

Malone fought back tears as he said, "Very bad, Nick. We're giving her oxygen through a mask, but she's barely conscious." He reached out and stroked Connie's hair, but she did not react. "She's not only having trouble breathing, but she can barely swallow. She was unable to speak by the time the ambulance arrived."

"What's the medical protocol here?"

"There are none, not locally. I've already phoned a friend at the CDC, Alan Cooper. When I described the symptoms and gave him the preliminary readings the EMT are getting, he agreed with my diagnosis. It's standard procedure for the CDC to become involved in a case like this. He and his team are flying up now. The key is for them to administer an antitoxin as soon as possible to stop the poison from moving through her system."

"They won't have a drug like that at the hospital?"

"Negative," Malone told him.

Reagan hesitated, almost unable to ask the next question. "You say this serum will stop the spread. What about reversing the damage?"

Malone's deep breath was audible. "That remains to be seen. At best this is a long-term recovery."

Reagan was not about to ask for the worst case outcome. "You said she's being taken to MedStar. You want me to get you into Walter Reed?"

Malone thought it over. "No, I know some of the staff at MedStar." Then he added, "At the moment I want as little to do with a government facility as possible."

"Loud and clear," Reagan said. After a pause, he said, "I know it's too early to consider this, but do you…"

"Have any idea how this happened?" Malone finished the thought, anger now rising in his voice. "Connie and I haven't been apart these past few days. We've been eating the same food, drinking the same drinks, so what do you think?"

"She was intentionally poisoned?"

"Or unintentionally."

"You're saying she might not have been the target."

"Think about it, Nick. Solares in Paris and Dr. Fontaine in New York City, both murdered. Solares and I were fighting against the new drug from within the company. Fontaine worked for a competitor and was issuing his own criticism. Including criticizing the use of lithium in the formula, by the way. If someone wanted to get rid of them, who would be the next logical victim? Not Connie."

Reagan could not argue the point. "What about the timing?"

"The gala, two nights ago, that would fit the progression of her symptoms. Yesterday morning she felt sick, last night she was worse, but this morning," he took a moment to collect himself. "Disaster," he said.

"Tell me more about this antitoxin. Can I send out an alert, see if any hospital in the area would have it?"

"Cooper did that. He's already texted me that he came up empty. These are all highly dangerous substances they keep under lock and key, even at the CDC in Atlanta. Now it's all about timing, and how soon he can get here with a supply."

"I'm sorry to go over this again, but if the serum won't cure her, what are the steps after it's administered?"

"Botulism attacks nerves throughout the system. If they have the right antitoxin—and if it works—it can only prevent the poison from damaging more of those nerve endings. Two big "ifs". It's then up to Connie's immune system to fight back against the damage she has already suffered."

"My God."

"God is right, because most of this is now in His hands."

With that, the ambulance screeched to a halt in front of the emergency room entrance of the hospital."

"We're here, Nick, I've got to go. I'm doing what I can on this end, but you know I'm counting on you to do what you have to do on yours."

"I'm on it," Reagan said. Then he called Erin, who had gone to Langley early that morning, and told her everything.

When he was done, she asked with obvious disbelief, "They tried to kill Derek?"

"That's our guess. That Connie took the wrong glass. Which means while Carol and I were threatening Paszek, they were carrying out a murder right there, right in front of us."

"How could you possibly know?"

The combination of anger, upset, and guilt made it hard for him to catch his breath. "It's my job to figure these things out," he finally said. "For now, the message is clear. We need to be extra careful, about every move we make, and everyplace we go." He hesitated. "None of us is safe," he told her.

PART THREE

CHAPTER FIFTY-FOUR

Hospital Emergency Room, Washington, D.C.

When the ambulance came to a stop, things began happening quickly. An orderly who had been waiting for their arrival yanked open the back doors of the vehicle, then worked with the two EMTs who were attending to Connie, sliding her onto a gurney and quickly wheeling her inside.

Malone jumped out and ran to the admitting desk. After identifying himself he hurriedly gave the nurse the names of several doctors he knew on staff, hoping to find one or more of them on duty. He was told that Dr. Sahith Kumar was in the building and the young woman promptly arranged to have him paged.

Meanwhile, Connie was taken to one of the rooms where she was being hooked up to devices that would monitor her blood pressure, heart rate, oxygen saturation, and breathing functions. Cooper had advised that she be quarantined, but by the time Malone got to her side, things were chaotic. Nurses and attendants were moving all around as the emergency room's attending physician was speaking with one of his residents.

Shaking his head, the young doctor was saying, "Labored breathing, heart rate, this paralyzed state could all indicate Guillain-Barré Syndrome. We should get her in for a spinal tap right now."

Malone, who had arrived at the foot of the bed where Connie's inert body lay, shouted, "Are you out of your fucking mind?" Then he looked around the emergency room, as if searching for someone with more sense than this young idiot. "Guillain-Barré? This is toxic poisoning,

257

and Dr. Cooper is already on his way from the CDC with a variety of antitoxin serums. Just take some blood and get us the results, stat!"

At that moment, Connie's body began to spasm, a violent shaking that caused the young doctor to call out, "Code Red."

His resident ran for the defibrillator paddles in the next room as other doctors arrived in what seemed mere seconds, assisting while the electric charges were applied to Connie's chest, until suddenly she settled back and her heart rhythms returned to normal.

Dr. Kumar arrived and—without even greeting Malone—had one look at Connie and said to the attending physician, "Get this woman into the ICU and onto life support. Immediately!" As they began wheeling Connie's bed toward the intensive care unit, he turned to Malone and asked, "What happened, Derek?"

Malone gave his opinion, that his wife had ingested a dose of botulism.

But Kumar wanted to know. "How?"

"We were at an affair a couple of nights ago, she must have eaten something that was contaminated."

"Do you know if anyone else who was there is experiencing these symptoms?"

Malone gritted his teeth, wanting to say that no one else was the target of a murder attempt, but said, "Not that I know of. Alan Cooper and his team are already on their way from CDC."

"I hope they get here soon," Kumar said. "If you're right—and your diagnosis is consistent with her condition—we have no antitoxin serum here."

"Understood," Malone said, then both men took off down the long corridor.

Inside the ICU, they found a nurse attaching Connie to even more computer apparatus and the emergency room doctor, who was looking concerned.

"What is it, other than the obvious?" Kumar asked.

"We're trying to intubate her, but her throat is already closed so tight we can't get the oxygen tube in."

"Well then, use a pediatric tube," Kumar ordered.

They watched as the child-sized tube was successfully inserted.

"The ventilator should be able to force air into her lungs," Malone said, as if speaking to himself.

Dr. Kumar agreed. "We should also administer nerve blocking meds, at least that will make her more comfortable. Get an IV set up."

Once again, his direction was followed. Then they stood and watched as the machines worked to help Connie Malone as she struggled to remain alive.

CHAPTER FIFTY-FIVE

The Gables, Virginia

As soon as Reagan finished his call with Malone, he phoned Kenny and told him what had happened. Then he said, "I need to speak with Khoury."

"What possible help could he be at this point? Right now things are quiet there. We have him under guard and, so far, Lawler is staying away."

"Khoury has answers he has yet to give us, and I need them now."

Kenny thought it over. "All right, let me call the director. Take Gellos with you, I don't want you going there alone."

"You think I'm going to need a witness?"

"In fact I do," the DD said.

"All right, but at least give me a head start. I don't want to meet anyone on my way there."

Reagan called Gellos and brought her up to speed.

"Wish I could be on the line when he calls Director Spinelli."

"You and me both," Reagan said. "For now, we need to get there before Lawler hears about this."

Gellos got her car from the garage, picked Reagan up at the Jefferson and they headed for the Gables.

When they arrived at the room where Khoury was being held, the prisoner asked, "What's going on? No one has spoken with me for two days."

"I'm not here to answer your questions," Reagan told him, anger in his voice and eyes. "It's time for you to begin cooperating. No more teasers, no more claims that you have secrets you're not going to share until we put you in the witness protection program. There have been developments and I need information. And I need them now."

"What do you want to know?"

"Let's start with Anatole Mindlovitch."

Khoury nodded. "Like most of the people I've named, he works both sides of the street. On one side, he's a legitimate businessman with successful companies, respected for a variety of technological innovations and all of that. His public face, if you will."

"And the other?"

"Like many men with power and wealth, it's never enough. Take the Ghost Chip, for example. The claim is that it renders any device untraceable, undetectable, and unhackable."

"I'm well aware," Reagan said.

"And I know you're familiar with the rumor that prototypes were stolen several months ago."

"I am."

"The thief was identified but never found, am I right?"

Neither Reagan nor Gellos replied.

"The investigation led to a woman who worked in his lab in China."

"The Suzhou lab," Reagan said.

"That's the story I've heard. But don't you find it odd she was never located? The People's Republic of China—an ironic name for a communist country, don't you think?"

"Go on," Reagan said impatiently.

"The PRC, as large and as heavily populated as it is, has an extensive database on its citizens, as well as its foreign residents. This is especially true for those who hold positions of importance or influence."

"Such as computer scientists."

"Exactly. Like Xia Chen," Khoury said.

Reagan did not betray his surprise that Khoury knew the name of the woman suspected of having stolen the prototypes. "You have a point?"

"What if Xia Chen does not exist? What if she was a fiction created to cover the fact that Mindlovitch actually sold those chips to a buyer who, shall we say, he did not want to disclose? A buyer willing to pay an extremely high price to have them before they become available to anyone else?"

"Another of your guesses?"

"What if I told you those chips were purchased by your steadfast ally, the Saudis?"

"I would ask what proof you have of that."

"Proof. Why must you always sound like some sort of police detective? Do you expect me to produce a bill of sale?" Khoury sighed. "We are in the information business, and often that consists of nothing more than discussions, or even rumors. My point, since you ask for it, is that Ms. Chen has never been found. Her family, assuming one exists, has likewise disappeared. And, in case you have not noticed, Mindlovitch does not seem to be pressing the search. That, in itself, should seem more than a bit strange."

Reagan and Gellos exchanged a glance before Nick said, "Go on."

"Whatever his intentions for the development and sale of the Ghost Chip, it is clear that one component remains essential, as it is for other battery-driven devices he manufactures."

"Lithium," Gellos said.

"Correct," Khoury said. "Which brings us to an intersecting line. Who else is anxious to increase their access to lithium?"

"John and Andrew Novak," Reagan said.

"Again, correct. The Novaks need lithium for many of their pharmaceuticals and, to use a time worn phrase, they will stop at nothing to secure that supply. Joining forces with Mindlovitch makes sense for both sides, because mining lithium is a nasty business. They'll need as much political clout as they can muster to obtain the rights to ravage new sites where this mineral can be found. As an example, are you aware that it takes approximately five hundred thousand gallons of water to extract one ton of lithium? Can you imagine the devastation to the surrounding area, the water supply, and the neighboring farmlands?"

"I'm familiar with the issues," Reagan said.

"Good, because you will then understand that these are people who care nothing for anyone or anything other than their own aims. To increase wealth and power, as I say, and in the process to create a new world order. Democracy be damned, they believe in an elitist rule where they will reside on a new sort of throne."

"When you say they care nothing for anyone..."

"I mean just that. When you arrived today, your rage was evident, which can only mean that someone you care about has met a violent end. Be assured, these are the people behind the attack at your home and on my way here the other day, and they will stop at nothing to silence those they see as a danger to their ends."

"Which includes you."

"Especially me."

Reagan sat back. "Let me make a point. I never lose sight of the fact that you're a Muslim extremist who engineered terrorist attacks on my country. Why should I believe anything you have to say and, perhaps more important, what do you have to do with all of this?"

Khoury shook his head. "Once again, Mr. Reagan, your tendency to see things in colors of pure good and pure evil could hinder your ability to take in the nuances of the full picture. For instance, you want to view me in one dimension, but that is never the reality. I was an investment banker who had dealings with these people and many others. Now some of those people want to prevent me from revealing what I know." He paused. "I had a wife and daughter who were murdered, then I remarried, and now have lost that wife to the exigencies of fate. You would like people to be simplistic, without texture or depth, because that serves your sense of morality."

Reagan leaned forward. "You expect me to sit through another ethics lecture from a mass murderer?"

"No, but I expect you to take the information I am willing to provide so you can protect me and, in the process, perhaps begin to prevent the spread of a cancer that is running rampant through your government." The three of them were quiet, until Khoury said, "You've asked for proof, which is difficult for me to provide, but you can get it."

"How?"

"First, you need to follow the money. Not an original concept, I grant you, but these people use it to build control. I will give you a lead and the name of someone that can start you in this endeavor."

And then he did.

CHAPTER FIFTY-SIX

MedStar Hospital, Washington, D.C.

The team from CDC arrived at the hospital, assisted by a police escort from the airport they had phoned ahead to arrange. The authorities at all levels took botulism very seriously.

Dr. Alan Cooper reviewed the blood test results, the vital signs being displayed by the beeping machines beside the bed, and conducted an examination of Connie's motionless body. There was no doubt in his mind that her condition resulted from poisoning.

He personally administered the antitoxin serum, then left his colleagues with Connie in the ICU, taking Malone by the arm and leading him out to the corridor.

"First and foremost, I don't want anyone saying anything negative in there," he told Malone. "Connie appears comatose, but she can hear everything."

Malone nodded, too emotionally spent to reply.

"I realize you know most of this, but I'm going to walk you through it anyway." Cooper paused. "It appears the botulism virus has moved throughout her body, which is why she looks paralyzed. Based on her blood tests, I'm confident we used the correct serum, which should stop the spread but will not reverse the damage. Our job is to keep her alive as she fights her way back."

Malone had been doing his best to hold it together but now, as his old friend verbalized what he already knew, tears welled up in his eyes. "She's going to have a long battle."

Cooper reached out and placed his hand on Derek's shoulder for a moment. "Yes, she is, but she's otherwise in excellent health, and we all know Connie is a fighter." He offered an encouraging smile. "Tough as nails, your girl. We both know that."

Malone felt unable to catch his breath as he fought the urge to break down. "It could be months before she can even speak."

"It's impossible to predict, since we have so few statistics on this. But optimism is appropriate, and it will be important that she gets as much positive feedback as possible. People who recover report that it matters. She really will hear everything."

"Give me the downside."

"To begin with, severe cases of botulism are so rare that there are hardly any doctors with experience in treating the condition. It was good that you reached out to us as soon as you did. Unfortunately, since we have no way of knowing the source of the infection, we do not know how much poison she ingested. I provided the amount of anti-toxin I believe appropriate, but we will even have to wait on that to see if another dose is indicated."

"How long?"

"Hard to say, Derek, as you know, but again, I think we gave her enough to stop things from getting worse."

Malone wanted to ask how much worse things could be.

"You believe this happened two nights ago? At a charity dinner, was it?"

"Yes."

Cooper shook his head. "How could she be the only one affected?"

Malone saw no point in discussing his suspicions with Cooper, but decided to ask, "What if someone intentionally gave her the toxin?"

"Who would do such a thing to Connie?"

"Put that aside for the moment," Malone said, fury beginning to replace sorrow. "What would you say about that?"

"The first thing I would ask is, where did they get it? They would need access to a highly controlled substance. You know that."

Yes, Malone said to himself. Then he said to Cooper, "I'm just trying to sort this out."

"Your focus should be on her recovery. I've already had my team call for an inspection of the ballroom and kitchen where you believe it happened."

"Will that really help? No one else has reported being infected, have they?"

"Any information we gather can be helpful," Cooper said. "Including where the poison came from."

Malone did not argue with that idea.

CHAPTER FIFTY-SEVEN

The Janus Building, Washington, D.C.

The Novak brothers were in a somber mood. Seated across from each other that afternoon at the small table in Andrew's office, neither seemed interested in speaking until Andrew finally said, "This is unacceptable."

"Exactly the word I've been looking for," his brother agreed.

"Connie Malone, for Chrissake? How is it even possible?"

"Paszek told me his man did exactly as instructed, served the drinks, and left the ballroom. He has no idea how or why Connie ended up with that glass."

"You've already explained this to me," Andrew replied. "I want to know why the idiot left without ensuring it was done correctly."

"Does it matter now?" John asked.

Andrew sighed. "I suppose not."

"The thing that matters is what we do now."

Andrew thought it over. "To begin with, we need a logical explanation of how we found out. Then we express our concern and support for Malone."

"We can say one of the doctors we know at MedStar heard about it and passed it on."

Andrew shook his head. "What if someone asks which doctor called us? We cannot do anything that is in the least suspicious or unverifiable. Until we can identify a credible source for the news on Connie, we keep our heads down and go about our business."

"You're right," John said.

"You had something else you wanted to tell me. Something Paszek said?"

"He had a discussion the other night, with this fellow Reagan."

"A discussion?"

"At some point Reagan caught up with him at the back of the room. Told Paszek he was keeping an eye on him, something like that."

"Really?"

"Paszek told him he had no idea what he was talking about and walked away."

"That was the entire conversation?"

"So he says."

"Why even bother to tell you?" Andrew wondered aloud.

"He saw Reagan when he came to our table a bit earlier, thought we should know."

Andrew nodded slowly. "It may be time to distance ourselves from Paszek. Just for now. Let him continue to run our security, but there's no need for us to be in regular contact, if you see my point."

CHAPTER FIFTY-EIGHT

En route to Washington, D.C.

On their way back from the Gables, Gellos was driving and Reagan was on the phone with Kenny.

"If someone tried to poison Derek Malone to shut him up, why wouldn't they take another run at him. Or at Khoury?"

"What do you suggest?" Kenny asked.

"I trust Dick Bebon, and we've already said that the Bureau has jurisdiction over the terrorist attacks Khoury engineered. What if we get him to the FBI, as you suggested, and they put him in a hole so deep that no one knows where he is? At least for now."

"How do we move him without Lawler getting involved?"

"We don't. We have Bebon go to his director, get the order to collect Khoury without our involvement."

"I'll need to run this by Spinelli."

"I understand that, but why would he object? The fact is, they do have jurisdiction over domestic attacks. And he gets rid of a headache."

"Meaning this in-fighting with Lawler."

"Precisely."

The DD paused again. "You're really convinced Khoury has more information."

"He gave me a name that might be very helpful. I'm going to follow that lead after I contact Bebon, provided you give this a green light."

"All right. I'd like to be rid of this headache myself. We have these recent attacks to address, and that should be our focus."

Reagan was not so sure about that, but he let it go for the present. His next call was to Bebon, for whom he laid out the situation, then waited.

After a few moments, Bebon said, "Tell you the truth, I'd like some time to interrogate Khoury myself. I'll make the request."

"You'll have to coordinate this with Langley, but my DD is already alerting the director."

"Understood."

Reagan paused. "I know I don't have to say this, but you need to keep Turnquist out of the loop."

"I'll keep you posted," he promised.

The call ended and Gellos asked if Bebon sounded positive about their idea.

"He's a low key guy, but I would say he's bought into the program."

Then Reagan called Langley and spoke with Sasha Levchenko. "I have name for you to run down for me."

"All right."

"You also need to get with Erin and do a deep dive into Ross Lawler's finances."

"Seriously?"

"It won't be easy. Lawler is no one's fool, and he's had a successful career in finance, so you need to be careful how you search this out. I want you to focus on any transaction between him and the Novaks. Including any companies any of them might have used."

"We're already at the edge of the limb, Nick."

"I understand that. The two of you will have to get out of the building and go somewhere else to do this research."

"I would say."

"Khoury also gave me some information I'll share with the two of you in person. Let me know where you're going to be once you're out of there."

"Will do," the tech expert replied.

"Relax, Sasha, you've got this."

"Right."

"The name I've got for you is Milos Gadzinski."

"Why does that sound familiar?"

"When Erin ran that background check on Bogdan Paszek, she found out his actual last name was Gadzinski."

"And Milos is…"

"His older brother. Khoury says he lives in Norwalk, Connecticut. I want you to find out everything you can about him."

"Then what?"

"That depends on what you dig up."

CHAPTER FIFTY-NINE

The Gables, Virginia

As requested, Richard Bebon initiated the dialogue between the two government agencies. The concept of handing Khoury over to the FBI was not a tough sell. The Bureau was eager to question him, and Director Spinelli was anxious to be rid of what was becoming an internal headache.

Rather than having curious FBI agents traipsing all over their property, the CIA arranged to have the Handler waiting at the entrance guardhouse when two large SUVs arrived and appropriate credentials were displayed. Khoury was then brought outside where they removed the plastic restraints from his wrists and were replaced with a pair of metal handcuffs provided by one of the FBI agents. Then Khoury was led to the first vehicle, where he was seated behind the front passenger seat.

There was an agent at the wheel, a second beside him in the back, and a third man directly in front of him. He could see that the third man was older than the other two, his salt-and-pepper hair visible above the headrest, so Khoury assumed he was in charge.

They began moving, prompting Khoury to ask the obvious question. "May I know where we are going?"

It was the man in front of him who replied. "You're not here to ask the questions, Mr. Khoury."

The Handler smiled to himself, by now accustomed to the tough talk favored by American law enforcement and intelligence personnel. "I'm sorry, I didn't think our destination was any sort of state secret."

The man in front of him took a moment to adjust his bulky frame so he could turn and face Khoury. "You'll have plenty of time to discuss secrets. For now, all you need to know is that I will be in charge of this interrogation, and whatever treatment you experienced from our friends at the CIA will seem like a birthday party when I'm done with you."

The two men stared at each other for a moment. Then Khoury said, "Might I know who you are, since you claim to hold the key to my future?"

The man's smile was as mirthless as Khoury's. "I am Victor Turnquist, executive assistant director of the FBI."

Khoury held his gaze, refusing to flinch at this unwelcome news, resisting the temptation to ask what the hell had happened to Reagan's friend Richard Bebon. Instead, he said, "Your reputation precedes you."

Turnquist nodded. "And you will find it is well deserved." Then he turned to the agent beside Khoury and said, "Tape his mouth shut, I don't want to hear another word out of him the rest of this trip."

Less than half an hour later, Bebon and two of his agents pulled up to the security gate at the Gables, showed their identification, and announced they were there to collect Walid Khoury on behalf of the FBI.

The two CIA agents standing outside their vehicle looked at each other, then back at Bebon. "You're going to have to wait here a moment, sir, we have to make a call."

CHAPTER SIXTY

The Jefferson Hotel, Washington, D.C.

Reagan and Gellos decided their meeting with the group would be more secure—if less comfortable—back at his hotel room rather than in her apartment. They were joined by Erin, Brandt, and Sasha, who brought with him two high-powered laptops and an untraceable internet link.

Their plan was to begin by focusing on three items—the real identity of Milos Gadzinski; financial transactions between the Novaks and Ross Lawler; and the poisoning of Connie Malone. Reagan had called for a couple of additional chairs, with the bed once again serving as their conference table. As they laid out some papers Erin had gathered and Sasha set up the two computers, Reagan received a call from Bebon.

He listened in silence as the FBI executive assistant director explained what had happened. When Bebon was done, Reagan was on his feet, too upset to remain seated.

"How could this possibly happen?"

"I don't know yet, but I'm going to find out. I promise you, Nick, I was beyond careful in limiting the people who knew of the handoff."

"Do we know who took him?"

"The men at your security checkpoint took screenshots of the two agents who identified themselves. I don't recognize either name, but I've checked them out. Totally legit, both working out of HQ."

Reagan shook his head. "Security didn't ask to confirm that you were part of the detail?"

"Not the way it was set up, apparently."

Reagan looked at the other people in the room, all of whom had all stopped and were listening to his end of the call. "And when you say these two agents work in HQ…"

"It's not unlikely they're connected to Victor Turnquist," Bebon said, anticipating the question.

"You're certain your director would not have copied him in on this?"

"I've known him a long time, and he trusts me. I specifically asked him not to include Turnquist in this operation—at least not yet—and he agreed."

Reagan nodded slowly. "Which means the leak came from our end."

"You think Spinelli spoke with Lawler?" Bebon asked.

"Or Lawler intercepted a communication about the move. Or someone between our director and Lawler passed it on. However he found out, all he would have to do is call his pal Turnquist and tell him to saddle up before you left."

"I don't know what to say."

"You have any sort of guess where Turnquist would take him?"

"There are any number of options I would choose, but knowing I was the one who was supposed to pick Khoury up, Turnquist will obviously go in another direction entirely."

"Makes sense," Reagan agreed.

"I'm going to have to report this to my director. I can't say I suspect Turnquist of anything, but at least I have the IDs for the two agents."

"Good idea. Let's see how your director reacts when he finds out."

"I'll let you know," Bebon said and signed off.

Reagan put down his cell. "You get most of that?"

"This guy Turnquist," Gellos said, "he got to Khoury before Bebon arrived."

"That's the gist. It's up to the FBI hierarchy how this is going to play out. After I hear back from Bebon I'll alert Kenny. Meantime, all we can do is wait."

The others agreed, so Erin said, "Shall we discuss Gadzinski?"

"What have you got?" Gellos asked.

"There are a lot of interesting details," Erin told the group. "But I'll start with the big picture Sasha helped me put together." She took a moment to pull a file from the pile of papers on the bedspread. "It appears Khoury told you the truth. Milos Gadzinski does seem to be Bogdan Paszek's older brother. They were born in Warsaw and came to this country as adults after their parents were both gone."

"Any other siblings?" Gellos asked.

"Negative," Sasha told them.

"Paszek served in the Polish military, then special forces, as we know. After they came to the States he dropped the last name, using his middle name instead."

"We've heard most of this before," Reagan said, obviously still disturbed by Bebon's call. "Get to the interesting details."

Erin looked at him with an understanding smile. "Will do, sir." Picking up another of the papers from the file, she said, "Gadzinski has been a stone mason his entire adult life, both in Poland and here. No military background. Just a laborer with only modest success. His tax returns, which Sasha retrieved, show a consistently middle-class income over the years."

"That sort of contracting can be a cash business," Gellos suggested.

"Maybe part of it, but hold on," Erin said. "He's been married for more than twenty-five years to a woman from back home who has never worked. They have a son and a daughter, each of whom went through a private college without taking out a single student loan. Both are now living in New York City, by the way, neither married yet. But get this—our man owns a house in an upscale part of Norwalk known as Silvermine. Not far from New Canaan, if you know the area."

The others waited.

"Here's the punchline. The house is worth well over a million dollars and has no mortgage. Better than that, it never did. Gadzinski bought the place for cash more than ten years ago. Before that he owned a house in a less expensive part of town, which was also purchased without a mortgage."

Reagan nodded. "We're supposed to ask, where does a stone mason get a million in cash to buy a house?"

"And the money to put two children through college, which is easily several hundred thousand more," Erin reminded him.

"Baby brother Bogdan," Gellos said.

"That's our guess," Erin replied. "Paszek has no other family and has done his best to shield the Gadzinskis from the sordid aspects of his life. Using a different last name, running the cash to his brother through third party entities," she said as she held up a different sheet of paper.

"Which means the Gadzinskis may be Paszek's Achilles heel," Gellos said. "I like that. And I really like the possibilities it presents."

"There's something else you'll find interesting," Sasha told them, as he pushed back some of the long, straight black hair that had fallen across his forehead, a habit he often engaged in when preparing to speak. "Mr. Gadzinski has an extra-large sized safe deposit box at a bank in Greenwich, which is about a half hour southwest of Norwalk for anyone who does not know the geography."

"Now what would a stone mason keep in there?" Erin asked the group, sounding like an elementary school teacher tossing out a soft-ball question.

"Surplus bricks?" Reagan suggested.

But Gellos did not laugh. She was thinking it over. "Under this fact pattern, we all understand that cash is the obvious answer. Or some other form of easily negotiated currency, such as gold coins or bearer bonds. But why such a large box? There would have to be a whole lot of money to require that." She paused. "The thing I find really fascinating is that this man and his brother are from the Old World, where Eastern Europe has a history of failed banks. A stone mason could easily install a safe in a slab of concrete in his own basement. Wouldn't that make more sense?"

"There's another interesting factoid that might inform your think-ing," Sasha said. "The safe deposit box is in Gadzinski's name, but there *is* a second person with authorized access."

"Bogdan Paszek," Reagan said.

"Yes."

Gellos pursed her lips as she considered the implications. "That makes more sense. The bank is not in his brother's town, in fact it's half an hour away. Paszek can come and go, dropping things off or taking them away, while minimizing visits to his brother, his brother's family, or their home."

"More insulation for his big brother's family," Reagan said.

"Right. Which brings us back to the size of the box," Gellos said. "I don't want to obsess over it, perhaps it was the only one available at the time, but from what we've learned so far about Paszek, he is extremely careful and does not do anything by accident."

"Which means," Reagan picked up the thread, "it's likely there's more than cash in there."

CHAPTER SIXTY-ONE

The Janus Building, Washington, D.C.

Malone tried to pull himself together. He had yet to tell their sons anything about this nightmare, waiting until he knew more about Connie's condition and prognosis. Now he realized that time had come, fearing his heart would break when he had to describe to them what had happened to their mother. That she was on the brink of death because of *him*. Because someone had tried to poison *him*. That she had ingested the toxin by mistake.

The mix of guilt and sorrow was overwhelming.

Rather than go through it twice, he went to the waiting area outside the ICU and tied both sons in on a three-way call. Michael and Jason, who were each married with a family of their own, immediately realized there must be a serious problem for their father to suddenly arrange a conference call in the middle of the afternoon.

"What is it?" Michael asked.

Malone could barely get the words out as he began, saying, "Your mother is…. She's very, very ill." Then he drew a deep, uneven breath and did his best to explain the inexplicable.

When he was finished, Jason said, "Don't worry, Dad, I just know everything will be fine." Then he said, "I'm coming down there right now." He lived in New York and would grab the Acela Express from Penn Station.

"Me too," Michael said. He lived not far from his parents, in West Palm Beach, and said he would grab the next flight up to Washington.

Malone began to say things like, "It's too early," and "There's no need at this point," but both sons cut him off.

Then Michael spoke for both of them. "This is about mom. And you, for that matter. We're on our way."

That done, Malone felt an odd sense of relief. Even with Connie unable to speak or react, he was not alone. His sons were coming, and she would love that, knowing they were in the room with her.

Then he began to feel a shift in his emotional turmoil. The anger rose up in his chest as he thought about what had happened, why it happened, and who was likely responsible. With nothing for him to do here but wait, he took his phone out again and called the limousine driver he always used in Washington.

"Eduardo, it's Malone," he said when the man picked up on the second ring. "I don't know what you're doing, but whatever it is you've got to drop it and come get me. Connie's in the hospital and you need to pick me up at MedStar. I'll be outside the Emergency Room entrance."

"Oh my, yes, I'll be there, Mr. Derek. Where will we be going?"

"The Janus Building," Malone told him.

They pulled up in front of the Janus Building and Malone told Eduardo to wait, then marched through the front doors past the security desk.

When one of the two guards on duty called out to Malone by name, he responded without turning around.

"Go fuck yourselves," Malone told them, then used his security card to push his way through the electronic gate.

Riding up to the penthouse floor, he was greeted by another Novak employee as the elevator doors slid open.

Before the man could speak, Malone said, "Get the fuck out of my way or you're going to have a major problem."

The man—not knowing how to react—simply stood there as Malone pushed past him and strode the length of the hallway to Andrew Novak's office. Novak's assistant began to greet him, but Malone held up his hand, walked past her, and shoved the door open, almost swinging it off its hinges as he barged into the room.

Not surprisingly, John Novak was also there, the two brothers standing in the middle of the room like some ersatz reception committee.

"I see your security downstairs warned you I was coming."

"Derek," Andrew began, "we just heard about Connie. One of the doctors we work with at MedStar called...."

"Stow it," Malone hollered at him. "You two pretend to embody the American Dream, but instead you betray every one of this country's finest values. You're the American Nightmare."

Andrew began to speak, but Malone shut him up again.

Looking from Andrew to John and back to the older brother. "I want you to listen to me very carefully, I don't want to say any of this twice. First, consider this my resignation from your board. Second, I am going to..."

"Derek—" Andrew interrupted, trying to halt the coming train wreck. "We know you're upset."

"Upset? You haven't seen me upset yet, Andrew. I told you both to shut the fuck up. Don't make me say it again." He felt barely able to breathe, but he continued. "Second, I am going to do everything I can to expose *Neulife* as a dangerous drug that should never be approved by the FDA, no matter how many people you've paid off to get it to market. And third—which I suggest you pay special attention to—if my wife does not survive this poisoning, if she suffers any permanent damage, I promise the two of you that you're as good as dead. You can hire all the protection there is in the world, but I will get to you."

Then he turned and stormed off, leaving them standing there, neither brother saying a word, and Malone feeling better than he had in two days.

CHAPTER SIXTY-TWO

The Jefferson Hotel, Washington, D.C.

Reagan and the team had moved from their speculation about Milos Gadzinski to the review of financial records involving Ross Lawler and the Novak brothers.

"Khoury was not wrong when he said to follow the money," Erin said. "They were careful in covering up these transactions, particularly by using a bank in the Cayman Islands, but eventually anything can be exposed."

"Interesting choice of words," Reagan said, but when no one reacted he felt the need to apologize. "Sorry gang, just trying to lighten the mood."

Gellos had been through enough with her partner to understand his impulse to make the occasional wisecrack, which did not mean he was not dialed in to the task at hand. "Maybe if you were actually funny it might help," she said with a smile.

Now everyone managed to laugh.

Returning to something Erin had showed them, Gellos said, "This house you're pointing us to, is it owned by Lawler?"

"By a company Lawler controls, or so it appears. There are also travel records showing he takes a number of trips down there."

"Not to defend Lawler," Reagan said, "but he was successful in business, right? If he has a vacation home, what do we think that proves?"

Sasha asked Erin if he might respond, and she told him to go ahead. "It turns out Mr. Lawler is not all he seems. It's true, he held some high corporate positions, but he never reached the top echelon of earners. Then we must take into account his two divorces and the last couple of

283

years earning a government salary here at the Agency, all of which does not paint a financial picture of someone who could afford that kind of house. We've reached the conclusion that he's far better at accumulating contacts than money. At least legal money. The transactions we're looking at over the past few years are definitely in the other category."

"That's correct," Erin agreed. "He's a classic schmoozer. Good golfer, big social drinker, heavy on name dropping, glad-handing, and arranging favors."

"And getting favors in return," Sasha reminded them. "The flow of some of these funds, including the purchase of that house in the Caymans, came from the Novaks. Put that together with his growing and considerable ownership of stocks in Novak Pharma and the conclusion is inevitable."

"He's on the take," Reagan said.

"And not just from the Novaks," Erin said.

Reagan sat back, tilting his chair onto two legs. "You all know I like a challenge as much as anyone, especially when I'm fighting for our country, but we're talking about slaying some huge dragons. The Novaks are almost unimaginably rich. Lawler is still the number two man at our Agency, and it looks like he continues to have the support of our director. This guy at the Bureau, Victor Turnquist, is another bad actor who's highly placed." He thought it over for a moment as the others did the same. "The unfortunate truth is that some of the wealthy and powerful who control America are capable of getting away with almost anything."

Gellos agreed. "It's one thing to prove the Novaks gave money to Lawler, assuming we can connect all of those links," she said. "But we also need to show that there were illegal acts underlying the payments. An improper *quid pro quo*."

"It's interesting, isn't it?" Reagan asked. "The higher up we go in society, the more sophisticated the crimes become and the tougher it is to hold people to account." Leaning forward and setting his chair down, he said, "Let's take some examples. Among the so-called underprivileged, what are the most common criminal offenses? Murder, theft, burglary, assault, carjacking, you get the idea. We all agree these felonies damage the quality of life for the victims as well as people around them, but they're fairly straightforward to investigate and prosecute."

"Find the perp, put together the evidence, and bring them to trial," Brandt said.

"Exactly my point. In the case of an assault, or even a murder, there might be a claim of self-defense, but things are usually pretty obvious. Someone was wronged, someone is responsible, and we ask for justice."

"We're with you," Erin said.

Reagan stood and began pacing around the small room. "Now let's look at how the mega-rich and well-connected operate. Let's say Mr. Smith invites Mr. Jones to play golf at his uber-exclusive country club. During the round they talk about something troubling Mr. Smith that he believes Mr. Jones might help with. A zoning project that's running into opposition on the local board. A new drug Mr. Smith wants the FDA to approve. An oil spill Mr. Smith's company is being blamed for. You get it."

"Got it," Gellos assured him with a chuckle.

"Don't worry, I'm coming to the point, which arises when Mr. Jones responds. He assures his host that the problem is something he indeed can address, and perhaps that he has other friends who are well placed and might also assist. The following week, the cloud over Mr. Smith's problem begins to lift, and a short while later Mr. Jones receives an invitation to join the club where they'd just played golf, his six-figure initiation fee having been inexplicably waived."

No one responded.

"Have we not just witnessed a crime? Or is that just influence ped-dling we think is all right? Is it just the natural by-product of our system?"

"The answer, I believe, depends," Brandt said.

"Go on."

"If Smith and Jones are two businessmen exercising their own judg-ments and using their influence, I think it's legal and, as you say, the way our world operates. It only rises to the level of criminality if the person being asked for the help is in a position of public trust, such as an elected or appointed figure in our government."

"Certainly that would be criminal," Gellos agreed. "But what if the help that Jones is giving Smith is illegal on some other basis. For instance, what if he helps Smith hide something about the zoning problem or the oil spill? That borders on the criminal as well."

"My point exactly," Reagan told them. "When you say 'borders on' that's where the trouble begins. Lawler, for instance, is not with the FDA. He cannot directly help the Novaks get a drug approved. He is also not in the Interior Department, so he has no direct influence on the Novaks' efforts to secure lithium mines. But he is part of our government and can provide other help or information or influence, and it seems they are willing to pay for that. The question for this group is whether that conduct constitutes a crime. Because, my highly ethical colleagues, that answer will dictate how we handle the information you're amassing."

"You're leaving something out that colors the entire situation," Erin reminded him, "which is our third major point of review for this meeting."

"The poisoning of Connie Malone," Gellos said.

"True," Reagan agreed, then sunk back down into his chair.

"Look, Nick," Gellos began, "there's value in everything you're saying. Corruption is the crime that exists at the upper levels of society in ways it cannot at the lowest levels. As the saying goes, power corrupts and absolute power corrupts absolutely. We need to dig further to see what Lawler and Turnquist might have provided the Novaks in exchange for payment. After all, we work for the Central Intelligence Agency, and it is critical to our responsibilities to gather that sort of information. But Erin is right, when the actions of these people become violent, we're operating in a different theater. The suicide bomber in New York, as well as the attacks in Paris and Moscow make all this another story entirely. And now Connie Malone may die because she took poison that was probably intended for her husband. There's no gray area when it comes to any of that."

"No," Reagan said. "There sure as hell isn't. Which means it's time for us to start doing what we do best."

CHAPTER SIXTY-THREE

Washington, D.C.

The group agreed with Reagan's thesis—that the first order of business was to find Walid Khoury. They had no way of knowing where Victor Turnquist was keeping him, or if he was still alive. As Reagan pointed out, the Handler had given them leads on Lawler's property in the Caymans and Bogdan Paszek's brother.

"If he has more intel to share, we need to find him," Reagan said.

"You have an idea?" Gellos asked.

"I do, and I believe it starts with Dick Bebon."

Not wanting to risk a phone call, Reagan texted his contact in the FBI a single word: Macallan?

Bebon's reply came quickly: Sixty.

Reagan entered a check mark on his cell and hit send. Then he told the group, "I'm going to meet Dick in an hour. I'd like Alex to come with me." Turning to Gellos, he said, "While I'm gone, I have something I'd like you to take care of with Erin and Sasha."

An hour later, Reagan and Brandt pulled up in front of Sequoia on K Street in Georgetown, the same restaurant where he and Bebon had met a few long days ago.

"Circle the block," Reagan told Brandt, "then park there, across the street. If you see anything suspicious, anyone looking like he's from the Bureau, call me immediately."

Brandt stared at him. "We're in D.C., Nick, everyone here looks like they work for the government, mainly because they do."

287

Reagan managed a chuckle. "Fair enough, but I think you'll be able to tell the difference between someone casually stopping by this place and someone on a hunt."

"Eyes wide open," Brandt said.

Reagan got out and entered the restaurant, where he found that his friend had again arrived first. This time, Bebon was already at a table at the far end of the outside terrace with a scotch in front of him.

"We've got to stop meeting like this," Reagan said, as he took a seat at the small table.

"I wish we didn't need to," Bebon said.

The waitress came by and took Reagan's order for a Bulleit on the rocks. When she walked off, he told Bebon, "We need to find Khoury."

"I assumed that's why you pinged me."

"Any word inside the Bureau about what happened?"

"Nothing," Bebon said. "And Turnquist is too highly placed for me to make an unsupported accusation."

"Unsupported? He abducted the man."

"That won't fly. He'll just say that he got word your director wanted to hand Khoury over to us for interrogation about those attacks, which is true. He'll claim he took the initiative and got there first. What do you expect me to say, that Khoury was my personal property?"

Reagan took a moment to gaze out across the Potomac. "I see your point," he said, then turned back to Bebon. "But there was no way he should have known about the exchange."

"He's my superior, Nick, who do you expect me to tell that story to?"

The young woman came back with Reagan's bourbon and the two men toasted. Then Reagan said, "I know what you're up against, believe me."

"Because you have Lawler to deal with."

"Precisely."

"But you asked me to meet you, so I assume you have an idea."

"I do. First, we need to go over a few things."

"I'm all ears."

"As far as we know, your director did not tell Turnquist anything about my agency delivering Khoury to the Bureau."

"I told you that when we spoke."

"Which means the information had to come from our end."

"Lawler again."

"That's the assumption," Reagan agreed, then had another taste of his drink. "Where does your director think Khoury is now?"

"Come on, Nick, you're talking about the FBI. We've got thousands of active cases. Investigations, preventive scenarios, and political issues up to our eyeballs. Even if the director had a discussion with Turnquist about Khoury, he would've been told the matter's being handled and he would believe him."

"Which leaves us with Lawler and Turnquist."

"As you said, that's the assumption."

"All right, what if we can prove that Khoury is being held incommunicado by Turnquist."

"Not unusual with a suspected terrorist."

"Understood," Reagan said. "But the Bureau must have protocols. No one is allowed to just keep him in in a dark hole."

Bebon smiled. "Unlike the CIA, you mean?"

Reagan let that go. "There are rules for detaining a suspect like the Handler, some sort of accountability for his location, who's assigned to guard him, whatever."

"Generally, I would say yes. What's your point?"

"My point is, you have no idea where he's been taken, nor does anyone else," Reagan said.

"True."

"Okay. Then what if we convince Turnquist to take Khoury somewhere he shouldn't be taking him? How far outside the norm would he have to go before we could nail him?"

"How do you propose to get him to move Khoury?"

"I have some ideas."

Bebon thought it over. "Turnquist is a smart bastard," he finally said. "Don't underestimate him."

"I don't intend to. I'm trying to figure out how we catch him doing something that will allow us to take him down."

"Murdering Khoury, that would work," Bebon suggested.

"I need Khoury alive right now. He's provided valuable intel and we believe he has more. Maybe enough to implicate some powerful players."

"And Turnquist is in your way."

"If he murders Khoury he is. For now, let's say he's part of a chain we absolutely need to break."

"I need more than that, Nick."

"You'll get it, as soon as we have a means of compromising Turnquist."

"I've obviously been thinking about this myself. Turnquist knew I was going to pick up Khoury, and he must realize that I know he got there first because I suspect Khoury poses a real danger to him. He can't afford to just let that be."

"Good, I like a motivated partner. Let me explain what I've come up with."

CHAPTER SIXTY-FOUR

MedStar Hospital, Washington, D.C.

Derek Malone was seated at his wife's bedside, their sons Jason and Michael with him, Michael tenderly holding her hand. They had moved her from the ICU to a private room, along with the various machinery and round-the-clock nursing care that was helping to keep her alive. Since she had descended into this comatose state, she had yet to speak, or even move, and the doctors all agreed the chances of recovery depended entirely on Connie. Certain that she could hear everything being said, the three men were careful to be positive and encouraging as they spoke to her in soft tones.

The ordeal had taken its toll on Malone. He had been sapped of his usual energy, had not shaved for the past couple of days, was wearing a running suit and sneakers, and looked haggard from the loss of sleep he was enduring as he spent as much time as possible with his wife.

One of the nurses, who had been just outside the door, came in and whispered to him. "There's a Dr. Roberts here to see you."

Malone looked up and nodded, then stood, told his sons he would only be a minute, and followed her into the corridor.

Phillip Roberts and Derek Malone had interned together in New York, went their separate ways, only to be reunited as research physicians at Novak Pharma. Although their collaboration on behalf of the Novaks led to the development of hugely profitable cosmetic applications, in the past year they found themselves on opposite sides of the internal debate over the efficacy and advisability of pursuing approval from the FDA for the drug being called *Neulife*. Malone only had a few vocal allies within the company, including Dr. Benjamin Solares, who had been killed in the pipe bomb attack at the café in Paris. There were others who shared Malone's concern about the side effects and long-term implications associated with the use of *Neulife*, but too many of them chose to remain silent. As Malone learned a long time ago, money does the talking, and many of the scientists saw what the Novak brothers saw—*Neulife* was going to be a bonanza.

When Malone stepped into the hallway he saw Roberts, dressed in a custom-made suit, freshly pressed shirt and French silk tie, leaning on the counter of the nursing station, chatting with a couple of young women there. After two failed marriages, and now in his late sixties, Roberts had become what Connie had long ago told him he was—a dissolute womanizer. Or perhaps he had always been, and Derek had just missed that aspect of his character.

Seeing Malone, Roberts came towards him with arms outstretched, about to embrace an old friend. But Malone was having none of that, holding up his hand to stop him in his tracks.

"What are you doing here?" he asked.

Roberts responded with an exaggerated look of surprise. "What am I doing here? I heard about Connie and I wanted to see if there's anything I can do."

Malone stared at him. "How did you hear?"

"From John Novak."

"And he sent you here to see me?"

"What are you talking about, Derek? I heard Connie had a stroke or something; John wasn't sure, but he said her condition was critical."

"A stroke? The Novaks know it's not a goddamned stroke. She was poisoned, Phillip. She was poisoned with a dose of botulism that was probably intended for me, so don't give me any bullshit about a stroke."

"I swear I had no idea," Roberts said, his look of surprise appearing genuine, and Malone realized it was possible the Novaks had told him exactly what he claimed.

"And you made no inquiries before you came here? With all your contacts, you didn't speak with anyone here at the hospital?"

"Derek, you have to listen to me. I came here as soon as I got John's call."

"I see. What else did he tell you?"

Roberts hesitated for the first time. "He said you went to see them. That you were in a rage, and that you somehow blame them for Connie's illness."

Malone's voice became louder as he said, "Stop referring to this as an illness. She is suffering from toxic poisoning. The CDC administered a serum to stop it from spreading, but while I'm standing here in the hallway listening to your bullshit, she's in that room fighting for her life."

"I don't know what to say."

"I have an idea," Malone said. "Why not tell me where the dose of botulism came from? We can't determine how much she ingested, so that might be helpful."

Roberts gaped at him in disbelief. "I realize you're beyond upset, Derek, I truly do, but I came here as a friend to offer my support, to see if there's any help I could provide. The first I'm hearing about botulism is from you, just now. What in the name of God would I know about the poison or where it originated?"

Malone stared directly into his eyes as he began nodding slowly. "Maybe you don't know, Phillip. But I believe you can find out." Then he turned and went back into Connie's room.

CHAPTER SIXTY-FIVE

Washington, D.C.

Even an agent as loyal as Nicholas Reagan would not argue that the Central Intelligence Agency had a checkered past. From well before the debacle at the Bay of Pigs, to promoting instability in foreign governments, to political assassinations—the Agency has had its share of immoral and incompetent moments. Nothing, however, has been as controversial as the Agency's sordid history of black sites, where they engaged in various means of physical and psychological torture. Locations have been maintained around the world, where suspects have been submitted to the most gruesome forms of interrogation man could devise. Perhaps the low point of that program existed when such a site was maintained on domestic soil, just on the outskirts of Washington, D.C. itself.

For years, the facility was hidden in the midst of an Agency adjunct, which was ostensibly dedicated to the analysis of photographs and videos taken from surveillance teams, satellites, and elsewhere. Known as the National Photograph Interpretation Center, it was created during the Eisenhower administration and proved a valuable resource. There was a time, however, when the center provided cover for a small suite of rooms in which every type of torture was practiced, from waterboarding, to sleep deprivation, to hanging prisoners from the ceiling of a dark room in various positions that eventually left them disoriented and delusional. Very few know exactly when that complex was created or exactly when it was dismantled, but the fact of its existence is indisputable.

How many of these enhanced interrogation techniques are still being practiced is an open question, but when Victor Turnquist received the text on his dedicated line from Ross Lawler, asking for them to meet, he was both relieved and pleased. First, it was going to be impossible for him to keep Walid Khoury hidden much longer without questions being asked. Second, he was eager to grill the man, and very much liked the idea that Lawler wanted to join him for the interview.

Turnquist obviously knew the stories of a black site in Washington, even if it no longer existed. In his exchange with Lawler, it was clear that his collaborator from the CIA was making appropriate arrangements, at an abandoned warehouse on Sixth Street that had once belonged to an automobile supplier.

Lawler also assured him there would be no one else in attendance.

* * *

WHEN REAGAN ASKED GELLOS to take Erin and Sasha to work on something for him, he had already devised the plan he was going to propose to Dick Bebon. The rest of the team did exactly what he needed to set things in motion.

Neither Reagan nor Bebon could be sure the Handler was still alive, but the entire team agreed the plan was worth the risks. As they had all discussed, taking down men in positions as powerful as Turnquist and Lawler, or the Novak brothers for that matter, was not as easy as pursuing an arrest for a garden-variety crime. These were sophisticated people engaged in complicated but illegal activities, and the quality of pursuit had to match the complexity of their actions.

Reagan called Gellos. "Seems everything is in place."

"Exactly as requested. Took a little doing, but we're ready."

"Great," he said, then asked her to meet Brandt and gave the address. "Please get there now and stay out of sight."

"Of course. Where are you going to be?"

"I'll stay with Bebon."

* * *

As THE TIME FOR HIS MEETING with Lawler approached, Turnquist drove to a private garage, where he pulled his SUV in beside a sedan he had rented a few days ago. After closing the garage door, he opened the trunk of the sedan, confirmed that Khoury was still breathing, then slammed the lid of the trunk shut again. After one more confirming text, Turnquist lifted the garage door and set off in the sedan to meet Lawler.

* * *

WHEN LAWLER RECEIVED Turnquist's first text earlier in the day, he felt much the same as his counterpart in the FBI. Time was not on their side, and they needed Khoury to talk. Once he did, they could dispose of him and move on.

It was that simple.

Since he did not have to stop and collect the prisoner, Lawler arrived at the deserted warehouse first. As agreed, he pulled inside, turned his car around for an easy exit, and stepped out.

Inside the old building it was dark and dank and quiet. Lawler had a look around, deciding this was as good a place as any to bring this drama to an end. He unholstered his automatic, made sure there was a round in the chamber, and that the safety was off. Lawler did not usually carry a weapon and was not generally comfortable with firearms; he thought it prudent to have protection. He trusted Victor Turnquist, but these were unusual circumstances and uncertain times.

Finding the staircase, he made his way up to the third floor where he located a room outfitted with a bench, rags, several extra-large plastic water jugs, a wooden chair, and rope. He took a moment to consider how easy it was to set up a waterboarding session, appreciating Turnquist's handiwork.

Then he sat on the chair and waited.

* * *

TURNQUIST SOON ARRIVED, maneuvering his car in position beside Lawler's. He took time to check his weapon, as Lawler had, then got out and opened the trunk.

296

It took a bit of effort to wrestle Khoury out of the well and onto his feet. Since Lawler indicated the room would be on the third floor, it was not practical for the prisoner to make his way upstairs with his ankles bound.

"I'm going to free up your legs," Turnquist said. "Get any stupid ideas and I'll end this without another word."

Khoury, whose mouth was still taped and still wore a blindfold, did nothing to react. When his ankles were released, Turnquist grabbed him by the arm and pulled him forward as they made their way up. It was a slow climb, since Khoury was still handcuffed and unable to see, but they finally reached the room where Lawler waited.

Without exchanging a greeting, Turnquist merely said, "Good idea."

"Yes, it was," Lawler agreed. "Let's get started, no sense spending any more time here than we need to."

They worked together in silence, Turnquist first removing the handcuffs from Khoury, then together laying him on the bench, face up. That done, they pulled his arms down so Turnquist could bind his wrists again, this time beneath the wooden plank, so he was tethered in place. Only then did Lawler pull off the blindfold as Turnquist ripped the tape from Khoury's mouth, provoking a short scream from the man.

"I hope you're ready to talk," Turnquist told him. "Be a lot easier if you just answer our questions."

Khoury blinked several times as he stared up at them. It did not take long to adjust his sight, since the only light in the room came through the rectangular frames where windows once existed. His lips ached, but there was nothing to be done about that. "What is it you want to know?" he asked.

It was Lawler who replied. "Let's start with everything you told Agent Reagan."

Khoury breathed deeply a few times before saying, "And after I've done that, you'll kill me and leave me here to rot. Am I right?"

"That depends on what you have to say." Pointing to the pile of rags and jugs of water, Lawler said, "If you've never been waterboarded, the alternative is not pleasant."

Turnquist, turning to Lawler, said, "By the way, nice job of pulling this all together so quickly."

Lawler appeared to have been stricken, his eyes widening as he stared at Turnquist. "What are you talking about? I thought you arranged all this…" he began to say, and then stopped.

In that instant both men knew they'd been had, but not how, or by whom. The two of them began looking around the four corners of the room as if there might be an answer there, each instinctively reaching for his weapon.

The next voice they heard came from an adjoining room.

It was Nick Reagan.

"I'd say we have enough to nail down their indictments," he said as he walked in with a Sig Sauer pointed at Lawler, who had instinctively reached for the gun he had holstered. "But if you make another move for your weapon, they'll be organizing your funeral and not your prosecution."

Turnquist had also began to pull out his automatic but was greeted by another voice that came from behind him.

It was Dick Bebon, who walked through the other door, his weapon aimed at Turnquist's head. "Same instructions for you, Mr. Executive Assistant Director."

Turnquist let go of the gun and dropped his hands to his side, then said to Lawler, "Say nothing, do not answer any questions."

Lawler stood there, frozen.

"They have nothing on us," Turnquist told him. "Nothing."

"Think so?" Reagan asked. "Did we mention we have everything recorded, since the moment each of you arrived?"

Smiling at Bebon, he added, "The immediate threat of waterboarding was unexpected, but a nice touch, don't you think? I thought these two geniuses would have at least asked Khoury some preliminary question before they cuffed him to the bench and started talking about torture. That really iced it for us."

Bebon was also smiling. "I even thought they might have figured out they'd been played long before that. Never thought you could pull off the dueling texts. I must give my congratulations to your tech team, maybe I could poach one of them for the Bureau."

Reagan, speaking into a mic, said, "You two can come up here now, we're going to take them in, and we'll need help with Khoury."

He and Bebon moved forward cautiously and relieved Lawler and Turnquist of their weapons, then told him to get down on their knees with their hands on their head.

"Don't you just love when a crooked cop finally gets treated the way he deserves?" Reagan asked Bebon.

"Especially these two. I'm going to enjoy cuffing them both."

"Go for it," Reagan said, then looked down at Lawler. "You two were so clever, with your dedicated phone lines and burner cells. It's the twenty-first century, men, don't you know that nothing is impossible when it comes to technology? Each of you believed you were texting back and forth with each other, but each of you was setting this up this little party with my team. The only thing we could not do is have one of you explicitly ask the other to make arrangements for this—what shall we call it—equipment. But that worked out as well, since neither of you would be idiotic enough to have a text exchange about waterboarding, even if you believed the lines were secure. We just used the codewords you've been using with each other to arrange the meeting place, you did all the rest for us."

"You're bluffing about recording anything," Lawler blurted out.

"Shut up," Turnquist told him.

"Entrapment," Lawler shouted.

"Come, come gentleman," Bebon said. "You'll have plenty of time to sell each other out later."

"Well said," Reagan agreed. "And as far as bluffing," he went on, then pointed to one corner of the room, then a second, "we have not one but two hidden CCTV cameras for the viewing pleasure of the prosecutors in the DOJ. We'll take them with us when we go."

When everyone was quiet, Khoury said, "If no one has an objection, could you please uncuff my hands? This is unbelievably painful. I feel like my arms are being pulled out of their sockets."

"Turnquist has the key," Reagan told Bebon. Then looking down at Lawler, he added, "Just in case you still think I'm bluffing, I knew he had the key because we watched the whole thing in the adjoining room, on my phone. Technology is a bitch."

Bebon unlocked Khoury's hands, and the man began swinging his arms and rubbing his shoulders.

"Just need to get some blood moving," Khoury explained. "I've been in the trunk of a car for I don't know how long."

"Get it done," Reagan said. "We're going to need to cuff you again. You're still in custody."

"Can you at least cuff my hands in front?"

Reagan smiled. "Only if you promise you're going to start talking."

Lawler could not restrain himself. "If you haven't told them anything, why didn't you just say that to us?"

Khoury looked him in the eyes as he replied. "I would have, but you had my mouth taped shut," he told him.

CHAPTER SIXTY-SIX

CIA Headquarters, Langley, Virginia

Kenny and Reagan were seated side by side in the office of their boss, CIA Director Anthony Spinelli. He was standing behind them, watching the video on a laptop. When it ended, Spinelli walked around his desk and slowly sank into his chair. "I can't believe it," he said.

"I'm sorry, sir," Kenny replied, "but Reagan has been right all along."

"As well as Walid Khoury," Spinelli admitted.

Kenny did not respond.

"I've known Ross Lawler for more than fifteen years," the director told them. "I would have trusted him with my life." After another moment he looked at Reagan. "You've spent more time questioning Khoury than anyone else. What do you make of all this?"

Reagan glanced at Kenny before answering. "It's a complicated situation, but a few things are clear. Lawler and Turnquist have been working together. Whatever they've been up to, it seems Khoury knows something about it that worried them. More than that, Khoury appears to know who else is involved."

"I certainly agree it's complicated. What have you learned?"

"As you know, sir, there are people who believe in a one world philosophy, who think nations are obsolete and that things should be run by an elite class."

"Klaus Schnabel," Spinelli said with obvious disdain.

"A good example. He's one of those people who buy their influence by paying off people in our government to do their bidding."

"Please spare me the political lecture and get to the point."

"Yes, sir." Having another look at Kenny, Reagan said, "Perhaps I should mention Mr. Lawler's house in the Cayman Islands. Which is owned in the name of an overseas LLC. The purchase of which was funded by another overseas entity, which is beneficially owned by Andrew and John Novak."

Spinelli shook his head. "The way you phrase it sounds sinister, but many people own vacation homes in corporate names. There's nothing inherently illegal about that."

"Even if it was purchased by industrialists seeking favorable treatment from our government?"

Spinelli responded with a skeptical look. "Far as I know," he said, "the Novaks are in oil and pharmaceuticals. Lawler doesn't work for the EPA or the FDA."

Reagan did not hear much conviction in the director's protest. "Our government is a tangled web of agencies, bureaucrats, and politicians. If someone is looking for help, the indirect route is logically the most effective." Spinelli did not disagree, so Reagan went on. "Let's say I wanted some off-the-books assistance in getting a new drug approved. The last thing I would do is go directly to someone in the FDA. The trail would be too easy to follow. But I might go to an elected official who is on a committee related to the subject. Or someone in another agency who has friends in other agencies, and so on."

Spinelli slumped in his chair. "The American way."

"Our system may not be perfect, but there are definitely lines that should not be crossed."

"Agreed," the director said. "When I look back, just over these past several days, it makes me ill. Lawler was the one who suggested you keep Khoury overnight."

"Followed by the attack on my home."

"Then there was the incident when Khoury was being transported to the Gables."

"He knew exactly when Khoury was being transferred," Reagan said.

"I was the one who told him," Spinelli admitted, then took a moment to compose himself. "What now? I understand both men are being held by the Bureau."

"Correct," Kenny said. "The early report is that Turnquist wants to make a deal."

"At the end of the video," Reagan said, "you could see Turnquist telling Lawler to keep his mouth shut, because Lawler was already acting like a sniveling child."

"Easy, Reagan," Kenny said.

"Sorry, sir, just calling it as I see it."

"I just watched it," the director said. "You're not wrong."

"This is just a guess," Reagan continued, "but Turnquist probably figured Lawler will go on talking, so he's trying to sell out before it's too late."

"Not a bad assessment," Spinelli agreed. "Maybe between the two of them we can move higher up the ladder, get to the people pulling the strings."

"My thought precisely," Reagan said.

Spinelli studied him for a moment. "You think you know who those people are."

"Yes, sir, I do."

"And you have a plan, I take it."

"Yes, sir," Reagan repeated, "I do."

CHAPTER SIXTY-SEVEN

New York City

It was time for Reagan and Erin to get back to New York City. Reagan had not been there since he left for London. Having returned from England without his travel bag, the small selection of emergency clothing he kept stashed at Carol Gellos' apartment was wearing thin. Erin also needed a change of clothes, as well as to stop by her office and take some time to decompress.

These past several days in D.C., the Gables, and Langley had been draining. Reagan was accustomed to intense action, but that normally occurred overseas, not on his home turf. The United States had enemies around the world, and he was sworn to gather intelligence that would prevent malicious actions being launched against America while doing his best to bring down the offenders. A different sort of action than required by the treachery of people like Victor Turnquist and Ross Lawler, who were enemies acting from within.

Reagan now understood that they were working from inside our own government, destroying the fabric of our principles, compromising our values, and violating the tenets of our Constitution—all from within. Worse than that, there was no indication their betrayal emanated from any ideological belief. It appeared they were nothing more than mercenaries, traitors who were highly placed in our bureaucracy, willing to sell the country out for money and power, without a scintilla of morality between them.

Having successfully unmasked Lawler and Turnquist, there were others who would be watching, and he wanted to flush them out of the weeds, like a pheasant hunter moving ever closer to his prey.

In the past several days, Reagan had worked hard to paint a target on his own back and then leave his calling card—such as with those guards at the Janus Building, for instance. He had purposely insulted the wealthy and powerful Novak brothers, given the mysterious Anatole Mindlovitch something to think about, and threatened a stone-cold killer in the person of Bogdan Paszek. Although the arrest of Lawler and Turnquist was being kept under wraps for now, with the kind of contacts they had, that group—the Novaks, Mindlovitch, and Paszek— would inevitably be getting the news straight away. It was going to be interesting to watch their respective actions—and, more importantly, reactions—and Reagan had bought himself a front row seat for himself.

Reagan decided to drive back to Manhattan from Washington and borrowed an Agency car for the trip; he did not want Erin to have to deal with any emotional distress from walking back into Union Station, and he did not favor the constraints of train travel, not with so much going on.

During the four-hour drive north, he and Erin had enough to discuss. As usual, her insights were spot on and her advice invaluable. At one point she again broached the difficult subject of Connie Malone.

"I know how you feel about her," Erin said. "But you can't blame yourself and you can't take it personally."

"It's clear to me they tried to kill Malone and now Connie is fighting for her life. I was the one who brought Derek into the line of fire, so who do I blame if not myself? And yes, I admit it, I take Connie's poisoning very personally."

"You won't be any help to them if you lose your objectivity."

He took his eyes off the road to have a look at her. "I'm listening," he said.

"I love you, Nicholas. And I believe you love me. Although, as love affairs go, you can be distant, withdrawn, and a real nuisance."

"I get it, you're trying to cheer me up."

"No, I'm trying to make a point."

"That you'd rather be involved with an investment banker?" Reagan asked.

"Would he be really rich?"

"Filthy."

Erin sighed. "Too boring for me."

"You said you were going to make a point," he reminded her.

"The point, Nicholas, is that you are at your best when you do what you do dispassionately. Logically. When you are thinking clearly. As I've said many times, those qualities do not generally make for a warm and nurturing personal relationship, but they are necessary for you to perform your job effectively. To survive," she added more softly. "Does that make sense."

"Yes, doctor, it does."

"Good, because you won't be any help to the Malones, or yourself, if you lose sight of your most valuable skill." She paused, expecting him to ask which of those she meant, but he stayed quiet. "The ability to manage your emotions in any situation."

"Except one," he said with a slight grin.

"Thank goodness for that," she responded with a smile.

When they arrived in Manhattan, their first stop was Erin's brownstone apartment building on West 76th Street. Reagan parked illegally, pulled down the visor with federal credentials attached, and escorted her upstairs—more about safety than chivalry.

"I'm going to arrange my clothing and take a long shower," Erin told him. "Then I'm heading to the office for a quick visit."

"Wish I could join you. For the shower, I mean, but we both have things to do. How about dinner at eight?"

"Done," she said, kissed him on the lips, and he left, having a good look up and down her street before heading out.

He had indoor parking at his place on East 55th Street so, after dropping the car off in the underground garage, he took the elevator up to the lobby, picked up more than a week of mail, then got back on and rode to the sixth floor.

Riffling through the bills and advertisements, he got to his apartment, put the key in the door and stepped inside.

Even from the entry foyer he could see the place had been tossed.

Quietly closing the door behind him, he silently engaged the inside security bolt. If someone was still inside, he wanted to keep them here. Then he removed the Walther PPK that was holstered inside his jacket.

Placing the mail on a glass etagere to his right, he moved forward a couple of steps with all of his senses on alert, then cautiously went past the dining area into the living room. It appeared everything had been turned inside out. His black leather couch was pulled apart, the cocktail table shoved aside, two chairs overturned, even the Asian area rug lifted and yanked out of position.

Reagan moved cautiously toward the bedrooms. Standing in the hallway, where he could get a good look inside both, it appeared they were even worse. The mattress in the master bedroom was upended, closets and dressers invaded, clothing scattered all over the place.

The second bedroom, which he used as his office, had been ransacked. His filing cabinets had been emptied, the leather chair knocked over, his desk searched, papers strewn across the room. Whatever they were looking for, it appeared this was the room where they thought they would be most likely to find it.

He remained quiet, his movements studied. He was still not certain the intruder had gone and, if an attack was coming, he was going to be ready. He next checked the master bathroom, then the guest bathroom, and finally the kitchen, ready for an assault to come from any corner of the apartment.

But none came.

Convinced he was alone, he went back and repeated the search of every room and closet. It appeared there was no place that had not been invaded.

He ended back in his office, where the intruders had ripped through and savaged the most intimate details of his private life. His writing, letters, even personal souvenirs had been examined. It left the apartment with an eerie coldness, as if he himself had been stripped and searched by faceless strangers, then left alone to suffer the sense of violation and indignity.

He went to the bathroom, placed his gun on the counter, and leaned over the sink to splash cold water on his face. He had a look in the mirror, staring at himself for a moment, studying his dark features, preparing himself.

Back in the bedroom, he sorted through the clutter of shirts and trousers that were scattered across the floor and put together a clean outfit of gray slacks, a long-sleeved black polo sweater, and black loafers. After a hot shower he quickly dressed, then returned to the living room to begin putting things together.

"What the hell did they think they'd find?" he asked aloud, knowing whatever it was, they did not find it.

CHAPTER SIXTY-EIGHT

New York City

More than an hour later, after doing his best to return his living room and bedroom to habitability and his office to a state of usefulness, Reagan's first call was to Carol Gellos. He did not want to upset Erin, and this was not something Brian Kenny was going to help him with.

"Sorry to be so obvious," Gellos said after he described the mess he had found, "but is anything missing?"

"Not that I can tell, although this was not a very professional job."

"How so?"

"I have a safe in the ceiling of my master bedroom closet. It's behind a sheetrock panel, so it's not immediately visible, but that wasn't even touched. Then there was the way they tossed things around, more haphazard than organized."

"I get the picture. What's your best guess of what they wanted?"

"Malone gave me something a couple of days ago. Haven't even mentioned it to you since I'm not sure how important it will be to us. Medical findings about that drug *Neulife* that Novak Pharma is developing."

"You told me about the drug."

"Malone says there are test results that were subsequently altered. He has the original data, date stamped before they made the changes. Could be embarrassing for the Novaks."

"Embarrassing or a game changer?" Gellos asked.

"I have no way of knowing, but Derek certainly thinks it's a big deal. I just find it hard to believe that's what they came after."

309

"Why?"

"First, Malone only gave it to me a few days ago, when I was still in D.C. I didn't have time to bring it here until today."

"They would have no way of knowing when he gave it to you, or where you might have left it."

"Fair enough, but then, it's only a copy. Malone has the original hidden away somewhere, and there may be other copies."

"They may be planning to collect them all, Malone's original and all the copies."

"That's a good point," Reagan conceded, "but copies would not be as persuasive as the original."

"True enough. Anything else you can think of they might have wanted?"

"That's all I've been thinking about for the past hour. It's not as if I keep classified documents in my apartment."

"Unlike certain other people," Gellos said with a laugh, then thought it over. "Maybe they were just sending you a message. Especially after you stuck your finger in their eyes at the charity event. Then we rousted Paszek and beat down those two clowns at the Janus Building."

"You think this is all about the Novaks."

"Of course, what do you think?"

"I think I agree, which means you also need to watch yourself."

"I'm on it," Gellos said.

"How do you think they found my apartment? Nothing is listed in my name."

"Lawler," she replied casually.

"You're probably right. If they could find my place on the Chesapeake, they could find me here."

"Which raises another thought. Maybe they weren't looking for a *thing*, maybe they were looking for *you*." She paused. "Where's Erin?"

"I dropped her at her place more than an hour ago. She was changing and heading to the office."

"Call her," Gellos said.

CHAPTER SIXTY-NINE

Washington, D.C.

After considerable debate between the brothers, the Novaks had finally agreed to meet with Paszek.

As Andrew said, "He is still our head of security."

John could not disagree.

Given the recent developments, they preferred a clandestine get together, selecting a small building they owned in Alexandria that would be undergoing renovations and was presently vacant.

As was their custom, the Novaks made a punctual arrival. As was his, Paszek was early.

The three men met on the second floor where there was a large drawing table with architectural plans and a number of chairs. None of them sat.

"Let's get right to it," Andrew said. "What the hell is going on, Bogdan?"

"Could you be more specific?" Paszek asked in his Eastern European accented English.

"Yes, I can. Let's take it in a reverse order of importance, beginning with two of your security guards being beaten to a pulp in the lobby of our building the other night."

"Nicholas Reagan. Claimed to be a federal agent. Left a card to that effect."

"We've heard," John told him.

"He's actually CIA. Accompanied by his woman partner, identified as Carol Gellos. She resides in D.C."

"Tell us something we don't know," Andrew demanded. "Such as, what level of security are you providing if two people can walk into our lobby and beat the living shit out of two of the men who are supposed to be providing the first line of security for our building?"

Paszek stared at him. "These were not just two people, Mr. Novak."

"All the more reason for our concern," John told him. "Your men are also supposed to be professionals. We don't need them to protect us from the average man on the street, do we? We can engage some rent-a-cop company for that level of safety."

"I will increase the staff and terminate those two individuals," Paszek said.

"All right," Andrew replied with a frustrated sigh. "Tell us about Connie Malone."

"She's at WebStar Hospital, likely to die from a dose of botulism."

"Damnit," John said, "tell us how she got there."

Paszek remained calm as he said, "I have already explained. The cocktail was delivered to Dr. Malone. How his wife came to drink it rather than—"

"We've got all that," Andrew said. "We're talking about the expected standard of performance. In this instance, why did your man leave before seeing his task though to the end."

"He served the drink. If the Malones switched glasses, what should he have done? Return to the table and say 'Excuse me Dr. Malone, you're supposed to take the cocktail with the poison, not your wife.'"

"Spare us the sarcasm," Andrew said. "Are you aware Derek Malone came to our office the other day and threatened our lives. Once again walking right past security."

"He has a pass," Paszek reminded them, "which you have not rescinded."

"Well rescind it now," Andrew ordered.

"Consider it done," Paszek said, his coolness only serving to further infuriate his employers.

"Let's get to the main point," John suggested.

"Yes," Andrew agreed. "Lawler and Turnquist have been arrested, are you aware of that?"

Paszek blinked for the first time. "When?"

"Yesterday," John told him. "Your friend Reagan set them up. Not only that, the authorities have Khoury back in custody."

"This I did not know," Paszek admitted.

"Well you know it now," Andrew said. "What do you propose to do about it?"

Paszek appeared to be considering his options. "Where are Lawler and Turnquist? Have they been released?"

"Released?" John asked as if it was the most ridiculous thing he had heard in a week. "There has not even been a formal announcement they were taken into custody."

"Word is they'll be charged with some sort of sedition," Andrew added. "They're going to be held without bail."

"Do we know who's holding them?"

"Our source tells us it's the FBI, which also now has Khoury."

"Making them almost impossible to reach," Paszek said, sounding more like he was thinking out loud than making a statement.

"That's our assessment," Andrew agreed. "What do you suggest?"

"I assume you want all three of them eliminated."

"Obviously," John replied. "You've already bungled two attempts to get rid of Khoury...."

But before he could give further vent to his anger, his brother reached out and touched his arm. John instantly became silent.

"You failed to take care of Khoury when he was in an isolated house on the Chesapeake and then on a quiet country road here in Virginia," Andrew said. "How do you propose to handle this while all three men are in federal custody? And, I am compelled to add, Lawler and Turnquist may already be trading information in the hope they can buy their freedom, or at least a reduced sentence."

Paszek smiled. "Trading. That's the important word here."

The brothers exchanged a glance but waited before reacting.

"This government does it all the time, exchanging dangerous criminals for worthless athletes or stupid tourists. Imagine what they would do to protect the secrets held by some of their most valuable operatives."

"You're saying—" Andrew began, but Paszek cut him off.

"You know exactly what I'm saying. They've taken two of your assets, as well as Khoury. That poses a danger to you because of what they know and what they might reveal. Reaching any of those three while in custody is impossible, as you say."

"Agreed," Andrew said.

"But taking some of their own so we can make a trade, that could be the answer."

Now Andrew and John looked at each other full on, before the older brother turned back to Paszek and replied.

"You're talking about kidnapping federal agents? That's insane. Even if you can make a trade, once it's done, they'll put us in jail and throw away the key."

Paszek smiled. "Only if they're able to prove who was behind the abduction. Which they will not. There will be no connection with you, because this is going to be the last discussion we ever have on the subject."

"What about the media? Bad publicity for us can be as bad as..."

"Who are the authorities going to tell?" Paszek asked with another grin. "You think they're going to let it leak that their agents were taken and then traded for criminals?"

"You already tried something like this, with that woman at Union Station."

Paszek waved that away, saying, "They were amateurs. This time I will handle things personally."

Andrew began nodding slowly.

"What do you think?" John asked him.

"I think it's worth a try. But if this is the last we talk of it, let's discuss the details because this time, Bogdan, there cannot be any mistake, none at all."

CHAPTER SEVENTY

WebStar Hospital, Washington, D.C.

Sitting at his wife's bedside, Derek Malone was as distraught as he had ever been. Even with his sons Michael and Jason there, he was consumed by sadness, guilt, and concern.

The three of them were in Connie's private room, the incessant beeping of the life support equipment providing a grim soundtrack to this unfolding tragedy.

Since Dr. Cooper and his colleagues from the CDC administered the antitoxin, Connie Malone had shown little sign of progress. Both Cooper and Malone's friend, Dr. Sahith Kumar, assured the family that the serum had effectively stopped the spread of the poison, which was as positive as they could be. As both physicians had repeated over the past few days, the ultimate prognosis depended entirely on Connie.

Malone and the treating neurologists were all convinced his wife could hear what was going on around her, and Derek spent hours speaking to her in soothing tones, encouraging her to keep fighting. He read to her from books he knew she enjoyed, as well as passages in the Bible. Neither of them had ever been particularly religious, but God could make His presence felt in the direst of circumstances.

"Dad," Michael said, as he placed a hand on his father's shoulder, "you should go back to your hotel and get some rest. Jason and I will stay here with mom."

Derek looked up at his son, his eyes moist, as he said, "I can't leave her son. I'm the one who should be in that bed, not her."

"Neither of you should be here," Jason said, "but we'll deal with all that later. For now, mom needs you to be at full strength. I'm sure that's what she wants."

Malone slowly shook his head as he turned back to his wife. Reaching out, he gently took her hand in both of his. "You don't want me to leave, do you sweetheart?"

And then, in response to the question, Connie squeezed his fingers.

CHAPTER SEVENTY-ONE

New York City

Reagan ended his discussion with Carol Gellos and immediately called Erin. He did not want to alarm her, but he needed to be sure she was safe.

"Missing me already?" she asked.

"I am. Everything good?" he asked.

"Everything's fine. I took some time arranging my wardrobe, had a shower, just about to head to the office."

"You're still in your apartment."

"Obviously. What's up with the monotone, Nicholas?"

"Nothing, sorry, just feeling a bit distracted. How about we have lunch?"

She treated him to one of her musical little laughs. "I would love to, but I have to show my face at work or they're going to think I retired."

"They know where you've been, Erin."

After a brief pause, she said, "True enough, and you obviously have something on your mind. Where do you want to meet?"

Reagan managed to smile at how well Erin knew him. "I'm coming to pick you up. Don't leave and don't answer the door to anyone but me."

"Nicholas..."

"Just wait for me, I'm on my way."

Reagan wasted no time driving across town, then ran up the stairs to Erin's apartment. Ringing her bell, he said, "It's me."

"How do I know it's really you?" she asked before opening the door.

"Come on, Erin."

"Sorry, couldn't resist." Opening up, she saw the look on his face. "You need to tell me what's going on."

"I will. Let's get in the car."

As they drove north, toward the Bronx, Reagan described what he found when he returned home.

"You really think they were after the papers Derek gave you?"

"Maybe, but I'm not convinced."

"Where are the papers now?"

"I put them in the safe."

Erin nodded. Then she asked, "Why would they go to all that trouble to retrieve a copy?"

"Precisely."

"Unless they're going after the original as well."

"The thought has crossed my mind."

"You've got to warn Derek."

"I know," Reagan said, "but with everything he's facing right now, I hate to create another issue for him."

"You have to tell him."

Reagan took a deep breath and exhaled slowly. "You're right."

"Let's assume for a moment these medical records are not what they were looking for. What else could they have wanted?"

"I don't know," he admitted. "It might've just been a fishing expedition, although that seems unlikely. Maybe they wanted to send a message."

They continued their discussion until arriving on Crescent Street, in the Arthur Avenue neighborhood, where Reagan parked around the corner from Roberto's. Consistently rated one of the best Italian restaurants in New York City, the place was typically jammed for dinner, but it was usually easy to get a table for lunch.

Inside, Reagan was greeted by one of the waiters he knew who showed them to a spot in the rear of the small dining room. They were seated, Erin ordered a glass of rosé, and Reagan asked for a Belvedere, straight up with onions.

Then she said, "Time to call Derek?"

Reagan nodded, pulled out his cell, and punched in the numbers. When the connection was made, he expected to hear Malone answer in a somber tone suited to the hospital setting and dire circumstances.

Instead, Derek sounded newly energized as he said, "Nick, I'm so glad you called, you're not going to believe this." Then he told him what happened. "At first no one believed me. The doctors came in, said it might just have been a muscular contraction. But I told them to watch, and asked Connie to squeeze my hand twice if she could hear me. And she did," he announced triumphantly, and Reagan could hear him begin to cry. "She can hear me," Malone said through his tears. "Can you believe it? And she can move her hand. Do you have any idea how incredible this is?"

Reagan was not sure of the medical implications, but felt himself choke up as he managed to say, "Miraculous."

"Exactly the word," Malone said.

Erin was watching Reagan, able to get most of the exchange. She lifted her hand to her mouth, unable to speak.

"This is the beginning of her recovery," Reagan said.

"Yes, yes, that's just what it is," Malone told him. "Thanks so much for calling to check in, I've got to get back in the room with the doctors. I'll call you later."

"Please do," Reagan said, but Derek had already ended the call.

"Oh my God," Erin said.

They were silent until their drinks came. Then they toasted Connie's health and Reagan had a large swallow of vodka.

"Now what?" Erin asked.

"First thing I'm doing is calling Dick Bebon and getting a protective detail assigned to Derek and Connie. I also want guards posted at his home in Palm Beach." He paused to have another taste of the frosty cocktail. "I told Director Spinelli that we have a plan, and now I'm convinced it's the right course."

"Care to share?"

"Carol and I need to find Bogdan Paszek," he said. "That's how we start."

CHAPTER SEVENTY-TWO

En route to Aspen, Colorado

Reagan was convinced that Bogdan Paszek was the key to bringing the Novaks to justice and ending their treasonous reign of violence in an effort to subvert American democracy. He had no way of knowing that Paszek was already looking for him and Carol Gellos. The only thing of which everyone could be certain is that all roads currently led to the world economic forum about to begin a week-long run beneath the regal mountains in the stylish town of Aspen, Colorado.

Considered by some as only a swanky ski destination, many residents and visitors regard Aspen as even more beautiful in the spring and summer. The crisp air, blue skies, and green hills capped in snow are a veritable postcard. The restaurants and shops epitomized elegance, and there is no lack of activities—from hiking, biking, and kayaking, to golf, tennis, fly fishing, and many other pursuits.

The symposium being held would feature Hollywood celebrities, business titans, and politicians. Reagan had already learned that Andrew Novak would be giving a keynote address; that the notorious enemy of the United States, Klaus Schnabel, would be in attendance; and that Anatole Mindlovitch was scheduled to sit in on a couple of the featured high-octane "talks" that hundreds would pay large sums to attend, hoping to glean a shred of information that would lead to the creation of their own fortunes.

Like many of the rich and famous—who espouse ideals regarding the environment, but eschew any sort of transportation that might bring them into contact with the lower classes—Reagan, Gellos, and

Brandt flew into the small, mesa-top airport in a private jet. Their flight was not arranged by the Agency, but by Derek Malone who was personally hosting them.

Over the past two days, Connie had made dramatic strides in responding to sounds and touches that astounded all of the doctors and nurses caring for her. She had yet to open her eyes, which continued to be a heartbreak for her husband and sons, but had already developed a means of communicating based on the number of times she could squeeze a hand. The neurologists agreed that Derek's enthusiasm helped to feed Connie's efforts to emerge from her comatose state, but cautioned him to be patient, which had never been Malone's strong suit.

His improved attitude persuaded Reagan it was time to let him know about the burglary of his apartment, his concerns for the Malones, and the arrangements he had made for their safety.

As raw as his emotions had been over these last several days, Malone took a deep breath, fearing he might tear up when Reagan described what he had done. "There are not many friends like you, Nick," he finally managed to say. Then, after another pause, Malone asked, "Now what are we going to do about these goddamned Novaks?"

"My team is heading out to Aspen for the forum. Everyone we need to deal with will be there. Seems like the place to be."

"For me too," Malone said.

"No way. This is going to be dangerous, and I've already put you and Connie in harm's way. Enough is enough."

"Bullshit," Malone said. "These bastards tried to kill me, they almost killed Connie, and if you're going to take them down I'm going to be there to help." He paused. "Connie is improving, my sons are there with her, and I know she would want me to go. I'm a hands-on guy, Nick, you know that about me."

"Derek, I appreciate your feelings, but it makes no sense."

"I thought you understood me better. This is my fight now, more than anyone else's." For the first time in almost a week, Derek Malone managed to laugh. "Not to mention, I have my jet to get us there, which will make it a lot easier for you to bring whatever you need, if you know what I mean. And I'll book us into the best hotel in town."

"I appreciate it, I really do. Anyway," Reagan added with his own chuckle, "everything in town was already booked ages ago. We're staying down the road, at a motel in Glenwood Springs."

"You forget who you're talking to, young man. I'll get us into The Little Nell, don't you worry. Meanwhile, I'll get my people to fuel the jet and be ready to pick us up here in D.C. When are we leaving?"

On one hand, Reagan knew that having Malone along might create a potential liability. On the other, it was helpful to be able to load their arsenal of weapons on a private flight, which the Agency had not yet authorized for them. And he knew his friend to be resourceful enough to provide them access to events where they might not otherwise be able to get in. Security at all the gatherings during the week would be extremely tight, and flashing federal credentials was the last thing they wanted to do.

That was how the three CIA agents came to be seated with Dr. Derek Malone in the cabin of his private jet the following morning, as they flew across the country, discussing what each of them would do when they arrived.

CHAPTER SEVENTY-THREE

Aspen, Colorado

Upon landing, a large SUV picked up the group and took them to The Little Nell, where Malone spoke to the manager and made quick work of checking them all in.

Malone would not say how he managed to get all of them into rooms at the last minute during a week like this, when the entire area was over-run with high achievers who expected to get their way at any cost.

And Reagan did not ask. He just smiled, reminding himself that the elite class, of which Malone was a member, had a way of opening locked doors.

If The Little Nell is not the best place to stay in Aspen, it would be hard to argue where that might be. The rooms are generous in size and well appointed, the suites large and luxurious, and the service impecca-ble. Fine dining is available at the restaurant inside. There is casual fare at the Ajax Tavern outside, where the quality is just as good. And the wine bar off the lobby is as popular a meeting spot as there is in town. The sprawling hotel, along with private residences, is located at the base of the mountain, right beside the base of the Silver Queen gondola, and provides a ski-out and ski-in concierge during the season.

After check-in, they each dropped their bags off in their respective rooms and agreed to regroup in the bar twenty minutes later. Malone had already arranged for a table in the corner and ordered a bottle of Champagne when Reagan showed up.

"I assume this geography suits you," he said when Reagan arrived.

"Perfect."

Gellos and Brandt arrived and they all took seats and began to review their assignments.

"When do we start?" Malone asked.

Reagan placed a hand on Malone's forearm. "As discussed on the plane, you will have an important but limited role. The last thing any of the three of us needs is to be worried about you."

"Trust me, you do not need to be worried about me," Malone said as he sat back with his Champagne flute in hand.

"We know our friends must already be here since Andrew's speech is later today," Reagan said.

"Got a text from New York," Gellos told him. "They have suites at the St. Regis."

"Good information," Reagan said, then asked Carol, "Are we sure that New York is being protected?"

Gellos smiled. "Just as I told you the first two times you asked, she is being guarded."

Reagan nodded. He was still concerned about Erin's safety.

Looking at Malone, Gellos asked, "Were you able to get those tickets to Novak's speech?"

"I got two seats in the front row, right in his face," Malone replied, happy to be back in the mix so quickly.

"Derek and I will be going there together," Reagan told them. "Give our man Andrew something to think about."

"Let's go over what you need from us," Gellos suggested.

Looking at Brandt, Reagan said, "Now that we know they're staying at the St. Regis, you should take a stroll over there. It's not far from here."

"Nothing is far from anything in this town," Malone told them.

"Hang around the lobby or the bar." Lowering his voice, Reagan added, "I assume you'll see the Novaks, but I want to find Paszek."

"Got it," Brandt asked. "Should I make any sort of move if I see him?"

"Follow him for sure, although we assume he'll be tailing the Novaks," Reagan said. "Since Derek and I will be in the auditorium, you can hang back. That'll give you a chance to see how much support they have coming up the rear. Take some photos if you can. The more we know about what we're up against, the better off we'll be. And text me if you see anything important."

"Such as an appearance by Paszek," Brandt repeated.

"Such as."

"You want me on the fringes?" Gellos asked.

"No. You can use the time to pay a visit to that private club at the top of the gondola, where Derek says there's a big dinner tonight after the speeches are done. Should be a lot of key players showing up for it."

"AspenX Mountain Club," Malone said.

"Got it."

"Do your best to get a layout of the area surrounding the building, the main room, the usual," Reagan said. "It will come in handy if that's where you and I decide to make our move on Paszek."

"Consider it done," Carol said. "That gondola looks like fun. As long as you don't mind heights."

"This entire operation is a bit unusual, especially since there's no need for us to be working from the shadows. To the contrary," Reagan said, "we want to be seen. We want them anxious. If possible, we want Paszek and his boys to make the first move."

"What can I do to help?" Malone asked.

"You've already done more than enough," Reagan told him. "Just don't lose your temper, no matter what. And do not, under any circumstances, confront the Novaks. The fact that you're here should be enough to rattle them. And remember what we told you on the plane. If things get hot, do not try and be a cowboy. Duck under a table or behind a rock until it's over."

Malone looked at him. "You know that's not my style, Nick."

"I do know that, but you need to be realistic. I realize you want your revenge, and no one wants you to have it more than I, but we're dealing with trained killers. It is not going to help our cause if you to turn from an asset to a liability. We clear about this?"

Malone knew he was right, frowning as he said, "Aye, aye captain."

"Good. Now let's go upstairs to my room and get ready."

That was where Reagan had left the duffel bag filled with the arsenal they brought. It was time to make their move.

CHAPTER SEVENTY-FOUR

Aspen, Colorado

It was a beautiful spring afternoon as Alex Brandt took a slow walk through the middle of town, from The Little Nell to the St. Regis. The streets were crowded with people eagerly patronizing charming shops, happily purchasing expensive items that ranged from jewelry to clothing to cowboy hats to exclusive cosmetics, their enthusiasm giving the impression that these assorted treasures were only available in Aspen.

Entering the hotel lobby, Brandt surveyed the place and quickly realized that remaining here—despite all of the people coming and going—would leave him looking like some old school house detective. Instead, he found a spot at the end of the crowded bar, which provided a fairly decent line of sight to the hotel entrance. He ordered a beer and settled in to wait and watch.

* * *

REAGAN REALIZED HE WOULD NOT be granted access to the auditorium if he was armed. Extreme measures were being taken to ensure the safety of the privileged throng populating the town this week, meaning that his federal credentials would do nothing more than get him an invitation to leave.

"I won't be surprised if they have us pass through metal detectors to get into some of the restaurants around here," Malone said.

Reagan reluctantly agreed, but for now he had his Walther PPK secured at the base of his spine as they engaged in their own exploration of Aspen. He would drop the weapon off at the hotel before heading to the conference center.

They passed the time, stopping in a couple of shops, checking out menus at a few expensive eateries, and walking through the lobby of the famous Hotel Jerome.

Just a couple of tourists out for the afternoon.

Malone ran into a couple of people he knew along the way, one from Novak Pharma. In each instance he paused, introduced Nick as a friend, then exchanged some pleasantries, after which they walked on.

All the while, each of them felt the clock moving slowly as they approached the time for Andrew Novak's speech.

* * *

"MALONE IS HERE?" Andrew Novak asked his brother for the second time.

They were standing in the bedroom of Andrew's suite as he finished dressing for his appearance, which was less than an hour away. John was already in his suit and tie.

"I just got the message. He flew in with his friend Reagan and some other people."

Andrew was having trouble getting his mind around the idea. "Who, exactly, are these *other people?*"

"One is a woman; we're getting confirmation on her identity."

Andrew waved the notion away with a flick of his hand. "No doubt it's Reagan's partner, something or other Gellos. Half of the tag team that roughed up our security guards."

"In all likelihood," John conceded. "The other was a younger man, no ID on him yet."

"Well let's get one, damnit. What the hell are we paying for?"

"They're on it," John said, then hesitated before going on. "I realize it's unsettling that Malone and his friend would show up here, but why does it matter? I mean, when you think about it, why should we care?"

"You're asking why we should care?"

"I am," John said. "To use the vernacular, brother, if they had something on us they wouldn't bother showing up at this forum. They would be issuing subpoenas, or asking us to come in for interviews, or whatever the hell process they would choose."

Andrew stopped fumbling with his cufflinks and stared at John. "Then why do you suppose they've come?"

"To do exactly what they're doing. To upset us. To make us nervous. To embarrass us. Perhaps to goad us into a mistake. That's why they're here. Isn't it obvious?"

Andrew thought it over, then resumed the insertion of his links a little more calmly. "You may well be right. If either of those idiots, Lawler or Turnquist, said anything damaging about us, there would already be legal action. Not some pathetic attempt at theater by having these people show up here in Aspen."

"That's my point, but it may even be better than that. This may present the perfect opportunity for Paszek to carry out his plan. It's as if they've been delivered to him on the proverbial platter."

Andrew nodded. "Especially since he's already identified them."

"Right."

His shirt now in place, Andrew began knotting his tie, then stopped and looked at his brother again. "What about Malone? Why, in the name of all that is holy, would he have left his wife to come here?"

"For the same reason. Harassment."

"Well said," Andrew agreed, then went back to tying his Hermès silk cravat. "Should we not get rid of that problem at the same time? Derek's become an absolute nuisance."

"Yes, he has," John agreed, "and yes we should. I'll find a way to convey that to Paszek."

* * *

Bogdan Paszek received a text from an unknown number—likely a burner phone—but it contained a familiar code and he immediately understood the message. In addition to abducting two federal agents, the Novaks wanted him to rid themselves, once and for all, of the burr under their saddle named Derek Malone.

Paszek was not happy about this new development. To start with, murdering someone without being caught, in the middle of all these people, with the large police presence and private security forces, was not going to be easy. Not to mention the difficulty in getting rid of the body.

Yet these were only tactical concerns. The truth was, of all the people he had met at the upper levels of the Novak universe, Derek Malone was the man he liked the best. Malone was not like the others, who looked through you rather than at you, those who behaved as if you were not really there. Malone treated everyone the same, no matter how important or inconsequential their positions, no matter how rich or poor. When he asked how you were, he expected an authentic exchange, not just a "fine" or "okay."

When Paszek had received the order to poison Malone, he considered intentionally botching the job, but quickly realized it would be of no use. When the Novaks made a command decision like that, they were not going to be satisfied until the job was completed. The accidental poisoning of Malone's wife had given them pause, not because of guilt—they seemed incapable of that emotion—but because they were concerned that moving too soon against Malone would be unwise. And in that regard, Paszek thought they were right.

Now that they had come to participate in this world forum, the Novaks were apparently annoyed that Malone had put in an appearance and were determined to be done with him.

Too bad, Paszek thought. He had always liked Malone.

CHAPTER SEVENTY-FIVE

Aspen, Colorado

When the others left The Little Nell, Carol Gellos went outside to enjoy the afternoon sun on the patio beside the base of the mountain. At an altitude of over seven thousand feet, the air is thin and the rays intense so, after a restful half hour, she decided it was time to take a ride up the mountain to conduct some reconnaissance of the club where the big dinner was being held that night.

The Silver Queen is the longest single-stage gondola in the world. Each car is designed to take as many as six passengers to the top of Aspen Mountain. In season, skis and poles are neatly tucked into the racks outside the car for the ride, which takes about fifteen minutes. Each of the gondolas glide above tall stands of pine while ascending to the summit, which reach more than eleven thousand feet.

Gellos bought a ticket and joined the queue for the next available gondola. There were not many people in line, and most of those there were in small groups. The attendant pointed Gellos to a spot up ahead and, when the next gondola came around the turn with its door open, she entered. Just before it closed, she was followed in by a small, dark-skinned young man. They sat on the benches opposite each other as the door slid shut and the gondola began its trip up the mountain.

Neither of them spoke for a couple of minutes, until the man smiled at her and said, "Never been on one of these before. They say the views are fantastic."

Gellos looked him over before saying, "Should be."

"They tell me from the top you can see the Maroon Bells Mountains. At least I think that's the name. Let me check." He reached into his jacket pocket, as if looking for a guide book, but pulled out an automatic handgun. "Don't do anything stupid," he told her, his demeanor instantly transformed. "I'm not here to hurt you. I just need to take you to someone who wants to talk with you."

Staring at the gun, which she could see was a Colt 1911, Gellos was feeling less afraid than annoyed. How had she allowed him to get the drop on her? Even as an experienced profiler—or perhaps because of those skills—she resisted the tendency to prejudge people, but there were tells she should have seen coming from a block away. His clothing was more like something a blue-collar laborer would wear, rather than someone sightseeing in Aspen. And his jacket was too bulky for the weather, obviously to hide the weapon. It was possible he could have been heading to work at the club on top of the mountain, but his affect belied that notion. He looked more like a Hispanic gang member than a dishwasher.

"You want to tell me who wants to speak with me?" she asked.

"Not my job. I just need to get you there."

Gellos responded with a thoughtful nod. "I suppose a simple invitation wouldn't have done the trick? They had to send you to pull a gun on me?"

"I do what I'm told."

"Well, aren't you a good soldier." She took a moment to look out the large plexiglass windows at the magnificent surroundings. "Can you at least tell me where this meeting is going to happen?"

"Not my job," he repeated. "My friends, at the end of this ride, maybe they answer your questions."

Gellos stared at him without speaking. If he was telling the truth, that there were others waiting for them at the end of this ride, it was valuable information. It also meant the best time for her to make a move—and she was definitely going to make a move—would be before she got there. With all of the law enforcement and private details blanketing the town below, there was little chance of much help at the mountaintop.

She let a few moments pass as he continued to hold the automatic at arm's length. "These friends of yours, they the people who want to speak with me?"

"Look, all I've got to do is get you there, that's my job. No need for you to..."

Before he could finish the sentence, Gellos lashed out with her right foot, kicking at his hand. Although he did not drop the gun, she knocked his arm far enough off-line to give her time to lunge across the small space and use the side of her hand to unleash a crushing blow across his windpipe.

As he gasped for air, she used her left hand to grab his wrist and keep the gun pointed up and away from her. Then she jabbed her right thumb into his eye, eliciting an anguished cry. Pulling her hand back, she grabbed a handful of his hair and smashed his head repeatedly against one of the gondola's metal supports behind him.

Before he had time to react to any of this, she pulled her Sig Sauer from its holster and pressed the barrel hard against his temple.

"Now drop the gun," she demanded through gritted teeth, "because I don't need to speak with anyone and I'm willing to blow your head off right here."

The man, in a state of pained confusion, did as he was told, and the Colt clattered to the metal floor.

Gellos moved back slowly, her weapon now pointed at his face as she picked up the Colt and sat back down on the bench across from him.

"You made an amateur's mistake," she told him. "Never hold your gun hand outstretched. First, your arm gets tired and second, it makes your weapon vulnerable, as you've just discovered."

The man responded with a scowl.

"We only have a few minutes, and if you want to live to enjoy those fantastic views at the top of this mountain, you're going to start answering some questions. Let's start with, who sent you?"

"Renaldo. I work for him sometimes. He brought me out here for this week, said we have some things to do. I don't know anything else."

"Is this Renaldo the man I'm supposed to speak with?"

He had one hand over the eye Gellos had gouged, using the other to rub the back of his head. "I don't know. Renaldo never tells me much."

"I wonder why," Gellos said. "And who's meeting us at the end of this ride?"

"Renaldo and one of our other guys, I think." He considered that for a moment. "They're not going to like this."

"No? What would they prefer, that you shoot me and send me down the mountain as a corpse?"

"I told you, they didn't want me to shoot you, they just wanted me to bring you to them."

"Why not just wait for me to get off the gondola?" Gellos asked, more to herself than him.

"I don't know. I do what I'm told."

Figuring she had learned as much as she was going to from her new friend, she said, "Well then, I'm telling you to have a nice nap." She stood and, before he could react, cracked him twice on the side of the head with the butt of her gun. As he fell to the side, unconscious, she sat back down and pulled out her cell, dialing Reagan as she wondered what to do about the reception committee that might or might not be waiting for her above.

CHAPTER SEVENTY-SIX

Aspen, Colorado

When Paszek got word from one of his scouts that Malone and Reagan were walking through town, he realized this was yet another complication he could have done without. His assignment was to capture Reagan, but now he had been instructed to kill Malone. No one had told him they were together.

He took out his cell and, calling the Novaks' coordinator for the upcoming keynote address, confirmed that Derek Malone had two front row seats for the event. He realized there was not enough time to arrange anything before the speech, but at least he knew where both men would be for the next couple of hours. Now he had to organize a means of intercepting both of them sometime and someplace after the auditorium emptied.

Knowing that would take every man he had brought with him, he would also need to take personal charge of carrying out his plan.

For now, his focus would remain on the abduction of Carol Gellos.

* * *

REAGAN AND MALONE had quickly tired of the window shopping and people watching, and were taking a circular route back to their hotel.

"I'm going upstairs to call the hospital and check on Connie," Malone said as they came through the entrance. "Then I'll take a quick shower and change into something befitting the honor being bestowed on my former partners."

Reagan nodded. "Guess I'll have to freshen up too. Don't want to embarrass anyone. Meet you in lobby a quarter to, does that work?"

"Perfect," Malone said and turned toward the elevators.

Before Reagan could follow him, his phone rang. Having a look at the screen, he said, "Go ahead, it's Carol." As Malone walked off, Reagan took the call and asked, "What's up?"

"We have a situation, and by my calculation I only have about six minutes before things get really bad, so we need to do something fast." Then she described what happened as succinctly as she could. She finished by saying, "When I get to the top, I have no idea who might be waiting for me."

"Understood. Which means we need to buy time."

"How?"

"Stay on the line, I'm putting you on speaker. I'm in the lobby of the hotel, so I'll head for the base of the gondola and see what I can do." With that, he shoved the phone in his pocket and raced for the back door of the lobby. Taking the stairs outside two at a time, he rushed past the line of people waiting for a ride and reached the young man who was in the booth operating the gondola. "We've got an emergency," Reagan told him. "You need to stop the gondola."

The young man blinked, obviously not knowing what to say. "What's the emergency?"

There was no time for a polite explanation. With his left hand, Reagan pulled out his federal ID, and with his right unholstered the Walther. Keeping the gun discreetly against his side, so the people on the other side of the base could not see, he said, "There's a federal agent up there and she needs you to stop this damn thing right now. Do it."

"I don't have authority to just…"

"I'm your goddamned authority," Reagan said, then looked past the young man to the assortment of buttons and levers on the large control panel. He was no engineer, but there was a large red handle under which a plate clearly said "FOR EMERGENCY USE ONLY." Pushing the operator aside, Reagan reached out and yanked it down, the line of gondolas immediately slowing to a stop. "Now what's the fastest way for me to get to the top of the mountain?"

"Is this really an emergency?" the young man asked, as if already worrying about the report he was going to have to provide when this was over.

"I already told you that. Now how do I get up there?"

The young man shook his head. "People take mountain bikes up…."

"Too slow. What about a dirt bike?"

"They rent them in town," he said with a nervous shake of his head, "but they're not allowed on these trails."

Reagan put his credentials away and pulled out his cell. "You getting all this?" he asked Gellos.

"Most of it," she said.

"I don't have a way to get up there fast enough to…"

"Hold on," Gellos said. "If you can get them to move this thing up around thirty yards, I can climb out onto one of the stanchions. I can see from here they have rungs I can use to make my way down."

Reagan turned to the young man who was still gaping at him. "You heard her. Can you get this thing to move up thirty yards and then stop it again?"

Just then a voice came over the communication system, asking, "What's going on down there, Taylor?"

Before Taylor could respond, Reagan grabbed the mic and said, "Federal agents here. The situation is under control and we'll have you moving again in a minute or so." Turning back to Taylor, he said, "You heard what she needs, now do it."

Taylor did not wait for his supervisor to weigh in. He hit a lever, pressed a large black button, and the gondola began moving slowly forward. After what he judged to be thirty yards he stopped it again.

"That enough, Carol?" Reagan asked.

"Perfect," she said.

By now, people in the other cars hanging high above the mountain were beginning to panic. Dozens of cell phone calls were being made to emergency numbers and Reagan saw two men, likely other employees for the system, hurrying up the stairs with a uniformed police officer in tow.

"Just let me know when you're out," Reagan told Gellos. Then, speaking to Taylor as the three men approached, he said, "You let me do the talking, but don't touch another thing until we hear my partner tell us she's clear."

* * *

GELLOS WAS LESS THAN THRILLED about doing a high wire act more than a hundred feet above the rocky trails below, but she figured it was a better option than being greeted by a group of armed henchmen at the end of the gondola ride. She used the emergency exit procedure to slide the door of the car open and began to climb out. Using the thick cable above to steady herself, she attained a sold foothold on one of the rungs of the support tower, which fortunately faced the upward cars. Reaching out, she had to negotiate a midair lunge, grabbing hold of a rung above her with both hands, steadying herself as she positioned both feet in place.

"Damn," she said to no one, but Reagan heard her on the phone she had placed inside her jacket.

"You all right?" he asked.

"Fabulous. Great views from up here, by the way."

He smiled. "You coming down?"

"Slowly, and one step at a time, I hope."

"You clear of the car?"

"I am. You can start them running again."

"All right, I'm heading up on foot, fastest way for me to get where you are."

"I'll be waiting. For now, I'm going to concentrate on my descent if that's all right. Over and out."

* * *

AS THE TWO APPROACHING EMPLOYEES and police officer were about to reach them, Reagan slipped his Walther back in its holster and pulled out his ID again. Before anyone else could speak, he held up his credentials and said, "I'm a federal agent. We had an emergency that has been resolved by the quick actions of Taylor, here. He should be congratulated. Now I need to get halfway up the mountain to meet another agent, and I want to know if there's a faster way than going by foot?"

None of them seemed to have any idea of how to respond.

"I guess in the winter I could take a snowmobile," Reagan suggested.

"That'd be right," the officer agreed.

"Okay, I guess I'm going by foot, but I'd like to speak with you privately for a moment." Before the policeman could respond, Reagan held out his hand to Taylor. "Nice work," he said. "We'll be sure your superiors know what you did here today."

Taylor shook Reagan's hand, the young man still looking as dumbstruck as he had when all this began just a couple of minutes ago.

Then Reagan took the officer by the arm and led him off to the side. "My partner was on assignment to meet someone at the club at the top of the mountain."

"The AspenX Mountain Club," the officer said.

"Precisely. On the way up she was assaulted at gunpoint in one of the gondolas."

"She all right?"

"She is, her attacker not so much. My partner is a skilled agent."

The officer responded with a dutiful nod.

"In about three minutes the gondola carrying this man will arrive at the top. We believe there will be other men waiting for him, expecting him to have my partner in his custody. You need to understand, these men are armed and, while my partner and I can take care of ourselves, the last thing we want is for any bystanders to become involved. You with me?"

The officer nodded, not admitting that the most violent incident he'd had to deal with in almost ten years on the force in Aspen was a drunken shoplifter who required three officers to handcuff him. "What do you want me to do?"

"I assume there's no police presence at the top of the mountain."

"Only private security at the club, which they've beefed up with all the high rollers in town."

"Got it." Reagan made a show of thinking it over, then said, "I'm not here to tell you your job, but I think you should take a few of your fellow officers and get up there. Just in case."

The man nodded, as if that made all the sense in the world.

"Just to create a law enforcement presence," Reagan told him. "Hopefully that's all you'll need to do to keep the peace."

"On it," the officer said.

"I'm Nick Reagan, by the way," he told him, and the officer gave his name. "We appreciate the help," Reagan said, "but I've got to get going. I've got a long hike ahead of me."

"Try to keep under the line of the cable," the officer said. "I'll try and reach one of the rangers on duty. They get around the mountain on small four-wheelers and might be able to pick you up."

"Much appreciated," Reagan said and headed off.

CHAPTER SEVENTY-SEVEN

Aspen, Colorado

Reagan wanted to reach Gellos as soon as possible, but realized it made no sense to try and run. The mountain was too steep and the path beneath the gondola too long. Pulling out his cell, he said, "Carol, I know you must be climbing down. Don't bother to answer, I'm on my way, will call you back in a few." Then he phoned Brandt.

"I saw the Novaks leave. No sign of Paszek," Alex told him.

"Okay, listen up," Reagan said, then filled him in.

"She's okay though?"

"Seems to be. As I said, I'm on my way."

"What do you need from me?"

"Call Malone, bring him up to speed. Then I want you to go with him to the conference center, don't let him out of your sight."

"Of course."

"Keep him in line, we've got enough to deal with right now."

"What are you going to do when you reach Carol?"

"We're going up. By the time we get there, this guy's friends are going to know he's been taken down and that Gellos is gone. We'll do our best to circle around and take a run at them."

"More of Paszek's men?"

"Obviously."

"Where the hell does he get them all?" Brandt asked. "He should be an Army recruiter for god's sake."

"Alex, I think you just made a joke in the middle of a crisis."

"I think you're a bad influence on me Reagan."

340

"I hope so."

* * *

THE GONDOLA CARRYING the unconscious man had arrived at the top of Aspen Mountain, where the cars slowed for people to step out. The young woman who assisted people with their exits was the first to see him as the door slid open. She gasped but, to her credit, did not scream or engage in any other sort of histrionics. She simply called out the name of the man operating the controls at this end of the line and told him to stop, that there was a body on the floor of one of the cars.

There were not that many people around. It was, after all, spring and not winter and, even with all the activity in town, this was not a busy place this time of day. There were, however, three interested observers standing off to the side. One was Renaldo, which was the name Gellos' would-be captor had given her as the person from whom he took orders. The second was a taller man his friends called Nando.

The third was Bogdan Paszek.

As soon as they realized their colleague had been taken down and that Carol Gellos was nowhere to be found, Paszek led them away from the area toward the building that housed the AspenX Mountain Club.

They walked around to the back and, when they were far enough away from everyone else so they could not be heard, Paszek said, "What the hell is this?" He was staring at Renaldo. "You told me your man was reliable."

Renaldo was literally speechless, shaking his head back and forth as if he wanted no part of this discussion.

"You have nothing to say?" Paszek demanded.

"Maybe he's not dead," Renaldo finally managed to reply.

"I don't care if he's dead or not. Where's the woman? Why am I dealing with this sort of incompetence?"

After a brief pause, Renaldo said, "I have no idea what happened."

Paszek began walking in a small circle, trying to comprehend how such a simple task could have gone so wrong. He finally stopped and said, "She got off. That much is obvious. She didn't just jump, which means she climbed out when the gondola stopped a few minutes ago." Nodding his head in affirmation of his own theory, he said, "That has to be what happened. Which means she's still on the mountain."

"But where?" Nando asked. "This is a huge mountain. She probably headed back down, maybe even got some help from one of the rangers."

Paszek disagreed, having received intel on every member of Reagan's team from Ross Lawler. "She's a CIA field agent, and she's going to come up here to find out where he was taking her. That's her training, that's what she'll do."

"Which means…"

"We need to be ready," Paszek said.

* * *

REAGAN'S HIKE UP THE MOUNTAIN was interrupted by the sound of an approaching ATV. Turning, he saw a four-wheeler being operated by one of the mountain rangers.

Pulling to a stop, the man said, "I assume you're Reagan."

"I am," he replied.

"I'm Adam, senior ranger on duty." He looked to be about thirty, with a solid build and a deep tan they called the Aspen Glow. "Got a call from the locals. How can I help?"

"Glad you showed up, I was starting to huff and puff."

"Mountains are easier to ski down than walk up," Adam said with a smile.

"My partner's further on, I need to get to her."

"I'm told she climbed down from the gondola. Not a great idea."

"She didn't have a lot of options."

"Guess not, from what I hear." With a slight shrug of the shoulders, he said, "Hop on."

They took off, and less than three minutes later they spotted Gellos. She was seated on a grassy area, leaning against the base of the support column she had scaled down.

When they pulled to a stop, she said, "I figured I could wait here as easily as anywhere else."

"Adam, meet Carol," Reagan said.

The ranger smiled at her. "My pleasure," he said.

Gellos returned the smile, then asked, "What now?"

Reagan climbed off the four-wheeler and had a look above them. "Whoever is waiting for you at the top had no way of seeing you leave the gondola."

"Agreed," Gellos said. "When I left the car I had a look up the mountain. No line of sight to the top from there."

"Too many rises and contours," Adam agreed.

"But when my car showed up a couple of minutes ago, with their friend on the floor, they would know I went somewhere."

Reagan nodded. "We need to get up there and find them, whoever they are."

"Paszek's men," Gellos said.

"That's my guess."

"I have no idea who this Paszek fella is," the ranger said, "but I can get both of you up there real quick, if it'll help."

"It would be great if your rig could carry all of us," Reagan said, "but we have to decide on the approach. These people are armed and dangerous, to borrow an old expression. I told that to the officer down below, hopefully he's got some help arriving on the gondola."

Adam nodded. "That's what I was told."

"Thing is, your buggy is a lifesaver, but in the open air it announces it's coming from half a mile away."

"No lie there," Adam said. "Let's start with exactly where you want to end up."

"The AspenX Club. These people are working security for some of the bigshots coming to dinner later. My guess is they'll stay close to that building."

"All right, then we can traverse the side of the mountain over there," Adam said, pointing off to his left. "There are trails we can take toward the top, and as long as we stay on that line, there won't be a lot anyone can hear on the other side." This time he pointed to his right.

"Sounds like a plan," Gellos said, getting to her feet. "And I'd much rather hang on to the back of your ATV than get on that gondola again."

"Climbing down from up there is no fun," Adam agreed.

"Have I mentioned that I hate heights?" she asked.

* * *

THE ASPENX MOUNTAIN CLUB sits at the top of Aspen Mountain. The interior of the building features a refined décor complemented by museum-worthy modern art. The elegant dining room can accommodate dinners for over 120 patrons, and tonight it would be packed with the rich and famous from business, media, and politics. Before that gathering took place, however, Nick Reagan and Carol Gellos had some of their own business to handle.

The ranger brought them up a path that circled toward a chair lift on the far side of the crest, away from the gondola's ending point. Having been given a general idea of what was at stake, Adam killed the engine on his ATV as soon as the mountaintop was in sight, bringing them to an abrupt stop.

"What else can I do to assist?" he asked, as Gellos and Reagan climbed off the vehicle.

"Offer appreciated, and you've already been tremendous help" Reagan said. "But as I've already mentioned, this is a nasty bunch and, with all respect, what comes next is likely to be outside your skill set."

Adam grinned as he pulled back the side of his jacket to reveal a holstered .45 automatic.

Gellos responded with an appreciative smile. "Never assume anything, right?"

"That's what they say," he replied, returning the warm look.

Regan was impressed as well, but needed to get back to business. "Tell you what you can do for us, then. Give us a couple of minutes to make our way over that hill. My plan is to come from around the back of the club building. You can start up again, make a normal appearance at the gondola to see what's happening, find out if any uniforms have arrived on the scene. If you've got the time to hang around, we may need a quick ride down the hill when we're done."

"You're covered."

Reagan thanked him, then he and Gellos started off toward the back of the mountain.

CHAPTER SEVENTY-EIGHT

Aspen, Colorado

Paszek had made his decision. There was going to be no better time and place for him to take Carol Gellos than if she appeared up here, as he expected she would. If she arranged for anyone else to join her, that would be their mistake. If it was Nick Reagan, even better.

He posted Nando off to the side of the huge deck that abutted the club building, facing the Elk Mountain range. He had Renaldo keeping an eye on the back of the building, just in case there was an approach from that side. He remained at the front, with a wide view of the entire area below.

The gondola station. A courtesy shack. And the expanse of mountain below.

If someone was coming this way, he would see them first.

* * *

THE CLIMB AROUND THE BACK was not as easy as Reagan had expected. The area was steep, with rocky footing and aspen trees everywhere. He took the lead as they made their way in a wide arc, through the dense forest, until they saw the club building.

They stopped to gauge their distance and the situation.

It was far too early for any of the dinner guests to have arrived, and staff making preparations would all be inside the kitchen, bar, and dining room. As they moved closer, to get a better view, they saw one man standing toward the rear of the building, leaning on a wood railing, smoking a cigarette.

346

"He looks a lot like my friend in the gondola," Gellos said quietly.

"He certainly doesn't look like he's going to be attending the dinner here," Reagan agreed.

"No telling how many others might be in the neighborhood," Gellos said, "but the way he keeps looking around, I would say he is one of their scouts."

"We're going to find out," Reagan said. "They know you got off the gondola, which left you two choices."

"I'd either head down the mountain, or make my way up here to find out what this is all about."

"And even if they're guessing you took door number two, that doesn't mean they would be expecting me."

"Probably not."

"Think about it. Not a lot of time has passed since you climbed down after the gondola stopped, the gondola started again, and they discovered you had knocked their man senseless when he arrived at the top." Reagan paused for a moment. "Give me two minutes to reach that stand of trees over there," he said, pointing further along the route they had been walking. "Then I want you to head straight for him, like you don't have a care in the world."

Gellos nodded, took out her Sig Sauer, and made sure a round was chambered and the safety was off. Placing it back in her jacket pocket, but keeping her hand on the weapon, she said, "Let's do it."

Reagan moved quickly now, staying low and out of sight, reaching a position that was far to the right of the scout as Gellos began walking through the trees, straight at the man.

Paszek's man, Nando, could not conceal his surprise at the site of this woman emerging from the forest and coming right at him. He tossed his cigarette away and reached inside his coat to draw his weapon. Before he could complete that motion, Reagan had come up from behind him and shoved the barrel of his Walther into the base of the man's spine.

No one spoke as Carol reached inside his jacket and took his weapon, while Reagan checked Nando's ears for any sort of transmitter. There was none.

"Don't say a word I don't ask for, or you're dead. Just nod if you understand."

The man nodded.

"How many men are with you?" Reagan asked.

Nando did not respond, so Reagan pressed hard on his automatic.

"It doesn't matter if there are fifty," Reagan said, "no one is going to get here in time to save you. Now, I repeat, how many others?"

"Two," Nando said as he glared at Gellos, who had taken two steps back and was watching their flanks.

"Names," Reagan demanded. When Nando hesitated again, Reagan said, "This is getting monotonous and you, my friend, are running out of time. Names."

"Renaldo and Paszek."

Reagan and Gellos exchanged a glance before he asked, "Where?"

"Paszek is going to kill me," Nando said, his resolve weakening.

"Not if we kill him first. Where?"

"Renaldo is by the deck, Paszek is out front."

"Any signals, any prearranged plans, or are you just a scout here?"

"Just a scout," Nando said.

"Then let me tell you something," Reagan said. "You're really lousy at your job." Then he lifted his gun and quickly hit him with two blows, one to the base of the neck and one to the side of the head, dropping him to the ground. Reagan then dragged him as close as he could to the railing, where he would not be easily seen.

"We going after Paszek next?" Gellos asked.

"That's my thought. Any ideas?"

"If he really is out front, why don't we try and get in through one of these back doors and come at him from behind."

"I like it," Reagan said. "Let's move."

As they hurried to the nearest door, Gellos said, "What I wouldn't give for a silencer right now."

"You and me both."

Since this was the rear of the building, they assumed the two doors there were intended as access for supplies and employees. They were not surprised to find them locked, nor by the fact that their gentle knocking on one of them was greeted by a security guard.

Reagan once again produced his credentials—wondering for a moment at the last time he had been obliged to show his identification this often in such a short period of time.

"We're federal agents, and we've got a situation here."

The burly man at the door said, "We've heard something's been going down. Unconscious man on the gondola, police officers arriving up here."

Reagan looked the man over, judging his posture and bearing, and said, "You're former military, am I right?"

"Army Ranger," the man said proudly. "Fought in Iraq and Kabul."

"I spent some time in both of those garden spots myself," Reagan said with a smile.

"Army?"

"Yes, sir. My partner too."

Gellos nodded.

"What's your sitrep, and how can I help?"

"Some bad actors up here. We believe the leader we're tracking is at the front of your building. We want a chance to make our way at him from behind. All we need is access through your building and out the front door."

"No trouble inside, then?"

"None."

"Then follow me."

Their guns out of sight, Reagan and Gellos followed the guard through the kitchen, into a dining area, and out to the main entrance.

"This is it," he told them.

"Mind if we have a look through the window before we step outside?"

"Go for it."

Reagan and Gellos each moved to the edge of a window, taking care not to be seen as they peered at the area out front.

"He's not there," Gellos said.

* * *

Paszek saw the police officers climbing off the gondola and knew he could not remain there, loitering in front of the club. There were not many people milling around, and he would make an obvious target for questioning about what he might or might not have seen, a discussion he did not want to have. He took a casual look at his watch, then began walking slowly toward the far end of the building. Around the corner there were a series of decks, the upper levels for outdoor dining, the larger area below where weddings and other events were catered.

Renaldo was standing off to the side of that lower structure, maintaining a good vantage point for approaches from either the front or rear of the club.

"Something happened?" he asked, as Paszek approached.

"Four uniformed cops just got off the gondola, obviously here to investigate."

Renaldo shook his head. "That makes things impossible for us."

"Not necessarily."

He stared at Paszek. "You're not serious? You want us to take a federal agent—assuming she shows up—in the middle of a police investigation, and get her down the mountain without being noticed?"

Paszek knew Renaldo was right. "Damnit," he said, unable to contain his frustration. First his man gets knocked unconscious and the woman escapes. Now they were wasting their time on the top of a mountain with no chance of capturing Gellos. "Let's grab Nando and get the hell out of here."

* * *

The security guard was cooperating, giving Reagan and Gellos the opportunity to look out some other windows in the hope of seeing their man. When the three of them got to the room leading to the upper deck, they saw Paszek with a second man as they started to walk toward the back of the building.

"Time to go," Reagan said.

"Why don't I walk out the door we came in through," Gellos suggested. "You can come around the back again."

"I like it," Reagan told her.

"Anything I can do to help?" the guard asked.

"We don't want anyone getting hurt, but it would be great if you would keep an eye on things as they develop. If things go south, call the police."

"You got it," the guard said.

Gellos ran for the back door while Reagan waited for Paszek and the other man to disappear around the corner. Then he stepped out onto the upper terrace and quietly made his way down the stairs.

* * *

AS SOON AS PASZEK AND RENALDO made the turn, they saw Nando's body on the ground.

"What the hell...." Renaldo began, but stopped as Carol Gellos emerged from the back door, automatic in hand.

"Looking for someone?" she asked.

"You..."

"Not another word and not another step," she told them. "Hands behind your heads or I'll drop you both."

Renaldo turned to Paszek, who was glaring at Gellos.

"You think you're that good from this distance?" Paszek asked her. "Take us both before we pull our guns out and fire back?

"She is," came a voice from behind them, "and I'm even better. Now you heard what she said, hands on your heads. Do it."

Renaldo slowly lifted his arms and laced his fingers together behind his neck. But Paszek wasn't moving.

"You've got nothing on me, you and your CIA. Nothing."

"You tried to poison Derek Malone and almost killed his wife."

Slowly turning to face Reagan, he said, "Prove it."

"One of your men just tried to abduct my partner."

Paszek responded with a nasty smile. "Another claim you can't prove."

"Really? When the idiot you hired wakes up and realizes he's facing thirty years in prison for trying to kidnap a federal agent, believe me, he'll be singing like Andrea Bocelli." Reagan paused, but this time Paszek had no answer. "Then there were those two attempts to murder Khoury, and me in the process, incidentally. And the attack on Erin David at Union Station. Once those two assholes find out you're under arrest, they'll start crooning as well, along with the Novaks' pals Lawler and Turnquist."

Paszek stared at him without speaking.

"What happened, Bogdan? No clever riposte. No snappy repartee? Because I've got another one for you that you're going to love." Reagan waited a beat, before saying, "Milos Gadzinski, and that safe deposit box you two share in Greenwich, Connecticut. The one you keep as your insurance policy."

The reaction was instantaneous, fury coming over Paszek like a storm. He raced forward, oblivious to the automatic Reagan was holding, lunging at him and taking both of them to the ground.

Reagan managed to hold onto the weapon as they went down but did not want to fire it unless he had no choice. He wanted Paszek alive to help him take down the Novaks.

Paszek, meanwhile, felt no such constraints. He had taken hold of Reagan's right wrist, his grip like a vise as he kept the gun pointed away, while he began to pummel Reagan with his right fist.

Gellos came rushing forward, executing a lateral kick across Renaldo's knees, dropping him to the rocky ground where she bent over and disarmed him.

"Don't make a move," she warned him.

Paszek was stronger than Reagan, and fought like a feral animal, but Reagan did what he could to ward off the punches as he made a deft maneuver to roll Paszek onto his back and try to pin the man's right hand to the ground.

Paszek responded with a vicious head butt and an unsuccessful attempt to knee Reagan in the groin. But even with the advantage of his strength and muscled physique, Paszek had made a critical mistake

Reagan had seen all too often in these situations—he was fighting with rage rather than skill.

When Paszek tried to turn them over again, Reagan suddenly let him, the move loosening Paszek's grip on his gun hand, which Reagan brought crashing down on Paszek's head, then hit him a second time. With his adversary momentarily stunned, Reagan used a scissor kick to immobilize Paszek's lower body and then pulled his gun hand completely free.

Pressing the barrel of the Walther into Paszek's forehead, Reagan said, "Stop moving."

Paszek stared up at him. "If you think I'm afraid to die, Reagan, you're very mistaken. But you leave my brother out of this. Do you hear me?"

Staring into Paszek's ferocious green eyes, Reagan did not see or feel him draw a knife from his hip before he used it to lash out at Reagan's side. The wound was not deep, but the thrust was painful, causing Reagan to reflexively pull the trigger.

CHAPTER SEVENTY-NINE

Aspen, Colorado

When Brandt accompanied Malone to hear Andrew Novak's keynote speech, he had no idea of all that was happening on the top of Aspen Mountain. From the look on Derek's face, the young agent's entire focus was on keeping his man from jumping out of his seat and rushing the stage.

Novak's talk was essentially a dull rehash of the questionable ideals being promulgated by those who no longer believed in the basic principles upon which the United States of America had been founded and on which it had been operating, through various edits and improvements, over more than two and a half centuries. Novak promoted impossible standards for climate change that flew in the face of everything he and his brother did to advance their gas and oil interests. He asked why borders are necessary in an age when men, women, and children should come together from all around the world, honoring the planet Earth rather than their own nations—not voicing the proviso that none of the invading hordes should settle in the neighborhoods where the Novaks and their elite brethren resided.

He spoke of all the miraculous pharmaceutical advances realized over the past few decades and the importance of making these drugs affordable to everyone, although never mentioning the high prices and enormous profits reaped by Novak Pharma. Then he congratulated those in the forefront of movements to defund the police, reform bail so that felons could walk free, and to defeat racism and gender inequality, without ever saying a word about the increases in violent crime and the continuing spiral of violence and drug abuse in our inner cities.

Throughout Novak's hypocritical oration, Malone stared daggers at him, in part because of his utter disagreement with everything Andrew Novak was saying, but mostly because he wanted revenge for what Novak and his brother had done to his beloved wife. He was convinced Andrew was doing all he could to avoid his venomous gaze, but there were moments when their eyes met, causing Novak to momentarily falter just a bit in his well-rehearsed presentation.

When the mind-numbing address finally concluded and the audience stood to applaud, Malone got to his feet, fists clenched at his side, and whispered to Brandt, "I would give anything to run up there and wring his fucking neck right now."

Brandt took him by the arm and said, "We'll get him, don't worry. Let's find Reagan."

With that, Alex's phone buzzed and he looked down at the text Reagan had sent:

"GELLOS FINE. PASZEK DEAD. GET MALONE BACK TO THE HOTEL ASAP."

* * *

THE SINGLE GUNSHOT that had ended Paszek's life was enough to bring a host of people running.

The guard inside the building had been watching things play out, and now burst through the door, gun drawn. Three uniformed police officers came from around the side, also armed.

Carol Gellos was already holding up her ID, calling out, "Everything's under control, gentlemen. Federal agents here."

The senior officer was a police captain, and he responded by holding up his left hand, telling everyone, "Let's all lower our weapons while you tell us what happened."

Gellos and Reagan holstered their weapons, and Gellos did as she was asked in her customarily concise manner. She was all about the facts, logical and clear, beginning with the man on the gondola and ending with the bullet to Paszek's head.

When she was done, the police captain moved forward to have a look at the body.

"You say you know who he is?"

"Bogdan Paszek," Reagan told them. "Sometimes the head of a security company, sometimes a paid assassin. As Gellos told you, I was trying to get him under control when he pulled a knife and slashed me in the side."

"And your gun went off," the captain said.

"Wish it hadn't. He would have been a lot more use to us alive than dead."

The captain, who still had his weapon in hand, walked over and nudged the inert form of Nando, who was still lying against the railing.

"Unconscious," Reagan said.

The captain nodded, then looked at Reagan's side. "You're bleeding pretty bad, son. First thing we need to do is get you some medical assistance."

"I can handle that for you," the security guard told him.

"Do it," the captain said.

The guard pulled the radio from his belt and called for help.

Turning to one of his men, the captain pointed to Renaldo who remained kneeling on the ground, and said, "Cuff that guy. Otherwise, no one touch anything."

Reagan gingerly took off his jacket, pain now replacing the initial shock of being stabbed. The left side of his shirt was covered in blood that was running down to his pants. Gellos stepped toward him and gave him a hand sitting up on the nearby steps.

"You all right?" she asked.

"I've been better."

The captain spoke to the guard who had helped Reagan and Gellos. "You see any of this?"

"All of it, and it's just as she described."

"That's helpful, that's very helpful." He had another look around. "We don't get many homicides around here. When we do, it tends to make national news, if you know what I mean."

They all knew exactly what he meant.

"Take photos from every angle," the captain told his men. "I'll call forensics so we can clear out of here as soon as possible. We only have an hour or so before the big gathering here tonight." Then he turned his attention to Gellos. "The guy they found in the gondola. He pulled a gun on you?"

She reached into her jacket and took out the Colt automatic, holding it with two fingers by the handle. "This was his," she said as she passed it to him.

Adam had also arrived, and watched the captain take the weapon from her. "You really are a pro," he said. "Disarming that guy, knocking him unconscious, and then climbing down the tower."

"That's what happened," she told him.

Adam nodded. "I have to say, that's some kind of work. If you ever think about moving to a quiet little resort town, you be sure to give me a call."

Carol looked into his eyes as she said, "Then maybe you should give me your number."

CHAPTER EIGHTY

En route to Norwalk, Connecticut

With Bogdan Paszek dead, Reagan knew there was only one possible path left on his journey to bring down Andrew and John Novak. Unfortunately, he had no idea how things would play out once he reached that destination.

By the time the authorities completed their investigation and cleared the scene outside the back of the AspenX Mountain Club, everyone in town knew that there had been multiple altercations ending in a homicide. As the police captain predicted, word of the situation was already making the evening news across the country.

Brian Kenny succeeded in keeping the names of his two agents out of the story, which was no mean feat since Reagan was the one who fired the single gunshot that brought the entire incident to a conclusion. The local police proved to be extremely cooperative, motivated in part by their desire not to have the matter become more complicated than necessary. A violent death outside the famous private club on the mountaintop was bad enough without adding the intrigue of federal agents in pursuit of assassins and all the rest that went with that. For now, it was being portrayed as a dispute among a group of men that were neither locals nor involved in any way with the world economic forum.

After Reagan received seven stitches for his wound, refusing any painkiller stronger than Advil, he and Carol Gellos got back to The Little Nell without anyone in the media knowing they had been at the center of the entire affair. They met in Malone's room, where Alex Brandt was still keeping his man under wraps.

After all of the details of what transpired in the past hour were dissected, Malone said, "I'm glad he's dead, now let's go after the Novaks."

Reagan, who was doing his best to find a comfortable position in the large armchair against the wall of the sitting room of Malone's suite, said, "We're going after them all right, you just need to be patient. They obviously know Paszek is dead, but these are men who always have contingency plans. Until we find out what those might be, you need to stay away from both them and trouble."

Malone responded with a reluctant nod.

"Right now, we have to get out of town and get you back to Connie. I want Alex to remain at your side until we're sure it's safe. Meanwhile, Carol and I have to make a visit."

"Here? Are you going to confront the Novaks?" Malone wanted to know.

"No, and I'm not telling you anything else, at least not yet. For now, I do need a favor."

"Name it."

"After you and Brandt are dropped off in Washington, I'd like to borrow your plane."

"You got it, but at least tell me where you're going? I'm entitled to that much."

Reagan nodded. "We need to take a quick trip to New Haven."

* * *

THAT NIGHT, AFTER MALONE AND BRANDT deplaned in Washington, the crew refueled and set off for Connecticut. It was just before nine when the driver they had arranged for dropped Reagan and Gellos at the home of Milos Gadzinski.

As Erin and Brandt had described from their research, there was nothing imposing about the colonial-style house, but it was clearly one of the nicer homes in the stylish neighborhood known as Silvermine. Reagan knocked on the door and waited.

When Gadzinski responded, he did not ask who was there, he simply opened the door.

Shorter and less muscular than his brother, he had the same broad features, the resemblance unmistakable. So was the look of sorrow etched into those features.

"You have come to tell me something I already know?"

"No, we've come to discuss what happens next."

Gadzinski looked them over, not with anger but with sadness. "Of course," he said. "And you are…"

Reagan gave their names, then said, "We're agents working for the federal government."

"As he always said it would end," he told them, then without hesitation, invited them inside.

"We can show you our identification," Gellos said as they followed him through the small foyer into a large, comfortably furnished living room.

"There's no need," Gadzinski told her, then pointed them to a sofa upholstered in a dark brown fabric where they sat side by side. He took a seat opposite them in a large wingback chair covered in brocade.

"Forgive my bluntness please, but is there anyone else in the house?" Reagan asked.

"Only my wife. I told her to stay upstairs, if that's all right."

"That's fine."

"Mind if we ask how you heard?" Gellos asked.

Gadzinski pressed his lips together before saying, "My brother knew many people. None of them friends, at least as far as I could tell, but one of them called me to say he was gone."

"Did they provide any details?" Reagan asked.

"They claimed not to have any."

"Do you want to know?"

Gadzinski responded with a sad smile. "I'm not sure. Will it matter?"

"I suppose not."

"Then, may I ask why you've come here?"

Reagan shifted his weight, still trying to find positions where his entire side did not ache. Then he said, "Your brother worked for Andrew and John Novak. I assume you know that."

"Oh yes, I am very aware."

"We have evidence that your brother has engaged in a series of unlawful activities, and we believe these actions were taken at the request of the Novaks."

Gadzinski waited.

"We recently learned that you are Mr. Paszek's brother."

"That was the name he has used for many years, but we are brothers, you are correct."

"We also learned that you maintain a safe deposit box in a bank in Greenwich, that your brother had access to that box, and that the contents likely belonged to him and not you."

"I assume, since you represent the government, that you have the means to discover whether that is true."

"Yes, we can," Reagan told him. "On our way here we made arrangements for that box to be locked, subject to a court order allowing us access. Do you want to tell us what we're going to find?"

Gadzinski looked away, as if he wanted to discuss anything but that. "I told him long ago to get away from those people. I told him it would end badly, that he had enough money, that he did not have to go on working for people like that. But in my brother's mind, it was never enough, there was always more money to be made." He turned back to them. "How much money is enough? When do you realize that there is no price to be placed on your soul?"

Gellos nodded her head in understanding, and Gadzinski replied with a sad smile of appreciation.

"When Bogdan brought me to this country, I thought we could work together. Build a life. Take advantage of the opportunities America offers." He took a moment to shake his head. "But Bogdan never recovered from his experiences overseas. He was trained to be a soldier where killing was part of the job, and that was all he truly knew how to do. We argued and argued about this, until there was no point in further discussion. He stayed away from me, my wife, my children. He was generous beyond all reason, but he was a man without a life of his own. You understand what I'm saying?"

For a moment, Reagan wanted to say that he understood more than this man could realize, but it was Gellos who spoke up.

"We do," she said.

Gadzinski uttered a long, heartfelt groan. "Now he is gone, and you want me to tell you what is in that strongbox he has kept for all these years. Would you like to guess?"

"I assume there's a great deal of cash there," Reagan said. When Gadzinski did not reply, he added, "I'm not interested in the money."

Gadzinski's eyes displayed the light of understanding, but he said nothing.

"Tell us what else is in there. Papers? Thumb drives? Videos? Discs?"

"You are obviously a bright young man and, since you will find out soon enough on your own, I have no reason not to tell you. Bogdan accumulated all of those things. He called that strongbox his safe place. He assured me, if anything ever went wrong, that the contents would be his ticket to freedom. You understand?"

Gellos said, "He was keeping records, proof that would incriminate other people."

Gadzinski nodded slowly. "I think you are correct, young lady. He believed he could buy his way out of trouble because, as he said, they always want the bigger fish. That was the concept. When people like you came for him, he would trade all of that so you could prosecute the bigger fish and let him be."

Reagan sighed. "Sometimes that works, but sometimes it does not."

"It cannot work if you are dead."

"No, it cannot," Reagan agreed.

Gadzinski paused again before saying, "Since you have already guessed all of this, may I ask why you have bothered to come and speak with me?"

"We have a few reasons," Reagan said. "To begin with, it would be better if you bring us to the box and voluntarily turn over the contents. If we have to resort to a court proceeding, there is the possibility the wrong people might find out, regardless of what might be done to seal the record. We are dealing with powerful people, and we want to be certain we have full control of these records before they can make any counter moves."

"The Novaks are very powerful people," Gadzinski conceded.

"Your cooperation will also make things move much more quickly. We can go there before anyone else has an idea of what is going on or who you are. As you know, courts move slowly, regardless of the circumstances."

Gadzinski nodded.

"There is also the matter of any cash that might be in the box. As I've said, that is not our concern. I am not from the IRS or connected to any agency that might be concerned about where those funds end up. From everything we have uncovered, you have never engaged in illegal activities and your only sin may have been that you could not convince your brother to give up the life he had chosen."

"He helped me purchase this house years ago," Gadzinski admitted, "and provided money for my children to go to college. I actually argued with him about both, but he insisted, and I did not have the character to refuse the sort of assistance that enriched life for my wife, my children, and for me. I know that was wrong, but I never took any of the cash from the strongbox. That is the truth."

Gellos said, "We've gathered a great deal of information about your brother, and it appears you and your immediate family were the only people he cared about."

Gadzinski hesitated again as a new wave of grief passed over him. "Can you tell me how he died?"

Gellos began to speak, but Reagan held up his hand. "He made more than one attempt on my life, arranged the attempted abduction of my girlfriend and my partner here. We confronted him."

"In Aspen, the man told me."

"Yes, we've just come from there to meet with you."

"I'm sorry I interrupted, please go on. What happen when you confronted him?"

"I was the one who tried to subdue him. I had my gun drawn and believed he was under control when he pulled out a knife and stabbed me in the side. The gun went off and he died instantly."

Gadzinski fixed him with a knowing look. "Life is strange, young man. When I opened the door to you and looked in your eyes, I knew that you were the man who killed Bogdan."

"For what little it's worth, I wanted very much to take him alive. I wanted him to testify against the Novaks."

"I'm not sure he would have. Not the way he saw himself, you see? I think he really kept all those records to protect me, rather than himself."

"I can understand that," Reagan said.

Gadzinski nodded, as if having made a decision. His features seemed to soften as he said, "Pick me up here, eight-thirty tomorrow morning. I'll take you to the bank."

Reagan and Gellos exchanged a look. Then she said, "We've made special arrangements with the bank. If it's not too much of an imposition, we'd like to go there now."

Gadzinski did nothing to hide his surprise. "My brother was right."

"About what?" Reagan asked.

"The power of the government. Even in what everyone claims to be a democracy."

Reagan did not argue the point. Instead, he said, "Better bring a bag with you." When Gadzinski responded with a confused look, he said, "I told you, I don't care about the money, and only the three of us will be in the room when the box is opened. Understood?"

"I do."

"Good, because you're never going back there after tonight," Reagan said.

CHAPTER EIGHTY-ONE

CIA Headquarters, Langley, Virginia

The following afternoon, the entire team was assembled in the conference room down the hall from Brian Kenny's office, the DD at the head of the table.

Reagan, Gellos, and Brandt were there, along with Erin and Sasha.

Kenny looked to Erin, who said, "First things first. I just got off the phone with Derek, and it appears Connie is going to be all right. The doctors are amazed at the progress she's making. They believe it was all about getting her the antitoxin serum in time." She paused. "Derek is convinced that it's all about the fighter in Connie. I agree with him."

As the others voiced their relief and gratitude at hearing the news, Reagan could not even bring himself to speak.

"Let's get to this business about Bogdan Paszek," Kenny told them.

"It's really about the Novaks," Gellos corrected him. "His strongbox was filled with all kinds of goodies. He'd been secretly taping his discussions with Andrew and John for years. There are even some videos. The records he kept are also a bonanza, but nothing like hearing the orders they gave."

"We've only begun compiling things," Sasha told them, "but he was very organized. Some of the recent conversations are dynamite, some go back over years."

"Share some highlights," the DD said.

"The attack on Reagan's house last week, when he and Alex were guarding Walid Khoury? There's an audio tape of all three of them

365

meeting, where they gave Paszek instructions to kill Khoury and any witnesses. They were the ones who gave him Nick's address."

"Which they obviously got from Ross Lawler," Reagan interjected.

"Same with the shooting near the Gables," Sasha told them. "Andrew Novak can clearly be heard on a phone call giving Paszek the time and address where the Agency car would arrive."

"He ordered the kidnapping?" Kenny asked.

"Hell no," Sasha said. "He told Paszek to liquidate everyone at the scene. Even referenced the earlier incident at Reagan's house. Told him in no uncertain terms not to screw up again."

"For careful men, they certainly made some big mistakes," Gellos observed.

"They not only trusted Paszek, but they underestimated him as well," Reagan said.

Kenny nodded. "Probably figured he was in even deeper than they were, since he and his men were the ones pulling the trigger."

Recalling what Gadzinski told them, Reagan said, "They forgot how the world works. If things went sideways, Paszek was betting he could always make a deal to save himself by giving up the big fish."

"He got part two of that equation right," Gellos said. "He just didn't live long enough to see it all the way through."

"I wonder if he believed he ever would," Reagan said.

The others looked at him as he turned to his partner.

"Remember when we confronted him at the gala?"

"I do," Gellos said.

"He was a pretty cool customer."

"Very."

"Even when we had the drop on him in Aspen. He never made a move, not until I mentioned his brother's name."

"You're right. That's the moment he flew into a rage."

"When he came at me, he had to know he had no chance. He was a professional. I mean, whatever he might have done to me, you were standing there with a gun."

"His brother," Gellos said. "He only lunged at you after he realized we knew about his brother."

Reagan nodded. "They were the only decent thing in his life, his brother and his family. Paszek had to know he was done back there in Aspen, meaning…"

"He didn't want his brother implicated."

"Precisely. He left him the money, the evidence he could trade if needed, and a road map to the Novaks."

Gellos said, "That was his real plan."

"Yes," Reagan said. "The box was always about his brother Milos."

The group spent the next hour reviewing the available evidence.

Lawler and Turnquist, still in FBI custody, were trying to outdo each other with offers of information in exchange for reduced sentences. Now, having all of the material in Paszek's safe deposit box, Reagan maintained that they did not need either of them to convict the Novaks.

"The only worthwhile intel they can provide would be the names of other traitors imbedded in our government," he said, and Kenny agreed.

After being shown evidence that their leader was dead, the two men who had tried to kidnap Erin were also willing to talk. It seemed they were more afraid of retribution from Paszek than any sort of prosecution by the feds. Unfortunately, their chain of communication did not extend above orders they received from him, so their testimony was not likely to reduce their time in jail.

The Bureau had identified the man who poisoned the drink Connie Malone had mistakenly ingested and, with Paszek gone, he was willing to make a deal. During discussions about the plan with Paszek, they learned the source of the botulism he had used—Malone's old friend and colleague, Dr. Phillip Roberts, had provided the lethal dose.

Derek Malone provided a couple of additional bombshells. First was about Novak Pharma and the test results for *Neulife* they were falsifying—the data he had shared with Reagan—while the Novaks were paying off any number of people to move their application forward. Second, as the Novaks were giving lip service to a "green agenda,"

Malone had managed to obtain reports on their plans to corner the market for mining lithium, which would be dependent on employing illegal child labor, destroying the surrounding agricultural areas, and decimating adjacent water tables.

By the time the group was done discussing and compiling evidence, there was no one in the room unwilling to take Andrew and John Novak apart, piece by piece.

The intercom buzzed, Kenny picked up the phone, listened, then announced that they had visitors.

There was a knock on the door, and Dick Bebon walked in with two of his most trusted FBI agents, one of whom was carrying a large briefcase. After introductions, Bebon and his men sat down.

"You get the warrant?" the DD asked.

"I did. Now you show me yours and I'll show you mine."

CHAPTER EIGHTY-TWO

The Janus Building, Washington, D.C.

It was nearly four in the afternoon when the joint task force descended on the Janus Building, several of the men and women with guns drawn, just in case. For good measure, Kenny and Bebon had provided advance word to various contacts in the media, about what they referred to as, "A developing story of national interest." A crowd was already gathering outside.

There were two security guards at the front desk who stood up as more than two dozen federal personnel poured through the front door. Bebon was in the lead, flanked by two armed agents.

He told them, "Sit down, put your hands on the desk, and do not speak or move." They did as they were told, as others in the large atrium also stopped in their tracks. Holding up the search warrant he had obtained earlier that day from a cooperative judge, Bebon said, "No one is to leave this building until we give permission. This is a legally authorized federal search. Unless anyone wants to face immediate arrest for obstruction, you will do as you are told."

No one responded.

Filling all three elevator cars, Bebon and most of his people headed to the top floor where the Novaks, having received no warning of what was going on downstairs, were in their offices. As the elevator doors slid open, Bebon held up his badge and hollered, "Federal agents with a search warrant. No one is to touch a computer or a phone or you will be subject to immediate arrest." Turning to the team around him, he said, "Get to work."

The Novaks, having heard the commotion, came into the corridor. "What is this?" Andrew demanded. "This is…"

But before he could continue, Bebon said, "Andrew Novak, you're under arrest for conspiracy to commit murder, conspiracy to murder a federal agent, conspiracy to kidnap, conspiracy to defraud the FDA, domestic and international terrorism, sedition, and a long list of other charges I don't have the patience to recite right now. Don't worry, your lawyers will get the entire menu. Now cuff him," he told his men, then repeated the same accusations and orders to take John Novak.

Brian Kenny had always done his job by the book, and the idea of his agents becoming involved in a domestic operation like this was normally out of the question. Then again, there were always exceptions, and sometimes rules needed to be broken. Nick Reagan had been the target of more than one murder plot, Gellos had been assaulted at gunpoint, and Erin David had been the victim of a failed kidnapping attempt. He concluded this was the time for an exception.

As Bebon's team began the time-consuming process of securing files, financial records, and other paperwork throughout all of the Novaks' cabinets and closets, Reagan and Gellos stepped from behind the group of operatives to confront the brothers.

"Can we have a moment?" Reagan asked Bebon.

Bebon nodded, allowing them to take the two handcuffed prisoners back into Andrew's office."

"You," John said, glaring at Reagan. "You're behind this nonsense?"

"Nonsense? I would hardly call it that. I simply decided to follow your company motto."

Both brothers looked confused. Reagan continued, "Be the change you wish to see in the world."

"Say nothing," Andrew told his brother, then turned to Reagan. "When this is over, you'll be lucky to get a job as a street sweeper at the National Mall."

Reagan ignored him as he watched Gellos open an iPad and fire it up. She hit a few keys, then turned the screen to face the brothers.

"Some of your greatest hits," she said, as she played the recording of the Novaks speaking about the poisoning of Derek Malone.

All of the blood drained from John's face, but Andrew remained defiant. "That's nothing more than a computer-generated copy of our voices. Our lawyers will have a field day with that bullshit."

Neither Reagan nor Gellos replied. She hit a few more keys and this time a video appeared on the screen. It showed the Novaks and Paszek, in the abandoned building they owned in Alexandria where the three of them had met just a few days before to discuss the poisoning of Malone and the plan to kidnap Reagan and Gellos and exchange them for Lawler and Turnquist.

When it was done, neither brother spoke.

Reagan said, "As my partner told you, these were just a couple of the gems in the treasure trove your man Paszek left for us, in case things went bad for him."

"And things went very bad," Gellos reminded them.

Andrew Novak's look hardened as he said, "This is less than nothing. You policeman still do not understand how our world works. People like us never get convicted, don't you know that? Our justice system is not designed to put the rich and powerful in jail. It's intended to do nothing more than keep the streets safe and allow for the occasional prosecution of a white-collar crime so the masses believe there is fairness after all."

Reagan nodded. "From everything you two have done, I think you really believe that. You really have no faith in this country or its principles. You believe that your wealth and position insulate you from the consequences of anything you do, no matter how evil, wrong, illegal, or damaging to others. But we believe just the opposite, and here is the message I want you to carry with you: I want you to suffer the full and complete punishment you deserve."

The Novaks stared at him without speaking.

"All yours," he told Bebon as he and Gellos headed back to the elevators.

Downstairs, Reagan and Gellos waited outside the building where the camera crews from a variety of media outlets were setting up their equipment and correspondents were testing their microphones. As Reagan had arranged, they were joined by Malone.

Gellos greeted him with a look of surprise, to which Malone said, "Wouldn't have missed it for the world."

"How is Connie doing this afternoon?"

"A miracle woman," Malone said. "She continues to recover movement, her eyes are open, amazing progress."

"We're all so glad," she said.

Malone nodded. "Speech is still an issue, but we're getting there."

It was not long before half a dozen men and women from the FBI escorted Andrew and John Novak from their building into a waiting van.

Malone stared at the brothers. He said not a word, but looked at both men with a mixture of hatred and victory.

Only John turned toward him, locking eyes with Malone for an instant, before entering the vehicle and being whisked away.

Behind them, Reagan, Gellos, and Malone could hear a reporter, who was standing nearby, making her report about the astonishing arrest of Andrew and John Novak for an array of crimes that were rumored to include treason and conspiracies to commit kidnapping and murder.

Reagan turned to them and said, "Our work here is done, and there's something far more important for us to do right now—let's visit Connie."

CHAPTER EIGHTY-THREE

The Capitol Building, Washington, D.C.

Several weeks later, as the prosecution of the Novaks was still in its early stages, the congressional subcommittee with oversight of pharmaceuticals was holding hearings about the revelations concerning Novak Pharma. The FBI investigation disclosed that the information provided by Malone represented only a fraction of the wrongdoing in which Andrew and John had engaged.

Their wonder drug, *Neulife*, was already dead on arrival. The dangerous side effects and addictive qualities were now well-documented, thanks largely to the continued efforts Malone devoted to the study. Since it had never hit the market, it was considered less of an issue than the numerous instances of overcharging for prescription medications and misrepresenting other results of their products.

Malone had been invited to testify, which he advised he would do voluntarily and with pleasure, requesting only that he could begin with a statement regarding all that had happened to his wife. That request was granted.

Malone wanted Gellos and Reagan to attend the hearing, and they agreed. When the day arrived, they showed up early, knowing how long it takes to get through the various checkpoints, and were surprised to find Anatole Mindlovitch there.

"Is this coincidence, or enemy action?" Reagan asked.

The Russian expat shrugged. "They want me to testify about lithium, and who am I to refuse? From what I understand, I should give your friend Dr. Malone some support."

Reagan asked Gellos to excuse them for a moment and took Mindlovitch down the hall where they found a private corner.

"Are you really here to testify about lithium?"

"I am," Mindlovitch told him. "As you know, I need it for my long-term batteries, and this committee is interested in where it comes from since it's also used in various pharmaceutical applications."

"Which is the reason your path crossed with the Novaks."

"One of the many," Mindlovitch admitted.

"In the mood to share?"

Mindlovitch smiled. "They wanted to buy into my Ghost Chip technology."

"And?"

"I wasn't interested."

"Keeping it all for yourself?" Reagan asked. "How selfish of you."

Mindlovitch responded with a look that said there was more to the story.

"You want to tell me anything about those missing prototypes?"

"Why would you ask that?"

"We did a deep dive on the young woman who supposedly stole the samples," Reagan said.

"Xia Chen."

"Yes, Xia Chen. And guess what?"

"Dazzle me," Mindlovitch said.

"She doesn't exist."

There was a slight pause, then Mindlovitch began laughing. "Serves me right for dealing with a spy."

"A spy who helped protect you when you were flat on your back in the hospital out there in California."

"Not forgotten," Mindlovitch said with a grateful nod. "Any chance we can keep this between us?"

"Honest answer? Whatever you tell me I'm going to share with my boss. As long as it does not pose a danger to this country, it will not go beyond that. And, before you ask, I trust Kenny with my life."

"All right. Since I know you now well enough to realize you're not going to let this go, I'll give you the short version." He took a deep breath. "The chip worked, doing everything we expected it to do. It prevented tracing, hacking, eavesdropping, all of it. But a couple of my people came to me and expressed a concern that it might not be bulletproof."

"That there might be a workaround?"

"Exactly. With all of the interest I had generated, I couldn't just come out and say that, but I had to know. I pretended there was a theft and had the twenty prototypes taken and brought to my facility in Silicon Valley. They went to work on it there, and in less than a month they cracked the code, so to speak."

"Which means a billion-dollar project went south."

Mindlovitch smiled. "You know what they say, Reagan. A billion here and a billion there, and suddenly it becomes real money."

"And you've managed to keep this quiet?"

"Known only to me and a select group of technicians, yes. They have no reason to admit we've got a problem, and they're trying to work out the glitches. But it was certainly a major step backward."

"While all that was going on, you could've sold a huge chunk of the action to my friends Andrew and John Novak."

Mindlovitch smiled again. "As they say in the press, Reagan, I'm a ruthless oligarch. But I'm not a crook."

"Good to know. And, by the way, glad you had no more to do with the Novaks than that. One needs to be careful about the company he keeps."

"As you told me the other night, which I take as good advice."

Reagan smiled. "All the same, I'll keep an eye on you."

"I feel safer knowing that," Mindlovitch said with a genial slap on his shoulder. "Meanwhile, I think your lovely partner is signaling you from down the hall."

Malone had arrived with Connie, who was still in a wheelchair, with a medical attendant. When Reagan reached them, he embraced Derek and bent down to kiss Connie on the cheek and give her a gentle hug.

"You guys ready for this?" he asked them.

"I'm ready as I can be," Connie said, although her voice was still thick and her speech slow.

"We're here for you," Gellos said, and the group made their way through the doors into the hearing room.

Inside, Malone wheeled his wife up to the front desk where they were warmly greeted by the Chairman of the subcommittee.

Reagan and Gellos chose seats in the last row where they had a full view of the entire room and spectators, tradecraft extending even to a Congressional visit. "This has certainly been a rough road," Reagan said to his partner.

"You mean Connie's recovery?"

"That, and taking down Lawler and Turnquist, nailing the Novaks."

Gellos nodded. "Those prosecutions are looking solid."

"Especially with everything Paszek left behind."

"And the information from Khoury," she reminded him. "Bebon's still got him in custody, that right?"

"Oh yeah, which is where he should stay until the trial begins. He's been cooperating, which should buy him his life, if not his freedom."

"The wheels keep turning," Gellos said, just as her cell phone lit up with a text. Looking down, she immediately broke into a smile.

"Don't tell me," Reagan said. "A message from your ranger friend in Aspen."

"Good guess," she admitted, "but not from Aspen. He's visiting me here in D.C."

Reagan responded with an approving grin. "Do tell."

Their attention was drawn to the front of the room, where the hearing was brought to order and Derek was asked to stand and was then sworn in. When it came time for Connie to take the oath, the Chairman explained that it would not be necessary to get up, but she insisted. Waving away her husband's offer to help, she braced herself on the edge of the table and bravely rose.

After she was sworn in, Connie said, "I hope you will allow me to make a few preliminary statements concerning what I know about Novak Pharma and the men who run it."

The audience became silent as the Chairman asked her to please proceed.

Before Connie began speaking, a nondescript man at the end of Reagan's row stood up, looked toward him and Gellos, then walked, with a slight limp, directly behind them and out the door in the back of the room. Moments later, Carol's phone lit up again, but this time Reagan's cell also buzzed. Discreetly looking down, they saw that they had each received the identical message from an unfamiliar number:

THIS IS NOT OVER.

THE END

ACKNOWLEDGMENTS

This is a work of fiction. The characters are my own invention and, although many of the locations are real, some of the details are invented to serve the plot and pacing. That said, I have some people to thank for the story lines that run throughout the novel.

Once again, this book could not have been written without Larry Garinger. As always, he provided a mixture of praise and criticism, suggestions and questions, and the occasional swift kick to keep me going.

Dr. Eric Kaplan and his elegant wife, Bonnie, provided incredible inspiration and expertise, much of it based on their own true-life saga. Please have a look at Eric's website, www.drerickaplan.com.

Thanks to my wife, Nancy, who is still the first to read whatever I write; my sons, Graham and Trevor, who keep pushing me; and so many dear friends, including Ed Scannapieco, Steve Weisblum, Eric and Melissa Thorkilsen, and Michele Poretto, all of whom provide endless support, advice, and encouragement.

My gratitude, as well, to Anthony Ziccardi and his entire team at Post Hill Press, who continue to endorse and back my efforts as a novelist.

A final thought—my interest in writing this book, and others in this genre, stems from my continuing admiration for the real American heroes who risk their lives to keep us and our great country safe. The men and women in the military and intelligence services, and those who support them, are owed a debt we can never repay—but we should strive to do better for them!

God Bless America.